the HEALING

WANDA & BRUNSTETTER

BARBOUR BOOKS
An Imprint of Barbour Publishing, Inc.

© 2011 by Wanda E. Brunstetter

ISBN 978-1-68322-362-7

eBook Editions:
Adobe Digital Edition (.epub) 978-1-68322-364-1
Kindle and MobiPocket Edition (.prc) 978-1-68322-363-4

All scripture quotations are taken from the King James Version of the Bible.

All German-Dutch words are taken from the *Revised Pennsylvania German Dictionary* found in Lancaster County, Pennsylvania.

For more information about Wanda E. Brunstetter, please access the author's website at the following internet address:
www.wandabrunstetter.com

Cover design: Faceout Studio, www.faceoutstudio.com
Cover photography: Steve Gardner, Pixelworks Studios

Published by Barbour Publishing, Inc., P.O. Box 719, Uhrichsville, OH 44683, www.barbourbooks.com

Our mission is to inspire the world with the life-changing message of the Bible.

Member of the
Evangelical Christian
Publishers Association

Printed in the United States of America.

DEDICATION/ ACKNOWLEDGMENT

To Irene Miller, one of my very special Amish friends.

*[God] healeth the broken in heart,
and bindeth up their wounds.*
PSALM 147:3

Fisher Family Tree

Abraham and Sarah (deceased) Fisher's Children

Matthew
(m) Abby Miller
(Fannie's daughter)

Stella
Derek
Joseph
Lamar
Brenda

Naomi
(m) Caleb Hoffmeir

Sarah
Susan
Josh
Nate
Millie
Kevin

Norman
(m) Ruth

Harley
Selma
John
Karen
Paul
Owen
Cora

Jake
(m) Darlene

Doris
Diane
Delbert
Duane
Debra

Abraham and Fannie Fisher's Children

Titus
(single)

Timothy
(m) Hannah

Mindy

Nancy
(m) Mark Stauffer

Stephen
Mavis
Lenore
Carl
Regina

Samuel
(m) Elsie

Marla
Leon
Penny
Jared

Mary Ann
(m) Abner Lapp

Lorie
Emma
Myron
Curtis

Zach
(m) Leona

Lucy
James
Jean

Fannie's Children from Her First Marriage

Abby (Miller)
(m) Matthew Fisher
(Abraham's son)

Stella
Derek
Joseph
Lamar
Brenda

Harold Miller
(m) Lena

Ira
Katie
Raymond

CHAPTER I

Paradise, Pennsylvania

A*lles is fix un faddich.*" Bishop Jacob Weaver clasped Samuel Fisher's shoulder and gave it a squeeze.

Samuel, who stood on his front porch with a few others from his community, gripped the railing so tightly his fingers ached. The last few days, and even now, he'd felt as if he were walking through a thick fog, barely able to hear what anyone had said to him. Yet the truth of the bishop's words—that all was completely done—slammed into Samuel with the force of a tornado. Overcome with emotion, he could barely manage a nod. They had just returned from the cemetery where they'd buried Elsie, his wife of ten years. He wasn't sure how he'd made it through the last couple of days, much less the funeral and graveside service, but frankly, he was too tired and too numb to care. Somehow, he was now expected to carry on without her, and that thought was overwhelming.

Samuel's mind hadn't rested since that awful day when he'd found his wife at the foot of the stairs. Over and over he kept asking himself, *How do I go on? How can I survive without my Elsie?* With his feelings so raw, he couldn't imagine where to begin. Constant thoughts and plaguing questions drained every bit of his energy.

Samuel realized he wasn't the first person to go through something like this, but even knowing that, all he felt was despair. The misery was more than he could bear. Well, he couldn't do it! The thought of caring for his and

7

Elsie's four children and going to work every day was too much to think about. But if he didn't work, who would buy food and pay their bills?

And if he stayed home from work and wallowed in self-pity, he'd only be reminded of Elsie. Everywhere he looked, he would see her face: in the kitchen, where she'd prepared their meals; in the yard, where she'd worked among the flowers; in their bedroom, where she would take down her hair at night and allow him to brush her long, silky tresses as they discussed the day's events and all their plans for the future—a future that would no longer include his beloved Elsie.

"I'll let you visit with your family now, but please remember, you can call on me or any of the ministers in our church if you need anything. Oh, and no matter how sad you feel, take the time to read God's Word and pray, because being alone with God is the only way you will find the strength to press on." The elderly bishop, who'd been a friend of the family for a good many years, gave Samuel's shoulder another firm squeeze and walked away, leaving Samuel to his disturbing thoughts.

Was it only last week that he and Elsie had discussed the approach of Thanksgiving and the huge meal they planned to have? They'd smiled and laughed as they'd reminisced about last year's holiday with their children and several of Samuel's family members sitting around the table. Elsie had commented on how she loved to watch the children's eyes grow big as saucers when the mouth-watering turkey, almost overflowing the platter, had been set in the middle of the table. All the laughter and chatter while they'd enjoyed the holiday feast was a special time for them as a family. Abruptly, those holidays and everything else Samuel and Elsie had shared had come to a halt. How quickly things could change.

In an attempt to force his thoughts aside, Samuel stared into the yard. A cold wind had scattered the fallen leaves all about. The trees were bare and empty—just like

Samuel's heart. He knew that some men who'd been wid-owed married within the first year of their wife's death, but Samuel was certain he would never marry again, for how could anyone fill the horrible void left by Elsie's untimely death?

He caught sight of his children playing in the yard with some other children as though nothing had hap-pened. Of course, the little ones didn't understand that Elsie was never coming back, but he was sure eight-year-old Marla and six-year-old Leon did. So how could they frolic about as if they hadn't just witnessed their mother's coffin being lowered into the ground? Surely, they must miss her as much as Samuel did. Maybe the only way they could deal with it was to run and play, trying to block it all out. Samuel wished he could find a way to block out the pain.

He looked away and sank into a nearby chair with a groan. *Nothing will ever be the same. I'll never be able to laugh with the children again. No more catching flies for their entertainment. No more walks in the woods, holding Elsie's hand. No more anything that used to be fun.*

Samuel closed his eyes, and a vision of Elsie's twisted body lying at the bottom of the stairs came uninvited into his head. Would he ever be able to get that image out of his mind? Would he ever know peace again?

Marla and Leon had seen their mother fall that day, and when Samuel rushed into the house after hearing their screams, he'd found them close to her body, sobbing and pleading with her to open her eyes. The two youngest chil-dren—four-year-old Penny and two-year-old Jared—he'd discovered in the kitchen, hiding behind the stove. Even before the paramedics arrived, Samuel had known Elsie was dead. He'd found no pulse, and she wasn't breathing. Later, Samuel learned that Elsie had suffered a broken neck from the fall, as well as severe internal injuries. Their unborn baby, still underdeveloped in his mother's womb, had also perished.

"Samuel, you shouldn't be sitting out here in the cold by yourself."

Samuel's eyes snapped open. When he looked up and saw his older sister, Naomi, looking down at him with concern, he mumbled, "Didn't realize I was alone, and I'm too numb to feel the cold."

Naomi seated herself in the chair beside him. "I feel your pain, Samuel. I truly do."

Samuel stared straight ahead. "How can you feel my pain? Your husband's still alive, and you've never lost a child—not even one who wasn't fully formed."

"I realize that, but I hurt with you, and I want to help ease your pain."

"There's nothing you can do."

She reached for his hand and gave his fingers a gentle squeeze. He could see the depth of Naomi's concern in her ebony-colored eyes. "God loves you, Samuel, and so do I."

"If God loves me, He wouldn't have taken Elsie away from me and the *kinner*," Samuel whispered, as the bitter taste of bile rose in his throat.

"Zach was unfairly taken from our family when he was a *boppli*, but it didn't mean God no longer loved us."

"That was different. Zach didn't die; he was kidnapped." Samuel pointed to the front door, where Zach and the rest of their family had gathered inside after the funeral dinner. "Zach came back to us. Elsie's gone from this earth forever."

"Her body's gone, but she was a Christian in every sense of the word, and I'm certain that her spirit lives on in heaven," Naomi said softly. "Someday you'll see her again."

"*Someday* could be a long time from now." Samuel swallowed hard, fighting to keep his emotions under control. "I wish it had been me who'd died. Why didn't God take me instead of Elsie?"

"You mustn't say such things. Your kinner need you now more than ever."

Samuel lowered his gaze to the porch floor. "They needed their *mamm*, and I can't take care of them without her."

"You don't have to, Samuel. God will see you through this. With the help of your family and friends, you'll make it."

Samuel rose to his feet, trying hard not to let the fear and loneliness he felt at the very core of his soul overtake him. "I can't talk about this right now. I need to be alone." Taking the porch steps two at a time, he hurried into the yard. He was halfway to the barn when his older brother, Norman, stepped up to him. "Are you okay, Samuel?"

"How can I be okay when Elsie's gone?" Just saying those words were hard enough, making him wish it was all just a horrible dream.

Norman's brown eyes became glassy as he put his hand on Samuel's shoulder and gave it a reassuring squeeze. "You have to accept her death as God's will. It's the only way you'll get through this."

Samuel's face heated, despite the chilly air. "What would you know about it? Your *fraa*'s not dead!" He shrugged Norman's hand away and stormed across the yard. It was easy for Norman to say such words when he'd never experienced the pain of losing his wife. Yet Samuel knew that his brother meant well, and if the tables were turned, he'd probably have tried to offer comfort to him in much the same way.

As Samuel moved on, he heard his brothers Jake and Titus, who stood outside the barn, talking about the upcoming Thanksgiving holiday.

"I wish I could stay and join you for the holiday," Titus said, "but we have a lot of orders that need to be filled in the woodshop before Christmas, so Suzanne, Allen, and I will have to head back to Kentucky tomorrow morning."

"It's good you could come for the funeral," Jake said. "I'm sure it made it easier for Samuel to have his whole family here."

My whole family's not here. Elsie was my family, and she's not here. Samuel's fingers clenched as he hurried his steps. When he entered the barn moments later, he was greeted by the soft nicker of the horses in their stalls. He dropped to a seat on a bale of straw and stared vacantly at Elsie's horse, Dolly, standing in one of the stalls, her head hanging over the gate. Did the mare know Elsie was gone? Did she miss her, too? He'd have to sell the horse now. If he kept the mare, he'd think of Elsie and be reminded that she would never hitch Dolly to the buggy again. Every waking hour, his thoughts were like a roller coaster, reflecting back over the ten years they'd been married. He wasn't ready to let go—he wanted to think about nothing but the memories they'd made together. But then his thinking would jump ahead, trying to imagine his life without Elsie. It was too much, too hard to grasp. For the last three days, he'd been falling into a fitful sleep at night, and finally, when he succumbed to exhaustion, it would be dawn. Mornings, he found, were the worst: his mind came to full alert, yet he still felt fatigued when he forced himself out of bed. He'd pace the floor, a million questions swimming in his head, wondering, *Where do I go from here? Will I always feel this restless and unsure?*

Halting his thoughts, Samuel noticed several pieces of hay falling through cracks in the loft above and was reminded of all the chores he had to catch up on. His pitchfork lay on the floor, where he'd dropped it the day he'd heard his children's screams that their mamm had fallen down the stairs.

A cat sprang down from the loft, and Samuel jumped. Purring softly, it rubbed its side against Samuel's legs. Elsie loved their cats, and they knew it. "Here, kitty, kitty" was all she had to yell, and the critters would come running, knowing their bowls had been filled. To Samuel, they were just plain old barn cats, good for only one thing—to keep the mice down. Elsie, though, loved all the farm animals and had a special way with them.

The barn door squeaked open and then clicked shut. Samuel looked up and saw Titus step inside. "I saw you come in here," Titus said. "I wanted to talk to you alone and thought this might be a good time."

"What'd you want to say?" Samuel asked. Truly, he just wanted to sit by himself for a spell, without interruption, but he didn't want to be rude—especially when his brother had come all the way from Kentucky to attend Elsie's funeral.

Titus took a seat on the bale of straw next to Samuel. "I'm real sorry about Elsie. It was a shock to hear that she'd died, and I know you and the kinner are really going to miss her." His dark brown eyes looked as sorrowful as the somber expression on his face.

Samuel, not trusting his voice, could only nod.

They sat for several minutes in silence until Titus spoke again. "If you ever feel the need for a change, I want you to know that you'd be welcome in Kentucky. I'd be pleased to have you stay with me for as long as you want."

"Me moving from here won't bring Elsie back." Samuel knew he sounded bitter, but he couldn't help it.

" 'Course not, but it would give you a new start. Maybe that's what you need." Titus leaned closer to Samuel. "Moving to Kentucky helped my wounded heart to heal after Phoebe and I broke up."

Samuel shrugged. "I'll give it some thought, but right now I just need to be alone." He couldn't imagine how moving to Kentucky could help his broken heart. Besides, his situation wasn't anything like Titus's.

"Okay, I'll head back to the house now, but remember, brother, I love you." Titus gave Samuel's arm a light tap and slipped quietly from the barn.

Dolly whinnied, and Samuel's vision blurred from the tears burning his eyes. *Oh Elsie, I'll never love anyone but you. Sweet Elsie, I'll always miss you.* He lowered his head into his hands and let the tears flow freely.

—w—

Pembroke, Kentucky

As Esther Beiler stood beside her mother at the counter near the front of their store, she sensed that something was wrong. Mom had been acting kind of strange all morning, as though a heavy burden lay on her heart. Esther had been tempted to ask what was wrong but figured if Mom wanted to talk about it, she would. Besides, they'd been busy with customers all morning.

"How long does Dad plan to be in Hopkinsville today?" Esther asked as she reached for a tablet and pen to start a list of supplies they needed for the store.

"Just long enough to run a few errands." Mom's dark brown eyes looked lifeless, as though she hadn't been getting enough sleep, and Esther couldn't help but notice the dark circles beneath her eyes.

The bell above the front door jingled, and Verna Yoder entered the store. "Brr. . ." she said, stepping up to the counter. "It's downright cold out there today. Bet it won't be long until we see some snow."

"I hope not." Mom shook her head. "I'm just not ready for *windere* yet."

"Well, like it or not, Dinah, winter's on the way. I can feel it in my bones." Verna rubbed her hands briskly over her arms, hidden beneath her black woolen shawl.

"Have you heard anything from Suzanne since she and Titus left for Pennsylvania?" Esther asked, curious to know when her best friend might be coming home.

Verna gave a nod. "She called when they first got there, and then I discovered another message from her this afternoon."

"How are things going for Samuel and his family?" Mom asked.

"Not so well," Verna replied. "Suzanne said Samuel's

14

taking his wife's death pretty hard, which of course is to be expected. The poor man didn't even want to talk to most of the folks who'd come to the house after Elsie's funeral. Suzanne said Titus was going to suggest that Samuel and his kinner move here."

"What? After just losing his fraa?" Mom clicked her tongue noisily. "I'm surprised Titus would even suggest such a thing."

"I'm sure he meant well," Esther was quick to say. "He probably thought it would be good for Samuel to get a new start—go someplace where there aren't so many painful memories." Esther didn't know why she felt the need to defend Titus. It wasn't like he was her boyfriend or anything. The short time they'd courted after Titus had first moved to Kentucky hadn't amounted to anything more than friendship. Now he planned to marry Suzanne, which made Esther happy, because she knew Suzanne and Titus were very much in love and seemed well-suited for each other.

"I think it might be good for Titus's brother to move to Kentucky," Verna said. "Look how well Titus has done here. Everyone can see how happy he and my daughter are when they're together."

"You do have a point," Mom said. "Guess we'll just have to see whether Samuel accepts Titus's invitation, and if he does, only time will tell how well it will go."

Verna smiled. "Well, I'd best get what I came here for." She turned and headed down the aisle where the cleaning supplies were kept.

Sometime later after Verna had left the store, Mom turned to Esther and said, "There's something I need to tell you."

"What is it?" Esther questioned.

"I spoke with Dan's wife this morning." Deep wrinkles formed across Mom's forehead. "Dan and Sarah have put off telling us for as long as they could, but she admitted to me that your brother's been having some health problems lately, and after numerous tests, they've learned that the reason for his unusual symptoms is because he has multiple sclerosis."

Esther gasped. "That's *baremlich*!"

"I agree. In some cases it can be a terrible thing, and from what I understand, the symptoms are often quite different for most people. Because Dan is so fatigued and suffering from such a loss of balance, he won't be able to keep his stands going at the two farmer's markets in Lancaster County." Mom drew in a quick breath. "So after talking with your *daed* about this, we've decided to sell the store and move to Strasburg so we can help out."

Esther's mouth dropped open. "After all these years of living here, you're moving back to Pennsylvania?"

Mom nodded. "Dan and Sarah need our help, and since we've had experience running our store, we ought to be able to handle the stands Dan has at Green Dragon and Root's Farmer's Market. Being in Pennsylvania will also put us closer to your brother James and his family, since their home in Lykens is only a few hours from Dan's."

Esther leaned heavily against the counter, feeling the need for support. It was bad enough that her older brother was ill, but if Mom and Dad sold the store and moved back to Pennsylvania, would they expect her to go with them?

CHAPTER 2

As Esther began washing the breakfast dishes, she glanced at the calendar on the wall to her right. It didn't seem possible, but Thanksgiving was over and Christmas was less than a month away.

It will be a difficult Christmas for our family this year, she thought. *For Dan and Sarah because Dan's health is failing; for Mom, Dad, and me because we're all worried about Dan and because giving up the store will be hard for my folks; and for me, too, since I'll no longer have a job.*

Tears welled in Esther's eyes and dribbled onto her cheeks. She'd never been one to give in to self-pity, but then she'd never felt so burdened.

A knock on the back door brought Esther's thoughts to a halt. When she opened it, she was pleased to see her friend Suzanne Yoder.

"Brr. . . It's sure cold this morning," Suzanne said as she stepped into the house and removed her black outer bonnet.

"I think winter's on its way." Esther led the way to the warm and cozy kitchen.

"Maybe we'll have a white Christmas." Suzanne's blue eyes twinkled, and a wisp of her pretty auburn hair peeked out from under her white head covering. It was in sharp contrast to Esther's dark hair.

Esther handed Suzanne a cup of tea. "Maybe this will warm you up."

"Danki." Suzanne set the cup on the table, removed

her black woolen shawl, and took a seat. "I haven't talked to you for a while. How are things going?"

"Not so well. Mom talked to my sister-in-law Sarah last week, and we learned that Dan has MS. Due to his loss of balance and extreme fatigue, he's not able to work like he did before, so my folks are planning to move to Strasburg to help out."

Suzanne's eyebrows furrowed. "I'm sorry to hear that— sorry about Dan, and sorry to hear that you'll be moving."

Esther shook her head. "I'm not going with them."

"They're leaving you to run the store by yourself?"

"No, they're selling it to Aaron and Nettie Martin, the Mennonite couple who moved here last month. I'll be staying here at the house, but I'll have to find some other job to support myself."

"Are your folks okay with that? I would think they'd want you to move with them."

"They do want that, but when I explained that I want to stay here with my friends in the place I love, they finally agreed." Esther sighed. "Now I just need to find a job."

Suzanne took a sip of tea. "Maybe Ethan Zook will marry you, and then you won't have to worry about finding a job."

Esther's eyebrows shot up. "Ethan Zook? Why would you think he'd be interested in marrying me?"

"You're a good cook, and he likes to eat, so—"

Esther held up her hand. "I'm not the least bit interested in Ethan, and I doubt he sees me as anything more than a friend."

"Let him taste some of your delicious boyfriend cookies, and I bet he'll be down on his knees, proposing marriage."

Esther giggled. "You're such a kidder."

"I'm glad you're staying. I'd miss you terribly if you moved away." Suzanne gave Esther a hug. "I'll keep my ears open about any jobs in the area, and of course I'll be praying."

"I appreciate that."

They sat quietly for a while, sipping their tea and nibbling on some banana bread Esther had made the night before. It was good to sit and be quiet with her friend. They'd always been there for each other, in good times and bad.

"What's new in your life?" Esther asked after they'd finished their refreshments. "Have you and Titus made any definite plans for the future?"

Suzanne's cheeks flushed as she gave a slow nod. "We've only told our immediate families so far, but we're planning to be married next fall."

"That's real good news. You two are perfect for each other, and I'm sure you'll have many happy years as husband and wife."

"I hope so. As you well know, our relationship got off to a rocky start when Titus first moved to Kentucky."

"That was only because you reminded him of his ex-girlfriend."

Suzanne nodded. "When Phoebe came here and tried to win Titus back, I thought I'd lost him forever."

"But he chose you over her, and soon he'll be your husband."

"*Jah.* I can hardly wait."

"Will you continue to work at the woodshop with Titus and Nelson after you're married?" Esther asked.

"We haven't discussed it, but I hope so. I love working with wood, and I'd miss being in the shop."

"You and Titus will work things out. Will he be going home to Pennsylvania for Christmas?" Esther asked.

Suzanne shook her head. "We're very busy in the woodshop right now, and since it's only been a few weeks since we were there for his sister-in-law's funeral, Titus will be staying here for Christmas."

Esther smiled. "I'm sure you don't mind that he'll be staying."

"I am looking forward to having Titus over to our

house for Christmas, but I know his family will miss him." Suzanne sighed. "I'm sure he'd like to be there for his brother, because from what Titus has told me, Samuel's still going through a really hard time."

"That's understandable."

"Titus is concerned because Samuel won't answer any of his phone calls. He knows from talking with his folks that Samuel's extremely depressed."

"I've never lost anyone that close to me, but I'm sure it's going to take some time," Esther said, wondering if she'd be able to cope with something as painful as losing a loved one. She thought about Dan and hoped he wouldn't lose his battle with MS.

"It was terribly hard on Mom and the rest of the family when my daed died," Suzanne said. "And when we lost Grandma, that was very difficult, too."

Esther wished no one ever had to die, but she knew that dying was a part of living, and for a Christian who had accepted Christ as their Savior, death meant leaving this world and spending an eternity in the presence of the Lord. She prayed that when the time came, those beliefs would give her strength and carry her through the days when she would need it most.

—⁓—

Paradise, Pennsylvania

Samuel moved slowly through the cemetery, weaving in and out among the plots until he came to Elsie's simple headstone. His throat constricted as he knelt on the cold ground beside it.

"Elsie May Fisher," he murmured, reaching out to touch the inscription on the headstone. "Loving wife and mother."

A gust of chilly wind blew, stirring up the dried leaves scattered around and whipping Samuel's straw hat from his head. He shivered and grabbed for it before it spun away. Winter was just around the corner, and soon it would be Christmas.

Hot tears pushed against his eyelids, and he blinked several times in an attempt to force them back. Thanksgiving had gone by in a blur, and Samuel didn't think he could deal with Christmas this year. He couldn't stand the thought of going to the kids' school Christmas program, knowing Elsie wouldn't be with him to watch Marla and Leon say their parts. Samuel felt as if his life had come to a screeching halt the day he'd lost his wife. He knew it was wrong to wish that he was dead, but he couldn't help it because that was still exactly how he felt.

He lifted his gaze to the sky and blinked against the snowflakes that had begun to fall. *Why, God? Why'd You have to take Elsie from us? Don't You know how much the kinner need her? Don't You care that my heart is breaking? How will I get through this? How do I go on?* Over and over, he kept asking the questions, hoping, praying his pleas would be heard.

No response. Nothing but the eerie sound of the wind whipping through the trees outside the cemetery fence.

He shivered again but knew it had nothing to do with the frosty air that engulfed him. The chill he felt was from his grief—a chill that went all the way to his heart, to the very core of his being.

Feeling the cold all the way to his bones and trembling badly, Samuel finally stood and made his way out of the cemetery. From there, he wandered aimlessly down the road, until he came to his folks' house. Samuel and the kids had been staying with his father and stepmother, Mama Fannie, ever since Elsie died. Samuel couldn't stand being alone in his house, and he couldn't deal with caring for the children. How could he, when he could barely care for himself?

He remembered how the other night, he'd stuck his head into the room Penny and Marla shared and seen them both kneeling on the floor by their bed with their hands folded. They'd obviously been praying. Were they asking God to give them their mother back?

Puh! Now that would take a real miracle, he thought bitterly. But God didn't give people miracles like that anymore. Just Lazarus and God's Son, Jesus—those were the only two people he knew about that had ever been raised from the dead. No, Elsie wasn't coming back, and he and the children somehow had to learn to live with that fact.

The stairs leading to his folks' back porch steps creaked as Samuel plodded slowly up them. When he entered the house, he heard voices coming from the kitchen.

"I'm worried about Samuel," Mama Fannie said. "I know he misses Elsie, but he's grieving so hard he can barely function. If it weren't for the fact that he's staying with us, I doubt he'd eat anything at all."

"I know you're concerned, Fannie, but try not to worry," Dad said. "It's going to take some time for Samuel to come to grips with Elsie's death. He'll come around eventually; you'll see."

"I hope so, because losing their mamm has been hard on the kinner, and if their daed remains in such a state much longer, they might think they've lost him, too."

Samuel's boots clomped noisily across the hardwood floor as he stormed into the kitchen. "My kinner are not going to lose me, and I'd appreciate it if you'd stop talking about me behind my back!" These days his guard was always up, feeling defensive about nearly everything. It seemed to be the only way he could protect his emotions and not allow his feelings to control him.

Mama Fannie blinked her dark eyes as she lifted her chin. "We're just concerned about you, son."

"Well, you don't have to be. I'm fine, and so are my kinner. Or at least we will be once we've moved."

"Moved where?" Dad asked, giving his beard, sprinkled generously with gray, a quick tug.

"To Kentucky."

Mama Fannie's eyebrows shot up. "What?"

"I've decided that if I'm ever going to move on with my life I need to get away from here so I can leave all the painful memories behind."

Mama Fannie jumped up and clutched the sleeve of Samuel's jacket. "You're not thinking straight right now. You need to give yourself more time to heal."

"I don't need more time. I need to get away—make a fresh start someplace else."

The wrinkles in Mama Fannie's forehead deepened, and when tears welled in her eyes, she covered her face with her hands. "I can't stand the thought of losing another one of my boys to Kentucky. Please, Samuel, won't you give this more thought?"

Samuel stood there, shaking his head.

"I've been taking care of your kinner since Elsie died, and if you take them to Kentucky, I'll miss them so much. Besides, they don't know anyone there and won't have the support of family and friends."

"They'll know Titus," Dad put in. "I'm sure they'll make friends with others in the community there, too."

"That's right," Samuel agreed. "And don't try to talk me out of it because I've made up my mind." He hated talking so severely to the dear woman who'd become his mother when he was a young boy, but being in the protective shell he'd put himself in, he couldn't let his shield of defenses down—not to anyone—not even his family.

Mama Fannie lifted her face and sniffed deeply. "Wh– when do you plan to leave?"

"We'll head for Kentucky after the first of the year. In the meantime, I'll get in touch with Titus and let him know we're coming. Hopefully, he or his contractor friend, Allen Walters, will be able to help me find a job."

"Shouldn't you at least wait until spring?" Mama Fannie persisted. "Traveling in the dead of winter could be dangerous. Besides, I've heard it said that when someone loses a mate they shouldn't make any major changes for at least six months. And in my opinion, it would be better to wait a whole year," she added with a decisive nod.

Making no further comment on the subject, Samuel moved quickly toward the door.

"Where are you going?" Mama Fannie called.

"Out to the phone shanty to call Titus." Samuel hurried away before she could say anything more, and at the same time, feeling terrible that he'd spoken so sternly to his folks.

CHAPTER 3

I still wish you weren't going," Mama Fannie said as Samuel and his children sat at the kitchen table having breakfast on the second day of January. "I wish you'd reconsider and stay here with your family."

Samuel's jaw clenched so tightly that his teeth hurt. Mama Fannie's constant badgering about moving to Kentucky was beginning to get on his nerves. Didn't she understand that he needed to get away? All his sisters and brothers and their families had come for supper last night so they could say good-bye. They'd shed lots of tears, but at least none of them had given him a hard time about moving.

"Samuel, did you hear what I said?" Mama Fannie reached over and touched his arm.

"Jah, I heard, but I'm not going to change my mind, so you may as well stop badgering me about it."

"Samuel's right," Dad said before she could respond. "He's a grown man, and he has every right to do what he feels is best for him and his children."

Mama Fannie looked up at Samuel and scrunched her nose. "How can moving to Kentucky be best for any of you? How can leaving your family here and moving two states away be a good thing?"

"Because I say it is!" It was so easy to say; he only hoped he could convince himself to believe it. This decision hadn't come easy, but he didn't know what else to do. He couldn't stand to stay here anymore—couldn't deal with anything that reminded him of Elsie.

"*Daadi*, please don't yell at Grandma." Marla began to cry, and then the younger ones, Leon, Penny, and Jared, followed suit.

Samuel felt like covering his ears. "*Es dutt mie leed*—I am sorry," he mumbled, looking first at Mama Fannie and then his children. "Now hurry up and eat your breakfast, kids, because our driver will be here soon."

"Grandma, will you and Grandpa come visit us in Kentucky?" Marla asked, swiping at the tears trickling down her cheeks.

"Of course we will," Dad was quick to say. "Maybe in the spring when the weather's better. And for sure when Titus and Suzanne are married in the fall."

Mama Fannie smiled, although there was no sparkle in her eyes. "I'm sure you'll be coming back here for visits, too."

"Can we come back to Pennsylvania for my birthday?" Marla asked, looking at Samuel with a hopeful expression.

He shook his head. "Your birthday's next month. That's too soon for us to be goin' anywhere."

"How come?"

"Because the weather will be bad, and hopefully I'll be busy working."

"The weather's bad now," Mama Fannie reminded. "And you don't even have a job yet."

Samuel's defenses rose once again. "I'll find something to do; you'll see."

"Since Zach's friend Allen is a general contractor, I'll bet he can find you some painting jobs," Dad said.

"Puh!" Mama Fannie dismissed the idea. "Who's going to want their house painted in the dead of winter?"

"Some folks want the inside of their houses painted," Samuel said. "Besides, we won't have many expenses because we'll be staying with Titus—at least until my house here sells and I can find a place there to buy or rent."

"At the very least, I'm sure you can find some odd jobs to do. You've always been pretty handy with things."

Dad thumped Samuel's back.

A horn honked outside, and Samuel jumped up and rushed to the window. "Our driver's here. Get your coats on kids, and then say good-bye to your *grossdaadi* and *grossmudder* so we can head out."

Marla started to cry again, and so did the others, including Mama Fannie, whose sobs were the loudest of all.

Unable to deal with any of it, Samuel grabbed his jacket from the back of the chair and hurried out the door. He figured Dad would get Mama Fannie and the kids under control, and then they could get on the road. For many reasons, he was unyielding in his decision to move to Kentucky. The most crucial, though, was for his children. He was sure he could be a better father to them there—where he wouldn't be thinking of Elsie all the time.

He paused a moment to look out across the land—a land he and Elsie had lovingly tended together. Like the hawk perched high on a branch overlooking the field, Samuel felt very much alone.

—⁓—

Pembroke, Kentucky

"Look at that." Esther pointed out the kitchen window. "Isn't that a sight to behold?"

"What is it?" Mom asked, while sponging off the table.

"Five does are in the yard, and they're playing in the snow like a bunch of frisky puppies."

Mom dropped the sponge and stepped up to the window beside Esther. "*Ach*! They're so cute!"

Esther smiled as she watched the deer kicking up their feet, looking like young fillies that had just found their legs.

"If you're done washing the dishes now, would you mind going to the store for me?" Mom asked. "I've made a list, and I need several things."

"Which store?" Esther asked. "The one we used to own or one of the stores in Hopkinsville?"

"Oh no, I don't expect you to hire a driver and go clear into town. The things I need can be bought at our old store."

"Okay." Esther turned away from the window, reluctant to leave behind the peaceful feeling she felt whenever she watched nature's antics. Those moments were cherished, and time seemed to stand still when she gazed out at the beautiful scenery surrounding them. She never forgot how truly blessed she was to have entertainment like that right outside their door. If only the distraction could delay her trip to the family business she'd grown to love. Truth was, she dreaded the thought of stepping into their old store and seeing someone else running it almost as much as she dreaded Mom and Dad leaving for Pennsylvania tomorrow morning. But now that the store was under new ownership, there was no reason for them to stay, because Dan's condition was worsening, and he needed them more than ever.

"Here's my list." Mom handed a piece of paper to Esther. "Take your time getting there. With all the snow on the ground, the roads might be slippery, so you'll need to be careful."

"I will." Esther slipped into her woolen jacket, put her black outer bonnet on her head, and went out the door. She figured Mom would probably worry about her even more after they moved and she was living on her own here at the house. But she'd be fine; she'd show herself, as well as them, how well she could manage on her own.

Esther stepped onto the porch and paused to watch the deer that had now moved out into the pasture. Grazing on what corn they could find after the harvest, they looked in her direction, watchful, yet undisturbed, as she made her way to the barn to harness her horse, Ginger.

When Esther pulled her horse and buggy up to the store's hitching rail sometime later, more than a few negative thoughts raced through her head. What if the new owners weren't as friendly to the people in their community as Mom and Dad had been? What if they decided to raise their prices and people couldn't afford to shop there anymore? What if they didn't keep the store adequately stocked, the way Mom and Dad had always done?

Shaking her disturbing thoughts aside, Esther entered the store, but when she saw Aaron and Nettie Martin behind the front counter, while their two oldest daughters, Roseanna and Lucinda, kept busy stocking shelves, she almost felt sick. It didn't seem right that someone else was running the store where she and her folks had worked so many years. It didn't seem right that one of her brothers was having severe health problems either.

Esther gave herself a mental pep talk. Her folks' help was needed—not only at Dan's place, but also at his two stands, where he sold soft pretzels, popcorn, and homemade candy. And for Esther. . . Well, she'd been working at the store most of her young adult life, so maybe it was time for a change. Now if she could only find a job that paid well and was something she truly enjoyed.

Esther had just gone down the aisle where the vitamins were kept when she noticed Titus Fisher come into the store.

"I figured you'd be hard at work in the woodshop by now," she said as he approached her.

"I'm heading in that direction but wanted to come by here first and pick up a few things. My brother Samuel and his kinner are moving here and should arrive within the next day or so. Of course, that all depends on how well the weather cooperates," he added. "If they have to deal with lots of icy roads, it could slow them down—especially the trailer that's hauling Samuel's horse, not to mention the truck with the buggy and other things in it," he added.

"When I last spoke with Suzanne, she said Samuel might be moving here, but I didn't think he'd be coming so soon," Esther said. "Why doesn't he wait until spring when the weather is better?"

"I think he's anxious to leave Pennsylvania and the painful memories of losing his wife."

"I guess that's understandable, but what will he do for a job?"

"Samuel's a good painter, and he also has some carpentry skills, so until he can find some paint jobs, he may be helping Nelson, me, and Suzanne in the woodshop. As soon as we have enough work for another person, that is."

"I see. Where will he and his kinner stay?" she asked.

"With me for now. . .until Samuel's able to either buy or build a place of his own. He's put his home in Pennsylvania up for sale, but until it sells he won't be able to afford to buy another place here."

"It's a good thing you have that nice double-wide manufactured home now, because there certainly wouldn't have been room for all of them in the dingy old trailer you used to rent from Allen."

"That's for sure. That place was so small there was barely room for me, let alone a family of five." Titus smiled. "Hopefully by the time Suzanne and I are married, Samuel will have his own place, but if he doesn't, then I guess we'll just have to make do."

Esther didn't say anything, but she wondered how everything would work out. Having Samuel and his kids living there could affect Titus and Suzanne's relationship—especially if Samuel's family wasn't able to move out before Titus and Suzanne got married.

Guess it's not my concern, Esther told herself as she looked over Mom's list and continued the shopping. *I'd better just concentrate on my own problems right now.*

CHAPTER 4

Portland, Oregon

Bonnie Taylor sat at her kitchen table, staring at the telephone. She'd just had a call from a lawyer in Hopkinsville, Kentucky, letting her know that her grandmother had died and left everything to her—including the old house that had been sitting empty since Grandma had gone to a nursing home several months ago.

Neither Bonnie nor her widowed father had gone to Kentucky to see Grandma after she'd gone to the nursing home. Bonnie's excuse was that she'd been working long hours for an advertising agency in Portland and couldn't get away. Dad had no excuse at all, other than the grudge he'd held against his folks ever since Bonnie could remember, which was why the few trips they'd made as a family to Kentucky while Mom was still alive had been brief. Bonnie was sure Dad had only agreed to go to make Mom happy, because she'd often said it was important for Bonnie, their only child, to get to know her grandparents on her father's side. Bonnie had never understood what the problem between Dad and his folks was about. She'd broached the subject with him once and had been told that it was none of her business and not to bring it up again.

Tears welled in Bonnie's eyes. At Mom's insistence, and despite Dad's disapproval, Bonnie had spent a week with Grandpa and Grandma almost every summer until Mom had died of a brain tumor shortly after Bonnie turned thirteen. Grandma and Grandpa had always been kind, and she'd enjoyed being with them. They'd taken her to church, where she'd learned about God, but she'd never mentioned it to Dad because after Mom died he'd become bitter and wouldn't let Bonnie visit his parents anymore. When Grandma sent Bonnie a Bible for her birthday that year, Dad threw it out and shouted some things Bonnie didn't care to repeat. Life had been terrible for Bonnie after that, and then two years before she'd graduated from high school, she'd made the biggest mistake of her life. But that was in the past, and she wouldn't allow herself to think about it right now.

Once Bonnie got her diploma and realized that she needed a fresh start, she'd taken some classes at the community college in Portland. When she landed the job at the advertising agency where she presently worked, she'd moved out on her own. Soon after that, she'd begun attending a church near her apartment, but she'd never taken an active part in any of the activities the church offered for people her age. Instead of socializing, she'd immersed herself in her job. It was better that way, she'd decided.

Bonnie's mind snapped back to the issue at hand. Grandma was dead, and she really needed to go to Kentucky—not only to attend Grandma's funeral, but also to sort through her things and decide what to do with them. Then there was the house; it would need to be sold.

Bonnie had some vacation time coming, so she'd use that to go to Kentucky for Grandma's funeral and then get the house put on the market. Hopefully, Dad would set whatever problems he'd had with his parents aside and go with her.

—⁓—

Paradise, Pennsylvania

Fannie entered the store her husband had given to his daughter Naomi and her husband, Caleb, several years ago.

"It's good to see you," Naomi said. "You must need

something badly to have braved the cold weather and icy roads today."

"The roads weren't so bad, and I do need a few things," Fannie said. "However, the main reason I came by was to see if you've heard anything from Samuel."

Naomi shook her head. "Have you, Mama Fannie?"

"No, and I'm getting worried. It's been two whole days since they left, and I would think they'd have gotten there by now."

"If the roads between here and Kentucky are icy, then they've probably gone slow." Naomi smiled, although her ebony-colored eyes showed a bit of concern. "I'm sure we'll hear something soon."

"I hope so." Fannie leaned on the counter. "How are things with you and your family? Is everyone doing okay?"

"With the exception of Caleb, everyone's fine," Naomi said.

"What's wrong with him?"

"He has a really bad cold, and last night when he coughed and bent over at the same time, his back spasmed." Naomi winced, as though she could almost feel her husband's pain. "He's hurting real bad so he stayed home to rest today."

"Has he been to see the chiropractor?"

"No. Said he figured it would get better on its own in a few days."

Fannie grunted. "Men. They can be so *schtarrkeppich* sometimes."

"That's for sure, and my husband is probably the most stubborn man of all."

The door jingled, and Timothy's wife, Hannah, entered the store with her pretty little blond-haired daughter, Mindy, who was two. Since Hannah's hair was brown, and so was Timothy's, Mindy took after Hannah's mother, whose nearly gray hair had originally been blond.

"Wie geht's?" Fannie asked.

"We're fine," Hannah replied. "How are you doing?"

"I'd be better if I'd hear something from Samuel."

Hannah rolled her eyes. "I still can't believe he moved to Kentucky. First Titus, and now Samuel. I sure hope Timothy doesn't get any ideas about moving there."

"That would be baremlich," Fannie said. "I don't think I could stand losing three of my boys and their families to Kentucky."

"I think you're worried for nothing," Naomi put in. "I'm sure Timothy has no plans to move."

Hannah wrinkled her nose. "He'd better not because I like it here in Pennsylvania, and I'd never agree to move to Kentucky."

Fannie was certainly relieved to hear that. "Think I'll say hello to Abby while I'm here," she said, moving toward the back of the store where the quilt shop was located. "Is she working today?"

"Jah," Naomi said. "She came in early this morning."

Fannie said good-bye to Hannah and hurried into the adjoining room, anxious to visit a few minutes with her daughter.

———— ⚋⚋ ————

Pembroke, Kentucky

"According to the directions your brother sent us, we must be close to his place now," Samuel's driver, Stan Haman, said as he turned his van onto Pembroke Road.

"It's right here." Samuel motioned to his right where he saw a mailbox with Titus's name and address on it. "We finally made it," he said, turning in his seat to look at the kids.

The children stared wide eyed out the window.

When they pulled into the driveway covered with several inches of snow, a double-wide manufactured home came into view.

Stan had no sooner stopped the van, when Titus came

out of the house, waving and smiling from ear to ear.

Samuel hopped out of the van and met Titus in the yard. After the long drive from Pennsylvania, it felt good to stretch his legs.

"It's great seeing you." Titus gave Samuel a hug. "Did you have a good trip?"

"It was slow because of the snow, and the kinner were fussy," Samuel said, "but we made it safely at least."

Titus opened the back door of the van, and the children scrambled out, squealing and running around in the snow. Their black Lab, Lucky, followed, barking and bounding at their heels.

"Guess I'd better get my horse, Socks, out of the trailer," Samuel said, shaking out more kinks in his legs as he walked to the back of the van where the trailer was hitched. "Do you have an empty stall for him in your barn?"

Titus nodded. "There's plenty of room, and I'm sure my horse, Lightning, will be glad for the company."

Sometime later, when everything had been unloaded and Samuel's driver had gone, Titus escorted everyone into the house and showed them around.

"I only have three bedrooms here," he said, "so the boys will have to share a room with you, and the girls can have the third bedroom."

"Guess that's how it'll have to be then," Samuel said as they walked down the narrow hall and looked into each room. He hoped it wouldn't be long before he could get a place of their own, but by living here, they'd not only have a roof over their heads, but he'd have Titus's help with the kids—at least in the evenings when Titus wasn't working. The question was who would watch them during the day once Samuel found a job?

Guess there's a lot of things I didn't think about before I decided to move, he thought as he watched the children play with two cats they'd discovered in the barn and brought into the house. *Sure hope I didn't make a mistake by coming here. Maybe I should have prayed about the move. But then,*

God doesn't seem to be listening to me lately, so what would have been the use?

Samuel knew he shouldn't let his thoughts go in that direction. They were here now, and as time went on, hopefully things would start falling into place. He'd just need to give it some time.

CHAPTER 5

"Have you called Mom and Dad yet?" Titus asked Samuel as they sat at the table, drinking coffee while the kids took the cats back to the barn.

"I suppose I should do that now. If I don't call them soon, Mama Fannie will probably leave a string of messages on your voice mail."

"She already has." Titus smiled. "You know how Mom tends to worry. Nearly hounded me to death when I first moved to Kentucky."

Samuel grunted as he forced himself to stand. He was bone-tired despite the fact that he hadn't done much all day other than to haul their things into the house and put his horse in the barn. He hadn't brought any of his household items or furniture along because he knew he wouldn't have a place to put them right now. Besides, when he'd put his house up for sale, he'd advertised it as fully furnished. He didn't want any of the furniture he and Elsie had chosen when they'd first gotten married. It would just be one more reminder that she was gone. So all he'd brought to Kentucky were his and the kids' clothes, some of his tools, his horse and buggy, a box of toys for the kids, their troublesome dog, and a few personal things that had belonged to Elsie. He'd asked his sister Mary Ann to put Elsie's things in a box because he hadn't had the strength or the courage to sort through them. He knew he'd have to do it at some point, but not yet. Right now, he wasn't even able to look at Elsie's things.

"You okay?" Titus asked, bringing Samuel's thoughts to a halt.

"Jah, sure. Why do you ask?"

"You said you were going out to the phone shanty to call Mom and Dad, but you've been standing there several minutes now, staring at the door."

"I was thinking," Samuel mumbled.

"About what you're gonna say to Mom and Dad?"

Samuel shook his head. "That's easy enough. I'm just going to tell 'em we got here okay. I was thinking about other things." He hurried out the door before Titus had a chance to question him further. He didn't want to talk about his feelings, and he hoped Titus wouldn't pry. He wanted the chance to start over and needed to concentrate on finding a way to earn a decent living so he could provide for his kids, because he wasn't about to let Titus support them very long.

Samuel stepped behind the barn to the phone shanty Titus had shown him earlier. After he'd made a call to his folks and left a message, he dialed his brother Zach's cell phone.

"Hey Zach, it's me, Samuel," he said, when Zach's voice mail came on. "Just wanted you to know that we made it to Titus's okay. Talk to you soon."

Samuel hung up the phone and trudged back through the slippery, wet snow toward the house. He was sort of glad he merely had to leave a message for his parents and brother. Right now, holding a conversation and answering a lot of questions would have drained him even more.

He'd only made it halfway there, when the two cats the kids had been playing with earlier darted out of the barn, followed by Lucky, who was hot on their heels. Hissing and meowing, the cats ran up the nearest tree. Lucky slid across the snow after them, bounced against the tree, and toppled over. He didn't stay down long though. He leaped to his feet and started barking frantically as he pawed at the trunk of the tree.

Samuel's son, Leon, dashed across the yard hollering at the dog, "*Kumme*, Lucky!" He slapped the side of his leg a couple of times. "Come to me now!"

The dog kept barking as he crouched in front of the tree, looking up at the cats huddled together on a branch high above.

"I was gonna play with the *katze* till Lucky came along and scared the life outa 'em," Leon grumbled.

Samuel bent down and grabbed Lucky's collar, but the dog growled and bared his teeth.

"Knock it off!" Samuel shouted. "You know better than that. Now come with me, you *dummkopp hund*."

"Lucky ain't stupid, Daadi. He's a very *schmaert* dog," Leon said, lifting his chin to look up at Samuel.

"He's not too smart when he doesn't do what he's told." Samuel pulled Lucky to his feet and continued slipping and sliding in the direction of the barn. He was almost there, when a horse and buggy rolled into the yard. He recognized Suzanne when she climbed down from the buggy, but he didn't know the young, dark-haired woman with her.

———

When Esther stepped out of Suzanne's buggy, she noticed a tall Amish man with light brown hair peeking out from under his dark blue stocking cap. He held onto the collar of a black Lab, thrashing about, kicking up snow with its back feet.

"That's Titus's brother, Samuel," Suzanne said to Esther. "I'd introduce you, but he seems a little busy right now."

Obviously struggling to gain control over the dog, Samuel leaned to the right, then to the left. With a sudden jerk, the dog pulled free, and Samuel fell, facedown in the snow. He came up, red-faced and hollering, "You dummkopp hund! I should have left you in Pennsylvania to fend for yourself!"

It was a comical sight, and Esther struggled not to

laugh. She could tell by the way Suzanne's face was contorted that she thought it was funny, too.

The young boy with sandy brown hair who stood nearby wasn't laughing. He looked up at Samuel and said in a pathetic little voice, "Daadi, please don't yell at Lucky. He just wants to be free to run."

"Well, he's not gonna be free. I'm puttin' him away in the barn so he can't terrorize those cats anymore!"

"Don't think he means to hurt the katze," the child said. "Think he just wants to play with 'em."

Ignoring the boy's comment, Samuel chased after the dog, grabbed hold of its collar, and pulled the struggling animal to the barn.

Feeling the need to comfort the boy, who appeared to be on the verge of tears, Esther knelt in the snow beside him. "My name's Esther. What's yours?"

"Leon." The child dropped his gaze to the ground. Was he shy or just upset about the dog and not wanting to let on?

"How old are you, Leon?" Esther asked.

"Six. I'm in the first grade at school."

"Is Lucky your dog?"

Leon lifted his head and looked right at Esther. "Nope. He liked our mamm the best, but after she went to heaven, he started hangin' around my daed." Tears welled in Leon's brown eyes, and he sniffed a couple of times. " 'Course Daadi don't like Lucky much. He don't like much of anything since *Mammi* died."

Esther's heart went out to the boy. She was sure that he wasn't just upset about the dog. He missed his mother and didn't understand the reason for his dad's behavior.

A few minutes later, Samuel reappeared—without the dog.

"It's good to see you, Samuel," Suzanne said, shaking his hand. "How was your trip?"

"It went okay."

Suzanne motioned to Esther. "This is my friend Esther

Beiler. We were on our way to the bakery but decided to stop here first and see if Titus wanted us to pick something up for him."

Samuel barely glanced at Esther. Then with a quick, "Nice to meet you," he tromped off toward the house.

"Maybe we picked a bad time to come," Esther whispered to Suzanne.

Suzanne shrugged. "We're here now, and I want to see Titus, so let's go inside." She looked down at Leon and held out her hand. "You'd better come with us. It's too cold to be out here in the snow."

When they stepped into the living room, Esther was surprised to see Titus sitting on the couch with two young girls, one with blond hair and one with brown hair, on either side of him. In his lap he held a small, blond-haired boy wearing diapers and a white T-shirt. Titus looked perfectly comfortable with the children.

He'll make a good father someday, Esther thought, *and Suzanne will be a good mother.*

"Did anything unusual happen outside?" Titus asked, looking at Suzanne. "When Samuel came in a few minutes ago, covered in snow, he tromped off to his room like he was really upset."

Suzanne explained what had transpired with the dog and went on to say how angry Samuel had gotten.

"My *bruder's* going through a rough time right now, so we'll need to be patient with him," Titus said.

Suzanne touched Leon's shoulder as she nodded at the three children sitting with Titus. "We need to help his kinner adjust to their new surroundings, too."

"Jah." Titus looked at Esther. "Would you like to meet my nieces and nephews?"

She smiled. "I met Leon outside, but of course I'd like to meet his brother and sisters, too."

"This is Marla." Titus motioned to the girl on his left. "She's eight years old, and here on my right is Penny. She's four. Now this little guy here is Jared, and he's two," he said, placing his hand on the boy's blond head.

Esther knelt on the floor in front of the couch, smiling up at the children. "*Mei naame* is Esther."

The children nodded as they stared at her with curious expressions.

Esther stayed like that for several seconds then rose to her feet. Samuel's children were obviously not comfortable around her yet. She'd always loved children and hoped she'd have the chance to get to know these four in the days ahead. But for now, not wanting to overwhelm them, the simple introduction would suffice.

CHAPTER 6

During Bonnie's first two days in Kentucky, she'd stayed at a hotel in Hopkinsville. The first day she had attended her grandmother's funeral—alone, without her father because he'd refused to come here for his own mother's funeral. The service had been held at the small church in Fairview where Grandma and Grandpa had attended. There wasn't a large crowd, since many of Grandma and Grandpa's friends were old and had passed on, but the people who had come seemed nice and offered Bonnie their heartfelt sympathies at her grandmother's passing.

The second day, Bonnie had met with Grandma's lawyer, Michael Givens, to go over the will and some other important papers. She still couldn't believe Grandma had left her the house, as well as all her money. It really should have gone to Dad, but when she'd called him the other day, he'd said he wanted nothing that was his folks, including their money—nothing at all. Mr. Givens had reminded Bonnie that since her father was Grandma and Grandpa's only child and was estranged from his parents, she should accept what had been left to her and be grateful.

This morning, Bonnie had driven out to her grandparents' home in the small town of Pembroke, where she'd been going through cupboards and closets and putting some things in boxes. It was a monumental job, but if she was going to get the place ready to sell, it had to be done. It was difficult sorting through these things—especially Grandma's, as she'd been the last one living in this cozy old house. In the dresser drawers, Bonnie had found an abundance of cotton hankies with lace edges, several sweaters and slippers Grandma had obviously knitted, two flannel nightgowns, and some of Grandma's lingerie.

As Bonnie sat on the edge of the bed in Grandma's room, which was on the main floor of the rambling old house, her fingers trailed over a pair of light blue knitted slippers. Grandma had taught her how to knit during a summer visit when Bonnie was twelve. She'd also helped Bonnie sew an apron, which she'd worn when she helped Grandma bake some cookies. Those were happy memories, and Bonnie wished she could relive them.

The rumble of a vehicle interrupted Bonnie's musings. She went to the window facing the front yard and looked out. A dark blue truck was parked in the driveway, next to the small red car she'd rented when she'd flown into Nashville. A young man with dark curly hair stepped out and trudged through the snow up to the house.

Bonnie left the room and hurried to the door before he had a chance to knock.

"Hi. I'm Allen Walters," the man said. "I was driving by and noticed a car parked in the driveway so I decided to stop."

Bonnie tensed and folded her arms. "If you're selling something, I'm really not interested."

He shook his head. "I'm not a salesman. I'm a general contractor, and I understand that the woman who used to live here passed away recently, so I was wondering if the place might be up for sale."

Bonnie relaxed a bit. She might be able to sell the place quicker than she'd thought. She smiled and extended her hand. "I'm Bonnie Taylor, and this house belonged to my grandparents, Andy and Margaret Taylor. I live in Portland, Oregon, but when I found out that Grandma had died, I came here for the funeral. Today I've been going through her things, trying to decide what I should get rid of and what I might want to keep."

"Did your grandmother leave the house to you?" he questioned.

Bonnie nodded.

"Are you going to sell it?"

"That's the plan." She hugged her arms around her chest, feeling the cold air penetrate her skin. "So if you bought the house, would it be for you?"

He shook his head. "I already have a house in Hopkinsville. However, I'm still interested in buying this place."

"How come?"

"I often buy homes that need fixing up. Then after I renovate them, I turn around and sell them again."

"In other words, you make a profit?"

Allen nodded, reached into his jacket pocket, and handed Bonnie his business card. "Give me a call once you've decided how much you want for the place."

"Okay."

As Allen walked away and Bonnie shut the door, a feeling of nostalgia washed over her. She didn't know why, but she was suddenly having second thoughts about selling the house. But if she didn't put Grandma and Grandpa's place on the market, what would she do with it?

She moved toward the fireplace to warm up and took a seat on the floor near the hearth. Looking about, despite the fact that the house was in dire need of repairs, it had a certain appeal and quaint-looking charm. The solid oak cupboards in the kitchen, with matching table and chairs; the spacious dining room with a built-in hutch; a roomy living room with a cozy window bench near the window; a simple, but beautiful, stained glass window above the front door—this homey place reminded her of a quaint bed-and-breakfast she'd stayed in once along the Oregon coast. She'd been relaxed and comfortable there and hadn't wanted to leave.

I wonder what Grandma would think if I turned her house into a bed-and-breakfast. There are no hotels nearby—the closest ones are in Hopkinsville. If I opened a B&B, it would give folks visiting this area a nice place to stay. Bonnie rubbed her hands together in front of the fire as she contemplated the idea. *But then, if I did that, I'd either have to hire someone to run the place or move here and run it myself.*

She stared at the flames lapping against the logs in the fireplace as she continued to ponder things. *I'm really not that happy living in Oregon anyway, so if I quit my job and moved to Kentucky, it would be a new beginning for me. I have fond memories here, and it would certainly be an adventure.*

———✧———

Samuel flopped onto the sofa in Titus's living room with a groan. He hadn't slept well last night, and it had been all he could do to hitch his horse to the buggy this morning and take Marla and Leon to school. As soon as he'd dropped them off, he'd come right back, prepared to spend the day resting. He knew he couldn't lounge around forever though. Once he found someone who'd be willing to watch his kids, he'd look for a job.

"Can Jared and me go outside and play?" Penny asked, tugging on Samuel's shirtsleeve.

Samuel shook his head. "You can play in here."

She thrust out her bottom lip in a pout. "We wanna play in the *schnee.*"

"I said no. It's cold outside, and you don't need to play in the snow."

"But there's nothin' to do in here. Uncle Titus don't have no toys for kids to play with."

"The toys we brought with us when we moved are in one of the boxes in my room." Samuel rose from his seat. "Let's go see."

Samuel headed for the bedroom, with Penny and Jared trudging after him. He looked through a couple of boxes that had been stacked along one wall, but the kids' toys weren't in any of them—just their clothes. When he opened another box, his breath caught in his throat. It was full of Elsie's things.

"What's this?" Penny asked, pulling a soft yellow baby blanket from the box. It was one Elsie had made for the baby she'd lost when she'd fallen down the stairs.

Samuel grabbed the blanket from Penny and clutched it to his chest. "It's nothing. Just a blanket, that's all."

She reached out her hand. "Can I have it, Daadi?"

"No!" he said a bit too harshly. Then, gaining control of his emotions, he put the blanket back in the box.

To Samuel's relief, he found another box marked KIDS' TOYS. Picking up the box, he hauled it out to the living room, set it on the floor, and opened the flaps. While the kids played with their toys, he would lie on the sofa and take a nap. Sleeping was the only way he could deal with his pain and escape from the raw emotions that still consumed him every waking moment and even in his dreams.

—⁓—

As Esther headed in her buggy down the road toward Titus's house, she thought about Samuel's children and wondered how they were doing. She'd done some baking this morning and had decided to take a batch of cookies to the kids.

Sometime later, Esther pulled her horse and buggy into Titus's yard and was surprised to see little Penny and Jared rolling around in the snow with only lightweight jackets and no mittens or boots.

"What are you two doing out here in the cold?" Esther asked after she'd tied her horse to the hitching rail.

"We're makin' snow angels," Penny said, standing up and pointing to her latest impression.

Looking around at all the imprints, Esther could see that the children had been quite busy. The urge to plop down and relive that special childhood memory was hard to resist, but right now she wanted to take the cookies inside and speak to Samuel about his two youngest children.

"Where's your daed?" Esther couldn't imagine him

letting them play out here by themselves. Especially little Jared, who was hardly more than a baby. What if he'd wandered off?

"Daadi's in there." Penny pointed to the house.

With the container of cookies tucked under one arm, Esther took the children's hands, and they trudged through the snow to the house, where she knocked on the door. When no one answered, she turned the knob and went in. Samuel lay asleep on the sofa. She didn't know whether to wake him or tiptoe to the kitchen and leave the cookies. Before she had the chance to decide, Samuel sat up with a start.

"Wh—what's going on? What are you doing here?" he mumbled, barely looking at her.

"I brought some cookies for your kinner," she explained. "When I got here, I was surprised to see the little ones playing in the snow by themselves, wearing only thin jackets and no boots or mittens."

"What?" He jumped up and glared at his children. "What were you two doing out there? I told you not to go outside!"

Penny and Jared turned red-faced and looked guilty. Crystals of snow slowly melted from their hair.

"Would you two like some peanut butter cookies?" Esther pointed to the container she held. "I made them this morning."

The children's eyes lit right up. "Can we have some *kichlin*?" Penny asked, looking up at her father.

"I should say no, since you disobeyed me and went outside, but if you promise to behave yourselves, you can have some cookies," he said. "Go to your rooms first and take off your jackets and wet shoes before you go to the kitchen."

"Okay."

Penny grabbed her little brother's hand, and they hurried down the hall.

Esther felt a bit awkward, standing there holding the

cookies, so she looked at Samuel and said, "Should I put these in the kitchen?"

"Jah, sure," he mumbled without looking at her.

I wonder who'll watch Samuel's kids once he gets a job, Esther thought as she headed to the kitchen. *I hope he's not foolish enough to leave them home by themselves.*

CHAPTER 7

"Hey Titus! How's it going?" Allen asked when he stepped into the woodshop where Titus knelt on the floor, sanding a cabinet door.

Titus looked up and smiled. "Pretty good. How are things with you?"

"Not bad." Allen looked at Suzanne's brother, Nelson. "How's business overall? Have you been keeping busy here at the shop, or do you need more outside jobs?"

"We can use all the work we can get right now." Nelson, who was just a few years younger than Suzanne, pushed his red hair off his freckled forehead and frowned. "Things were real busy before Christmas, but they've slowed down a lot since then. Suzanne's not even working here in the shop this week."

"That's too bad. Things have been a little slower for me, too, but hopefully work will pick up in the spring." Allen smiled. "When it does, I'm sure I'll have a lot more jobs for you."

"I hope so." Titus swiped a hand across his sweaty forehead. "With five more people living in my house right now, I need to keep working steady."

"Hasn't Samuel found a job yet?" Allen asked.

Titus shook his head. "He's been here two weeks already, and as far as I know, he hasn't really been looking."

"How come?"

"Says he doesn't have anyone to watch the kids, but I'm sure if he finds a job we can find someone willing to watch them," Titus replied.

"I understand he's done some painting for Zach."

"That's right. He also has some carpentry skills, and we'd hoped to hire him to help out here, but as I said before, we don't have much work right now."

"If I hear of anything, I'll be sure to let him know." Allen turned toward the door. "Guess I'd better get going. I've got several errands I need to run yet today."

———✴———

Two weeks ago, Bonnie had returned from Portland, where she'd put in her resignation at the advertising agency, told her landlord she was moving, and packed up her things. She'd also told her dad good-bye, which of course, hadn't gone well at all. Even though he'd tried to dissuade her, she'd returned to Kentucky and spent the last few days cleaning and organizing more things in her grandparents' home. Some things she'd tossed out, some had gone to a charity organization in Hopkinsville, and some—like dishes, glassware, and linens—she would put to good use. Even with everything she'd done, there were more closets and cupboards she hadn't gone through—not to mention all the stuff in the attic.

Bonnie had also applied for a business license and taken care of some other necessary paperwork involving opening her new business, but there were still some major repairs that would have to be done to the place before she could even think about advertising or opening for business. She'd also have to hire someone to help at the B&B—cleaning the guest rooms and hopefully helping her prepare the food she would serve for breakfast every morning.

"So much to do," she muttered as she made her way to the kitchen to clean out a few more cupboards. "Sure hope I haven't bitten off more than I can chew."

She found one of Grandma's aprons in the pantry and slipped it on. *Oh Grandma, I miss you and wish I'd come to visit while you were in the nursing home. Were you lonely there? Did you think no one cared?*

Bonnie remembered the day of Grandma's funeral when one of the women who'd attended the service had mentioned that she'd gone to the nursing home to visit Grandma at least once a week. *I'm thankful Grandma's friend was there for her, even though I wish now it had been me. So many regrets. Why do I always look back and wish I could do things differently? Why can't I make wise decisions at the right time, and do things I won't later regret?*

Knowing she couldn't undo the past, Bonnie resolved to keep a positive attitude and stay busy for the rest of the day. She'd just taken a sponge and some cleanser from under the kitchen sink when she heard a vehicle pull into the yard. She peered out the window and noticed a pickup truck parked in the driveway. When a young man with curly dark hair, wearing a baseball cap got out, she realized it was the same man who'd stopped by two weeks ago asking about buying the house.

Bonnie slipped into her sweater, hurried to the door, and opened it just as he stepped onto the porch.

"Good morning," he said. "Remember me?"

She nodded. "Allen Walters, right?"

"That's correct." Allen offered her a wide smile, revealing two deep dimples. "I was in the area and thought I'd stop by and see what you've decided about selling this place."

She leaned against the doorjamb. "I've actually decided not to sell."

"Really? I'm surprised. This place is so big, and unless you have a large family then—"

"I'm not married. It'll just be me living here—at least until I get the place ready to open for business."

He tipped his head. "What kind of business?"

"I've decided to turn my grandparents' home into a bed-and-breakfast."

"Are you sure that's a good idea? I mean, this place

is old, and from what I can tell, it needs a whole lot of work."

"I realize that, but it's roomy and has lots of charm. Besides, from what I've seen, there aren't a lot of places for visitors to stay in the area unless they go to a hotel in Hopkinsville."

"You do have a point, but bringing this place up to code would involve quite a bit of money and time."

"I quit my job in Oregon, so I have the time. Between what I have in my savings and the money my grandparents left me, I should be able to live comfortably for a while and also pay for any necessary repairs that need to be done." She folded her arms. "Since you're a contractor, would you be interested in doing the work for me?"

"I might be able to do some things, but I couldn't do everything because before I came here this morning I got a call about remodeling a house not far from where I live, and I'll have to start on that right away." Allen gave the brim of his baseball cap a tug. "Come to think of it, I do know someone who's a qualified painter, and he's also done some carpentry work. He's a widowed Amish man with four kids. He's new to the area and needs a job right now. His name is Samuel Fisher, and he's living with his brother whose home is not too far from here."

"That sounds like a good possibility. From what I understand, the Amish are really hard workers."

"You're right about that. Any of them I've ever known do quality work. Would you like me to bring Samuel by so you can talk to him?"

She nodded. "I'd appreciate that very much."

—⁓—

Realizing it was time to fix Penny and Jared some lunch, Samuel forced himself to head out to the kitchen, where he fumbled around in the propane-operated refrigerator, searching for something the kids would eat. Penny liked most things, but Jared was picky.

He finally decided on peanut butter and jelly sandwiches, knowing both kids liked that. He'd just gotten the kids seated at the table when a knock sounded on the door.

"I wonder who that could be." Samuel ambled over to the door, and when he opened it, he was surprised to see Allen Walters standing on the porch. He'd met Allen when he'd brought Titus and Suzanne to Pennsylvania for Elsie's funeral, but Samuel hadn't said more than a few words to him. Of course, he'd been so consumed with his grief, he hadn't said much to anyone that day. Even now, he found it hard to make conversation. He just wanted to be left alone.

"Hi, Samuel. How are you doing?" Allen asked as he brushed some fresh-fallen snow off his jacket.

"Gettin' by," Samuel mumbled.

"Any leads on a job yet?"

Samuel shook his head. " 'Course I haven't looked that hard since I have no one to watch my kids." He glanced over his shoulder and frowned when he noticed that Jared had a blob of strawberry jam stuck to his chin and some sticky peanut butter on the front of his shirt.

"I was wondering if you'd be interested in doing a remodeling job at a house not far from here. The young woman who lives there is planning to turn the place into a bed-and-breakfast."

Samuel knew he needed a job—he couldn't lie around here forever, sponging off Titus. "I am interested in the job," he said, "but as I said, I'll need to find someone to watch my kids while I'm at work."

"I think I know someone who'd be perfect for the job," Allen said. "If it's all right with you, I'll head over to her place now and talk to her about it."

Samuel gave a nod. He hoped whoever Allen had in mind was good with kids, because Jared could be a handful at times.

CHAPTER 8

The following morning while the kids finished their breakfast, Titus and Samuel sat on the sofa in the living room, drinking coffee and visiting before Titus left for work.

"Sure hope this snow goes away soon," Titus said with a frown. "Makes me wish I was in Sarasota, Florida right now."

Samuel winced at the mention of Sarasota. Elsie had always wanted to visit there, and Samuel had promised to take her and the kids someday, but of course, it hadn't happened. So many regrets. So many wishes that never came true.

Titus nudged Samuel's elbow. "Did I say something wrong? You look *umgerennt*."

Samuel shook his head, keeping his regrets to himself. "It's nothing. I'm not upset."

Someone knocked on the front door, and Titus rose from his seat. When he returned, Allen was with him.

Allen smiled at Samuel and said, "I've got good news. I found someone to watch your kids, so as soon as she gets here, I can take you over to the Taylor place so you can speak to the owner about what she needs to have done. If she hires you, then you can begin right away, since the kids will have a sitter."

Samuel sat a few seconds, letting it all soak in. He hadn't expected Allen would find him a job, much a less a sitter. But this was the chance he needed, so he couldn't turn it down. "Sure," he said with a nod. "That sounds good."

Titus thumped Samuel's arm. "I knew God would provide a job for you."

"I don't have the job yet." Samuel shrugged, not wanting to get too excited about it. He'd had too many disappointments already. "I have to speak with the owner first and see what she needs done. Maybe it's something I'm not qualified to do. Or maybe she's interviewing other people and will hire one of them."

"Don't sell yourself short," Allen said. "I'm sure you're more than qualified, and as far as I know, Bonnie hasn't interviewed anyone else. In fact, she asked if I knew of someone who could do the work, and my first thought was you."

"Even so, that doesn't mean she'll hire me. And there may be things I might not be able to do." Samuel wouldn't give in to the mounting hope of this job, fearing it would be snatched away from him before he had the chance to even meet the woman.

"You sound like me when I first moved to Kentucky," Titus interjected. "I didn't have much confidence in myself and was always afraid I'd mess up."

Samuel knew his brother was right. Since Elsie had died, he didn't feel like he could do much of anything right—especially where his kids were concerned.

Another knock sounded on the door. "I'll get it." Titus hurried out of the room. When he returned, Esther Beiler was with him.

"If you came to get the container you brought the cookies in the other day, it's in the kitchen." Samuel stood. "I'll get it for you."

Esther shook her head. "I'm not here for my container. I came to watch your kinner while you go with Allen to see about a possible job."

"Oh, I see." Samuel knew from what Titus had told him about Esther that she wasn't married and lived alone because her folks had moved to Pennsylvania. Since she was single, he didn't know how much experience she'd had with children. He'd give her a chance, but if it didn't work out, he hoped he could find someone else.

———⚎———

Bonnie had just stepped outside to feed a stray cat that had been hanging around the place the last couple of days, when she saw Allen's pickup pull into the yard. She waited on the porch, watching as Allen and a tall Amish man got out of the truck and sloshed their way through the wet snow to the house.

"I'd like you to meet Samuel Fisher," Allen said to Bonnie when the men joined her on the porch. He gestured to Samuel, then to Bonnie. "Samuel, this is Bonnie Taylor, and this old house that needs fixing used to belong to her grandparents."

Bonnie smiled and shook Samuel's hand, noting the strength in his handshake. She also noticed that he barely made eye contact with her. Was he shy, wary of strangers, or just an unfriendly sort of person?

"Come in out of the cold," Bonnie said. "I'll show you what I think needs to be done inside."

Allen motioned to the broken railing on the porch and the peeling paint on the side of the house. "Looks like there's a lot to be done out here as well."

"You're right about that," Bonnie said as the men followed her into the house. "Let's start in the kitchen." She led the way and pointed out all the things she felt needed fixing: walls to be painted, stained and torn linoleum to be replaced, an electric stove with only two burners that worked, and the need for a second oven.

"I can do the painting no problem, because I did a lot of it when I lived in Pennsylvania and worked for my older brother," Samuel said. "I can also replace the linoleum, but the stove and oven will involve electrical hookups, which I know nothing about."

"No problem," Allen said. "I can talk to Adam Jarvis,

the electrician who does most of my work, and see if he can take care of any electrical problems for you."

Bonnie smiled. "I'd appreciate that."

"What else needs to be done in the house?" Samuel asked, looking around.

"Well, there are six large bedrooms here, a living room, dining room, and two full bathrooms. As near as I can tell, every one of them needs some kind of updating or repairs. That should keep you busy throughout the rest of winter, and then this spring, when the weather improves, you can start on the outside of the house."

Samuel leaned against the kitchen counter and gave her a nod. "I'm willing to do whatever I can."

"Great!" Bonnie clapped her hands and then motioned to the kitchen table. "Let's have a seat, and we'll talk about your wages."

—m—

Esther smiled as she watched Jared and Penny sitting on the living room floor, each holding one of Titus's cats. The one Penny held was Callie, an orange, black, and white calico. The cat in Jared's lap had white hair with a black spot on his head. That cat Titus had named Buttons. Esther figured the cats would be in for a challenge with the feisty black Lab she'd seen out in the yard. The dog obviously belonged to Samuel, because Titus only had cats.

Jared got up off the floor, set Buttons on the sofa, and climbed up beside him.

"I don't think your uncle Titus allows the cats to be on the furniture," Esther said in German-Dutch, so that Jared, who hadn't learned English yet, would understand. "Please put the cat on the floor."

Jared just sat there, stroking the cat's head, as though he hadn't heard a word she'd said.

"Jared, did you understand me?"

The boy gave no reply, nor did he make any effort to put the cat on the floor.

"His thinker ain't workin' so well today," Penny said. "Fact is, he don't do much of anything he's told—not since Mammi died anyways. I think he misses her, same as me."

Esther's heart went out to Penny and Jared. No doubt the two older children missed their mother as well. After all, she'd only been gone a little over two months. Poor little Jared wasn't much more than a baby, and what child of his age didn't need his mother's nurturing?

"Why don't we all go into the kitchen and have a snack?" Esther suggested.

Penny jumped up, raced to the front door, and put the calico cat outside. Jared climbed down from the sofa and put his cat outside as well. Then both children followed Esther into the kitchen. Penny climbed onto a chair, and Esther picked Jared up and lifted him into his high chair. Then she gave them each a glass of milk, some crackers, and a few apple slices.

The kids were just finishing their snack when the back door opened and Allen stepped in. "I came by to tell you that Samuel's going to start working for Bonnie right away—that is if you're free to stay here with the kids for the rest of the day."

Esther nodded. Now she'd just need to think of something to keep Penny and Jared occupied for the next several hours.

CHAPTER 9

By the time Bonnie dropped Samuel off at Titus's, after he'd worked at her place most of the day, he was exhausted. It was a good kind of exhaustion though—the kind that comes from working so hard that your muscles ache—the kind that keeps a person so busy there's no time to think or dwell on the past. Besides securing a position that would give him a steady income for the next few months, putting in a good day's work helped take his mind off Elsie and how much he missed her. Sleeping and working. . .those were the only times when he felt free of his pain and despair. Well, if working was what it took, then he'd keep busy doing something from now on.

Samuel was almost to the house when he decided to give Zach a call. He hadn't talked to anyone from home in several days and wanted to let them know he'd found a job.

He crunched his way through the snow, and when he entered the dilapidated-looking shanty, he flipped on the battery-operated light sitting beside the phone.

He could see his breath in there, and the small wooden structure seemed even colder than it was outside, so he wasted no time in making the call. When Zach answered, Samuel told him about Bonnie Taylor and the work he'd be doing at her house, and how it would eventually be turned into a bed-and-breakfast.

"That's good news about the job," Zach said. "Finding work during the winter months is sometimes hard to do."

"Bonnie said she'll have work for me in the spring, too.

She wants the outside of the house painted and also any necessary repairs that will need to be done. Plus, there's an old guest house on the property she wants me to fix up. Your friend, Allen, will do some of the carpentry work when he's able to fit it into his schedule, and one of the electricians he knows will do all the electrical work."

"When does she plan to open the B&B?"

"Hopefully by late spring, but not until all the repairs and remodeling have been done. The place is pretty run down right now and needs a lot of work, so it could take longer than planned, I suppose."

Woof! Woof! Samuel's black Lab bounded in through the open door and flopped a wet, snowy paw on Samuel's knee, obviously wanting his attention.

"Get down, Lucky," he grumbled. "Guess that's what I get for not shutting the door."

"What's up with the dog?" Zach asked.

"He's just making a nuisance of himself, like usual." Automatically, Samuel scratched behind the dog's ears as Lucky leaned in closer for more. Lucky used to love it whenever Elsie petted him. He'd been her dog from the time he was a pup, and it had been comical to watch the mutt follow her all over the place.

"How are the kids adjusting to the move?" Zach asked. "Do they like it there?"

"I guess they're okay with it." Truth was, Samuel hadn't bothered to ask any of them if they liked their new home or not. Even if they didn't like it that much, they were kids, and kids adjusted to things easier than adults. They seemed to have adjusted to their mother's absence, because they rarely mentioned her name. But then of course, Samuel didn't talk about Elsie either. It was better that way. Better to deal with the agony of losing her in silence.

"Guess I'd better let you go," Zach said. "It's probably cold out there in the phone shed."

"They call 'em shanties here, and you're right. It is pretty cold."

"I'll let the rest of the family know about your new job," Zach said.

"Okay. Talk to you later then."

Samuel hung up the phone, but before he could stand, Lucky whimpered and flopped his other paw on Samuel's knee. Samuel knew the dog missed Elsie and wanted more of his attention, but he didn't feel like it right now. He just wanted to get into the house where it was warm. So he pushed Lucky away, stepped out of the shanty, and sloshed his way through the snow. These days even their family pet seemed like a nuisance—and at times like now, he was the biggest nuisance of all.

When Samuel entered the house and stepped into the living room, he halted. Esther was seated in the rocking chair with Jared asleep in her arms. A wisp of Esther's dark hair had escaped her head covering and lay across her slightly pink cheek. She looked so content holding Jared like that.

A lump formed in his throat. Seeing Esther with Jared made him think of Elsie, and how she used to rock Jared to sleep each night. It didn't seem right that someone else should be holding his little boy. It didn't seem right that Elsie wasn't here to care for him and the other children.

Samuel took a step, and the floor creaked beneath his feet.

Suddenly, Esther's eyes snapped open. "Oh, you're home!" She glanced at the battery-operated clock on the far wall. "I—I didn't realize it was getting so late."

"Guess you wouldn't, since you've been sleeping."

"I must have dozed off after Jared fell asleep in my arms." Esther looked down at the rosy-cheeked boy and smiled. "He's sure a cute little guy."

Samuel just removed his hat and jacket and draped them over a chair.

"How'd it go today?" Esther asked.

"Fine. I'll be going over there every day until the work's all done. Can you keep watchin' the kids for me? I'll pay you a fair wage of course."

"I'd be happy to watch them. I enjoyed myself today, and I think the kinner and I got along quite well."

"Where's Penny?" he asked, glancing around the room.

"She's in her bedroom with Buttons."

Barely looking at Esther, Samuel scratched the side of his head. "Buttons?"

"One of Titus's cats has a mark on its head that looks like a black button."

Samuel raised his eyebrows, as irritation set in. "I hope that cat's not on the bed, because Penny knows her mamm doesn't approve of pets on the furniture. I—I mean, when Elsie was alive, she didn't approve." Embarrassed and angry, Samuel whirled around and headed down the hall toward the room Penny shared with Marla.

—⁓—

Seeing the angry look on Samuel's face, Esther was afraid Penny might be in trouble with her father. She wished there was something she could do to intercede on the child's behalf.

It's probably best if I don't say anything, she decided. *Samuel might not appreciate my interference with the discipline of his children.*

A few minutes later, Penny appeared red-faced and sniffling as she carried Buttons to the front door and put him outside.

"Would you like a cookie?" Esther asked after Penny had closed the door.

Penny nodded soberly. "Okay."

Esther rose from her seat and placed Jared on the sofa. Taking Penny's hand, she went to the kitchen.

Penny took a seat at the table while Esther got out the cookie jar. She'd just placed two cookies on a napkin in front of Penny when Samuel stepped into the room.

"What's goin' on?" he questioned.

"I'm giving Penny a little snack." Esther motioned to

the cookies. "Would you like some?"

He frowned as he shook his head. "She shouldn't be eating anything now either. We'll be having supper soon, and too many cookies will spoil her appetite."

"Oh, I didn't realize you'd be starting supper so soon. Your two oldest children aren't home from school yet."

Samuel slapped the side of his head. "Oh, great! I forgot about picking them up. I should have asked Bonnie if she'd mind stopping by the schoolhouse before she dropped me off here." He looked at Esther, then dropped his gaze, the way he'd done when she'd first met him. "Can you stay awhile longer—while I go get the kinner?"

"Certainly."

Samuel started for the door, but turned back around and pointed his finger at Penny. "No cookies for you! You need to learn to follow the rules."

Esther flinched as the door slammed behind Samuel. If she hadn't known that he was still grieving for his wife, she'd have thought he wasn't a nice man. Hopefully after he'd worked through his grief, he would be kinder to his children, although since the kids were grieving, too, Esther thought Samuel should be more tolerant and kind. But she chose to keep her opinion to herself.

—⁓—

Bonnie stared out the kitchen window in awe. The shadows from the fence outlining her grandparents' property made incredible patterns on the glistening snow in the front yard. It made her wish she was a child again and could go outside and romp in the snow. She remembered when she and her parents had come here for Christmas one year, and she and Grandpa had made a snowman together. It had been so much fun. But then it was always more fun to do something like that when you had someone to share it with. She wished her dad, who had always seemed to be working when she was a child, had spent more time with her.

I suppose I could go outside and make my own snowman, she thought, *but it's so cold out there now, and I really should fix something for supper. When Samuel comes tomorrow, maybe I'll suggest that he bring his children over here on Saturday. We can all build a snowman, and afterward I'll fix them hot chocolate with marshmallows.* That's what Bonnie's grandma had fixed her and Grandpa when they'd come in from the snow, and it had added to the special memory of the day.

Bonnie turned away from the window, opened the pantry door, and took out a jar of spaghetti sauce and a package of angel-hair noodles. She'd just placed them on the cupboard, when she heard a dog barking in the backyard.

She opened the door to see what was going on, and a shaggy-looking, brown-and-white terrier of sorts bounded onto the porch. She'd never seen a dog quite like him before and figured he was probably a mixed breed.

"Shoo! Go on now!" Bonnie waved her hand, took a step forward, and tripped on a loose board.

"Oh!" She grabbed the handle of the screen door just in time to keep from falling on her face. Here was another job that couldn't wait until spring. She'd ask Samuel to fix it first thing tomorrow morning.

Bonnie turned her gaze on the dog again. It had plopped down on the porch and was lying there with its nose between its paws and a forlorn look in its cocoa-colored eyes. The poor thing looked unkempt and underfed. Could it be a stray someone had abandoned? Or maybe it had gotten away from its owner and become lost. Bonnie didn't want to take the dog in—especially if it belonged to someone else. Besides, she already had a stray cat to feed.

She stepped back into the house and shut the door, certain that the dog would get tired of lying there and hopefully would go back to wherever he'd come from.

Bonnie opened the jar of spaghetti sauce and got it heating on the stove; then she took out a kettle to cook the noodles in and set it in the sink. When she turned on the faucet to fill the kettle with water, she heard the dog again.

Woof! Woof! Woof! The loud barking was followed by scratching at the door.

With an exasperated groan, and determined to send the dog on its way, Bonnie turned off the water and opened the back door. When she stepped onto the porch, being careful to avoid the loose board, the dog leaped up and put both paws on her knees.

She looked down at her jeans and grimaced. They were wet!

She leaned over, picked up the dog, and tromped down the steps. Then she set him in the snow. "Go home!" she said, pointing to the road.

The dog just sat there, looking up at her with such forlorn-looking eyes. With his tail swishing against the snow, he stayed put, watching as if patiently waiting for Bonnie to change her mind.

Bonnie tried again. "Go home!" She clapped her hands and stomped her feet a few times—partly to get the dog moving, and partly to keep herself warm. She'd been foolish to come out here without a jacket.

Despite more coaxing, clapping, and pointing to the road, the dog wouldn't budge.

"Suit yourself," she said with a shake of her head. "If you want to sit out here in the cold snow, that's up to you." With all there was to do around the house, as much as she'd like to, she couldn't let herself get attached to a dog, because dogs needed a lot of care.

Bonnie turned and hurried back into the warmth of the house. When she stepped into the kitchen, she let out a shriek. Water was all over the kitchen floor!

"Now how could that have happened?" she fumed, instantly forgetting about her four-legged visitor. "I know I turned off the water before I went outside."

It didn't take long for Bonnie to realize that there was water seeping out from under the sink. "Ugh!" She slipped off her shoes and socks, and then waded through the water in her bare feet. When she opened the cupboard door beneath the sink and leaned over, she knew immediately what the problem was. A rusty-looking pipe had sprung a leak. "That's just great," she said with a moan.

Bonnie reached in and closed the shut-off valve, thankful that it wasn't stuck, because she had no idea where any of Grandpa's tools might be. Even if she had known where they were, she wasn't sure she'd know how to use them. Since she wouldn't be able to use the kitchen sink until the pipe was repaired, she'd have to use the sink in the bathroom. Now that was convenient!

Once the water was off, she sloshed her way back across the wet room, grabbed a mop from the utility porch, and started sopping up the water. This was just one more thing she'd have to ask Samuel to do. At this rate, she would never get the place ready to open as a bed-and-breakfast this spring.

She groaned. "I wonder what else will go wrong."

CHAPTER 10

Samuel shook the reins and clucked to his horse to get him moving quickly down the road. He was on his way to Bonnie's with the kids, and they'd all been chattering away like a bunch of magpies ever since they left Titus's place. They were obviously excited about going to Bonnie's, but Samuel couldn't help feeling irritated by their exuberance. It was as if they didn't miss their mother anymore. Could they have forgotten her so quickly?

I wonder why I let Bonnie talk me into bringing the kids over today, he thought with regret. *The last thing I want to do is build a snowman. Think I'll just let the kids play in the snow while I do some work on Bonnie's place.*

Samuel thought about some of the things he'd done there this past week. He'd put a new pipe under her kitchen sink, repaired several loose spindles on the banister leading upstairs, stripped some wallpaper in the kitchen and then painted the walls, replaced all the loose boards on the porch, and hauled some boxes up to the attic for Bonnie. The house was old, and it seemed like there was no end to the work that needed to be done. He figured he might not to have to look for any outside paint jobs until late spring or early summer because he'd probably be working for Bonnie that long.

"Daadi, Leon keeps pokin' me!" Penny shouted, bringing Samuel's thoughts to a halt. "Would ya make him stop?"

"Knock it off, Leon," Samuel called over his shoulder, "or you won't be making a snowman when we get to Bonnie's. You'll be in the house, workin' with me."

"But she started it," the boy complained. "She's hoggin' the seat."

"Huh-uh. He's the one hoggin' the seat," Penny retorted.

Samuel gritted his teeth. He didn't have the patience to deal with this right now. If only Elsie were here, she'd know what to do to quiet the kids and make them stop arguing.

"Stop pinchin' me!" Penny's piercing squeal sounded like a baby pig that had been cheated out of its mother's milk.

"I didn't pinch ya," Leon countered. "Jared's the one who pinched you, and that's the truth."

All was silent for a few seconds; then Jared started to cry. Samuel figured Penny had probably pinched him.

"If you three don't stop it, you're gonna be in trouble," Marla, who sat in the front of the buggy beside Samuel, said in her most grown-up voice.

"Ya can't tell us what to do, Marla." Leon said.

"Daadi, Leon just leaned over the seat and poked my shoulder," Marla tattled.

"Knock it off!" Samuel hollered at the top of his lungs. "If I hear one more peep out of any of you, I'll turn this horse and buggy around and head back to Titus's place. Is that clear?"

Except for a few sniffles, all was quiet.

I'm starting to sound like an angry, mean man, Samuel thought as he clenched the reins tighter. *But these petty little issues between the kids are really getting on my nerves.*

───∾───

Bonnie glanced out the kitchen window, wondering if Samuel and his children would be here soon. She looked forward to meeting them and hoped they were looking forward to making a snowman today.

She thought this would be a good chance for Samuel to relax and have a good time. He seemed so sullen and kept to himself much of the time. With the exception of discussing the repairs that needed to be done, they'd had very little conversation.

A whimper pulled Bonnie's thoughts aside and she looked down. The stray terrier she'd found earlier in the week cocked his head and looked up at her pathetically. She'd asked around the neighborhood and hadn't been able to find the dog's owner, so she'd finally weakened and taken him in. After all, she couldn't leave the poor pooch outside in the cold, nor could she stand the thought of the dog going hungry. She'd ended up giving him a bath and trimming his matted hair. The little fellow was really quite cute once all that dirt was gone. She'd even named the mutt Cody, which she certainly wouldn't have done if she hadn't decided to keep him.

"What's the matter, Cody?" Bonnie asked, reaching down to pet the dog's silky head. "Do you want to go out, or are you just looking for some attention?"

Cody whimpered and nuzzled her hand.

Bonnie continued to pet the dog a few more minutes; then she went to the front door to see if he wanted to go out. When she opened it, she caught sight of Samuel's horse and buggy heading up the driveway.

Woof! Woof! Cody raced out to greet them.

Bonnie grabbed her coat and stocking cap, slipped into her boots and gloves, and hurried outside. As soon as Samuel pulled the horse up to the hitching rail, his four children clambered out of the buggy and started frolicking in the snow. Bonnie waited on the porch until Samuel and the children walked up to the house.

"This is Marla, Penny, Leon, and Jared," Samuel said, motioning to each of the children.

Bonnie smiled. "My name's Bonnie Taylor, and I'm glad you could come over to play in the snow today."

The children stared up at her without saying a word.

Samuel nudged the oldest girl. "Say hello to Bonnie."

"Hello," she said in a voice barely above a whisper. The other children echoed her greeting.

"It's nice to meet you, and now I'm wondering—is everyone ready to help me make a snowman?" Bonnie asked.

All heads nodded. All except for Samuel's, that is. He was staring at the front of the house where the paint was peeling in several places.

"You're going to help us build the snowman, aren't you?" Bonnie stepped up to Samuel.

He shook his head. "Thought I'd get some more work done inside while you and the kids are out here playing in the snow."

"Are you sure you want to work today? You've worked hard all week, and I think you should take the day off."

He shook his head. "There's a lot to be done here, and the sooner I get it finished, the sooner you can open your bed-and-breakfast."

"Okay." Bonnie figured he wasn't going to change his mind, so she bent down, scooped up a clump of snow, and formed it into a ball. "Come on, kids, let's get that snowman started!"

Yip! Yip! Cody raced around the yard, running circles around the children. Then he leaped up and grabbed the edge of Marla's scarf.

"Hey! Come back with that!" Marla dashed after the dog, waving her hands, and Leon did the same.

Woof! Woof! Woof! Cody circled the yard a few times, dragging the scarf through the snow.

Bonnie clapped her hands and shouted, "Cody, drop that scarf!"

When the dog didn't listen, she joined Marla and Leon in the chase. She knew they'd all be exhausted by the end of this day.

—⁓—

As Esther's horse and buggy approached Titus's house, she was filled with a sense of excitement. Since Samuel paid his children so little attention, she'd decided to see if the kids wanted to help her build a snowman today. That was something she hadn't done in several years, so it should be fun for her as well.

When Esther pulled into Titus's yard, she spotted him out by the barn. He waved and then secured her horse, Ginger, to the hitching rail.

"What brings you by here this morning?" he asked when she climbed down from the buggy.

"I came to see if Samuel's kinner would like to help me make a snowman."

"That's too bad, because they're not here right now."

"Where'd they go?"

"Samuel took 'em over to Bonnie Taylor's. They're gonna make a snowman over there."

"Oh, I see." Esther couldn't help but feel disappointed. She'd really been looking forward to spending time with the children today.

"Say, I have an idea," Titus said. "Why don't you go over to the Taylor place and join them? Do you know where the house is located?"

She nodded. "Margaret Taylor used to come into our store sometimes, and when her husband, Andy, was ill, I made a delivery to their house a few times."

"Well, good. You'll know how to get there then."

"I wouldn't want to intrude." Esther felt a bit awkward and tried to hide her disappointment.

Titus shook his head. "I'm sure Bonnie wouldn't mind, and I know the kinner would be glad to see you."

"I'd be glad to see them, too."

"So if you're going, would you mind taking Penny's mittens? She forgot them this morning."

"I'd be happy to take them to her." Esther was glad

for a legitimate excuse to show up at Bonnie's. That way it wouldn't look like she was trying to interrupt the fun Bonnie had planned for the kids.

———ɯɯ———

When Esther arrived at the Taylor place sometime later, she spotted Samuel's children out in the snowy front yard. Marla and Jared were rolling a good-sized snowball, although the little guy seemed to be more of a hindrance than a help. Leon and Penny, with the help of a young woman with curly blond hair peeking out from under her stocking cap, rolled another.

"Hello," Esther said as she approached the group. "It looks like you have a good start on a snowman."

The kids stopped rolling their snowballs long enough to tell Esther hello, and the woman held out her mittened hand. "I'm Bonnie Taylor. Are you one of my neighbors?"

"I'm Esther Beiler," she said as she shook Bonnie's hand. "My folks used to own the general store in the area, and your grandparents shopped there sometimes." She gestured to the children. "I've been watching Samuel's kids while he's working for you, and when I stopped by there this morning, Titus said Samuel had brought the kids over here."

"That's right." Bonnie offered her a friendly smile. "We're building a snowman."

Esther held up the mittens she'd brought along. "Titus gave me these and said they were Penny's."

"It was nice of you to bring them by," Bonnie said. "When they got here, and Penny realized she'd left her mittens at home, I gave her a pair of mine, but as you can see, they're much too big for her small hands."

Esther handed the mittens to Penny, and the child smiled appreciatively.

"Where's your daed?" Esther asked.

Penny pointed to the house. "He's in there, workin'."

"Oh, I see. I figured he'd be out here helping you build the snowman."

"Nope," Leon chimed in. "Our daadi's always workin' now."

"Workin' or sleepin'," Marla interjected. "He hardly talks to us anymore, and when he does, he usually yells."

Esther glanced at Bonnie and noticed the concern showing in her dark brown eyes. Was she worried about Samuel, too?

"I tried to talk him into playing in the snow with us, but he insisted on working today," Bonnie said.

"That's 'cause he don't like bein' with us no more," Leon said with a tone of sadness in his voice.

Esther's heart clenched, and Bonnie gave the boy's shoulder a squeeze. "I'm sure that's not the case. I think your daddy just likes to keep busy."

Leon silently started rolling his snowball again.

"Would you like to join us?" Bonnie asked Esther. "I think Marla and Jared could use some help."

"I'd be glad to help out." Esther felt an immediate connection with Bonnie and hoped she would have the chance to get to know her better.

As they worked on the snowman, Bonnie told Esther about her plans to open a bed-and-breakfast. "Of course," she added, "once the place is ready to go, I'm not sure what I'll do about fixing my guests their breakfast." She wrinkled her nose. "I get by in the kitchen, but I'm definitely not the world's best cook, and I don't think my guests would be satisfied with cold cereal and toast every morning."

"Last year I taught my friend, Suzanne, how to cook, and she's doing real well on her own. I'd be happy to give you some pointers as well."

Bonnie smiled. "That'd be great."

"Whenever you're ready, just let me know. I could come over some Saturday or in the evenings after I'm done watching Samuel's kids."

"When you mentioned that your folks had a store in

the area, I thought you might be working there."

Esther shook her head. "They sold the store not long ago and moved to Pennsylvania to help my brother, because he has MS and can't manage on his own anymore."

"I'm sorry to hear that. I know a young woman in Oregon who has MS, and she's really struggling with it."

"Dan's doctor bills are mounting up already, so besides the fact that I enjoy being with Samuel's children, some of the money I earn watching them will be sent to my brother to help with his medical expenses."

"Doesn't he have any health insurance?"

"No. We Amish don't believe in buying health insurance. We take care of our own."

"Oh, I see. I guess there's a lot about the Amish I don't know. Maybe while you're teaching me to improve my cooking skills, you can enlighten me about the Amish who live in this community. After all, if we're going to be neighbors, it would be helpful if I understood the people living around me."

Esther smiled. "I'd be happy to answer any questions you might have."

"I appreciate that, and I'll be happy to pay you for helping me learn my way around the kitchen." Bonnie stopped rolling her snowball and let the kids take over. "In fact, once the B&B is up and running, would you be interested in coming to work for me here?"

"That's a tempting offer, but if Samuel finds another job after he's done working for you, I'll probably still be watching his children."

"Maybe you could come over here in the late afternoons or early evenings to clean the guest rooms and help with the preparation of the food I'll be serving my guests for breakfast the next day."

"I'm sure I could manage, but I'll have to get permission from my folks first," Esther replied. "Some Amish families in our church district don't approve of their daughters working in English people's homes. And even if they do say it's okay for me to work for you, I won't be allowed to listen to the radio or watch any TV."

"That's fine," Bonnie said. "I don't watch much TV myself."

Esther smiled. "While I'm waiting for Mom and Dad's answer, if there's anything you need my help with right away, I could probably do that."

"Actually, there is. I'm still going through my grandparents' things, so you could help me with that, as well as some of the cleaning I still haven't done."

"That sounds good to me." Esther felt sure God had provided more work for her, and she looked forward to calling Mom and Dad and hopefully beginning a second job soon.

She smiled to herself. All those concerns in the beginning—wondering what she would do after her parents left and how she would earn money—were now being lifted because everything seemed to be working out well.

CHAPTER 11

E sther was relieved when she received permission from her folks to work for Bonnie, with only a caution about not using anything in the house for worldly pleasures. Esther didn't think she'd have a problem with that because she was content to do without modern things.

So for the next two weeks, Esther went over to Bonnie's every day after Samuel got home from work. She enjoyed spending time with Bonnie, as she was doing now, and was impressed at how quickly they had become friends. Not that Bonnie would replace Esther's friendship with Suzanne—she was sure nothing could ever come between them.

Esther glanced at Bonnie, who stood at the kitchen counter kneading bread dough. "You're doing well, but be careful not to work the dough too much," she said. "My mother taught me when the dough feels elastic and quits sticking to your fingers, then it's ready and time to let rise."

Bonnie smiled. "I can't tell you how much I appreciate you teaching me how to do this. It'll be so nice to offer my B&B guests homemade bread every morning."

"In the spring, when the rhubarb in your grandma's garden patch ripens, maybe we can make some rhubarb jam."

"I remember Grandma serving that on toast when I was a girl and came here to visit. It was so good." Bonnie smacked her lips. "She made strawberry-rhubarb pie, too."

"Then there must be some strawberry plants hidden under all that snow in the garden."

Bonnie nodded. "I believe there are."

The rumble of a vehicle interrupted their conversation. "It's Allen," Bonnie said, peering out the window. She smiled. "I'm so thankful he introduced me to Samuel."

The smile on Bonnie's face when she mentioned Samuel's name made Esther wonder if Bonnie might have a personal interest in him.

Surely not, she told herself as Bonnie went to the door to let Allen in. *Bonnie's English and Samuel's Amish, so I'm sure she wouldn't be romantically interested in him. She probably just appreciates all the work he's doing for her. I shouldn't let my imagination get carried away like I sometimes did when I was a child.*

"Sorry it's taken me so long to get over here," Allen said when Bonnie opened the door. "I got busy all of a sudden with work I hadn't expected."

"It's okay," Bonnie said. "Nothing I've needed you to do has been critical, and Samuel's been a big help to me in so many ways."

"Hi, Esther," Allen said when he and Bonnie entered the kitchen. "I wondered if that was your buggy I saw parked outside."

Esther smiled. "I came over to help Bonnie do some baking."

"I'm not much of a baker," Bonnie said, "so I appreciate Esther's lessons."

Allen sniffed the air. "I can tell. Is that fresh bread I smell right now?"

"Yes, it sure is." Bonnie motioned to the loaf of bread she'd already baked. "If you're still here when it's cooled, maybe you'd like a piece."

"That'd be nice. There's nothing quite like eating fresh bread." Allen looked over at Esther and said, "I've had some of the good-tasting breads and cookies you taught Suzanne to make, so I'm sure that whatever you and Bonnie make will be real good, too." He grinned and gave her a wink. "I must say though, there's no better smell wafting through a house than bread baking in the oven."

Esther's face heated. Was Allen flirting with her? *Of course not, silly. There goes my wild imagination again.*

—⁓—

Samuel stepped into Titus's phone shanty with a feeling of dread. He'd received a voice mail from Mama Fannie a few days ago asking him to call at 9:00 a.m. on Saturday morning, when she would be in the phone shed. Since he knew Mama Fannie had disapproved of him moving to Kentucky, he figured he might be in for a lecture on how foolish he'd been for leaving Pennsylvania.

"Guess I may as well get this over with," he mumbled as he dialed the number.

"Hi, Mama Fannie. It's me, Samuel," he said when she answered her phone.

"It's good to hear from you. How are you and the kinner doing?"

"Okay."

"I talked to Zach the other day, and he said you've been working for an English woman in the area."

"That's right. Her name's Bonnie Taylor, and she's planning to open a bed-and-breakfast in the spring."

There was a pause, and then Mama Fannie said, "How old is she?"

"Beats me. I've never asked."

"You must have some idea how old she is. Is she older than me?"

"I'd say she's probably in her late twenties or early thirties."

"Is she married?"

"Nope." Samuel put his hand to his forehead. He already knew where this conversation was headed.

Another pause. "Do you think it's a good idea for you to be alone with her all day?"

Samuel felt his defenses rise. "You have nothing to worry about, Mama Fannie. Bonnie's a nice woman, and most of the time she's not even around when I'm working. She's often out shopping or working in some other part of the house."

"Can't you take one of the kinner with you when you're over there? That way no one can say anything about you being alone with a woman."

"As you know, my two older ones are in school all day, and I'm not about to bring the younger ones to work with me." Samuel grunted. "They'd only get in the way."

"But don't you think—"

"I hate to cut this short, but there are some things I need to get done yet today, so I'd better go," Samuel said, cutting her off in mid-sentence.

"Oh. I see."

Samuel knew from the tone of her voice that he'd hurt her feelings, so he quickly added, "It's been good talking to you, Mama Fannie. Tell Dad and the rest of the family I said hello."

"Okay. Tell your kinner I said hello, too. Oh, and tell Marla I'll be mailing her birthday card out to her soon."

"I will. Bye." Samuel quickly hung up the phone. If Mama Fannie was going to badger him about working for Bonnie, he might make fewer calls home. He knew her intentions were good, but sometimes she didn't know when to quit. He didn't remember her being this way when he was young and figured it might have something to do with her age. Their bishop said once that the older a person got, the more they worried about things.

———∿∿∿———

Paradise, Pennsylvania

When Timothy arrived home after helping Zach and his crew paint the inside of a grocery store, he was disappointed that he didn't find Hannah in the kitchen. He was tired and hungry and hoped she'd have supper waiting for him. Painting all day was hard work, but the money he earned paid the bills and kept him busy during the winter months when he wasn't able to farm.

He was about to head down the hall to see if she was in the living room when he spotted a note on the kitchen table. It was from Hannah and said that she'd taken Mindy and gone to her folks' house to help her mother clean and do some baking. She also said there was a container of vegetable soup in the refrigerator that Timothy could heat for his supper.

He frowned. It seemed like Hannah's mother was more important than him. But then that was really nothing new. Hannah was tied to her mother's apron strings and thought she had to be over there nearly every day. When Hannah wasn't at her folks', her mother was over at their place. It was getting old, and Timothy was tired of it.

He draped his jacket over the back of a chair and took a kettle and a bowl out of the cupboard. He'd just started heating the soup when the back door opened and his mother entered the house.

"I'm surprised to see you, Mom. What are you doing here at this time of the day?" he asked.

Her forehead wrinkled. "Is that any way to greet your mamm?"

"Sorry. I just figured you'd be at home having supper right now."

"We already ate, and when your daed fell asleep in his recliner, I decided to come over here and talk to you about something." She glanced at the single bowl he'd set on the table. "Where's the rest of your family? It looks like you're planning to eat alone."

He nodded. "Hannah and Mindy are at her folks' house."

Mom's lips compressed. "Again? She seems to go there a lot."

Timothy merely shrugged and said, "What'd you want to talk to me about?"

"Not what, but whom. Samuel, to be exact."

"What about him?"

"Did you know that he's been working for an English woman who's planning to open a bed-and-breakfast this spring?"

"Jah, I heard about that. From what Samuel said, Bonnie Taylor's a very nice woman."

"Well when I spoke with Samuel on the phone earlier today, I told him that I didn't think it was a good idea for him to be alone with this woman, and he got defensive."

"Can you blame him, Mom?"

"What's that supposed to mean?"

Timothy could see by his mother's pinched expression that he'd hurt her feelings. "I just think you to need to remember that your boys are grown men now, and we have the right to make our own choices—even if what we decide doesn't go along with your thinking."

"I don't mean to be overbearing," she said sincerely. "I'm just concerned."

"I know your intentions are good, but I'm sure there's nothing to be worried about where Samuel's concerned. I think you ought to concentrate on keeping Dad happy."

Her eyes narrowed. "What do you mean? Has your daed told you he's unhappy?"

"No, no, of course not. I just meant that Dad should be your primary concern, not your grown children."

"Are you saying I shouldn't be concerned about my kinner?"

"I'm not saying that at all, but I think you worry too much." Timothy wished they could start this conversation over. Every word he said seemed to make Mom more agitated.

"I probably do worry too much," she admitted, "but I can't seem to help it. I just want what's best for everyone."

"God doesn't want us to worry, Mom. You've told all of your kinner that at one time or another."

"You're right, I have, and I'll try not to worry or

interfere." Mom gave Timothy a hug. "I love you, son."

"I love you, too."

She smiled and turned toward the door. "Guess I'd better head for home now, before your daed wakes up and misses me. If you talk to Samuel anytime soon, please don't mention that I spoke to you about him working for that English woman," she requested as she went out the door.

"I won't say a thing," he called to her retreating form.

As Timothy continued to heat his soup, he thought about his conversation with Mom and hoped she would be careful not to pester Samuel about working for the English woman. Samuel wore his emotions on his sleeve since Elsie died, and if Mom wasn't careful, she might push him away. Could Mom's constant pressuring be one of the reasons Samuel had moved to Kentucky, or was it simply because he needed a fresh start?

Wish I could start over someplace new, Timothy thought. *If Hannah wasn't so dependent on her mother, I might think about moving to Kentucky, too.*

CHAPTER 12

Pembroke, Kentucky

Esther smiled to herself as she guided her horse and buggy down the road toward Titus's house. It was the first Saturday in February, and she had plans to meet Suzanne and take Samuel's kids sledding. Esther had enjoyed sledding since she was a girl and used to race her older brothers, James and Dan, down the hill behind their house. Besides, a day of sledding meant she wouldn't have to be alone. It was quiet and lonely in the house since Mom and Dad had moved to Pennsylvania. She missed them both so much. At times she found herself wishing she'd moved there with them, but if she had, she wouldn't have met Samuel's children. Spending time with them had filled a void in her life that she hadn't even realized was there. The children seemed to need her—especially since Samuel paid so little attention to them.

Esther thought about the other day when she'd been holding Jared in her lap as she visited with Penny, who sat on the floor playing with her doll. Both children were equally sweet, each in a different way. Even though Jared could be a bit rambunctious at times, he always obeyed, as did Samuel's other children. Esther had noticed that they weren't nearly as obedient with their father, but maybe that was because he ignored them so much of the time. Could they be using their disobedience as a way to get his attention? She knew Samuel was still grieving over his wife's death, but she wished he would wake up and realize all that he was missing by ignoring the children and being so harsh when he was with them.

When Esther had seen Titus the other day, he'd agreed to go sledding with them and said he'd try to talk Samuel into joining them, too. From what she'd observed and what the children had told her, Samuel did nothing for fun. He was either working or sleeping. That meant when Titus got home from work each day, he not only had the responsibility of doing the cooking and cleaning, but he had to keep an eye on Samuel's children. Esther wondered how things would be once Samuel had a place of his own.

If he ever gets a place of his own, she thought. *What if Samuel plans to stay with Titus indefinitely? Poor Suzanne might end up with a ready-made family. Would that mean she'd have to quit working with Titus and Nelson at the wood-shop in order to care for the kinner, or will Samuel want me to continue caring for them?*

Esther's horse snorted, pulling her thoughts aside. Ginger seemed to like the snow, prancing along with her head held high, blowing what looked like steam from her nostrils.

It is beautiful, Esther thought as she noticed the trees along the road, heaving with snow, bending down to touch the glistening ground. Seeing the beauty God had created made Esther feel closer to Him.

Ginger whinnied a greeting as they passed another horse and buggy, and Esther waved when she saw it was Ethan Zook, one of their minister's sons. Ethan waved in response and tipped his hat in her direction. Apparently he'd left his buggy outside last night and hadn't taken the time to clean the snow off this morning, for it was covered with white.

Esther knew that some folks saw the snowflakes pil-ing up into drifts across the road as a nuisance, but she saw the beauty in it. The frosty cold clung tightly to the earth now, but in another month spring would be here and all signs of snow would most likely be gone. *Spring,* she thought wistfully. *Even in the oldest folks, it brings out a burst of youthful energy. I think just about everyone loves the feeling of freedom after being cooped up during the cold winter months.*

Lost in thought, Esther smiled at what spring would bring when it arrived in all its glory. She could almost hear the bubbling sounds as streams flowed from the melting snow and the birds singing joyfully as they migrated home. Oh how she welcomed spring's unfolding splendor and the warmth in the breeze. But for now, she was content to enjoy the moment of this winter's solace.

Esther breathed in the scent of pine, heavier in the air from branches recently broken with the weight of ice and snow. Overhead, a hawk's shrill cry was joined by the crows announcing their protest.

When she pulled into Titus's yard a short time later, she noticed Suzanne's buggy parked outside the barn.

She climbed down from her own buggy and was about to unhitch the horse when Titus stepped out of the barn. "I'll put Ginger away for you," he said, joining her beside the horse.

"Danki." She motioned to the back of the buggy. "I brought three sleds with me, so while you take care of my horse, I'll get them out of the buggy. Oh, do you know if Suzanne brought any sleds we can use?"

Titus shrugged. "I'm not sure. She's in the house right now, helping the kinner get into their boots."

"Is Samuel going with us today?"

Titus turned his hands palm up. "I don't know. I asked, but he never said. You can ask him, too, if you like."

"I might do that." Esther hurried to the back of the buggy, took out the sleds, and leaned them against the side of the barn. Then she trudged her way through the drifts up to the house.

When she stepped inside, she was greeted by four exuberant children wearing boots, heavy jackets, stocking caps, and mittens. All except for Penny, who only wore one mitten.

"I can't find my *fauschthensching*," Penny said, holding up her hand.

Esther chuckled. "It's right here." She reached around behind the child and lifted the mitten that dangled down her back from under her hat.

Penny squinted. "Now how'd that get there?"

Everyone laughed. Everyone but Samuel, who sat slouched on the sofa, looking like he was half asleep.

"Are you going sledding with us?" Esther asked.

He shook his head.

"What do you plan to do all day?" Titus asked when he entered the house.

"Ich daed yuscht so lieb gear nix duh," Samuel said.

Esther looked at Suzanne and slowly shook her head. She couldn't believe Samuel had said he would just as soon do nothing, when he could spend the morning having fun with his children. Was he really that depressed?

"Please come with us, Daadi," Leon pleaded. "You never do nothin' fun with us since Mammi died."

"Ich fiehl saddle schlect heit." Samuel stood and ambled out of the room.

Titus turned to Suzanne. "Since my bruder has just told the kids that he feels out of sorts, I think I'd better forget about sledding and stay home with him today."

"Oh." Suzanne's look of disappointment, as she dipped her head, was as clear as the sorrowful expression on Leon's face. Esther's heart ached for her friend. Suzanne had obviously counted on Titus joining them. Esther felt bad for Samuel's children, too. Didn't Samuel realize that going sledding with the children might lift his spirits? He'd never recover from his loss if he didn't do anything fun. Esther remembered that after Suzanne's dad died, their whole family grieved, but when her Grandpa suggested they all go fishing one afternoon, there had been a change in Suzanne's mother, who seemed more positive about life after that, which in turn, caused everyone else in their family to become more joyous.

"Sorry about the change of plans," Titus said, looking sincerely at Suzanne, "but as long as Samuel's still having bouts of depression, I wouldn't feel right about leaving him here alone."

"I understand that, but I wish. . ." Suzanne's voice trailed off, and then, turning away from Titus, she motioned toward the door. "Come on, kids; let's go sledding."

———⁂———

Tap! Tap! Tap!

"Samuel, can I come in?"

Samuel rolled over on his side so that he faced the wall. He didn't want to talk to Titus right now. He just wanted to be left alone.

Tap! Tap! Tap!

Samuel figured if he didn't respond, the tapping would only continue. So he pulled himself to a sitting position and called, "Come in."

The door opened and Titus stepped into the room. "You know, you're not doing yourself or the kinner any good by pulling away like you have," he said, taking a seat on the edge of the bed.

"I'm not pulling away."

"Jah, you are. You won't join the kinner in anything they do that's fun, and—"

Samuel leaped to his feet and started pacing. "I can't do anything fun! I'm miserable without Elsie. Not that I'd expect you to understand." He stopped pacing and whirled around to face Titus. "You've never lost a mate, and you have no idea how empty I feel without Elsie. The pain is unbearable. It's like my heart has been torn in two."

"I know you're hurting, and you're right, I don't

understand, but Mom and Dad do. As you well know, they both lost their first mates, and I'm sure it wasn't easy for either of them." Titus stepped up to Samuel and placed his hand on his shoulder. "Maybe someday, when the time is right, you'll find someone else, the way our folks did."

White hot anger boiled in Samuel's chest as he glared at his brother, hoping he would get the point. "I am never getting married again. Don't you get it? No one could ever take Elsie's place in my heart!"

Titus blinked and held up his hand. "Of course not. You don't have to get so riled. I just meant—"

"I don't want to talk about this anymore. I need to be alone." Samuel grabbed his jacket and stormed out of the room. "Why can't everyone just leave me alone and quit telling me how I'm supposed to feel?" he mumbled under his breath.

—m—

"Sorry I forgot to bring my sled," Suzanne said as she and Esther trudged through the snow behind the children and Lucky, their exuberant Lab.

"That's okay. We can manage with the three I brought." Esther smiled. "I think this is going to be a fun day for all of us, don't you?"

Suzanne exhaled, releasing a sigh. "I suppose."

"Are you disappointed because Titus didn't come with us?"

"Jah, but I understand why he felt the need to stay with his bruder."

"Do you think Samuel will ever get over his wife's death?" Esther asked, knowing everyone dealt with grief in their own way, at their own pace.

"I hope so, but I think it'll take some time, just as it did for my mamm when my daed died. From what Titus has told me, Elsie was the love of Samuel's life, and the two of them were really looking forward to having another child, so losing the boppli she carried made it that much harder for Samuel."

"I'm sure it did. I just hate to see him looking so sad."

"I know, but until he's able to come to grips with his loss, there isn't much any of us can do but pray for him and offer support."

They walked in silence for a while; then Esther said, "I don't think Samuel likes me."

"How come?"

"He doesn't say much whenever I'm around, and when he does, he won't look at me."

"Titus was like that with me when he first moved to Kentucky," Suzanne said. "It really bothered me, too."

"But that was because you reminded him of his ex-girlfriend, Phoebe."

Suzanne nodded. "I was so relieved when he chose me over her."

"Have you heard anything about how she's doing since she went back to Pennsylvania?"

"From the few things Titus's mamm has told him, I gather that Phoebe's getting along pretty well and has even decided to join the church."

"Is she being courted by anyone there?"

Suzanne shrugged. "I don't think so, but I don't know for sure. Titus doesn't talk about her much anymore, and I'm glad. When Phoebe showed up here out of the blue, it was hard for me, and I felt insecure about my relationship with Titus."

"But things are okay between you now, aren't they?"

"For the moment, they are. If Samuel doesn't mess them up, that is."

"What do you mean?"

"Samuel's always around, and I miss not having the quality time Titus and I used to have together." Suzanne bumped Esther's arm with her elbow. "Speaking of Samuel, if you think he doesn't like you, then maybe you should ask him why."

Esther shook her head. "I don't think that's a good idea."

"Why not?"

"Samuel's hard to figure out, and I don't want to say or do anything that might make him angry at me. I enjoy watching the kinner and wouldn't want to lose my job."

"I don't think you have to worry about that. Samuel needs someone to watch them while he's working, and since you're so good with the kinner, he'd be foolish to let you go."

Esther was about to comment, when Penny stopped walking, turned toward Esther and Suzanne, and pointed upward. "Look there—some *gens*!"

Esther leaned her head back. Sure enough, there was a flock of honking geese cutting across the sky. "Looks like spring can't be too far off now." She smiled. "They're heading back north."

"And look over there." Suzanne pointed to her left. A small doe pranced into the empty cornfield, now covered with snow.

"Ach, how cute!" Penny watched the doe a minute, then she hurried on.

After they'd gone a bit farther, Marla handed her sled rope to Leon and joined Esther and Suzanne. "I'm hopin' I get a sled of my own for my *gebottsdaag*," she said.

"When is your birthday?" Esther asked.

"I'll be nine years old next Saturday. Daadi hasn't said a thing about it, though, so I'll bet he forgot." Marla frowned deeply and scrunched up her nose. "He don't remember much of anything anymore."

Esther gave the girl's shoulder a gentle squeeze. "I'm sure he won't forget something as important as your birthday."

Marla shrugged. "We'll see."

As they continued on, Esther determined in her heart that she would do something special for Marla's birthday.

That way, if Samuel should forget, the child wouldn't be quite so disappointed.

"Since we only have three sleds, we'll have to take turns," Suzanne said when they came to the top of a hill that looked perfect for sledding.

"Me first! Me first!" Leon shouted, hopping up and down. He raced for one of the sleds and took off down the hill before Esther had a chance to respond. Barking and nipping at the back of the sled, Lucky followed.

Marla grabbed another sled and went right behind him. "Look out, Leon—here I come!"

"Penny's kind of little to manage the sled by herself," Esther said to Suzanne, "so maybe I should ride down the hill with her."

"That's a good idea," Suzanne agreed. "When one of the others gets back with their sled, I'll take Jared for a ride with me."

Esther seated herself on the sled, situated Penny in front of her, and pushed off with her feet.

"Whee. . . This is *schpass*!" Penny hollered.

"Jah, it's a whole lot of fun." Esther giggled as they gathered speed and the snow sprayed back in their faces. The faster they went, the more she laughed, enjoying the memory of her youth when life was so simple and carefree.

When they reached the bottom of the hill, Lucky was there, ready to slurp Penny's cheek.

Penny giggled as she turned her head. "Get away, Lucky! You're gettin' my face all wet."

Woof! Woof! The dog wagged his tail, and with one final slurp, he dashed up the hill behind the others.

They went up and down the hill several more times, with Esther taking turns with Suzanne as they gave Penny and Jared rides on the sled.

"I wanna ride by myself now." Before anyone could stop her, Penny grabbed hold of the sled Marla had been using and took off down the hill in a flash. Lucky raced ahead of her, barking excitedly and zigzagging through the snow.

"Penny, look out!" Esther shouted.

It was too late. Lucky bumped the sled, and Penny screamed as her hat flew off. The sled flipped over, and Penny landed at the base of a tree with a horrible thud!

CHAPTER 13

E sther raced down the hill and dropped to her knees beside Penny, who was laying facedown in the snow. Lucky stood over her, whimpering.

Esther pushed the dog aside and quickly turned Penny over. "Ach, my!" she gasped when she saw blood oozing out of a gash in the little girl's forehead.

Penny's eyes opened and she looked up at Esther with a blank stare. "Wh–what happened?"

"You flew off the sled." Esther removed the scarf she wore around her neck and wrapped it around Penny's forehead to stop the bleeding.

"Is she okay?" Suzanne asked, kneeling on the snow beside Penny. Marla and Leon had joined them now, too, wearing worried expressions.

"There's a nasty-looking cut on her forehead. I think she either hit the runner of the sled or the tree." Esther felt deep concern, but she tried to remain calm for the children's sake, as she didn't want to frighten them. "She could have a concussion, and I'm sure she's going to need stitches," she whispered to Suzanne. "We need to get her back to the house right away."

"Let's put her on the sled, and I'll pull it to the house. That'll be quicker and easier than one of us trying to carry her," Suzanne said.

Once they got Penny situated on the sled, Esther carried Jared, while Marla and Leon pulled the other two sleds, and as quickly as possible they headed for the house.

"Sure wish we didn't have to quit sleddin'," Leon complained as they trudged along.

"We can't sled no more, dummkopp. Penny's been hurt." Marla's chin quivered. "You don't want her to die, like Mammi did, do ya?"

"I ain't no dunce, and Penny ain't gonna die," the boy shot back.

"She might. Mammi died when she fell down the *schteeg*."

Leon's face turned white as the snow beneath their feet. "Ya really think so?"

"Your sister is not going to die," Esther was quick to say. "She'll be fine once we get her cleaned up and see if she'll need to go to the doctor for stitches."

Marla gave a nod, but Leon didn't look one bit convinced. It was obvious that the pain of losing his mother was still very real. Esther wished there was something she could do to bring healing to Samuel's children. Samuel, too, for that matter, but she didn't think he'd ever let her get close enough to offer comfort. He didn't seem to let anyone get close to him—not even his children or Titus.

Esther had a tender heart toward those who were hurting. She'd been like that since she was a child. She remembered once when her brother James had broken his arm after falling from a tree in their yard. She'd felt his pain as if it were her own. Then there was the time her dog, Rascal, had gotten hit by a car. When they'd brought Rascal home from the vet's, she'd stayed by his side for hours on end.

"We're almost there," Suzanne said, pointing to the house as it came into view. "I think I see Samuel out by the barn."

~⚬~

When Samuel spotted Suzanne pulling Penny on a sled, he knew something was wrong. They hadn't been gone very long, and he was sure the kids wouldn't have agreed to quit sledding so soon.

As the group drew closer, he noticed that Penny had a scarf wrapped around her forehead, and both Suzanne and Esther wore looks of concern.

"Was is letz do?" he asked, dropping to his knees beside the sled.

"Penny fell off the sled and cut her forehead on either the runner or a tree," Suzanne replied, explaining what was wrong.

"Wasn't anyone watching her?"

Esther stepped forward. "We were, but she jumped on the sled and took off down the hill, and then before we hardly realized what had happened, Lucky darted in front of the sled and Penny flew off."

"I ought to get rid of that good-for-nothing mutt!" Samuel's hand shook as he removed the scarf from Penny's head. There was a fairly deep gash on her forehead, and he knew immediately it was going to need stitches. "I'll take you into the house where it's warm, and then I'm going to call a driver so we can go to the hospital in Hopkinsville, where you can be seen by a doctor."

He scooped Penny into his arms and hurried into the house. When he placed her on the sofa and took a seat beside her, everyone gathered around, exchanging concerned glances.

"What's going on?" Titus asked, stepping out of the kitchen. He halted when he looked at Penny. "What happened to her?"

Samuel repeated what Suzanne had told him about the accident, and then he added, "They weren't watching the kinner close enough. I shouldn't have let 'em go sledding."

"Don't blame Esther or Suzanne," Titus said. "It sounds like Lucky was the cause of the accident, and I'm sure he didn't run into the sled on purpose."

Samuel grunted. "I realize that, but it wouldn't have happened if they'd been watching Penny closer. She's too young to ride on the sled alone." He stood. "I'm going out to the phone shanty to call one of your drivers so I can take Penny to the emergency room at the hospital." Samuel turned and rushed out the door.

He was almost to the phone shanty when Allen's truck pulled into the yard. Allen waved at Samuel and called, "I was at Bonnie's doing some work for her and decided to stop by here on my way home to see how everyone's doing."

Samuel raced over to Allen. "Penny cut her head on the sled, and I need someone to take us to the hospital. Would you be able to do that?"

Allen hopped out of the truck. "Of course I can."

"Thank you," Samuel said, relieved that Allen had shown up when he did. "I'll get Penny and meet you in the truck."

—⁂—

Esther glanced at the clock on the wall in Titus's kitchen, where she and Suzanne had begun making lunch while Titus kept the children entertained in the living room. "Samuel and Penny have been gone two hours already. I wonder what's taking so long."

Suzanne shrugged. "Maybe they had to wait awhile in the emergency room. This time of the year, more people seem to get sick."

Esther frowned. "I'm afraid Samuel thinks I'm not a responsible person. I'd be really disappointed if he won't let me watch his kinner anymore because of this."

"I don't think you have to worry about that. Samuel was just upset when he saw the gash on Penny's forehead, and he needed someone to blame." Suzanne placed a loaf of bread on the counter. "One good thing came from Penny's accident though."

"What's that?"

"Samuel pulled out of his depression long enough to focus on something other than his own pain."

"I suppose that's true, but it's too bad it took Penny getting hurt to get his attention."

"Is lunch ready yet?" Titus asked, poking his head into the room. "The kinner say they're feeling *hungerich*." He thumped his stomach. "To tell you the truth, I'm kind of hungry myself."

Suzanne laughed. "You're always hungry, so what else is new?"

"Guess you're right about that," he said with a grin, and they all laughed even harder when his stomach let out a growl of protest.

"We'll call you as soon as we have everything on the table," Suzanne said after their laughter died down.

When Titus returned to the living room, Esther and Suzanne finished making tuna fish sandwiches. They'd just called everyone to eat when Samuel returned home with Penny. Allen was with them.

"How's Penny?" Esther asked before anyone else could voice the question.

"She doesn't have a concussion, but she did need several stitches." Samuel pointed to the bandage on Penny's forehead. "She was a brave little *maedel*."

"They gave me a lollipop," Penny said with a nod. "So I didn't cry no more after that."

Esther was relieved to hear that Penny was okay. She left her chair and bent to give the sweet little girl a hug; then she motioned to the table. "We were just about to eat some lunch, so why don't you both take a seat and join us?"

"No thanks. I'm not hungry." Samuel barely glanced at Esther before hurrying out of the room, but Penny didn't hesitate to find a chair.

Esther grimaced as she gripped the edge of her apron. *He's obviously upset, and I'm sure he still blames me for Penny's accident. Everything had been going so well, and the kinner were having some much-needed fun this morning. Now I wish we'd never gone sledding.*

CHAPTER 14

"Don't forget about the birthday supper I'm fixing for Marla tomorrow evening," Esther said as she and Bonnie sat at the kitchen table, having a cup of tea in Bonnie's kitchen.

"Thanks for the reminder," Bonnie said, watching the steam rise from her cup. "I've been so busy with things around here all week that I'd almost forgotten about the birthday supper. I'll have to go shopping tomorrow morning and see what I can find to give Marla for a present." She lifted her teacup and took a drink. "Do you know what she might like?"

Esther blotted her lips with a napkin. "I'm giving Marla a drawing tablet and some colored pencils. Suzanne said she'd bought a couple of puzzles, and I think Titus is giving her a sled, which I know she really wants. I'm not sure what, if anything, Samuel will give her."

"I'll need to get her something different than the others then. Any suggestions at all?" Bonnie asked.

"She might like a doll or a game."

Bonnie gave a nod. "I'll drive to Hopkinsville in the morning and see what I can find."

"The party's a surprise, so I haven't said anything about it to any of Samuel's kids, because they'd probably tell Marla."

"I assume Samuel knows though."

"I hope so. Titus was supposed to tell him." Esther's furrowed brows showed her obvious concern. "Samuel seems to be living in a world of his own most of the time, so it's hard to say whether he'll remember his daughter's birthday or not."

"I think the grief he feels over his wife's death has taken a toll on him." Bonnie finished her tea and set the cup down. "I can understand that, because when my mother died from a brain tumor, my father sank into depression, and I don't think he's ever fully recovered. I believe he may have felt guilty because they argued so much when she was alive."

"I'm sorry about your mother." Esther placed her hand on Bonnie's arm and gave it a couple of soft pats. "It must have been hard on you to lose your mother, too."

Bonnie gave a slow nod. "I was only thirteen, and it was rough going through my teen years with only a father who barely knew I was alive. At least Samuel has the support of Titus, as well as his family in Pennsylvania. My dad's an only child, and he really had no one after Mom died; although I'm sure my grandparents would have offered him support if he'd let them." She pushed away from the table and stood. "That's enough talk about death for one day. Shall we get started on my baking lesson?"

"I'm ready if you are." Esther stood, too. "Would you like to make Marla's birthday cake?"

Bonnie nibbled on her bottom lip as she contemplated the idea. "I'd better not. It would probably turn out to be a flop."

Esther went to the cupboard and took down a sack of flour. "I don't think it will be a flop, and you'll never learn to bake a cake unless you try."

Bonnie smiled. "With your help, I'll give it a try."

—⁂—

The following evening as Esther set the table in Titus's kitchen, she hummed softly. The chicken and potatoes baking in the oven were almost done; a tossed green salad was chilling in the refrigerator, along with some cut-up pickles and carrots sticks; and a kettle of creamed corn simmered on the stove. Marla and Leon had been home from school for about an hour, and as soon as Suzanne, Titus, Bonnie, and Samuel got here, they could eat.

"Somethin' smells really good in here." Marla sniffed the air as she entered the kitchen. "How come you're cookin' supper, Esther? Uncle Titus usually does that."

"I thought your uncle deserved a little break tonight," Esther replied.

"How come you're puttin' so many plates on the table?"

Esther smiled, watching the youngster's expression. "Because I'm staying for supper, and a few others are coming to join us."

"Who's coming?" Marla questioned.

"Bonnie Taylor and Suzanne."

"Are they comin' because it's my birthday?"

"Jah."

The little girl's eyes lit up, and her face broke into a wide smile. "I got a couple of cards in the mail yesterday, but I didn't think anyone was gonna do anything special for my birthday. Last year Mammi made a chocolate cake with vanilla icing, and all my cousins came over for my birthday." Her face sobered. "Since Mammi's gone and we've moved here, I guess there won't be no more parties like that anymore."

Esther's heart clenched. One minute Marla had seemed so happy, and the next minute her joy had turned to sorrow. Samuel wasn't the only one who missed Elsie. His children were still grieving, and he was too immersed in his own pain to see theirs.

"I know you must miss your mamm a lot, and I'm sure it's been hard for you to move away from all your family and friends in Pennsylvania." Esther bent down and gave Marla a hug. "I know I can't take the place of your *mudder*, but I would like to be your friend, and I want to make your birthday a special one."

Tears welled in Marla's eyes, and she sniffed a couple

of times. "Danki, Esther."

The back door opened just then, and Titus entered the kitchen, along with Suzanne.

"Umm. . . Something smells real good in here," Titus said, sniffing the air. Then he leaned over and gave Marla a hug. "Happy birthday, Marla."

She grinned up at him, all tears forgotten. "Did Daadi come with you?"

Titus shook his head. "But I told him about your birthday supper, so I'm sure he'll be here soon."

Just then, a knock sounded on the back door.

"Come in," Titus said, looking to see who it was.

A few seconds later, Bonnie stepped into the room, carrying a box with Marla's birthday cake inside. With Esther's help, she'd made a chocolate cake with vanilla icing, and they'd decorated it with little heart-shaped candies, since tomorrow would be Valentine's Day.

Marla seemed excited when she saw the cake and ran into the other room to get her brothers and sister. After everyone had made over the cake awhile, Esther mentioned to Suzanne that supper was ready, and she wondered if they should eat or wait for Samuel.

"I say we eat," Titus said before Suzanne could respond. "The kinner are hungry, and there's no point in making 'em wait or letting this fine meal be ruined trying to keep it warm for Samuel. He can eat when he gets here."

Esther didn't feel right about having supper without Samuel, but Titus was right: the children needed to eat. So with the help of Suzanne and Bonnie, the food was quickly put on the table and everyone took their seats. They were almost finished with the meal when the back door opened and Samuel stepped into the kitchen.

"What's goin' on?" he asked, looking at the table as everyone watched him.

"We're eating supper." Titus's tone sounded a bit miffed as he motioned to the platter, where only a few pieces of chicken were left. "And you're late."

"Uh—well—the paint job I was working on today took longer than I expected. Then my driver was late pickin' me up," Samuel mumbled as he set his lunch pail on the counter. "Besides, I didn't realize we were having company for supper."

Esther was about to say something, but Suzanne spoke first. "We're celebrating Marla's birthday tonight. Titus said he told you about it."

Samuel's face turned bright red as he looked at Marla with a guilty expression. "Happy birthday."

She smiled, although it didn't quite reach her eyes. Did she realize that her father had obviously forgotten about her birthday supper? It was certainly evident to Esther.

"We're just about done here," Esther said, "but there's still some food left, so if you'd like to take a seat at the table, we'll wait until you're done eating before we cut the birthday cake."

"No, that's okay. Go ahead and serve the cake. I'm not that hungry anyway."

"You're gonna have a piece of birthday cake, aren't you, Daadi?" Marla asked, turning to her father with a look of anticipation.

"Jah, sure." Samuel took a seat and leaned his elbows on the table. He looked tired and a bit befuddled. Esther was even more sure that he'd forgotten today was Marla's birthday.

"Bonnie made this beautiful cake," Esther said, placing it on the table in front of Marla.

Bonnie smiled. "I couldn't have done it without Esther's help, and I hope it tastes as good as it looks."

"Esther's a great teacher, so I'm sure the cake will be delicious," Suzanne said.

All heads bobbed in agreement. Everyone's but Samuel's, that is. He sat staring at the empty plate in front of him as though in deep thought.

"Now for the candles," Esther said, placing nine candles in the center of the cake. Then Titus lit a match to light the candles, and everyone sang "Happy Birthday" while Marla beamed from ear to ear. When the singing ended, she closed her eyes and blew out the candles with one big breath.

"Did ya make a wish?" Leon asked his sister.

"I did, but it's a secret, and I can't tell ya what it is or it won't come true."

"You can't get what you want from blowin' out birthday candles and makin' a wish," Samuel mumbled. "If you could, I'd bake a cake myself and put a hundred candles on it."

The room got deathly quiet, as all eyes became fixed on Samuel.

He lifted his shoulders in a quick shrug. "I'm just saying. . . I don't believe in wishes."

Marla's chin trembled, and so did Penny's. Esther figured if she didn't do something quick, she'd have a couple of crying girls on her hands.

"Let's cut the cake now so we can taste how good it is," she said, taking a knife from the kitchen drawer. "Suzanne, would you get us some dessert plates?"

Suzanne hurried over to the cupboard and took out enough plates for everyone at the table. Then, as Esther cut the cake and handed each one a piece, Suzanne served up scoops of vanilla ice cream.

"Umm. . . This cake is *appeditlich*," Titus said, smacking his lips.

All heads bobbed again—even Samuel's this time. "It is delicious, and you did a good job making it," he said, looking at Bonnie with a grateful expression.

Bonnie smiled. "Thank you, Samuel."

Esther couldn't help but notice how comfortable Samuel seemed to be around Bonnie. Not like when he was with her—stiff, as though he could hardly stand to look at her.

Esther mulled things over as she ate her cake. *Why would an Amish man be more comfortable around an English woman than he is with an Amish woman? Is there something he finds more appealing about Bonnie than me?* Esther picked up her glass of water and took a drink, forcing her troubling thoughts aside. This evening, she needed to keep her focus on Marla and on making her birthday special.

When everyone finished their cake and ice cream, Suzanne gave Marla her gift.

"Danki. I like it," Marla said after she'd opened a box with two puzzles in it. Then Titus presented Marla with a sled, which he said Suzanne had helped him pick out. Marla seemed quite happy with that gift as well.

Next, Esther handed Marla the present she'd bought. When Marla opened it and removed the drawing tablet and colored pencils, she fairly beamed. "Danki, Esther! Now I can draw a whole bunch of pictures."

Esther smiled. She was pleased that she'd given Marla something she liked.

"Now it's my turn." Bonnie pushed away from the table and returned with the beautifully wrapped gift she'd brought into the house before supper. "I hope you like this," she said, handing it to Marla.

Marla quickly tore off the pink tissue paper and gave Bonnie a happy smile when she pulled out a cute little doll dressed in Amish clothes. "Danki. I really like it. I like everything I got." She turned and looked expectantly at her father, as though waiting to see if he had a gift for her, too.

Esther held her breath, wondering what Samuel would do.

———《∭》———

Samuel, feeling guilty and stupid for forgetting his daughter's birthday, didn't know what to say or do. Truth was, he didn't have anything to give Marla. *Elsie would never have forgotten one of our kinner's birthdays*, he thought. *What's wrong with me?*

Suddenly, an idea flashed into his head. There was that

box in his room with Elsie's things that he hadn't gone through yet. "I'll be right back," he said, rising from his chair.

"Where ya goin'?" Penny called as he started out of the room.

"To get your sister's present."

Samuel hurried to his room, pulled the box away from the wall, and flipped open the flaps. After a bit of searching, he located one of Elsie's favorite teacups. Thinking Marla might like to have something that belonged to her mother, he returned to the kitchen and gave it her. "This was one of your mamm's favorite *kopplin*," he said.

Marla smiled and lifted the delicate china cup to her lips, as though pretending to drink from it. "Danki, Daadi. Knowin' this was Mammi's makes it my best gift of all."

"Let me see it." Penny reached across Jared, and he turned his head sharply, bumping Marla's arm and knocking the cup out of her hand. It landed on the floor, shattering into several pieces.

Marla gasped and burst into tears.

"Now look what you did!" Samuel pointed at Penny. "You not only took away your sister's birthday present, but you broke your mamm's favorite cup!"

Hands shaking, and forehead beaded with sweat, Samuel stormed out of the house.

CHAPTER 15

I'd better go talk to Marla and Penny," Esther said after the two girls had gone tearfully to their room. "This was not a good way for Marla's party to end, and I'm sure she and Penny both could use a bit of comforting right now."

"I'll stay here and clean up the broken cup," Suzanne said.

"I'll clear the table and do the dishes," Bonnie spoke up.

Titus pushed his chair away from the table. "Think I'd better go outside and have a talk with my bruder. No doubt, he could use a bit of comforting, too."

Esther glanced at the boys. Leon sat with his head down, staring at his half-eaten piece of cake. His father's outburst had no doubt upset him. Little Jared, however, seemed unaffected by the whole ordeal. Wearing a grin on his chocolate-smudged face, he sat in his high chair happily eating the piece of birthday cake Esther had given him before Samuel stormed out of the house.

Esther gave Leon's shoulder a tender squeeze. "Would you like some more ice cream?"

He shook his head. "I ain't hungry no more. Think I'll get ready for bed." He leaped off his chair and hurried out of the room.

Esther sighed. Three upset children, and one angry father. What a terrible way for the evening to end. She wished now that she hadn't even planned a party for Marla. But if she hadn't made the effort, there probably wouldn't have been a party at all.

Esther left the kitchen and hurried down the hall to the bedroom the girls shared. She found them both curled up on the bed, crying as though their little hearts had been broken.

"It's all right," she said, taking a seat on the bed beside them and gently patting their backs. "Don't cry."

Penny sat up and hiccupped on a sob. "Daadi's m—mad at me. He thinks I—I broke the kopplin on purpose."

Marla sat up and leaned against Esther. "He don't love us no more."

Esther slipped her arms around both girls' waists, drawing them closer to her. "It was just an accident, and neither of you is to blame. I'm sure once your daed calms down he'll realize that." Esther hoped she was right, and she prayed that when Titus spoke to Samuel, he'd make him understand that it was just an accident.

—⁓—

Samuel paced back and forth in the barn for a while; then he plopped down on a bale of straw. He'd been stupid to give Marla one of Elsie's cups. She was still a little girl and didn't know how to take care of such a delicate thing.

But of course, he reminded himself, *it wasn't really Marla's fault she dropped the cup. If Penny hadn't reached across Jared, and if Jared hadn't turned his head, he wouldn't have bumped Marla's arm and she wouldn't have let go of the cup. I realize now that none of my kinner are old enough to be anywhere near such a delicate cup.*

Samuel leaned forward and let his head fall into the palms of his hands. He should have left all of Elsie's things with Mama Fannie for safekeeping. Then when the girls were old enough, he could have let them choose whatever they wanted.

"I'm so stupid," he muttered. "Seems like I always make bad decisions, especially where my kinner are concerned."

A cold, wet nose brushed against Samuel's hand, and when he lifted his head, he saw Lucky at his side.

"Go away!" Samuel pushed the dog away. "I don't want to be bothered with you right now."

The dog whimpered and dropped his head onto Samuel's knee, looking up at him with understanding eyes. Did the critter realize Samuel needed some comfort, or was Lucky simply in need of attention? He figured it was probably a bit of both.

With a groan of resignation, he patted the dog's head. After all, the poor critter had done nothing wrong. Truth was, sitting here petting Lucky's silky head felt kind of nice. It was a good way to relieve some of his stress. Maybe he ought to pay the dog more attention from now on instead of always hollering at him to get out of the way or go lie down. In spite of everything, he knew Lucky had to get used to his new surroundings, just like the rest of them. The only thing left that was familiar to the poor dog was Samuel and the kids.

Lost in thought, Samuel sat for several minutes, scratching behind Lucky's ears, until the barn door opened and Titus stepped in. *Oh, great. I hope he didn't come out here to lecture me.*

"You okay?" Titus asked, taking a seat on the bale of straw beside Samuel.

Samuel motioned to Lucky. "I wasn't until the mutt came and offered me some comfort. After sitting here petting him awhile, I've calmed down a bit."

"You were pretty upset in there." Titus reached over and put his hand on Samuel's arm. "What happened with the teacup was just an accident, you know."

Samuel nodded. "I probably overreacted, but I wanted to give Marla something special that belonged to her mamm, and I'd hoped it would mean as much to her as it did to me."

"I'm sure it did. Didn't you see the way her eyes lit up when you handed her the kopplin?"

"Jah. She's probably just as disappointed as I am that it broke."

"I know she is. She and Penny both ran crying to their bedroom after you yelled and stormed out of the house. I'm sure they both feel responsible for the cup being broken."

"Guess I'll need to apologize to the both of them, and then I should find something else to give Marla." Samuel gently pushed Lucky aside and stood.

"Where are you going?"

"To the house, to talk to the girls."

"Can it wait awhile? Esther's in with 'em right now."

Samuel frowned, as irritation welled in his chest. "They're my kinner, not hers. It ought to be me talking to them, don't you think?" More annoyed with himself that he'd forgotten his daughter's birthday and the fact that he'd been pushing everyone close to him further and further away, even their beloved pooch, had made Samuel feel more agitated when he'd heard that Esther was comforting the girls. Then again, why shouldn't they be comforted by her? In their own little ways, all four of his children had tried reaching out to him, but instead of giving comfort to the children as a dad should, Samuel had once again reacted harshly. His children were trying to go on with life the best they could without their mother—why couldn't he?

"I do think you need to talk to them, but right now what they need is a woman's gentle touch." Titus motioned for Samuel to take a seat. "And I think you and I need to talk."

"About what?"

"Sit down, and I'll tell you what's on my mind."

Samuel wasn't used to having his younger brother tell him what to do, and it kind of irked him. But since he was beholden to Titus for allowing him and the children to stay with him, he figured he'd better at least listen when Titus said he wanted to talk.

He returned to the bale of straw and leaned his head against the wall behind him, figuring he was probably in for a long lecture about what a rotten father he was. Well, he felt like a rotten father, so he might as well admit it.

"I forgot it was Marla's birthday today, and I gave her the cup so she wouldn't know I'd forgotten," Samuel said.

"I figured as much." Titus pulled a piece of straw from the bale of hay he sat upon and stuck it between his teeth. "I wanted to suggest that unless you can find something of Elsie's that's not breakable, you probably should wait until Marla's older to give her more of Elsie's things."

"I've already come to that conclusion." Samuel groaned and slapped the side of his head. "I'm not a good daed anymore."

"You are a good dad," Titus said. "You're just dealing with your own grief, and I don't think you realize how much your kinner are hurting."

"They don't act like it. They carry on like they don't even miss their mamm."

"Do you remember what it was like when you lost your real mother?"

"Jah, I do."

"How old were you when she died?"

Samuel shrugged. "I was pretty young—maybe seven or eight, and I missed her a lot—especially at first, but I kept it pretty much to myself."

"How'd Dad deal with it?"

"He didn't talk much about Mama—at least not to me. Things didn't get a whole lot better till he met Mama Fannie and they decided to get married."

"Maybe you ought to think of getting married again."

Samuel's face heated, and his whole body tensed. "I've told you before—I'll never love anyone the way I did Elsie, so I won't be gettin' married again!"

CHAPTER 16

Paradise, Pennsylvania

On a Friday morning in the middle of March, Timothy knew the minute he stepped into his parents' house that his mother had been doing some baking. The delicious aroma of ginger and cinnamon wafted up to his nose, causing his mouth to water.

"Is that gingerbread I smell?" he asked when he entered the kitchen and found Mom bent over the oven door.

She whirled around, nearly dropping the pan in her hands. "Ach, Timothy! You shouldn't sneak up on me like that!"

"I wasn't sneakin'," he said with a grin. "I'm surprised my noisy boots didn't alert you to the fact that someone was coming."

"I did hear some clomping but thought it was your daed."

"Nope. After we came in from the fields, Dad went out to the barn to feed the horses." Timothy sniffed deeply and pointed to the pan she held. "That looks like gingerbread."

"You're right; it is." She placed a cooling rack on the counter and set the pan of bread on top of it. "Would you like some after it cools?"

He smacked his lips. "Sounds good to me."

"Are you and your daed done for the day, or just taking a break?" Mom asked.

"We're finished. The ground's too wet to get much plowing done. Guess that's to be expected when spring finally comes." He went to the cupboard, took out a glass, and filled it with water. "Mind if I ask you a question, Mom?"

She motioned to one of the chairs at the table. "Have a seat and ask away."

Timothy set his glass down on the table and seated himself. "Do you think it's normal for a married woman to spend more time with her mother than she does her husband?"

"I assume you're talking about Hannah?" Mom asked, taking a seat across from him.

He gave a nod. "As I've told you before, it seems like every time I turn around, Hannah's either over at her mamm's or her mamm's at our place."

"She and Sally do seem to be very close."

"Jah, but you and Abby are close, and she's not over here all the time."

"That's true. Abby's husband and children come first, and if I thought she was spending more time with me than them, I'd say something about it."

Timothy grunted. "I doubt Hannah's mamm would ever say anything to Hannah about her not spending enough time with me. Fact is, I think Sally would have preferred that Hannah stay single and livin' at her parents' home for the rest of her life."

Mom waved away the idea with her hand. "I don't think it's that bad, son."

"Maybe that was a bit of an exaggeration, but I think Hannah and her mamm are too close, and I wish there was some way I could stop it."

"Have you tried talking to Hannah about the situation?"

"Many times, and she always gets defensive. Even said I was selfish and wanted her all to myself." He took a drink of water and frowned. "I just want to know that the woman I married would rather be with me than anyone else. If Dad didn't need my help farming this place, I'd consider selling our home and moving my wife and daughter to Kentucky."

Mom's eyes widened as she drew in a sharp breath.

"Oh, don't worry," he was quick to say. "Hannah would pitch a fit if I even mentioned the idea."

"Can't say as I'd blame her for that." Mom's eyebrows drew together so they nearly met at the bridge of her nose. "Don't forget, your daed and I visited Titus in Kentucky last year, and I didn't see anything there that would make me want to move."

"Land's cheaper, and it's less populated in Christian County than here. Titus has said so many times."

"Jah, well, just because your twin likes it there doesn't mean you would." Mom leaned forward with her elbows on the table and looked at him intently, the way she had when he was a boy about to receive a stern lecture for something he'd done wrong. "If you think things are bad between you and Hannah now, just move her two states away from her mamm and see what happens."

"I didn't say I was planning to move. Just said I'd consider it if Dad didn't need me here. 'Course, I'd have to talk Hannah into it first, which would be nigh unto impossible."

Mom pursed her lips, causing the wrinkles around her mouth to become more pronounced. "I don't think it's right for Hannah to spend so much time with Sally that she's begun to ignore you, but if it's affecting your marriage, then you'd better have a talk with Jacob Weaver or one of our other ministers. Running from one's problems is not a good idea."

Timothy nodded, but didn't say anything. Truth was, he didn't think his mother would be any happier about them moving to Kentucky than Hannah's mother would be. Well, she didn't have to worry, because short of a miracle, Hannah would never agree to move anywhere that was more than five miles from her folks. What he needed to do was figure out some way to get Hannah paying more attention to him and less to her mother.

———⟨⟩———

Pembroke, Kentucky

"Would you like to have supper with us this evening?" Suzanne asked Titus as the two of them worked on a set of new cabinets one of their neighbors had recently ordered.

"Sorry, but I can't," he said, reaching for another piece of sandpaper. "I need to fix supper for Samuel and the kinner."

Suzanne's frown was so intense that deep lines were etched in her forehead. She looked downright miffed. "You've got to be kidding. Surely Samuel can fix supper for his family."

Titus shrugged. "He probably could if he set his mind to it, but it's all I can do to get him to eat a decent meal, let alone cook anything."

"I know you're concerned about your bruder, but you can't do everything for him. Since Samuel and his kinner moved here, we hardly see each other anymore."

"That's not true." Titus gestured to the cabinets they'd been sanding. "We see each other here at work almost every day."

Her nose wrinkled, like some foul odor had permeated the room. "That's not the same as spending time together doing something fun. Thanks to Samuel, you haven't taken me anywhere or come over for supper even once."

"I'm sorry about that, but it won't always be this way. Once Samuel works through his grief, I won't feel like I have to be there for him all the time."

"What if he never gets over Elsie's death?"

"I'm sure he will. He just needs a little more time." Titus started sanding again. "I talked with Allen the other day, and he's going to ask Samuel to paint a couple of rental houses he recently bought in Hopkinsville. So if Samuel keeps busy, I'm sure that'll help with his depression."

"I thought he was painting the outside of Bonnie's Bed-and-Breakfast."

"He has started on that, but he can't work on it when it's raining. The painting he'll do for Allen will be inside work." Titus stopped sanding and reached over to touch Suzanne's arm. "Are you *missvergunnisch* of the time I spend with Samuel?"

She looked at him intently. "I'm not envious, but I am afraid that because of him, we might never get married."

"That's *lecherich*. Samuel won't stop us from getting married this fall."

"It's not ridiculous. Samuel's been here over two months already, and he's made no effort to find a place of his own."

"His house in Pennsylvania hasn't sold yet, and even if it had, I doubt he could handle raising the kinner on his own."

Suzanne's cheeks flushed a bright pink. "There's no way I can think of moving into your house and starting a family of our own if Samuel and his kinner are still living there. Your place isn't big enough for that, and I'm sure it would eventually cause tension in our marriage."

Titus knew Suzanne was right. After the last couple of conversations he'd had with his twin, he knew Timothy and Hannah's marriage was full of tension. He didn't want to start his marriage out with differences between him and Suzanne, but he couldn't push Samuel and his kids out of the house either.

"I'll have a talk with Samuel about looking for a place of his own as soon as I feel he's ready," he said.

"What if he's not ready before fall?"

Titus took Suzanne's hand and gave it a gentle squeeze. "Let's pray that he is."

CHAPTER 17

Esther's stomach growled as she stepped into the kitchen, devoid of any pleasant smells. Even though Mom and Dad had been gone for two months, it still seemed strange not to have Mom here fixing breakfast in the mornings. She and Mom had always been close. Not an unhealthy kind of close, where she couldn't do anything without asking her mother first. No, she and Mom had a special bond—an understanding of one another's needs. Whenever Esther had been afraid as a child, Mom had always been there to calm her fears. When she'd had trouble making a decision, she'd gone to Mom for advice.

It wasn't easy to do that now, since Mom and Dad lived two states away. Of course, she could always write Mom a letter or leave her a message on Dan's voice mail. But it wasn't the same as sitting down with a cup of tea and having a good heart-to-heart conversation.

Knowing she needed to set her thoughts aside and fix something for breakfast so she could get over to Titus's to watch the children, Esther heated some water for tea, fixed herself a plate of scrambled eggs, and paired it with a slice of the delicious raisin bread Suzanne's mother had given her last night.

When she took a seat at the table and bowed her head, the first thing she prayed about was her brother.

Dear Lord, please help the doctors find something that will make Dan feel better. Help him find new ways to do things. If he has to begin using a wheelchair, help the transition to be easy. Help Sarah and their kinner to accept the changes and be an encouragement to Dan.

Be with my brother James and his family at their home in Lykens, and of course bless and be with Mom and Dad.

Help Samuel through his struggle with grief, and I pray that I may be a blessing to his kinner today. Help me know what to do to help them through their grief. Amen.

—◦∿◦—

"That looks really good, Samuel," Bonnie said when she'd finished spading her garden plot and joined Samuel on the side of the house where he'd been painting.

Samuel gave a nod and stopped painting long enough to move the ladder to a different spot.

"I'm glad I chose a pale yellow for the color."

"Jah, it looks pretty good," he said.

"Jah, means yes, doesn't it?"

"That's right."

"Esther's been explaining some things to me about the Amish way of life, and I'm hoping to learn some Pennsylvania-Dutch words. She's already taught me a few, but if you're willing, I'd be happy if you'd teach me some, too."

"Why would you want to learn Pennsylvania-Dutch?"

"Since so many of my neighbors are Amish, I thought it would be a good idea if I was able to understand some of their words."

Samuel picked up his paint brush. "We do speak English, you know."

"Of course, but when my Amish neighbors are talking among themselves, they usually speak their own language."

"So you want to know what they're saying?"

She chuckled. "Jah. That way I can be sure they're not talking about me."

He smiled. At least it felt like a smile. He hadn't found anything to smile about in such a long time he wasn't sure he knew how to smile anymore. "You seem like a nice person, Bonnie. I can't imagine anyone saying anything negative about you."

Bonnie's cheeks flamed. "That's kind of you, but I'm no saint. I'm sure there a few things about me that some folks might not like."

"Sure don't know what it'd be. You've been nothing but kind to me."

"Well, that's because you're such a nice man."

Samuel felt kind of embarrassed by that comment and wasn't quite sure how to respond, so he just shrugged and said, "Guess I'd better get back to work or this house will never get painted."

Paradise, Pennsylvania

"How come you're home so early today?" Hannah asked when Timothy entered the kitchen and found her fixing a sandwich for Mindy. "I figured you and your daed would be working in the fields until late now that the weather's improved."

"We've been pushing the horses hard all morning, so we're giving them a rest," Timothy said. "Thought I'd grab an early lunch while I'm here."

"Oh, I see. Would you like me to fix you a sandwich?"

"That'd be nice." Timothy leaned over and kissed the top of Mindy's head; then he looked back at Hannah. "I'm surprised to see you here."

Her brows furrowed. "Where else would I be?"

"Figured you'd probably be over at your mamm's. That's where you seem to spend all your time these days."

"That's *narrisch*, Timothy. I'm not over at Mom's all the time."

He moved over to the sink to wash his hands. "Jah, you are, and my comment may seem foolish to you, but it's not to me."

"What's that supposed to mean?" Hannah placed Mindy's sandwich on the tray of her high chair and poured her a glass of milk.

"When we got married, I figured I'd come first and then any kinner we had." He glanced back at Mindy, now eagerly eating her sandwich.

Hannah plopped her hands against her slender hips and stared up at him innocently. "I've always put you and Mindy first."

"Oh really? Is that why I've come home so many times and discovered that you were over at your mamm's?" He shook his head. "I hardly ever get to visit with my wife anymore, and I'm gettin' mighty sick of it." Timothy's voice grew louder, and Mindy's eyes widened as she looked up at him fearfully.

"It's okay," he said, gently patting her plump little arm. "Daadi's not mad at you."

"No, he's mad at me," Hannah mumbled, turning her back to him.

Timothy took hold of his wife's arm and turned her to face him. "I think we need to talk."

"Not if you're going to yell." Hannah motioned to Mindy. "I don't want to upset her."

"Let's go in the living room," he suggested.

She hesitated but finally nodded.

After they'd both taken a seat on the sofa, Timothy turned to Hannah and said, "I think we should move."

Her mouth dropped open. "What?"

"I think we should move."

"Where?"

"To Kentucky."

She shook her head vigorously with a determined set of her jaw.

"We need a new start."

Hannah's eyes filled with tears. "It's because of my mamm, isn't it? You want to move to Kentucky to keep me away from her."

Timothy wasn't sure what to say. He didn't want Hannah to think he disliked her mother, but he needed her to understand that her place was with him.

"Will you give up the notion of moving to Kentucky if I agree to stay home more?" she asked tearfully.

Timothy flinched. He hated it when Hannah cried. It always made him feel guilty—like he'd done something wrong. "Even if you stayed home more, your mamm would end up over here," he said, keeping his voice down.

"No, she wouldn't. I'll ask her not to."

"Oh, great. Then she'll think it's my fault and that I'm trying to come between the two of you. As it is, I'm not sure she likes me all that well anyhow."

"That's not true. Both of my parents like you just fine. And Mom won't think you're trying to come between us."

"How do you know that?"

"Because I'll tell her it was my idea—that I've come to realize that I need to spend more time with you, and that she needs to be with Dad more." Hannah clutched Timothy's shirtsleeve. "Please don't make us move. We wouldn't be happy in Kentucky; I know we wouldn't."

"Maybe you're right," Timothy said. "It would be hard to start over in a new place."

A look of relief spread across her face as she bobbed her head. "That's right. Look what a hard time Samuel's having. He's no better off now than he was when he lived here."

"I guess you have a point." Timothy pulled Hannah into his arms. "If you're willing to give me more of your time and put my needs ahead of your mamm's, then I'll forget about moving."

She smiled up at him sweetly, and his heart nearly melted. "Danki, Timothy. You won't be sorry; you'll see."

Chapter 18

Pembroke, Kentucky

Esther was pleased when she stepped into the phone shanty and discovered a message from her mother, asking her to call.

She reached for the phone, dialed Dan's number, and was surprised when Mom answered the phone.

"Mom! It's so good to hear your voice. I got your message but never expected you'd be near the phone when I returned your call. I figured I'd have to leave a message for you."

"I just came out to the phone shanty to make a call, and the phone rang as soon as I stepped inside. It's so good to hear from you, Esther."

"It's good hearing from you, too."

"How are things going?" Mom asked. "I've been concerned because I haven't heard from you in several days, so that's why I left a message."

"Everything's fine. I'm keeping busy with my two jobs. Oh, and Samuel finished painting the outside of the B&B yesterday, so Bonnie will be opening for business soon—hopefully within the next week or two."

"Does that mean you'll be working there more?" Mom asked.

"I believe so. Bonnie mentioned the idea of me moving into the guest house on her property so I could be closer and help her fix breakfast for her guests every morning."

"But if you did that, our house would be sitting empty,

and that might make it easy for someone to break in and steal things."

"I hadn't thought of that. So I'll just keep getting up early and going over there to help with breakfast whenever she needs me to."

"I'm glad you're keeping busy, Esther."

"How's Dan doing?" Esther asked, while watching with fascination as a spider created an intricate web in the corner of the shanty.

"About the same. The new medication he's taking is helping some, but I think he may have to start using a wheelchair soon, because he's still struggling with extreme fatigue and is very wobbly on his feet. Your daed's keeping busy at the two farmer's markets where Dan has his stands, and I've been helping him some there whenever I can."

They talked awhile longer, catching up on things, until Esther glanced at the battery-operated clock sitting on the phone table and realized what time it was. "I'm sorry, Mom, but I'm going to have to hang up now. It's time for me to go over to Titus's to watch the kinner. Allen lined up some paint jobs for Samuel, and I need to get there before his driver picks him up."

"Okay, I'll let you go," Mom said. "Take care, and do keep in touch so we know how you're doing."

"You do the same. I miss you and Dad, and it's been good talking to you. Bye, Mom."

When Esther hung up the phone, she hurried to the barn to get her horse. She had taken the buggy out of the shed before coming to the phone shanty, so all she had to do was hitch Ginger to the buggy. She looked forward to spending another day with Samuel's children because she was becoming more and more attached to them—especially Penny and Jared, who were with her most of the day. Caring for them gave her a taste of what it would be like if she had children of her own.

"I wonder if I'll ever fall in love and get married," she murmured as she stepped into Ginger's stall.

The horse whinnied and nuzzled Esther's hand.

"What do you think, Ginger?" Esther asked, patting the gentle mare's flanks. "Will any man ever ask me to marry him?"

With a shake of her mane, and a little nicker, Ginger answered, as if telling Esther not to worry.

———

Bonnie had just taken a seat on the window bench in front of the dining room window to have a second cup of coffee, when a knock sounded on the front door. She set her cup down and went to see who it was.

When Bonnie opened the door, she was surprised to see a young Amish boy wearing a bedraggled-looking straw hat standing on the porch, holding a fat red hen. When she'd first heard the knock, she'd thought it might be Allen, as he'd stopped by to say hello to her several times in the last few weeks. But since she hadn't heard a vehicle pull in before the knock sounded on her door, she'd quickly dismissed that idea.

Bonnie had never seen the young boy who stood staring up at her now, but then there were a lot of Amish in the area she hadn't met yet. "May I help you?" she asked.

"Ya need any chickens? We've got more just like her in our coop at home, and ya can have as many as ya like for a fair price."

"I don't know what I'd do with even one chicken," she said.

"Ya raise 'em for the eggs. . .and for eatin' of course." The boy tipped his head back and grinned up at Bonnie. "Ya got a husband I can talk to 'bout this?"

Bonnie shook her head. "I live here alone. This was my grandparents' house, and it'll soon be turned into a bed-and-breakfast." She gestured to the sign Samuel had put up on the front of the house that read: BONNIE'S BED-AND-BREAKFAST.

The boy glanced at the sign then back at Bonnie.

"How many beds have ya got for sale, and are ya chargin' folks to eat breakfast here, too?"

She bit back a chuckle. "I don't sell beds. I'll be renting rooms to people who need a place to stay when they're visiting this area, and I will also feed them breakfast."

"What about supper? Ya gonna feed 'em supper, too?"

"No, just breakfast."

"Don't ya think folks oughta have some supper? They'll get awful hungry if all they get is breakfast every day."

Bonnie was sure the boy didn't understand the concept of a bed-and-breakfast. He was young and probably quite innocent to the things of the modern world. "I might consider offering supper to my guests sometime in the future, but for now, I'll only be serving breakfast."

"If ya had some chickens, you'd have plenty of eggs to fix for breakfast." He looked down at the chicken he held and grinned.

Bonnie mulled the idea over a few seconds and finally said, "How many chickens do you have for sale, and how much would you charge me for them?"

"We've got fifteen hens we could sell ya for three dollars each, and we'll throw in a rooster for free, 'cause you're gonna need them eggs fertilized if you're plannin' to raise more chickens. If ya say yes, I'll run home and tell my dad; then he'll haul the chickens over to ya after he takes me to school."

"That's fine." Bonnie smiled, tickled by the young boy's salesmanship. "What's your name, anyway?"

"Amos Bontrager. What's yours?"

"I'm Bonnie Taylor, and you know what I think, Amos?"

"What's that?"

"I think you're a pretty good little salesman."

Amos shook his head. "Naw, you're just a good customer." He turned and bounded down the stairs.

"What in the world have I gotten myself into?" Bonnie muttered as she returned to the house. "I don't know the first thing about raising chickens, but I guess that's about to change."

———m———

"I hope you're in the mood for oatmeal this morning, because that's what I fixed," Titus said, placing a bowl on the table in front of Samuel. He gestured to the children, already gathered around the table. "As you can see, they're waiting to eat."

"Oatmeal's fine," Samuel said with a shrug. "It really doesn't matter to me."

"I don't like *hawwermehl*," Leon complained when Titus placed several more bowls on the table. "Makes me think I'm eatin' horse food."

"Oatmeal's not horse food." Marla poked her brother's arm. "Just eat it and be thankful."

"Nobody's eating anything until we've prayed." Titus gave Penny and Jared their bowls; then he pulled out his chair at the head of the table and took a seat.

All heads bowed, and when their time of silent prayer was over, Titus picked up the container of brown sugar and handed it to Leon. "If you put some of this on the oatmeal, it'll taste just fine."

The boy scowled. "Nothin' can make horse food taste fine."

"It's not horse food," Marla insisted.

"Jah, it is."

"No, it's not."

"If Leon's not eatin' horse food, then neither am I," Penny said with a shake of her head.

Marla's face turned red. "It's not horse food!"

Leon bobbed his head. "Uh-huh."

"You like Esther's hawwermehl kichlin, don't ya?"

"Jah, but that's different."

"No, it's not. Oatmeal cookies have brown sugar and raisins in 'em, same as what ya can put on oatmeal cereal."

"It's not the same, and I don't like hawwermehl cereal!"

"That's enough!" Samuel slammed his fist down on the table so hard that his glass of milk toppled over.

Jared let out a piercing howl, and Samuel thought his head might explode.

Titus jumped up, grabbed a dishtowel, and quickly mopped up the mess. "It's okay, Jared," he said. "There's nothing to cry about."

Jared continued to howl, and Samuel wanted to scream. It seemed like he could never say or do anything right where the kids were concerned, and all their fussing really got on his nerves.

I wish it had been me who'd died, instead of Elsie, he thought. *She was always better with the kids than me.* He grimaced, as another thought popped into his head. *But if I had died, then Elsie would have had the responsibility of trying to raise and support them by herself. Dear Lord, why couldn't You have let Elsie live? How can I can accept her death as Your will? Will I ever feel at peace and happy again?*

CHAPTER 19

Esther took a seat on the sofa in Titus's living room and reached into the satchel she'd brought with her. Penny and Jared were both taking naps, so this was a good time to write a few thoughts in her journal.

> *As much as I miss Mom and Dad,* she wrote, *I'm glad I stayed here in Kentucky. This is home to me, and I enjoy coming over here each day to care for Samuel's kinner. With each passing day I've become more and more attached. When school's out near the end of April, I'll become better acquainted with Marla and Leon. I just wish I could get to know. . .*

Esther paused and lifted her pen. Did she dare write everything that was on her heart?

It's all right, she told herself. *No one but me will ever see what I've written in my journal. No one but me will know my deepest thoughts.*

> *I have the strangest feeling whenever I'm around Samuel,* she continued to write. *I know he's hurting, and it's as though I can almost feel his pain. I want to reach out to him, but I'm not sure how. He keeps his distance and will barely look at me whenever we speak. Yet he doesn't seem that way with Bonnie. He's always willing to help or answer any of her questions.*

A sense of anxiety clutched Esther's heart. Maybe what she'd imagined before wasn't so crazy. Samuel might actually have a personal interest in Bonnie, and she could be interested in him as well. The other day, Bonnie had told Esther that Samuel had taught her some Pennsylvania-Dutch words, and she'd also made some comment about how comfortable she felt when she was around Samuel.

Why would Bonnie ask him to teach her some of our words when she had already asked me? Esther wondered. *Is the reason Bonnie wants to learn our language so she can understand what we're saying, or is she thinking of leaving her modern, English world and—*

"Mammi! Mammi!" Penny's shrill voice echoed down the hallway.

Esther slipped the journal into her satchel and hurried toward the bedroom Penny shared with Marla. She found the little girl curled up on her bed, sobbing.

"What's wrong?" Esther asked, leaning over the bed and gathering the child into her arms.

"I—I miss my mamm." Penny's shoulders shook, and she turned her face toward the wall.

Esther took a seat on the bed. "I know you do," she said softly. "I'm sure your sister and brothers miss her, too."

Penny sniffled. "I–I'm afraid I might forget her." She sat up and rubbed her eyes. "Sure don't wanna forget my mamm."

"Of course not, and if you talk about your mamm, it will keep her memory alive in your heart." Esther patted Penny's back, hoping to offer the comfort she needed. "You can talk to me about your mamm anytime you like."

"Danki, Esther." Penny leaned against Esther's shoulder with a sigh. "I like you a lot."

"I like you, too," Esther murmured.

"Will you be my new mamm?"

Esther's throat tightened as she slipped her arm around Penny's waist. "I can't be your mamm, sweet girl, but I will be your friend."

—m—

Bonnie had just picked up her laundry basket and was about to head to the basement, when she heard the whinny of a horse outside. She put the basket on the floor and went to the kitchen window to look out. A horse pulling an open wagon was coming up the driveway. She didn't recognize the Amish man driving the rig, but when she saw several wooden crates in the back of the wagon, she knew it must be Amos Bontrager's father bringing her chickens.

Bonnie slipped into a sweater and hurried out the door.

"You must be Amos's father," she said, when the man halted the horse and climbed down from the wagon.

He gave a nod. "My name's Harley Bontranger. Where do you want the chickens?"

Bonnie gulped. Until this minute, she hadn't realized she didn't have any place for chickens. "Umm. . . Let me see." She glanced around the yard. She couldn't put them in the garage; they'd make a mess and probably hop all over her car. She couldn't let them run free, because she was sure they'd never stay in the yard. Then, too, if she was going to run a B&B, her guests wouldn't want chickens running all over the place, leaving their droppings. *Oh dear, what was I thinking when I agreed to buy these chickens?*

Her gaze came to rest on the storage shed, where Grandpa had kept his lawnmower and yard tools. It wasn't a large structure, but she was sure it was big enough to temporarily house sixteen chickens.

"We can put them in there for now." She gestured to the shed. "I'll have to take out the mower and other tools first though."

Harley tipped his head, and his pale blue eyes seemed to be sizing her up. He probably thought she was a city slicker who didn't have a clue how to raise chickens. Well, it was true; she didn't. But she'd let Amos talk her into buying the chickens so she'd have fresh eggs, and now that the critters were here, she felt obligated to take them.

"Can you wait a few minutes while I clear out the shed?" she asked Harley.

"Sure. I'll help you clear it out, and then I'll need to be on my way. I have to get back to plowin' my fields soon before it starts raining."

Bonnie glanced up. There wasn't a cloud in the sky, but maybe Harley knew something about the weather that she didn't. Or maybe he was just anxious to be on his way.

"I appreciate your help," she said, hurrying toward the shed.

"Where do you want me to put everything?" Harley asked when she opened the shed door.

"I guess we can put them in the garage for now, but I'll have to pull my car out first."

One thing always leads to another, she thought, as she hurried toward the garage. *I have to clear out the shed to make room for chickens and clear out the garage to make room for the yard tools. What next?*

By the time Bonnie had moved her car out of the garage, Harley had the lawnmower, several shovels, a pair of hedge clippers, and two rakes out of the shed. While he put them in the garage, Bonnie went into the shed to see what else needed to go. She figured she'd better remove several clay pots that sat on a shelf. She'd heard that chickens liked to roost, so they might get up on the shelf, and she wouldn't want the pots to get broken because she might want to fill them with flowers and set them out on the front porch for a bit of color.

After she'd hauled the pots to the garage, she returned to the shed, where Harley was gathering more tools. When they'd gotten everything out, she turned to him and said, "I guess you can bring the chickens in now."

"Have you got any nesting boxes?" he asked.

"What are those?"

"Small wooden boxes where the hens can lay their eggs."

"There are some boxes in the attic. I suppose I can use those."

"You'll also need some chicken feeders, watering trays, cracked corn, and laying mash."

She sighed. "Oh my, I am unprepared. I sure hadn't figured on all of that."

"You can't expect chickens to survive if you don't feed and water 'em. And if you want plenty of eggs, you'll need to give 'em some laying mash." Harley's dark eyebrows drew together. "You sure you wanna do this?"

Bonnie thought about the desperate look she'd seen on Amos's face this morning and knew she couldn't say no. She had a hunch that the Bontragers needed money, and even though they weren't charging her a lot for the chickens, she wanted to help out.

"I know it seems that I didn't think things through very well, but I haven't changed my mind," she said, more determined than ever. "So let's get those chickens unloaded, and I'll pay you for them."

After Bonnie got her laundry started, she would head to Hopkinsville and see about getting the things she'd need for the chickens. She also thought she'd better buy a book that would tell her everything she needed to know about raising chickens. Then later, she'd drop by Samuel's and see if he would be willing to build her a chicken coop. It was a cinch she needed one, and soon.

CHAPTER 20

A cold foot pushed against Samuel's side, jolting him awake. "How many times have I told you to stay on your own side of the bed?" he grumbled as Leon looked at him with sleepy eyes.

"Sorry, Daadi," the boy mumbled. "Don't know where I am in the bed when I'm sleepin'."

Samuel couldn't dispute that fact. He'd found the boy on the floor a few times since he'd begun sharing a room with him and Jared. He glanced at the other side of the room, where Jared lay sleeping on a cot. Bunking in with two active boys wasn't the best arrangement—for him or them. But what else could he do? His house in Pennsylvania still hadn't sold, he wasn't making enough money yet to build or buy a home, and there was nothing for rent in the area right now. Besides, if he moved out on his own, he'd have to deal with the kids by himself, not to mention cleaning, cooking, and doing whatever other chores needed to be done. Right now, the thought of him and the children being on their own seemed overwhelming to Samuel.

He looked at the battery-operated clock on the table by his bed and realized it was only 5:00 a.m. The kids didn't usually get up for school until six.

"I'm awake now, so I may as well get up." Samuel poked Leon's arm. "You, too, since you're the one who woke me."

Leon yawned. "I'm sleepy."

"That's because you've been thrashin' around all night."

Samuel pulled the covers aside. "Now climb out of bed and get dressed. You've got chores to do."

Leon clambered out of bed and plodded over to the window. Lifting the shade, he said, "It's still dark outside, and it's Saturday, so there's no school. Can't I sleep awhile longer?"

"No." Samuel put on a shirt, slipped into his pants, and pulled his black suspenders over his shoulders. How could he have forgotten that today was Saturday?

"I'm hungerich," Leon complained. "Can I wait to do my chores till we've had breakfast?"

"No!" Samuel didn't know why, but every word the boy said made him more irritated. He couldn't remember feeling so impatient with the kids when Elsie was alive. He wasn't so forgetful then either.

"Should I wake Jared?" Leon asked.

"You'd better not. If you wake him now, he'll be cranky and out of sorts all day." The last thing Samuel wanted was another issue to cope with. He might not know much about caring for the kids on his own, but he knew that his two-year-old boy needed eight to ten hours of sleep at night, plus at least one nap during the day, or he was impossible to deal with. At least for Samuel, he was. Elsie never seemed to have a problem with Jared. He also knew that Jared was a heavy sleeper, and even loud voices in the room didn't wake him. You had to shake the boy's arm and practically shout in his ear to get him awake.

'Course Jared wasn't like that with Elsie. All she had to do was pick him up and carry him across the room, and he woke right up—in a pleasant mood, too. Not like with me; he usually cries whenever I hold him. Guess that's because I don't have Elsie's gentle touch.

Samuel jammed his feet into his boots. *Stop thinking about Elsie. You need to find something to do to keep your mind busy.*

He turned to face Leon, who was still standing in front of the window. "I asked you to get dressed!" Didn't the boy do anything he was told?

Leon's chin quivered. *"Ich bin mied wie en hund."*

"I don't care if you are tired as a dog. You woke me out of a sound sleep, and since I'm getting up, you are, too."

"But, Daadi. . ."

"Don't argue with me. Just do as you're told."

"You're a *schtinker*," the boy said defiantly.

Samuel stomped across the room and grabbed Leon's arm roughly. "So you think I'm a mean person, do you? Well, I'll show you how mean I can be." He lifted the boy off his feet, flopped him facedown on the bed, and gave his backside a couple of well-placed swats.

He didn't think he'd hit the boy that hard, but Leon let out a yelp that could have woke the soundest sleeper. In fact, it did. Jared sat straight up and started howling like a wounded heifer.

Unable to deal with it, Samuel rushed out of the room. He'd be heading over to Bonnie's after breakfast to build her a chicken coop, and he could hardly wait to get there. He was glad Titus didn't have to work on Saturdays and would be here to watch the kids, because right now, he didn't have the patience to deal with even one of his kids, let alone all four!

—m—

Bonnie was surprised when she looked out the kitchen window and saw Samuel's horse and buggy pull into the yard. It was only 7:00 a.m. She hadn't expected him until nine, which is when he said he'd be over.

She set her coffee cup on the counter and stepped outside onto the porch. Despite the early morning chill, there wasn't a cloud in the sky, and no wind at all. It looked like the promise of a beautiful spring day.

"Guder mariye," Bonnie said, joining Samuel near the garage, where he'd tied his horse to the hitching rail he'd constructed several weeks ago. "Did I say 'good morning' right?"

Samuel gave a nod. "Good morning to you, too. Hope it's okay that I came early," he said, without offering an explanation.

"It's fine. I've been up since five. For some reason, I couldn't sleep."

"I can relate to that," he muttered. "I was up early, too."

Cock-a-doodle-do! Cock-a-doodle-do!

Bonnie grimaced. "That noisy rooster's probably the reason I woke up at the crack of dawn."

Making no comment about the rooster, Samuel moved to the back of his buggy and removed a box of tools. Having grown up on a farm, he was probably used to many strange animal sounds. "Where do you want me to build the chicken coop?" he asked.

Bonnie studied the expansive yard a few minutes. "I don't want it too close to the house. It might turn guests away if they can smell the chickens."

"I'd think about getting rid of the rooster if I was you," Samuel mumbled. "Some folks might not appreciate getting woke early in the morning by an irritating rooster."

Bonnie could see by Samuel's sour expression that he was agitated about something, and she was fairly certain it had nothing to do with roosters. She was tempted to ask but figured if he wanted to talk about it, he would.

"Guess I'll keep the rooster for a while and see how it goes," she said. "If any of my guests complain, then I may need to get rid of him though."

Samuel nodded at the box of tools he held. "So where do you want the coop?"

"How about there?" Bonnie pointed to a patch of ground several feet behind the garage. "That should be far enough from the house that my guests won't have to deal with the chicken smells."

"Okay. How big do you want the coop to be?"

"I hadn't thought about that. How big do you think it needs to be?"

"I'd say an eight-by-twelve chicken coop ought to be

big enough," he said as he started walking toward the area she'd suggested.

Bonnie followed, and when they got there, he set the tool box on the ground and turned to face her. "I'm guessin' you'd like an outside run for the chickens, too?"

"I suppose that would be a good idea. I can't keep them cooped up all the time, and I certainly don't want them running all over the place."

He tipped his head and stared at her strangely. "I've been wondering. . . Have you ever had chickens before?"

"No, and it shows, doesn't it?" She grinned. "Truth be told, the only experience I've had with chickens are the ones fried golden brown." Bonnie hoped her comment might bring a chuckle from Samuel, but he never even cracked a smile.

"Where's the lumber you want me to use?" he asked. "When you called and left a message for me the other day you said you'd ordered some wood for the coop."

"I did. The Amish man who owns the lumber mill in the area had it delivered for me yesterday. It's piled up on the other side of the garage."

"Okay. I'll cut the pieces I need then start hauling 'em over." Samuel started walking in that direction.

"I'll be in the house. Esther's coming over soon to help me do some more cleaning before I open for business," Bonnie called. "If you need anything, just let me know."

Okay now, she thought as she hurried along. *That's one more thing taken care of. Let's see what I can get into next.*

As Bonnie neared the front door, she stopped and traced her finger on the porch table, leaving a streak of pollen dust. She sneezed. "Yep. Spring is definitely in the air."

CHAPTER 21

W hen Esther pulled into Bonnie's yard, she saw Samuel's horse and buggy parked at the hitching rail. He'd no doubt come to build a chicken coop, as Bonnie had mentioned he was going to do when she'd spoken to Esther yesterday.

When she stepped down from the buggy and heard a steady—*Bam! Bam! Bam!*—she knew for certain that was why Samuel had come.

Curious to see how things were going, Esther made sure her horse was secure and headed around the garage. In a clearing several feet away, she saw Samuel hard at work.

"Looks like you have a good start on the chicken coop," she said, stepping up to him.

"It's comin' along," he mumbled without making eye contact.

"How big is it going to be?"

"Eight by twelve feet." Still, he wouldn't look at her.

Bam! Bam! Bam! He hammered another piece of wood to the frame.

She figured she probably wasn't going to get much more out of him, so she turned and headed for the house. She wished he'd be a little more sociable.

Esther found Bonnie in the kitchen, scouring the kitchen sink. "Looks like you're hard at work," she said, removing her black outer bonnet and placing it on one end of the counter.

Bonnie pushed a strand of her curly blond hair away

from her face. "Seems like there's always something to do around here." She nodded toward the window. "Now that I've got chickens, it means even more work for me. Lately, I find myself asking, 'What was I thinking?'"

"You could have said no when that little boy came by with his chicken and sales pitch."

"I know, but he was so cute, and I figured his folks probably needed the extra money."

Esther smiled. "You have a tender heart, Bonnie."

A blotch of red erupted on Bonnie's cheeks. "I just care about people. My grandma used to say that if a person loves God, they'll love His people."

"That's what I believe, too, and it's what the Bible teaches." Esther made a sweeping gesture of the room. "Now, what would you like me to do today?"

"With all the renovations that have been done, there's dust everywhere," Bonnie said. "So it would be good if you dusted the living room, dining room, and the banister on the stairs."

"Sure, I can do that." Esther found the dust rag and some furniture polish in the utility room, and then she quickly set to work.

She started in the living room first, and when all the dust had been cleared away from the furniture, window ledges, and fireplace mantel, she moved on to the dining room. Finished with that, she went up the stairs and was about to start working her way down, cleaning the banister rungs, when she heard Samuel come into the house.

"I came for a drink of water," she heard him say to Bonnie when he entered the kitchen.

"Would you rather have a glass of iced tea?" Bonnie asked.

"That sounds good."

"Have a seat, and I'll fix you a sandwich to go with your tea," Bonnie said. "When Esther finishes up with what she's doing, I'll fix her one, too."

"I appreciate the offer, but you don't have to do that."

"It's no trouble. You've been working hard all morning, and I'm sure you're hungry by now."

"Guess I am at that."

Esther tried not to eavesdrop, but their voices floated out of the kitchen and up the stairs. So while she continued to dust and unavoidably listened, she wondered once more why Samuel was so talkative to Bonnie but would barely say more than a few words to her.

"When you first got here this morning, you seemed kind of down," Bonnie said. "I wasn't going to bring it up, but I've been wondering if there might be something wrong."

"Actually, there is. I had a little trouble at home this morning with Leon," Samuel said. "When I told him to get dressed and do his chores, he smarted off to me, so I gave him a spanking."

"Oh, I see."

"I don't normally lose my temper so easily, but it irked me when he said I was a mean person." Samuel groaned deeply. "Guess I *was* mean to him, and now I feel like a bad father."

Esther grimaced. *Poor Leon must have been upset when Samuel spanked him. But the boy shouldn't have said what he did. Even so, I've seen how short Samuel can be with the kinner. Maybe he overreacted, the way he did the night Marla dropped her mother's cup.* She was pleased when she'd learned that Samuel had apologized for that and had bought Marla several new books for her birthday present, but he obviously had a long way to go if he was going to establish a loving relationship with his children.

"You're not a bad father because you disciplined your son," Bonnie said. "Besides, kids usually get over things quickly and don't hold grudges the way some adults do. Well, most kids, anyway," she added.

"That may be, but I plan to apologize to Leon as soon as I get home."

"When I was little and my dad got mad at me, he

never said he was sorry for anything he said or did."

Esther could hear the hurt in Bonnie's voice. No wonder she'd decided to leave Oregon and move here.

Samuel and Bonnie continued to talk for a while, as Bonnie shared with him some details about her childhood. She'd told Esther a few things during the times they'd spent working together, but not nearly as much as she was sharing with Samuel right now. Apparently Bonnie's father had been very harsh. . .especially after his wife died.

"It's hard to live in the same house with someone when there's a lot of stress and undercurrent going on," Bonnie said.

"I know what you mean." Samuel paused. "There's been a lot of tension at Titus's house these days—between me and the kids and between me and Titus."

Esther thought about a conversation she'd had with Suzanne the other day, remembering how upset Suzanne was because Titus spent all his free time with Samuel and the kids instead of her. Esther figured the solution to the problem would be for Samuel to find a place of his own. If things didn't get better soon, she was afraid Suzanne might break her engagement to Titus.

—⁓—

"I can't believe you're stuck watching Samuel's kids again," Suzanne said when she dropped by Titus's house that afternoon and he said that he couldn't go shopping with her because Samuel was over at Bonnie's, building a chicken coop.

Titus put his finger to his lips. "Be careful what you say. The kinner are playing in their rooms. All except for Leon, that is. He went outside some time ago. Did you see him in the yard?"

Suzanne shook her head. "Couldn't Esther watch the kinner today?"

"Nope. She was supposed to go over to Bonnie's to help her clean."

Suzanne folded her arms and tapped her foot impatiently. "Are we ever going to start courting again?"

"Sure. Just as soon as Samuel finds a place of his own."

"When's that going to be?"

Titus shrugged.

"Have you asked him yet?"

"Well no, but. . ."

"What happens if he gets too comfortable with these living arrangements? He'll never move out if you don't ask, and you promised you would."

"I will when I think he's ready. Once Samuel's home in Pennsylvania sells he'll have enough money to start looking for a place of his own."

"With the economy what it is, his house may never sell, and I doubt he'll ever start looking for a place of his own here. Not unless you say something to him."

Titus's teeth snapped together with a click. "What do you want me to do. . .throw my own bruder out of my house?"

"Of course not, but. . . Oh, never mind." Suzanne's shoulders slumped as she turned and opened the front door.

"Where are you going?" he asked, stepping onto the porch behind her.

"Shopping. Alone!" Suzanne hurried off, leaving Titus there, shaking his head. *She doesn't understand. If she's not going to be more understanding, then maybe she's not the right woman for me.*

Before Titus went into the house, he decided to go outside to see if Leon was ready to come in for lunch. When he didn't see any sign of the boy, he stepped into the barn to look there. It was dark and quiet. The horses were in the pasture, so it made sense that he didn't hear them, but if Leon was in here playing, there ought to be some sign of him.

Titus cupped his hand around his mouth. "Leon! Are you in here?"

No response.

"Are you hungry for lunch?"

Still no reply.

Thinking the boy might be hiding somewhere, Titus looked around the barn, checking in every nook and cranny. When he'd searched in all the obvious places, he left the barn and walked around the yard again, calling Leon's name. There was no sign of Leon at all.

The hair on the back of Titus's neck prickled. What if Leon had wandered off by himself? With the exception of walking to and from school now that the weather was warmer, the boy didn't know the area that well.

Titus dashed down the driveway and looked up and down the road. No sign of Leon there either.

He raced back to the house and spotted Marla in the living room, sitting on the sofa, reading a book to Penny and Jared. "Have you seen Leon?" Titus asked.

Marla shook her head, but Penny nodded.

"When did you see him?"

"He came in the house awhile ago. Said he had to get somethin'. After that he went outside and never came back."

A shiver of fear shot up Titus's spine. *If Leon doesn't show up soon, I don't know what I'm going to tell Samuel when he gets home.*

Chapter 22

Whe n Suzanne got home from Titus's, she hurried to put her horse away and then went straight to the house. She was still upset about the argument she'd had with Titus and hoped her mother was home so she could tell her about it.

She found Mom in the kitchen, cutting up pieces of chicken.

Mom turned and smiled. "I've got the chicken almost ready to go in the oven, so supper should be ready in about an hour. Did Titus come home with you?"

Suzanne shook her head.

"Is he coming over later then?"

"No. He's watching Samuel's kinner again while Samuel builds a chicken coop for Bonnie Taylor." Suzanne dropped into a seat at the table. "I'm sure Samuel will be home by suppertime, but I guess Titus figures he needs to be there to cook the meal."

"Doesn't Samuel know how to cook?"

Suzanne shrugged. "He probably could if he set his mind to it, but why would he want to when Titus is there to do it all for him?"

Mom placed the chicken in a baking pan and put it in the oven. After she'd washed and dried her hands, she poured them some tea and took a seat beside Suzanne. "You're upset with Titus again. I can see it on your face and hear it in your voice. Did you two have an argument about Samuel?"

"Jah. It seems like all we do anymore is argue." Suzanne blinked as tears pricked the back of her eyes. "I—I don't think we're going to be married this fall. I think he loves his bruder more than he does me."

Mom placed her hand on Suzanne's arm. "I don't think Titus loves Samuel more than you. He loves him in a different way and no doubt feels a sense of responsibility to be there for Samuel and his kinner, because he knows they're still grieving."

"I understand that, but Titus isn't helping Samuel by doing everything for him or being there all the time. If something doesn't change for the better soon, I'm going to break up with him."

"Ach, Suzanne! You can't mean that."

Suzanne reached for a napkin and blew her nose. "I want things to be the way they were before Samuel and his family moved to Kentucky. I want to go places with Titus and have him come here to visit and share meals with us like he used to do."

Mom took a sip of her tea. "Have you tried talking to him about this—let him know how you feel?"

"Of course I have. That's why we keep arguing. Every time I express my feelings, Titus gets upset and says I need to be more understanding." Suzanne paused and drew in a deep breath. She was so upset her hands had begun to shake. "I do feel sorry for Samuel, and I know losing Elsie couldn't be easy for him, but he shouldn't expect Titus to sacrifice his own life to care for him and his kinner."

"Have you prayed about this matter?" Mom asked. "Have you asked God to give you more patience and understanding?"

Suzanne hung her head in shame. "I have prayed, but my prayers have always been that Samuel will find a place of his own and that Titus and I can begin courting again." She blotted the tears streaming down her face. "I—I guess I do need more patience and understanding. Guess I'm not setting a very good Christian example."

Mom lifted Suzanne's chin and looked like she was about to say something, when Grandpa entered the room.

"Where's Titus?" he asked. "I thought he'd be joining us for supper this evening."

"I invited him, but he said he couldn't come because he had to watch Samuel's kinner." Suzanne felt her cheeks to see if all the tears were gone. She hoped Grandpa wouldn't know she'd been crying.

"He must not be watching 'em too well because when I was on the way home from visiting the bishop just now, I saw Samuel's boy, Leon, getting into someone's car."

"Whose car was it?" Mom asked.

Grandpa shrugged. "Beats me. I've never seen it before. Thought at first it might be someone Titus knows, but the more I think about it, the more concern I feel."

Alarm rose in Suzanne's chest. She was sure Titus would never allow any of the children to go off in a car without him or Samuel accompanying them—much less with a stranger.

"Do you know the make or color of the car?" Suzanne asked.

He squinted and rubbed the bridge of his nose. "The car was kind of a silver gray. It was one of those little compact cars, but I don't know the make, and I didn't take notice of the license plate number either."

"Did you get a look at the driver?" Mom questioned.

"Not a good one. Just saw the back of his head. I think his hair was blond, and he wore a baseball cap."

As fear gripped Suzanne, she pushed her chair quickly aside and stood. "I'm going back over to Titus's. He needs to know about this!"

—∾—

"Where's Bonnie?" Samuel asked, poking his head into the living room, where Esther was cleaning the brick on the front of the fireplace.

"Upstairs. Do you need me to get her?"

He shook his head. "That's all right. Just wanted to tell her I'm done with the coop and am heading home now."

"Okay. I'll let her know." Esther was tempted to mention what she'd heard Samuel and Bonnie talking about earlier, but didn't want him to think she'd been eavesdropping. Besides, he might not want to talk to her about the problem he'd had with Leon this morning, although he sure hadn't minded discussing it with Bonnie.

Samuel hesitated, like he wanted to say something more, but then he turned and headed out the door.

Esther's stomach growled noisily, and she glanced at the clock on the mantel. No wonder she was hungry. It was almost five o'clock. She should head home soon and start supper, but the thought of eating alone held no appeal.

"Was that Samuel's voice I heard?" Bonnie asked when she came downstairs a few minutes later.

"Yes, he wanted me to tell you that he'd finished the chicken coop and was going home."

"Oh, good. Would you like to go outside with me and take a look at it?"

"Sure." Esther put her cleaning supplies aside and followed Bonnie out the door.

As they approached the new chicken coop, Esther heard the chickens clucking. "Sounds like they're in there already," she said to Bonnie. "Samuel must have transferred them from the shed to the new coop before he left."

Bonnie opened the door, and as they stepped inside, they were greeted by a cackling hen that managed to slip between her legs. "Shut the door, quick, before she gets out! She might be hard to catch."

Esther complied, and in so doing, she spotted a straw hat on the floor. "Looks like Samuel left this behind," she said, bending to pick it up. "I'll drop it off to him on my way home. Speaking of which, I should probably be heading out soon."

Bonnie smiled. "No problem. You've done enough for

today. I wouldn't be this far along with all the cleaning if it weren't for you."

As Samuel headed for Titus's place, he rehearsed what he was going to say to Leon. The boy needed to know he was loved but that he couldn't talk disrespectfully to his father—or any other adult, for that matter.

First off, I need to apologize for being so harsh, Samuel reminded himself. *I should never have lost my temper like that with him this morning.*

When Samuel guided his horse and buggy into Titus's yard a short time later, he saw Titus step out of the phone shanty.

"I've got some bad news," Titus said, joining Samuel beside his buggy.

"What's wrong?"

"Leon is missing."

"Wh–what do you mean?"

"He disappeared. I've searched everywhere for him—in the house, in the barn, all around the yard. He's nowhere to be found."

Samuel leaped out of the buggy. "He's got to be somewhere. Have you checked with the neighbors?"

Titus nodded. "I've made several phone calls, but no one's seen Leon."

"I'm going down the road to look and call for him. He might be hiding in the woods."

Clippety-clop! Clippety-clop! A horse and buggy pulled into the yard. It was Esther.

"You left this at Bonnie's," she said, leaning out the buggy and holding Samuel's straw hat out to him.

"Just leave it somewhere," Samuel said, barely looking at her. "I'm heading out to look for Leon."

"Isn't he here?" she asked.

Titus stepped forward and explained the situation.

She gasped. "I hope he's okay."

"Esther, could you stay with the kinner so I can go with Samuel to look for Leon?" Titus asked.

"Sure, no problem. I'd be happy to stay. I can fix the kinner their supper, too."

Just then, Suzanne's horse and buggy pulled in. She jumped out quickly and dashed up to Samuel. "Is Leon here?"

Samuel shook his head.

"He's missing," Titus said. "I've looked all over for him. Samuel and I are going to search along the road and in the woods if need be."

She drew in a quick breath. "I hate to tell you this, but my grandpa just told us that he saw Leon getting into someone's car."

"Whose car?" Samuel asked.

"He didn't recognize it, and he didn't get a good look at the man who was driving the vehicle either."

Samuel's heart pounded like a herd of stampeding horses as he broke out in a cold sweat. "I'm sure Leon wouldn't have gotten into the man's car unless he'd been forced." He squeezed his fingers into the palms of his hands until they dug into his flesh. "I think my boy's been kidnapped, and I'm the one to blame."

CHAPTER 23

W hat'd the sheriff have to say?" Titus asked when Samuel stepped out of the phone shanty.

"He said they'd be searching for Leon, and that we should also keep looking. He wanted me to give him a picture of Leon, but I told him I didn't have any." Samuel frowned. "Sure wish I did though."

"You gave him a good description of Leon, didn't you?" Titus asked.

"Of course, but I'm not sure how much it'll help." Samuel moaned deeply. "I can't believe my boy's been kidnapped. Makes me think about how everyone in my family felt when Zach was snatched from our yard."

Titus placed his hand on Samuel's shoulder and gave it a squeeze. "We don't know for sure that Leon's been kidnapped."

"Suzanne said her grandpa saw Leon get into a stranger's car. I've warned my kinner many times not to go anywhere with someone they don't know, so I'm sure Leon didn't get into the car willingly." Samuel drew in a quick breath and released it with another moan. "I was pretty young when Zach was taken, but I can still remember how upset everyone was, and Naomi blamed herself for it. She felt like everyone else blamed her, too." He rubbed his forehead, where sweat had beaded up, feeling more anxious by the minute. "I can understand that now, because I blame myself for Leon being taken."

"It's not your fault. You had no way of knowing some-one would come along and coax the boy into their car."

"What makes you think he was coaxed? Maybe Leon was forced." Samuel clenched his fingers as he held his arms tightly against his sides in an effort to keep from shaking. "Either way, I'm the one to blame. If I hadn't gotten angry with him this morning, he wouldn't have taken off."

"He might not have taken off. He may have just gone outside to play."

Samuel wrung his hands as he shook his head. "I don't think so. If he'd been playing, he wouldn't have been out by the road; he'd have been in the yard or barn."

"You're upset and need to calm down. I think you ought to go in the house and be with your kinner while we wait for the sheriff."

"Of course I'm upset. You'd be upset, too, if you had a son who'd gone missing." Samuel glared at Titus. "And I'd appreciate it if you'd stop tellin' me what to do. I'm going to get my horse buggy so I can look for Leon by myself." Samuel hurried away. *Lord, help me. I'd never be able to live with myself if anything happens to my boy.*

—᠁—

"I'm glad we're both here right now," Esther told Suzanne as they scurried around Titus's kitchen getting supper ready. "Not only do the kinner need to be fed, but someone needs to be here to watch them while Samuel's out looking for Leon and Titus is in the shanty making phone calls."

"Titus will probably be awhile calling his family back home, and I'm sure they'll be quite upset when they hear the news," Suzanne said. "I just hope Leon is found soon and that he hasn't been harmed. Titus and Timothy weren't born during the time of their brother Zach's kidnapping, but from what Titus has been told, the whole family was in a terrible turmoil after Zach disappeared. It took twenty years for him to be reunited with them. Can you imagine that?"

"That's baremlich. Sure hope things turn out better for Leon. Samuel's suffered enough over the loss of his wife and unborn baby. I can't imagine how he'd deal with losing Leon, too."

"Let's not think about that." Suzanne took out a loaf of bread and stacked several slices on a plate. "We need to think positively and pray for Leon."

Esther nodded. "I have been praying, and will continue to do so until he's found."

The back door swung open just then, and Titus stepped into the kitchen, looking very upset.

"Did you get ahold of your family in Pennsylvania?" Suzanne asked.

He nodded soberly. "They took it pretty hard—especially Dad. I think it brought back memories of when Zach was taken."

"I figured it might," Suzanne said.

"Then when I hung up from talking to Dad, the sheriff called."

"What'd the sheriff say?" From the grim expression on Titus's face, Esther feared it wasn't good news.

He leaned against the wall as though needing it for support. "Some English fellow came into his office awhile ago and said he'd seen a young Amish boy walking along the side of the road. Since the boy was alone and appeared to be crying, the man stopped to see if he was okay."

"Was it Leon?" Suzanne questioned.

"From the description the man gave the sheriff, I'd say it was." Titus moved over to the table and took a seat. "Anyway, the man tried to get the boy to give him his name, but he wouldn't. When he asked where the boy lived, he said Pennsylvania."

"Why would Leon say something like that?" Esther asked.

Titus shrugged. "Maybe because he's from Pennsylvania."

"Or maybe he was trying to get to Pennsylvania," Suzanne put in.

Esther drew in a sharp breath. "Could Leon have been running away from home?"

"That's a definite possibility. I heard some raised voices this morning, and Samuel told me awhile ago that he'd lost his temper with Leon." Titus pinched the bridge of his nose. "Anyhow, thinking the boy was lost, the man decided to take him to the sheriff's office."

Hope welled in Esther's chest. "Is Leon with the sheriff now?"

Titus shook his head. "As the man neared Hopkinsville, he realized that he was almost out of gas. So he stopped at a station just inside the city limits, and while he was pumping the gas, the boy hopped out of the car and took off down the street."

"Did the man catch up with him?" Esther asked, hoping against hope that he had.

"Afraid not. Leon must have hidden somewhere, because the man lost sight of him real quick." Titus continued to rub his nose. "So the man went on to the sheriff's office and reported the incident, and the sheriff called here because the description of the boy fit Leon."

"If Leon's somewhere in Hopkinsville, surely he'll be found," Esther said, again feeling hopeful.

"I hope so." Titus frowned. "Trouble is, there are so many places he could hide."

"At least we know he hasn't been kidnapped, and I'm sure he'll be found." Suzanne's voice sounded optimistic, but the look of doubt on her face cancelled it out.

Esther moved over to the table to stand beside Titus. "You don't suppose Leon will try to get to Pennsylvania."

Titus shook his head. "I don't see how he could. He's only six years old and wouldn't even know where to catch a bus. Besides, he has no money."

"Jah, he does," Marla said, entering the room. "Penny

said she saw Leon with Daadi's wallet earlier. Guess Daadi must have forgot to take it with him today."

Esther gasped, and Suzanne's mouth dropped open.

Titus pushed his chair back and stood. "I'd better go out to the phone shanty and leave a message for my folks again. They need to know about this latest information, just in case Leon somehow ends up in Pennsylvania. Sure wish Samuel would get back so I can fill him in on all this."

"I don't understand why Samuel went out looking for Leon," Suzanne said. "He had to know that if someone picked Leon up in a car, there was no way he could catch up to them in his horse and buggy. Especially after so much time has gone by since Grandpa saw Leon."

"My bruder's no dummkopp. He's just concerned about his son and is desperate to get him back." Titus shot Suzanne a look of irritation then rushed out the door.

Suzanne groaned and thumped her head. "Oh, great. He's mad at me again."

Esther put her arm around Suzanne's waist, hoping to offer some comfort. "I'm sure he didn't mean to be so sharp. He's obviously worried about Leon, and Samuel, too. Everything will work out as soon as the boy is found."

"*If* he's found," Marla said. "What if my bruder never comes home?"

CHAPTER 24

Samuel hated to give up his search, but it was dark and he couldn't see much of anything. Discouraged, yet trying to remain hopeful that Titus might have heard something from the sheriff by now, he turned his horse and buggy in the direction of Titus's house. He couldn't shake the nagging fear that he might never see his son again, and he couldn't stop blaming himself.

Dear Lord, he silently prayed, *please take care of my boy, and bring him safely back to us. If You'll grant me this one request, I promise I'll be a better daed from now on.*

When Samuel stepped into the house a short time later, he found Titus sitting in the living room by himself.

"Where is everyone?" he asked.

"Suzanne and Esther were exhausted, so I told 'em to go home, and the kinner are all in bed," Titus said.

"I went a long ways up the highway and stopped at every house I saw," Samuel said. "No one has seen Leon or the car he was riding in." He sank into the rocking chair and leaned his head back. He, too, was exhausted. "Have you heard anything from the sheriff?"

"He said Leon wasn't kidnapped. The man who picked him up thought he was lost so he decided to take him to the sheriff's."

"Is he here? Did the sheriff bring my boy home?" Samuel leaped out of the chair, feeling truly hopeful for the first time since he'd learned that Leon was gone.

"No, he's not here. When the man stopped for gas,

Leon hopped out of the car and ran."

"Where is he now?"

Titus shrugged. "We don't know. The man lost sight of him, but the sheriff and his deputies are out searching for Leon. I'm sure it's only a matter of time before he's found."

Samuel's shoulders drooped as he glanced at the clock on the far wall. It was almost ten. The later it got, the worse he felt. Leon had to be frightened out there by himself.

Samuel began to pace—praying, thinking, and praying some more.

"You're not doing yourself any good by doing that," Titus said. "We just need to pray."

Samuel's jaw clenched as he whirled around. "I've been praying. Not that it's gonna do any good. God sure didn't answer my prayers when I asked Him to keep Elsie and our unborn boppli safe from harm, now did He?"

"God's ways are not our ways."

Samuel dropped into the rocking chair again and let his head fall forward into his hands. There wasn't much else he could do for Leon right now except pray, so even if he had lost faith in receiving an answer to his prayers, he closed his eyes and continued to plead with God.

—∞—

Heavenly Father, Esther silently prayed as she knelt on the floor beside her bed, *please be with Leon tonight. He must be so scared out there all alone. Help the sheriff, or someone else, to find Leon and bring him safely home.*

When Esther's prayer ended, she stood and moved over to the window. It had started raining, and she shivered as she listened to the splattering raindrops hitting the window. It was a chilly spring night—too cold and wet for a little boy to be out on his own.

I wonder if Samuel gave up his search and came home. If I feel this bad about Leon, I can only imagine how terrible Samuel must feel.

Esther folded her arms across her chest. She knew

Samuel loved his children, even though he often ignored them. Perhaps the pain of losing his wife had caused Samuel to pull so far into himself that he'd forgotten that his children missed their mother and needed their father. During the time Esther had spent taking care of them, she'd seen how needy they were—especially little Jared, who often called her "mammi." The poor little fellow still sucked his thumb and had a hard time falling asleep unless he was rocked. Not that Esther minded rocking him. She enjoyed holding Jared on her lap and stroking his soft skin. His hair smelled so good after a bath, and his warm, steady breathing nearly lulled her to sleep. She enjoyed everything about caring for Samuel's children, and the more she was with them, the more she longed to become a mother.

Heavenly Father, she prayed once more, *please, please keep Leon safe.*

—⁓—

Paradise, Pennsylvania

The sound of heavy footsteps woke Fannie from a restless sleep. In the darkness of the room, lit only by the glow of the moon shining through their bedroom window, she could see her husband's silhouette.

"Abraham, what are you doing up?" she whispered.

"I'm standing by the window."

"I can see that, but why?"

"I couldn't sleep. I'm worried about Samuel and think we ought to go to Kentucky to be with him."

Fannie slipped out of bed and made her way across the room to stand beside Abraham. He was in the middle of planting season and never would have considered going anywhere unless it was an emergency. "I'm worried about Samuel and Leon, too," she said, "but when Titus called to tell us about Leon, he said we should wait until tomorrow to make a decision about going there. By morning, we may have received word that Leon's been found."

"Maybe some stranger will find the boy and take him away. Maybe our family will have to suffer through yet another kidnapping."

Fannie could hear the fear and desperation in Abraham's voice. Even after all these years, the pain of having his own son kidnapped had truly never left him. It was as if Leon's disappearance had stirred up all the old hurts and doubts from the past.

She slipped her arm around his waist. "We must trust God, Abraham. He knows where our grandson is, and if it's His will, then Leon will be found."

"And if it's not?"

"Try not to think about that," she said. "Let's keep our thoughts positive and pray for the best. If we don't have some good news by tomorrow morning, we'll call our driver and head to Kentucky."

Abraham grunted. "Let's hope we're not too late."

CHAPTER 25

Pembroke, Kentucky

A knock sounded on the front door, causing Bonnie to jump. She'd been lying on the sofa, reading a book, and hadn't expected any company this late at night.

She rose from the sofa and padded across the room in her bare feet. Peeking out the little window near the top of the door, she was surprised to see Allen standing on the porch. Quickly, she opened the door.

"I hope I'm not disturbing you," he said. "I went by Titus's place, but it looked dark, so I figured they'd probably all gone to bed. Then when I came by here and saw a light in your window, I decided to see if you'd heard the news about Samuel's boy."

Bonnie nodded. "Esther stopped on her way home from Titus's this evening and told me Leon was missing, but I haven't heard anything since then. Have you?"

He shook his head. "I can only imagine how Samuel must feel."

"I know, and I've been praying for him, as well as Leon."

"Me, too."

"Would you like to come in for a cup of coffee or some hot chocolate?" she asked.

"Hot chocolate sounds good. I could use a little pick-me-up before I head home."

Bonnie led the way, and Allen followed her into the kitchen.

"Have a seat," she said, motioning to the table. "I'll heat some water for the hot chocolate. All I have is the instant kind, but with a couple of marshmallows on top, maybe you won't know the difference."

He chuckled.

"What's so funny?"

"I was just thinking about how Samuel's brother Zach and I used to get into his mother's cupboards when we were kids. One of our favorite things to snack on was marshmallows. We'd eat 'em till our stomachs were nearly bloated."

She smiled and tossed the bag of marshmallows on the table in front of him. "Here you go. Take as many as you like."

"I've got better sense than to eat the whole bag, but I will have one while we're waiting for the water to heat." Allen opened the bag, reached inside, and popped a marshmallow into his mouth. "Yum. It's been too long since I've had one of these."

Bonnie took two mugs down from the cupboard and emptied a package of hot chocolate mix into each. When the teakettle whistled, she poured the hot water in and stirred it well. The delicious aroma of chocolate wafted up to her nose as she handed Allen a mug.

"I assume since you knew Samuel's brother when you were a child, you must have grown up in Pennsylvania," Bonnie said, taking a seat across from him.

Allen shook his head. "I grew up in Washington State. So did Zach."

She tipped her head in question.

"It's a long story, but to give you the shortened version, Zach was kidnapped when he was a year old, and the man who took him lived in Washington. Zach grew up thinking his name was Jimmy, and that Jim and Linda Scott were his parents."

Bonnie's eyes widened. "That's terrible! No one in their right mind would steal a baby from his family. How did Zach end up back in Pennsylvania?"

Allen added a marshmallow to his hot chocolate and stirred it around. "After Linda died from cancer, the truth came out, so Jimmy, who was twenty-one at the time, went to Pennsylvania in search of his real family."

"Did he find them right away?"

"Nope. He didn't even know their names, so he had no idea where to look. I believe it was God's divine intervention that brought the pieces of the puzzle together for Zach. In the end, the bishop in their church district identified him by a birthmark on his neck."

Bonnie leaned back in her chair. "That's the most incredible story I've ever heard! Someone should write a book or make a movie about it."

"Yeah, it probably would make a good story." Allen's forehead wrinkled. "I missed Zach after he moved to Pennsylvania, but I knew he was where God wanted him to be, and he seems very content to be Amish."

"You've mentioned God twice now. Do you have a personal relationship with Him?"

He nodded. "I accepted Christ as my Savior when I was a boy, and Zach did, too."

"So do you have a church home?"

"Yeah. I attend a great Bible-preaching church in Hopkinsville. How about you? Have you found a church to attend since you moved here?"

She nodded. "I've been going to the church my grandma attended in Fairview. The people there are nice, and I enjoy the sermons, as well as the music."

"Have you gone to church most of your life?" he questioned.

"No, not really. My mother took me a few times when she was still alive, but it wasn't until I was seventeen that I found the Lord," Bonnie said. "I went to church with a friend of mine, and when the pastor talked about the need to seek God's forgiveness for our sins, it was as though he was speaking directly to me, because I felt so terribly guilty."

He leaned forward and stared at her intently. "I know we've all sinned and need God's forgiveness, but I can't imagine that a woman as nice as you would have anything to feel terribly guilty about."

She dropped her gaze to the table, unable to share the details of her shameful past with him. Instead, she changed the subject. "After my mother died, my dad became bitter and angry. I was worried at first that he was going to drink himself to death and I'd become an orphan, but then he got control of his drinking and became a workaholic instead." She lifted her gaze and picked up her mug. "Dad and I had never been very close, but after he started working long hours at the bank he manages, we drifted even further apart." Tears sprang to her eyes, and she blinked to keep them from falling onto her cheeks. "To make things worse, he's had a grudge against his parents for many years, so when Grandma died, he wouldn't even come here with me to attend her funeral."

"Sounds like what your dad needs is the Lord."

She nodded. "I've been praying for that since I accepted Christ, but Dad's so stubborn and thinks he can do everything in his own strength. He won't even go to church, much less talk with me about spiritual things."

"Well, don't give up praying," Allen said. "In 2 Peter 3:9, God's Word tells us that it's not His will that any should perish, so maybe God will bring someone into your dad's life or cause something to happen that will open his eyes and give him peace."

Yes, Bonnie thought, *and I hope that someday God will give me a sense of peace.*

―⁊―

Samuel's eyes snapped open, and he glanced at the clock on the far wall. It was almost midnight. Apparently he'd dozed off. He looked over at Titus, sprawled out on the sofa with his eyes closed. He'd obviously fallen asleep, too.

I wish we'd hear something from the sheriff, Samuel

thought. *I wish God would answer my prayers.*

Tap! Tap! Tap!

Someone was at the front door. What if it was the sheriff and he'd brought bad news?

Samuel rose to his feet and hurried to the door. Good or bad, he had to know.

When he opened it, relief flooded his soul. There stood the sheriff with a tired and very guilty-looking Leon at his side.

"Oh, thank the Lord!" Samuel scooped the boy into his arms and hugged him tightly. "Where was he? Where'd you find my son?" he asked the sheriff.

Before the sheriff could respond, Titus woke up and joined them. "Praises to God, our prayers have been answered!" He put his hand on Leon's head. "I'm going out to the phone shanty and leave another message for the family in Pennsylvania, letting them know you've been found." He slipped past them and hurried out the door.

Samuel turned to the sheriff and asked again, "Where'd you find my son?"

"Inside Walmart. One of the employees found him in the men's room about an hour ago," the sheriff replied. "The man called me, and I went there right away. After questioning the boy, his story was pretty much the same as what the man who'd picked him up in his car earlier today told me."

"What were you doing at Walmart?" Samuel asked as he seated Leon on the sofa.

The boy dropped his gaze to the floor. "I—I was hungerich and *vergelschdere.* Figured I could find somethin' to eat in the store. When I got there, I had to go to the bathroom."

"Well, if you were hungry and scared, you should have told someone you were lost and needed to go home. What possessed you to run off like that?" Samuel's voice shook with all the emotion he felt.

Leon's chin trembled. "I—I thought you didn't love

me no more. I was gonna head on back to Pennsylvania."

"Pennsylvania's a long ways off, and you would have gotten lost for sure. You should have known better than to try something like that, and you ought to know I still love you."

Leon's eyes filled with tears that quickly spilled onto his cheeks. "I'm sorry, Daadi. You're always hollerin', and after you gave me a *bletsching* this mornin', I figured you'd be better off without me around." He sniffed and leaned his head against Samuel. "I'm sorry for spoutin' off and callin' you a schtinker. Guess I deserved to be punished."

Guilt as heavy as a load of hay weighed in on Samuel. "I'm the one who should be sorry, son." Choking with emotion, he pulled Leon into his arms. "I've been hurting so much since your mamm died, and because of my grief, I haven't been a good daed to you, Jared, or your sisters. With God's help, I promise to do better from now on."

CHAPTER 26

"Has there been any word on Leon?" Suzanne asked when she arrived at Titus's house on Sunday morning and found him standing on the porch, looking out into the yard.

"Jah. An employee at the Walmart in Hopkinsville found Leon in the men's room last night."

"That's sure good news. What was he doing there, anyway?"

Titus gave Suzanne the details on Leon's adventure, and ended by saying, "It was close to midnight when the sheriff brought him home."

"I'm sure Samuel was very relieved."

"We all were." Titus shuffled his feet a few times. "There's something I need to say to you, and I think I'd better say it before we go to church this morning."

"What's that?"

"I'm sorry for the disagreement we had yesterday. You were right. I've been neglecting you lately, and I'll try to do better from now on." Titus took a step toward her. "Am I forgiven?"

Suzanne nodded. "I'm sorry for my part in the argument as well. I should be more understanding of Samuel's situation, because I know he is relying on you and really has no other place to go right now."

"What do you think about me hiring a driver so we can go to Ryan's Steakhouse in Hopkinsville for supper one evening?"

"That'd be nice. When did you want to go?"

"How about this coming Saturday? We can go in a little early and do some shopping and then eat supper around five."

"What about Samuel and the kinner? If we're having supper at the steakhouse, who'll fix their supper at home?"

"Samuel's planning to take them to the pond near my place this Saturday so they can do some fishing and have a picnic supper."

"Won't he expect you to fix the food for their picnic?" she asked.

"Nope. Samuel said he's gonna ask Esther to fix the meal."

"Oh. Well he won't be sorry about that, because Esther's a wonderful good cook. If it weren't for her teaching me how to cook, I wouldn't have agreed to marry you this fall."

His forehead wrinkled as he stared at her with a look of confusion. "Is the only reason you said yes to my proposal because you know how to cook?"

She swatted his arm playfully. "Of course not, silly. I said yes because I love you and want to be your wife, but if I hadn't learned to cook, I wouldn't make a good wife, and you deserve to be fed well after we're married."

Titus moved closer and put his arms around her waist. "I'd marry you even if you didn't know how to boil water and I had to do all the cooking myself."

Since no one else was outside and could witness their display of affection, Suzanne melted into his embrace, thankful that everything was all right between them again.

—∾—

Paradise, Pennsylvania

"Our prayers have been answered," Abraham said when he entered the kitchen where Fannie stood at the stove, stirring a kettle of oatmeal.

She whirled around. "Was there a message about Leon?"

A wide smile stretched across his bearded face. "Titus left a message saying the boy's been found and is back with Samuel again."

Fannie crossed both hands over her chest and looked upward with gratitude. "Thank You, Lord!"

"It's not good that he ran away, but it's a relief to know he wasn't kidnapped." Abraham slowly shook his head. "I'd never want anyone to go through the misery I went through after Zach was stolen. There were times when the pain was almost unbearable. I always wondered where he was and whether he was okay or not. Until he came home to us, I was never completely at peace."

Fannie gave Abraham a hug. "I know what a terrible time that was for you. I, too, am relieved that Leon's been found." She pulled back slightly. "Where was he, anyway?"

Abraham told Fannie everything Titus had said. "I'm sure the boy was pretty scared out there on his own."

Fannie clucked her tongue. "Things must be really bad between Samuel and Leon if he was so upset that he decided to run away."

Abraham's face sobered. "Titus said Leon had been trying to come here."

"What?" Fannie's mouth opened wide. "How did he think he was going to get here?"

Abraham shrugged his broad shoulders. "From what Titus said, Leon had Samuel's wallet, and I believe he thought he could either catch a bus or hire a driver to bring him here."

Fannie sank into a seat at the table. "I think Samuel ought to move back to Pennsylvania so we can help with the kinner like we did before."

"That's not the answer, Fannie. What the kinner need is Samuel's attention. Those kids suffered a great loss when their mamm died, and they need their daed now more than ever." Abraham joined her at the table. "From what Titus said in a previous phone conversation, Samuel's been so immersed in his own pain that he hasn't paid much attention to the needs of his kinner. He even blamed Suzanne and her friend Esther when Penny got hurt on the sled awhile back."

"Which is exactly why he needs to be living closer to us—so he can be sure they're getting the proper attention."

"He'll be fine, Fannie. This thing with Leon really gave him a scare, and Titus said that Samuel's planning to spend more time with the kinner from now on. Fact is, he's taking them fishing and on a picnic this Saturday."

"That's good, but it's just one day of fun. The kinner need someone with them all the time—someone who'll give them every bit of the love that they need."

"They have Esther to care for them," he reminded.

Fannie brushed his words aside. "That's not the same as having someone in their family with them. Besides, if Esther's doing such a good job, then why'd Leon run away?"

"I told you before. He was upset with Samuel, and Esther wasn't even watching the kinner that day; Titus was in charge of them."

Before Fannie could comment, the back door opened and Timothy entered the kitchen. "Since it's our in-between Sunday and there's no church in our district today, Hannah and I thought we'd visit at her brother's church," he said, looking at Abraham. "Just wondered if you and Mom would like to go with us."

"Not today," Abraham said. "Your mamm and I didn't get much sleep last night on account of Samuel's Leon."

Timothy's eyebrows drew together. "What's wrong with Leon? Is he sick?"

"He went missing yesterday," Abraham replied. "We left a message on your voice mail last evening. Didn't you get it?"

Timothy scratched his head. "I haven't checked for

messages since yesterday morning." He took the cup of coffee Fannie offered him. "Danki, Mom."

"You're welcome."

"So tell me about Leon. Is he still missing?"

Abraham shook his head. "Thank the good Lord, Leon is back where he belongs, and I think things are going to be better between him and his daed from now on."

"Well, I think we ought to plan another trip to Kentucky soon, even though our grandson is home safe and sound," Fannie said. "I want to see for myself if things are any better."

Abraham shook his head. "Timothy and I are too busy planting the fields for me to go anywhere right now."

"But you were all set to go when you first heard Leon was missing."

"That was different. It was an emergency."

She frowned. "If you won't go to Kentucky now, then how are we supposed to help Samuel with the kinner?"

"We can pray for them." Abraham gave Fannie's arm a gentle pat.

—⁓—

Pembroke, Kentucky

Anxious to know if there had been any word on Leon, Esther decided to stop by Titus's place before going to church. She figured if Leon hadn't been found, everyone would be in a state of grief—especially Samuel, who she knew blamed himself for Leon's disappearance. If only there was something she could do to make Samuel and the children feel better, but she realized that no one in Samuel's family would ever feel better until Leon had been found.

Esther stepped onto Titus's porch, and was about to knock, when the door opened and Samuel appeared.

"Esther, I—I didn't know you were here." His face

turned red, and he looked a bit befuddled.

"I came by on my way to church to see if there's been any word on Leon."

Samuel smiled widely. It was the first time Esther had seen him smile like that—at least when he'd been looking at her. "The sheriff brought Leon home last night."

Esther appreciated the way Samuel's appearance changed when he allowed himself to smile. "Where was he?" she asked.

"At Walmart." Samuel gave Esther the details of Leon's disappearance. "I'm ever so thankful my boy's okay. Don't know what I'd do if I lost another member of my family right now."

Esther reached out her hand to offer comfort, but when he stepped back, she quickly pulled it away. "I'm glad Leon's okay," she murmured.

He gave a slow nod. "Me, too."

"Will you be going to church today?" she asked.

"Jah. Wouldn't feel right about staying home. Especially after God answered my prayers and brought Leon home."

She smiled. "I understand. It was an answer to all our prayers."

"The whole ordeal left me pretty shook up, and it's made me realize that I need to spend more time with my kinner." Samuel folded his arms and leaned against the door. "I've decided to take the kinner on a picnic supper at the pond this Saturday, and while we're there we'll do a little fishing."

"That sounds like fun. I'm sure you will all enjoy the day."

Samuel shifted his weight slightly. "Say, I. . .uh. . .was wondering. I'm not much of a cook, so would you be willing to fix us something we could take along to eat?"

"You want me to make your picnic supper?"

"Jah, if you don't mind."

"I'd be happy to do that, Samuel." Esther smiled. She

figured if Samuel was asking her to fix the food for the picnic supper, he probably meant for her to go along. She hoped so, anyway, because a picnic with Samuel and his children would certainly be fun.

CHAPTER 27

O n Saturday afternoon, Esther arrived at Titus's house, filled with anticipation. She'd fixed a nice picnic supper for Samuel and his children—fried chicken, potato salad, baked beans, dill pickles, and carrot sticks. For dessert she'd made a pan of brownies and two dozen of her favorite boyfriend cookies. Knowing how much Samuel's children yearned to spend time with him, she figured they were probably looking forward to today even more than she was.

Esther reached into the back of her buggy to get the box of food she'd prepared just as Titus stepped out of the barn.

"Need some help?" he asked.

"I'd appreciate it."

He sniffed the box. "Whatever's in here sure smells *gut*."

"Samuel asked me to fix the food for their picnic, and I hope they'll all think it's good. You're a pretty good cook yourself," she added. "I'm surprised he didn't ask you to make the picnic supper."

"I'm taking Suzanne out for supper this evening, so that's why he didn't ask me." Titus picked up the box and started walking toward the house. Esther followed.

"I'm glad you and Suzanne are going out," she said. "It's been awhile since the two of you went anywhere alone."

He nodded. "After what happened with Leon, I think Samuel plans to spend more time with the kinner and keep his focus on them instead of allowing himself to be so consumed with grief over losing Elsie."

"I'm glad to hear he wants to spend more time with the kinner. I've tried to give them lots of attention, but it's not the same as spending time with their daed." Esther smiled. "I'm also glad things are better between you and Suzanne. I've been worried about you two."

"No need to worry," he said. "I think everything with us is back on track."

Esther opened the door for Titus, and when they entered the house, Titus took the box of food to the kitchen. Esther found Samuel sitting on the living room sofa, with all four of his children gathered around.

"Wie geht's?" she asked.

Samuel looked up. "We're doing good now that Leon's back home. Everyone's looking forward to going to the pond today."

The children bobbed their heads in agreement.

"I brought the food for your picnic supper," she said.

Samuel smiled. "We appreciate that."

Penny looked up at her father. "Is Esther goin' with us, Daadi?"

Samuel's face turned bright pink. "Well, I. . .uh. . . thought it would be good for us to spend some time alone together."

Esther placed her hand on Penny's shoulder. "I'll be with you on Monday." She hoped the disappointment she felt about not being included in their plans didn't show on her face.

"Is everyone ready to go?" Samuel asked, thumping Leon's shoulder.

The children all nodded and climbed down from the sofa.

"All right, let's get the food Esther prepared, grab our fishing poles, and we'll head for the pond." Samuel stood and turned to Esther. "I sure do appreciate your being willing to fix the picnic supper and also for allowing me to spend some time alone with my kinner."

Esther managed a weak smile. It was the best she could do to hide her disappointment. "I hope you have fun and catch lots of fish." She followed them out the door and watched as they scrambled into Samuel's buggy. It was good to see the children so happy today, and she hoped they'd have a good time at the pond. She was glad to see Samuel take an interest in the children, too. She'd seen a different side of him since Leon had run away—a softer, more sensitive side. Truth was, Esther had begun to have feelings for Samuel that she could no longer deny. Of course, she'd never admit that to anyone, because she was sure Samuel had no interest in her other than as someone to watch his children—and fix their picnic supper.

As Samuel's rig pulled onto the road, Esther started walking toward her horse and buggy. She was almost there when Titus came out of the house and called out to her. "Have you got a minute? There's something I'd like to talk to you about."

"Sure." Esther stopped walking and waited until Titus joined her. "What's up?"

He ran his finger down the side of his nose, looking a bit unsure of himself. "I'm. . .uh. . .not quite sure how to say this, but I'd like to hear your thoughts on something."

"What's that?"

"As much as I enjoy having Samuel and the kinner living with me, I'm afraid if they're still here by the time Suzanne and I are wed, it will put a strain on our marriage. Even though things are better between Suzanne and me now, I don't think she'd be happy sharing a home with my bruder and his four active kinner."

"You're probably right, but if Samuel isn't able to buy a place by then, I'm sure Suzanne will learn to deal with it."

"Maybe so, but. . ." Titus kicked at a stone beneath his feet. "The thing is. . .I was wondering. . ."

"Is there something you think I can do to help Suzanne adjust to the idea that she might have to share her home with Samuel and the kinner?" Esther questioned.

"No, but I was wondering if your folks might be interested in renting their place to Samuel."

Esther's eyebrows lifted. "How could they do that? I'm living there, remember?"

"I was thinking since you're working at the B&B, maybe you could stay there."

"Bonnie mentioned the idea of me living in the little guest house on her property, but I'd have to get Mom and Dad's permission to do that. I'd also have to ask if they'd mind renting their place to Samuel."

"Well, let me know what they say, and if they're agreeable to the idea, we can mention it to Samuel." Titus started to turn toward the house, but then he stopped and motioned to a fishing pole leaning against the barn. "Oh, oh. Looks like Samuel forgot one of their poles."

"I'll be going near the pond on my way home," Esther said. "So unless you have some objections, I'll take the fishing pole along and give it to him."

"That'd be great. Danki, Esther."

―――∞―――

"Be careful not to get too close," Samuel warned Jared, who was edging near the water. "Marla, keep an eye on your bruder, please."

"Okay, Daadi." She turned to smile at Samuel, and then she darted after her little brother.

Samuel took a seat on the blanket he'd spread on the ground and leaned back on his elbows. The warm spring sun shining down on his face felt so good, and for the first time since Elsie died he allowed himself to fully relax.

"Daadi, aren't ya gonna fish with us?" Leon asked, bumping Samuel's arm.

"I'll fish in a minute, son. I want to sit here awhile and enjoy this nice spring day."

Leon took a seat beside him while Penny went off to play with Marla and Jared. "I wish Mammi could be here with us," the boy said. "I sure do miss her."

Samuel's throat constricted. "I miss her, too, but I'm glad I have you and your brother and sisters."

Leon gave a nod. "Jah."

They sat quietly together, watching as the girls and Jared pitched rocks into the pond. The birds in the nearby trees chirped happily while the bullfrogs sang their deep-throated chorus, but the peacefulness of the moment was interrupted by a noisy vehicle pulling in.

Samuel turned his head and was surprised to see Bonnie climb out of her car. Frolicking at her side was her little mixed-breed terrier, Cody.

Marla, Penny, and Jared rushed excitedly toward the dog, but Leon remained on the blanket with Samuel.

"Wie geht's?" Bonnie called, waving at Samuel.

"Doin' pretty good. How about you?"

"Just fine. I've been wanting to check out this pond for a while but haven't taken the time until now." When Bonnie took a seat on the blanket beside Samuel, Leon gave her a strange look, but she didn't seem to notice.

"I'm surprised to see you here," she said to Samuel. "I thought you might have a paint job to do somewhere today."

He shook his head. "I wanted to spend the day with my kinner."

"Kinner means children, right?"

"Jah."

"Are ya learnin' the *Deitch*?" Leon asked.

She laughed. "Well, I'm trying to anyway. Your daed's taught me a few Pennsylvania-Dutch words."

"How come?" the boy asked.

"Because she asked me to," Samuel replied.

Leon looked at Bonnie and squinted. "Why do ya wanna learn Amish words?"

Samuel gave Leon's arm a light tap. "How come you ask so many questions? Are you writing a book?"

Leon shook his head. " 'Course not. I'd never be able

to think up enough words to write a whole book."

Samuel lifted Leon's straw hat from his head and ruffled his light brown hair. "Why don't you join the others for a while? I'll call you when it's time to eat."

"I thought we was gonna fish."

"We will. After we've eaten."

Leon shrugged and shuffled off toward his brother and sisters, who were kept busy chasing after Bonnie's dog.

Bonnie looked over at Samuel and smiled. "I was glad when I heard that Leon had been found. I'm sure you must have been very worried about him."

"I was, and Leon's disappearance opened my eyes to the fact that I need to spend more time with my kinner."

"Like you're doing today?"

"Jah. We came here to do a little fishing and enjoy a picnic supper." Not wishing to appear rude, he motioned to the cooler he'd brought along, full of beverages and the food that needed to be kept cold, as well as the box of picnic food Esther had prepared that didn't need cooling. "If you don't have other plans for supper, you're welcome to eat with us 'cause there's more than enough food."

"That'd be nice. I really wasn't looking forward to going home and eating by myself."

"Should we call the kinner and eat now?" he asked.

"I'm ready to eat whenever you are."

—⁓—

When Esther pulled her horse and buggy into the clearing near the pond, she was surprised to see Bonnie's car parked next to the tree where Samuel's horse and buggy had been tied.

She stepped out of the buggy, tied Ginger to another tree, and reached inside the buggy to get the fishing pole. As she headed across the clearing toward the pond, she saw Samuel, his children, and Bonnie sitting on a blanket together. Her heart felt like it had plummeted all the way to her toes. They were eating the food that she'd prepared!

"It's nice to see you." Bonnie smiled up at Esther. "Would you like to join us?"

Esther shook her head. "I just came to bring this." She held the fishing pole out to Samuel. "It was left by the barn."

"Guess I forgot it. Danki, Esther," Samuel said.

Esther gave a nod then turned toward her buggy.

"Are you sure you won't join us?" Bonnie called.

"No thanks. I'd better get home."

As Esther climbed into her buggy, a lump formed in her throat. Samuel was obviously interested in Bonnie, or he wouldn't have invited her to join them for supper. What hurt the most was the fact that he'd asked Esther to fix the picnic supper when he'd planned to invite Bonnie to join them all along.

CHAPTER 28

As Esther sat at the desk in her room one Saturday evening, writing in her journal, she felt as if a heavy weight rested on her shoulders. Ever since Titus had suggested she rent her house to Samuel, her mind had been swirling with unanswered questions. She'd been praying about it, too, but was still unsure what to do. It would be hard to leave the roomy home she'd lived in since she was a young girl and move into the small guest house on Bonnie's property.

Of course, Esther reasoned, *if Mom and Dad agreed to rent their house to Samuel, that would mean more money coming in to help with Dan's medical expenses.*

As Esther's thoughts shifted gears, she wrote in her journal:

> *I'm confused about so many things. Even though Bonnie later explained that Samuel hadn't invited her to join them at the pond until she'd shown up there with her dog, it hurt my feelings.*
>
> *I'm concerned that there might be something besides friendship between them. Is it my imagination, and am I the only one who sees it? Would Bonnie be willing to give up modern things and join the Amish faith? Could Samuel give up his Plain way of life to go English?*

Knowing she needed to focus on something else,

Esther glanced at the calendar on her bedroom wall. Monday would be her twenty-fourth birthday, and so far she hadn't received even one card in the mail—not even from Mom and Dad. Had everyone forgotten about her birthday? Mom and Dad had a good excuse, she supposed, because they were so busy helping out at Dan's. Last year Suzanne had given Esther a surprise party and invited all their friends. This year, her birthday would probably go right on by, unnoticed. She thought about the birthday supper she'd made for Marla and how Samuel had forgotten his daughter's birthday. Maybe this was the year for forgotten birthdays.

Tears slipped out of Esther's eyes, dribbling down her cheeks, and she sniffed and wiped them away. *I'm just feeling sorry for myself. I'm sad because I have feelings for Samuel and he doesn't even see me. I'm also struggling with the idea of moving out of my home. But if I don't ask Mom and Dad about letting Samuel rent their house, then Suzanne and Titus's relationship will be affected when they get married. I really need to talk to Mom and Dad soon.*

―――∽∿∽―――

On Monday morning, before Esther headed to Titus's to watch Samuel's children, she spotted the mail carrier in front of their box. As soon as he pulled his vehicle away, she hurried down the driveway to get the mail. She was pleased to find a birthday card from her folks, as well as one from both of her brothers. At least her family had remembered her birthday, which made her feel much better.

She rushed back to the house and took a seat at the kitchen table so she could read the letter Mom had enclosed with the card. Things were about the same with Dan, and Dad was keeping busier than ever at the two farmer's markets. Mom ended the note by asking when Esther might be able to come for a visit.

I need to call Mom and Dad right now, Esther decided.

———∿———

"Are you sure you have time to help me with this today?" Samuel asked Allen as they started painting the inside of a two-story home in Fairview.

"I have some extra time this morning, so it's not a problem. Besides, the Carsons want the job done by the end of the week, and since Frank, the other fellow who does painting for me, is tied up with another job right now, I figured I'd help you here today." Allen dipped his brush into the can of off-white paint. "Painting's not my specialty, but I think I know enough about it to do a fairly decent job."

"I'm sure you do. Would you rather paint the stairwell or the dining room?" Samuel asked.

Allen shrugged. "It doesn't matter to me, but since you're a better and faster painter, maybe you should tackle the dining room."

"Okay."

As Samuel and Allen worked, they visited about the warm spring weather they'd been having.

"It was just starting to turn warm when I took my kids to the pond for a picnic a few weeks ago," Samuel said.

"I never did ask you about that. Was it fun?"

"It was a good day, and Bonnie was there, too. After we ate, she tried her hand at fishing."

"Oh, really?" Allen took a step back, and the next thing Titus knew, the poor fellow was bouncing down the stairs on his backside. He hit the bottom with a sickening *thunk*!

Samuel dropped his paintbrush and rushed forward. "Allen, are you all right?"

"Oh, my aching back! I don't think I can move," Allen groaned.

Samuel grabbed Allen's cell phone from his shirt pocket and dialed 911.

Chapter 29

Sorry I'm so late," Samuel said to Esther when he arrived home from work that afternoon. "Allen fell down the stairs while we were painting that house in Fairview, and now he's in the hospital."

Esther's eyes widened. "Oh my! Was he seriously hurt?"

"He's not critical, but his back is sure sore and spasmed up."

Esther frowned. "That's awful. Is he going to be all right?"

"I think so, but it'll take some time. They gave him something for the pain and swelling, and I think they may put him in traction for a while."

"That's too bad." Esther slowly shook her head. "Allen won't be able to work for a while I guess."

"No, he sure won't. I'll have to finish the paint job we were working on by myself, which means I might be late getting home for the rest of this week. Will that affect your job at Bonnie's Bed-and-Breakfast?"

"I don't think so. As long as I go over there sometime every evening to help Bonnie get things ready for her guests the next morning, it doesn't matter what time I get there." She shrugged. "Besides, I only have to go when she has guests."

"Well, good." Samuel removed his straw hat and set it on the small table by the sofa. "It's sure quiet in here. Where are the kinner?"

"They're out in the barn, playing with the katze."

"Guess I'll wander out there and say hello." He moved toward the door. "You're free to go now, Esther."

She hesitated a minute, then nodded. "I'll see you tomorrow, Samuel."

———

"I'm sorry I'm late," Esther said when she arrived at Bonnie's that evening. "Samuel got home later than usual because Allen got hurt today."

Bonnie's forehead wrinkled in a worried frown. "What happened to Allen?"

Esther explained what Samuel had told her. "I can't imagine how much pain Allen must be in," she said.

Bonnie grimaced. "A back injury can be painful all right. Does Samuel know how long Allen will be in the hospital?"

"I guess it all depends on how long it takes for his back to heal."

"From what I've observed, Allen probably won't make a good patient."

"What makes you think that?" Esther asked.

"He seems to be a workaholic, and workaholics don't like to be laid up very long." Bonnie pointed to herself. "I tend to be like that, too."

Esther smiled. Bonnie was a hard worker, but she'd never thought of her as a workaholic.

"I have two couples arriving later this evening," Bonnie said. "So are you ready to help me whip up a tasty breakfast casserole I can serve them tomorrow morning?"

"I'm ready if you are."

They headed for the kitchen, and as they prepared the vegetables and meat that would go into the casserole, Esther mentioned that she'd spoken to her folks about renting their home to Samuel, and they'd agreed. "That is, if you're still willing to let me stay in your guest house," she quickly added.

"That would be fine with me." Bonnie smiled. "And if you stayed there, you'd be close to the house here, which would make it easier for you to help me prepare breakfast for my guests and get the rooms serviced."

"Would it be possible to remove the wiring in the guest house so I could live in it without breaking any of our church rules?"

"I don't think that would be a problem at all. I can speak to Allen's electrician about it. The guest house is pretty small, but with some elbow grease I think we could make it quite livable."

"That'd be great," Esther said. "I'll talk to Samuel soon about the possibility of him renting my folk's house."

A knock sounded on the door just then.

"That must be one of my guests." Bonnie hurried into the living room to answer the door. She returned a few minutes later with Suzanne at her side.

"You're not one of the B&B guests," Esther said when Suzanne set a paper sack on the table.

Suzanne chuckled. "No, I'm sure not. I came over to give you this." She reached into the paper sack and handed Esther a wrapped present. *"Hallich gebottsdaag."*

Esther smiled. "I didn't think you remembered that today was my birthday."

"Of course I remembered. I could never forget my best friend's birthday." Suzanne gave Esther a hug.

Esther unwrapped the present and was surprised when she discovered a leather journal inside the box.

"I know you have one already," Suzanne said, "but you write in it so much, I figured you'd probably be needing a new one soon."

Esther smiled. "You're right about that."

"There's also a Walmart gift certificate in there."

Esther reached into the box again and pulled the certificate out. It was for twenty-five dollars. "Danki, Suzanne. I'm sure I can put this to good use."

Bonnie stepped forward then. "Happy birthday, Esther.

If I'd known today was your birthday I'd have baked you a cake or taken you out somewhere special to eat."

"It's okay," Esther said. "I don't need a cake or supper out. I'm just happy to be here with good friends like the both of you."

CHAPTER 30

"Any word on Allen?" Esther asked the following morning when she entered Titus's house and found Samuel in the living room putting on his work boots.

He shook his head. "But Titus and I have a driver coming to pick us up soon so we can go to the hospital to see Allen."

"You're going this morning?"

"Jah. Figured we'd go before we started work for the day, because with the job I'm on I'll probably be working late, and then Titus can watch the kinner this evening while you're at the B&B, helping Bonnie."

Titus entered the living room just then. "With all the practice I'm getting watching my nieces and nephews, I ought to be pretty good at bein' a daed by the time Suzanne and I have kinner."

Esther nodded and smiled. Then she looked at Samuel and said, "There's something I'd like to discuss with you."

"What's that?" he asked.

"I've been thinking about moving out of my house and staying in the guest house on Bonnie's property."

"Why would you want to do that?"

"For one thing, there's just one of me roaming around in that big old house, and I think the place would be better for someone with a family. I thought maybe you and the kinner would like to live there. I've already spoken to my folks about it, and they're fine with the idea. The rent they would charge wouldn't be too much either."

Samuel scratched the side of his head. "Well, I don't know. . . ."

"It sounds like a good idea to me," Titus chimed in. "I think it'd be better for you and the kinner than staying here with me where there's not nearly as much room."

Samuel's forehead wrinkled. "Are you trying to get rid of me, Titus?"

" 'Course not, but wouldn't you like to have a place of your own?"

"It wouldn't be mine," Samuel said with a shake of his head. "I'd only be renting the house, remember?" He looked over at Esther and frowned. "Did you come up with this idea for my benefit or yours?"

"Wh–what do you mean?" she stammered.

"Figured maybe you needed the rent money. Am I not paying you enough to watch the kinner?"

She shook her head. "That's not it. I just thought. . ."

"And why would you want to stay in that little guest house when you can have a big house all to yourself?"

"I've only been sleeping at home. Quite often I eat supper with Bonnie, and then I go home, only to sleep, feed my horse, and do a few chores. If you and the kinner were living in my folks' house, I could come over there to watch them and make sure the house is clean, and I can even see that your laundry is done."

"That's a lot more work than you're doin' right now," Samuel said. "You're gonna wear yourself out if you're not careful."

Esther looked at Titus, hoping he'd speak on her behalf. To her relief he did.

"I really do think it's a good idea, Samuel, and I don't think Esther will have any more work than she does now. Maybe less, since she won't have to come over here every day and keep this place clean, too."

A horn honked, and Samuel went to the window. "Our driver's here. We'd better go."

"Will you at least give the idea of renting Esther's

folks' house some thought?" Titus asked.

Samuel nodded and hurried out the door.

"It'll work out; you'll see," Titus said to Esther before he followed Samuel outside.

Esther hoped she hadn't made a mistake suggesting that Samuel rent the house. He was obviously not too thrilled about the idea.

She turned toward the kitchen to start breakfast for the children and was surprised to see Leon already sitting at the table with a bowl of cold cereal.

"How long have you been up?" Esther asked.

"Got up when Daadi did." He shoveled a spoonful of cereal into his mouth. "We sleep in the same room, and once he starts movin' around, I wake up."

"I'll bet you'd like to have a room of your own, wouldn't you?" she asked.

He bobbed his head. "Used to have one when we lived in Pennsylvania."

Maybe I should have mentioned to Samuel that my house has five bedrooms, she thought. *That might have given him more incentive to move there.*

"I'm hungerich," Penny said when she and Jared bounced into the kitchen a few minutes later. "What's for breakfast?"

Esther motioned to Leon. "Your bruder's having cold cereal. Would you like that, too, or should I fix you an egg?"

"I want *pannekuche*!" Penny announced.

Esther smiled. "I think that's a good idea. In fact, I didn't have much for breakfast this morning, so I might have a couple of pancakes, too."

Marla entered the room just then, yawning and rubbing her eyes.

"Would you like to help me make some pannekuche?" Esther asked.

Marla grinned and rubbed her stomach. "I sure would! Our mamm used to make pannekuche, and they were real good."

I wonder what it would be like if I were these children's mother, Esther thought as she went to the cupboard to get out the flour and other dry ingredients. *I wonder how it would be if I were Samuel's wife.*

"Did ya hear what I said?" Marla tugged on Esther's apron, pushing her foolish thoughts aside. Marrying Samuel and becoming these children's mother were nothing but silly dreams.

—⁓—

Soon after Bonnie's B&B guests left the house to do some touring of the area, she decided to head for Hopkinsville and see how Allen was doing. By going early in the day, she would have time to do some shopping and get back to the B&B before her guests returned this afternoon.

As Bonnie pulled her car out of the driveway and headed in the direction of Hopkinsville, she thought about the pot of pansies she'd put in the backseat and wondered if Allen would like them. He'd worked hard helping Samuel get the repairs and remodeling done on the B&B, so going to see him and taking a little get-well gift was the least she could do. Allen seemed like a nice man who cared about others and wanted the best for everyone. It was too bad he'd injured his back. She was sure he was anxious to start working again. If she were in his place, she certainly would be.

It seemed odd that a man as attractive as Allen wasn't married. As far as Bonnie knew, he didn't even have a girlfriend. If he did, he'd never mentioned it, although they'd talked about lots of other things when he'd been helping remodel her grandparents' house.

Of course, she reasoned, *I never said anything to him about why I'm still single. Would someone like Allen show an interest in me if he knew what I'd done in the past? Would I even want him to?*

She gave the steering wheel a tap. *The best thing I can do is just concentrate on my new business and forget about love and marriage, because I decided a long time ago that I would never get married.*

—⁓—

Hopkinsville, Kentucky

"How are you feeling this morning?" Samuel asked when he and Titus entered Allen's room.

Allen groaned. It was nice to see his friends, but he wasn't sure they'd enjoy his company much. He'd been irritable ever since the accident happened—partly from the pain, but mostly because he didn't like being laid up. "I've been better," he mumbled.

"Any idea how long you'll have to be here?" Titus asked.

"Nope, but since I'm in no shape to go home yet, I may as well accept the fact that I'm here, albeit against my will."

Samuel took a seat in one of the chairs beside Allen's bed, and Titus sat in the other chair. "Is there anything we can do for you?" Titus asked.

"Not unless you can figure out a way to take charge of all the jobs I've got going right now." Allen winced as a spasm of pain shot through his back. "I should have been watching what I was doing yesterday. Just one false step, and wham!" He winced again. "Don't know what I'll do if I can't get back to working soon."

"I'll do whatever I can to help out, but what about one of the English fellows you have working for you?" Samuel asked. "Can't one of 'em take over till you're back on your feet?"

"Maybe Ron. I called him last night, and he said he'd come here sometime today to talk about it."

"If there's anything I can do, let me know, too," Titus added.

"Thanks, I appreciate both of your offers."

The door to Allen's room opened just then, and Bonnie

entered. "How are you feeling?" she asked, stepping up to Allen's bed.

"I've been better, but I guess I'll live."

"I was sorry to hear about your accident." She lifted the pot of pansies she held. "I thought maybe these might cheer you up a bit, and they'll certainly add some color to the room."

"Thanks. That was nice of you." Allen motioned to his bedside table. "You can put them over there."

Bonnie set the pansies on the table, and Samuel offered her his chair.

"I assume Esther's watching the kinner today," she said, taking a seat and directing her question to Samuel.

He nodded. "She got there a few minutes before our driver showed up."

Bonnie looked back at Allen and said, "Any idea how long you'll be in the hospital?"

"My muscles are really in spasm, so I'll probably be here a few more days." He frowned. "I'm not sure how well I'll do on my own after they let me out of here though. With all this pain, I can barely think, let alone fend for myself."

"Do you know someone you could ask to come in and help out?" she questioned.

"I think my mom might come. I had one of the nurses call her and Dad after I got settled in here yesterday, so I wouldn't be surprised if they don't catch the next plane out so Mom can take care me."

Bonnie nodded affirmatively. "It would be good if you had the help."

"I do need help," Allen said. "What I don't need is my mom hovering over me and telling me what to do, which I'm sure is exactly what she will do."

CHAPTER 31

Allen rolled onto his side, trying to find a comfortable position on the sofa. It had been a week since he'd come home from the hospital, and his mother had been hovering over him the whole time the way she'd done when he was a boy. Dad had gone home three days ago, saying he needed to get back to work.

Allen thought about the time last year when Titus's folks had come to see him after he'd been hit by two men who'd broken into his house. Titus had complained that his mother hovered over him too much while they were there to help out. Allen guessed maybe that's what most mothers did when their kids—even the grown ones— became sick or got hurt.

"I'm going out for a while to do some shopping," Allen's mother said when she entered the living room. "Do you need me to do anything before I go?"

Allen shook his head.

"Would you like a cup of tea?"

"No, Mom. You ought to know that I don't drink tea."

"Of course I do, but this is iced tea, and since it's such a warm day, I thought it might be refreshing."

"No thanks." He nodded at the half-empty bottle of water on the coffee table. "I'm fine with that."

Mom pushed a wisp of graying blond hair away from her face and smiled. "You know what I think you really need, Allen?"

"What's that?"

"You need a wife to take care of you."

Not this again. How many times had she pestered him about finding a good Christian woman and settling down? Did she really think that would make him find a wife any sooner?

He forced a smile. "You know I have nothing against marriage, but I haven't found the right woman yet."

"You're not still grieving over Sheila's death, are you?"

"No, Mom." Truth was, Allen had pined for his girl-friend long after she'd been hit by a car and killed. But he'd come to grips with it and was ready to get married, if and when he fell in love again.

Mom's forehead wrinkled. "You're not interested in that Amish woman you told us about, I hope."

"You mean, Esther?"

She gave a quick nod.

"If I was interested in her, would you have any objections?" he asked.

"From what you've said about her, she seems like a very nice young woman, but I can't imagine you leaving your way of life to join the Amish faith. I wouldn't think she'd want to leave her faith to become part of the English world either."

"No, I don't suppose she would."

"Then you won't pursue a serious relationship with her?"

"There's no need to worry about that. Esther and I are just friends."

"What about the woman who runs the B&B? When she stopped by here the other day, she seemed quite friendly, and she's very pretty, too."

"Bonnie and I are just friends, same as me and Esther." Allen pulled himself to a sitting position and gritted his teeth. His back still hurt whenever he moved the wrong way, but it felt stiff if he didn't get up and walk around once in a while.

Mom rushed forward with a look of concern. "Do you need some of your pain medicine?"

He shook his head. "I thought you were going shopping."

"I am. Just want to be sure you're okay before I leave."

"I'm fine. If I need anything, I can get it myself." Allen offered her what he hoped was a reassuring smile and motioned to the front door.

"Okay, I'm going." She gave him a quick peck on the cheek. "I'll see you later then."

When Mom went out the door, Allen made a trip to the kitchen to refill his water bottle and then returned to the sofa. It wasn't that he didn't appreciate all his mother had done for him. He probably couldn't have gotten through this past week if it hadn't been for her. But he was anxious to get better so she could go home to Dad and he could get his life back as it had been before the accident.

———— ⁓⁓⁓ ————

Pembroke, Kentucky

"There's a *fliege* in the house." Penny pointed at the buzzing horsefly circling the kitchen. "Can you get it, Daadi?"

"It's not bothering anyone. Just eat your breakfast," Samuel mumbled after he'd spooned some cold cereal into his mouth. They'd moved into Esther's house a few days ago, and he was having a hard time coping with things by himself. He hadn't realized how much he'd relied on Titus until they'd moved out on their own.

"If ya don't get the fliege, it might land in my cereal," Penny complained.

"If you're that worried about it, then get the fly swatter and take care of the critter yourself," Samuel said.

"You're the bug master," Leon said. "If anyone can get that nasty old fliege, it's you, Daadi."

Samuel grunted. He knew he was good at catching bugs, but did that mean he had to catch every spider and fly that came along? He had better things to do than catch a pesky old fly this morning.

Bzz. . . Bzz. . . Bzz. . . The fly buzzed noisily over Samuel's head, and then it swooped down, almost landing in his bowl of cereal. "All right, that does it!" Samuel dropped his spoon to the table, reached out, and scooped the fly into his hand.

The children clapped. "You got that old fliege!" Penny shouted. "Are ya gonna take it outside?"

"That's exactly what I'm going to do." Samuel pushed away from the table and headed for the door. He smiled to himself. It felt kind of nice hearing his children cheering him on and clapping with delight just from him catching a fly, rather than looking at him and wondering when he was going to yell next.

Opening the door, he held his head a bit higher, and when he stepped onto the porch, he spotted Esther's horse and buggy coming down the lane. She was here early today.

———※———

As soon as Esther turned up the lane to her house she spotted Samuel on the porch. Her heartbeat picked up speed the way it always did whenever she saw him. The more her heart ached to be with him, the more convinced she was that they'd never be together, for Samuel still hadn't shown her the least bit of interest—at least not in a romantic sort of way. She figured the only way she and Samuel would ever be together was in her dreams. Could it be that she was only attracted to him because of his children, or was it the look of hurt she still sometimes saw on Samuel's face that drew her to him?

No, she told herself, *my attraction to Samuel goes much deeper than that. I've noticed a gentleness and deep sense of devotion to his kinner that I didn't see when he first moved here. He's a hard worker, too, who takes his responsibility for his family seriously. He's also quite nice looking and more mature than so many of the young men in our church district who like to show off and fool around while trying to get a girl's attention.*

She thought about Ethan Zook, who'd wanted to bring her home from the last young people's singing. Esther had turned him down, saying she'd brought her own horse and buggy. She was glad she'd had that as an excuse. While Ethan was a nice enough fellow, she wasn't the least bit interested in him, and they had nothing in common. Ethan didn't like dogs or cats, and as far as she could tell, his primary interest was in food—mostly how much and how often he could eat the food.

Bringing her thoughts to a halt, Esther pulled her horse and buggy up to the hitching rail and climbed down. When she joined Samuel on the porch, she smiled and said, "Are you headed to work already, or am I late today?"

He shook his head. "You're not late, and I'm not headed to work yet either. Just came out here to dispose of a pesky old fliege." He opened his hand and released a big, black horsefly into the air.

"What were you doing with a fly in your hand?" Esther asked in surprise.

"Caught it with my bare hand. Been catchin' flies that way ever since I was a boy."

Esther's eyes widened. "I've never known anyone who could capture a fly like that."

He grinned. "My boy Leon calls me the bug master. Guess that makes me the bug master from Lancaster."

She giggled. It was nice to see Samuel smiling and making a joke. "Have you heard how Allen's doing?" she asked.

"I talked to him yesterday. Said he's getting along fairly well, but I think he's impatient and anxious to get back to work."

"Is his mother still there with him?"

Samuel nodded. "He said he appreciates her help, but she's beginning to get on his nerves because she fusses about everything and won't let him do a thing for himself."

"She's no doubt concerned that he'll do too much."

"You're probably right. I remember once when my

back went out, Elsie fussed over me like I was an invalid." Samuel's face sobered, and he dropped his gaze to the porch. "I'd give anything to have her here, fussing over me right now."

Impulsively, Esther reached out and touched his arm. "I'm sorry for your loss, Samuel."

He just turned and opened the door.

As they entered the house, a feeling of nostalgia washed over Esther. It seemed strange to have someone else living in the home she'd grown up in, and it seemed equally strange to come over here to watch Samuel's children after spending the night in the little guest house at Bonnie's. She knew it was foolish to daydream about impossible things, but she secretly wished she and Samuel were married and that they lived here, raising his children together. But of course, that was nothing but a silly dream—just like it was crazy that her legs were still shaking after touching Samuel's arm.

CHAPTER 32

As spring turned to summer, Esther developed a routine. Up early in the morning to help Bonnie serve breakfast to her guests, head over to her house to watch Samuel's children, then back to the B&B when Samuel got home from work.

Since this was Saturday and all of Bonnie's guests had just checked out, Esther and Bonnie decided to visit some yard sales.

"Every June there's a forty-mile stretch of yard sales along one of the highways in the area," Esther told Bonnie as they climbed into Bonnie's car. "Lots of Amish people hire drivers so they can go to as many yard sales as possible, looking for the best bargains."

"Everyone likes a bargain." Bonnie chuckled. "Me most of all."

"Are you looking for anything in particular?" Esther asked.

"Not really, but I'm sure I'll know what I want when I see it." Bonnie glanced over at Esther. "What will you be looking for today?"

Esther shrugged. "I don't really know. Maybe something for Samuel's children. They don't have a lot of toys. In fact, I found Jared playing with a can full of rocks the other day."

Bonnie's dark eyebrows shot up. "Surely Samuel's not so poor that he can't afford to buy his kids a few toys."

"They do have some, but I think they get bored playing

with the same toys all the time."

"I'm sure they'll appreciate whatever you might buy for them, but you know kids are funny. Back home, I knew a family that gave their children every toy imaginable. Their mother would find it so amusing when her kids asked to play with some of her pots and pans instead of the new toys. She'd laugh and tell me how the pots and pans would entertain them for hours at a time. So who knows, maybe Jared was really having fun with that can of rocks."

After they'd both had a good laugh, they rode in silence for a while. Bonnie concentrated on the road while Esther enjoyed the beauty of a lovely summer day. "How can one look around and not see all the wonderful things God created for our enjoyment?" she said after they'd passed a farmhouse with a garden full of colorful flowers.

"I don't know," Bonnie replied. "God is everywhere—in the sun, moon, and stars. His artistic hand can be seen in every changing season, too."

"Which season do you like best?" Esther questioned.

"I think summer, when everything is in full bloom. I love watching the hummingbirds flit from one flower to the next. How about you?"

"I like summer, too, but autumn is my favorite time of the year, when the leaves are changing colors and the weather's begun to cool. There's so much beauty to take in. It's like a vibrant quilt blanketing the trees."

"That's a descriptive way of saying it, Esther," Bonnie said. "You certainly do have a way with words."

Esther smiled. "Or sometimes I think of it as God taking a paintbrush to create a beautiful masterpiece."

"Yes, that's right." Bonnie pointed to her left. "Oh, there's a yard sale at that house. Should we stop now or check it out on the way back?"

"Let's stop now. If we wait until later, all the good stuff might be gone."

"You do have a point." Bonnie turned into the driveway and parked the car. When they hurried across the lawn, Esther noticed several tables full of various items, and on the grass sat furniture and decorator items for the yard.

"Oh good, I see some Christmas decorations." Bonnie rushed to one of the tables and scooped up a box of colored lights, a couple of large red bows, and a fake snowman with an odd-looking nose. "These will look great when I decorate the B&B for Christmas this year. I hope I get some guests over the holidays to enjoy the decorations."

"Will your dad be coming for Christmas?"

"I doubt he'll ever come here." Bonnie moved toward the woman who was taking the money. "Guess I'd better pay for these and put them in the car. Did you see anything you want to buy?"

Esther shook her head. "I don't think so, but I'll continue looking while you pay for the decorations."

As Bonnie walked away, Esther offered a silent prayer on her friend's behalf. She couldn't imagine how it would feel to be shut out of her parents' life like that, and it was obvious by the way Bonnie so quickly changed the subject that it hurt to talk about it.

—w—

"Where's Jared?" Samuel asked after he'd finished giving Leon a haircut. "I need to cut his hair next."

"He's in our room, hidin' under the bed."

Samuel's forehead wrinkled. "What's he doing there?"

"Guess he don't want his hair cut."

"Well, he's beginning to look like a shaggy dog, and it's way past time for a haircut." Samuel left the kitchen and tromped up the stairs to the bedroom Jared and Leon shared. Leon had wanted his own room, but Samuel felt better about having Jared in with his brother. He was too young to be alone yet, and Samuel was glad when Leon agreed to the arrangement.

It was nice living in a house where there were enough bedrooms so Samuel could have his own room. With the girls sharing a room and the boys sharing a room, there were still two more bedrooms he could use when any of his family from Pennsylvania came for a visit, which he hoped would be soon, because he really did miss them. He was sure most of his family would come for Titus's wedding in the fall, if not before, so that was something to look forward to.

When Samuel entered the boys' bedroom, he knelt on the floor and peered under the bed. Sure enough, there lay Jared. "Kumme. Come out," he said.

Jared said nothing; he just started to cry.

Samuel reached under the bed and touched Jared's arm. "*Haar schneide*—haircut," he said in a much softer voice.

Jared still wouldn't budge. "Esther," he said with a whimper. "I want Esther."

Samuel frowned. If Esther were here, would Jared be willing to let her cut his hair? Probably so, since he clung to her whenever he could. Samuel had to admit, Esther was real good with the kids. She was a capable young woman, a real good cook, and she was pretty to look at, too.

Shaking his thoughts aside, he decided to try a new approach and promised Jared that if he let him cut his hair, he could have some of the cookies Esther had baked when she'd been here yesterday.

When Jared finally crawled out, Samuel picked the boy up and carried him downstairs to the kitchen. Then he set him on a wooden stool, draped a towel around his shoulders, and picked up the scissors.

For the first few minutes everything went fine, but when Penny dashed into the room saying Lucky was chasing a bird, Jared whipped his head around.

Snip!

"Oh no," Samuel groaned. He'd taken a hunk out of Jared's hair that he hadn't meant to. He made a few more snips, trying to even it up, but with little success. "I can't glue it back on, so I guess we'll just have to live with it till it grows out." He sent Jared into the other room while he went to wash clothes.

Downstairs in the basement, Samuel fumbled with the washer but couldn't get it started. "What on earth is wrong with this thing," he grumbled. This was turning into a frustrating day!

"How come the washer's not goin'?" Marla asked when she joined him in the basement a few minutes later.

"Beats me. I can't get the crazy thing to work."

"It won't start till ya turn on the gas," she said, pointing to the valve.

Samuel frowned, feeling pretty dumb. He should have known to check for that.

"I'll bet if Esther was here she woulda known what to do," Marla said. "Esther seems to know everything about runnin' a house."

Samuel couldn't argue with that, but Esther wasn't here now, and he had to learn to do some things by himself.

—∾—

"Whew! I can't believe how long we've been gone or how much we bought today," Bonnie said when she and Esther returned to the B&B that afternoon.

"We did find some pretty good bargains." Esther placed a large paper sack on the table. It held the toys she'd bought for Samuel's children: two dolls—one for Marla and one for Penny; a set of building blocks for Jared; and a baseball, glove, and bat for Leon.

"Guess I'd better haul the box of Christmas decorations I bought up to the attic," Bonnie said. "Then I'll need to go outside and feed the chickens. I've gotta keep my hens happy so they'll continue laying eggs. My guests seem to enjoy having fresh omelets for breakfast, and so do I." She chuckled. "No one's complained about the rooster crowing yet either."

"That's good. Personally, I enjoy the crow of a rooster greeting me in the morning."

Bonnie smiled. "Same here."

"Would you like me to put the decorations away while you're outside?" Esther asked.

"I appreciate the offer, but you look tired. In fact, I'm concerned that you've been doing too much these days."

"What do you mean?"

"I'm wondering if it's become too much for you to keep working two jobs."

Esther shook her head. "I enjoy what I'm doing here and at Samuel's, too. Besides, going over to my old house during the weekdays is closer to the B&B than it is to Titus's place, so it's been working out real well for me. Since I've been sending some of the money I make to my folks to help with my brother's medical expenses, I really need the income from both jobs."

"I understand, but if things get to be too much, you can always bring the kids over to the B&B for part of the day and they can play outside while you do the cleaning."

"I'll think about it, but right now, I'm going to take these decorations up to the attic for you." Esther picked up the box and carried it upstairs.

When she entered the attic, her foot bumped the door. *Bam!*—it slammed shut.

She set the box on the floor, grabbed the door handle, and gave it a yank, but the door wouldn't budge.

Feeling a little bit desperate, Esther pounded on the door and hollered for help, but there was no response. Of course not—Bonnie was outside feeding the chickens.

Don't panic, Esther told herself. *Bonnie will come in soon, and then she'll hear me calling and open the attic door. I just need to relax and stay calm.*

Whoosh! Something flew past Esther's head. She thought it was a bird at first, but when it swooped past her again, she realized it wasn't a bird at all—it was a bat!

CHAPTER 33

Esther dropped to her knees and tried not to panic. While one of her biggest fears was high places, at the moment, being trapped in the attic with a bat seemed much worse.

I need to get out of here now! Several minutes went by, and Esther pounded on the door. "Help! I'm trapped in the attic with a bat!"

No response. Where was Bonnie? Surely she couldn't still be out feeding the chickens.

The bat made another pass over her head, and Esther screamed. If she didn't get out of here soon, she didn't know what she would do.

She thought about Samuel and the way he'd caught that fly the other day. If only catching a bat could be as simple. Not that she'd have the courage to do it of course. She might be brave enough to whack the bat though—if she could find something suitable to use.

Esther glanced around the attic but didn't see anything that would make a good club. *I wish I had that baseball bat I got for Leon with me right now,* she thought. *Maybe there's something in one of the boxes up here I can use.*

She crawled over to the box closest to her and was about to open the flaps, when the bat swooped in front of her face, brushing her nose with the tip of its wing. She screamed and covered her head with her hands. Being trapped in the attic was definitely worse than her fear of heights!

———m———

Bonnie's stomach rumbled as she entered the house. It was past time to fix supper. *I think I'll fix some spaghetti tonight,* she decided. *That's one of my favorite meals, and it appeals to me right now.*

She checked in the pantry for some tomato sauce, but seeing none there, she decided to go to the basement, where she kept her excess canned goods as well as the strawberry-rhubarb jam she and Esther had made this spring.

She opened the basement door and turned on the light, then carefully descended the stairs. Heading toward the shelves where the canned goods were kept, she spotted an old pie cupboard in one corner of the basement. She'd been meaning to take a closer look at it for some time, thinking that if it was in good enough condition she would put it to good use in the kitchen.

Think I'll take a minute and check it over right now, she decided.

Bonnie knelt on the floor beside the cupboard. The outside appeared to be in pretty fair shape. Just a little bit of sanding and a coat of varnish and it should be good as new.

She opened the cupboard doors, and when she looked inside, she was surprised to see a stack of old newspapers. "I think Grandma must have saved just about everything," she said with a chuckle. She pulled out the newspapers and was even more surprised when an envelope fell to the floor. She soon realized that it was a letter addressed to her dad.

Bonnie slipped the envelope into the pocket of her jeans, took three cans of tomato sauce from the shelf, and then headed upstairs.

Back in the kitchen, she placed the sauce on the counter and took the letter from her pocket. She noticed that the postmark on it was older than she was, and the envelope was still sealed shut. *I wonder who it's from and if Dad even knew about this letter.*

She stared at the letter several seconds then tore it open and read it silently.

> *Dear Ken,*
> *When you told me that you and your folks were moving to Kentucky, I wanted to tell you that I'd been secretly going out with Dave, but I didn't have the nerve to say it to your face. So I hope you'll forgive me, but I decided the best way to tell you was to send this letter instead of saying it to your face before you moved. I hope you'll be happy living in Kentucky, and I'm sure someone as nice as you will find another girlfriend who'll care as much about you as I do Dave.*
>
> > *Wishing you all the best,*
> > *Trisha*

Bonnie sat staring at the letter. *Trisha must have been Dad's girlfriend before he and his folks moved to Kentucky. Obviously Dad didn't know about Trisha's letter, since it's never been opened. I wonder what he would say about this now. Did Trisha write to Dad again, or was this the only time? Should I tell Dad about the letter or pretend I never saw it? Would he even care after all these years?*

Unsure of what she should do, Bonnie placed the letter on the counter and flipped the radio on to her favorite Christian station. When a song of worship and praise came on, she turned up the volume and sang along: "I will give you all my worship. I will give you all my praise. You alone I long to worship; You alone are worthy of my praise."

By the time the song was over, Bonnie had the water boiling for the spaghetti and was about to put it in the kettle, when the lights flickered then went out. She groped around in the top drawer below the counter and was relieved when she found the flashlight. Then she made her way slowly to the living room and discovered that the lights were out there, too. Since it was a calm evening with no wind or rain, she figured someone in the area must have run into a pole and knocked the power out.

Remembering that Esther had gone up to the attic with the box of Christmas decorations, and seeing no sign of her now, Bonnie called Esther's name as she swung the flashlight around the room.

No response. Could Esther still be in the attic, or had she gone out to the guest house?

Bam! Bam! Bam!

Bonnie tipped her head and listened. The sound seemed to be coming from upstairs. She returned to the kitchen, turned off the stove since there was no power, and went up to investigate. When she reached the top of the stairs, the pounding grew louder, and she heard Esther's voice calling for help.

Bonnie rushed to the attic door and turned the knob. Nothing happened. It appeared to be locked. "Esther, are you in there?"

"Yes, and the light blew out so now I'm in the dark with—"

"The lights are out throughout the house. I think someone may have hit a pole." Bonnie grabbed the doorknob and pulled again, but it still wouldn't budge. "The door must be locked from the inside. Try to open it, Esther."

"I have tried, but there's no button to unlock it, and if there's a key somewhere, I can't find it in the dark."

Bonnie grimaced. If there was a key to the attic door, she didn't know about it, and if the door was locked, short of taking it off the hinges, she had no idea how to get it open. The job would require more strength and expertise than her limited handywoman skills. Besides, with it being so dark, she'd never be able to see well enough to do anything constructive. What she needed right now was a man's help.

"Hang on, Esther," she called through the door. "I'm going to get you some help."

—∞—

Samuel and the kids had just finished supper when someone knocked on the back door. He opened it and was surprised to see Bonnie on the porch holding a flashlight.

"Esther's locked in the attic and our power is out," she said breathlessly. "Can you come help me get her out?"

Samuel glanced over at his children sitting at the kitchen table. "I'd like to help, but I'm not comfortable leaving my kids here alone."

"I'll stay with them while you're gone," Bonnie offered.

Samuel hesitated a minute and finally nodded. "They're almost done eating supper, so if you'll make sure they clear the table and that the dishes get done, I'd appreciate it."

"Sure, no problem."

"Hopefully I won't be gone too long." Samuel grabbed his straw hat and hurried out the door.

—∞—

Whoosh! The bat swooped past Esther's head once more. It was so close that she could hear the flutter of its wings. *Dear Lord, don't let it touch me again.*

As Esther's fear escalated, she crouched closer to the floor.

Sometime later, Esther heard footsteps clomping up the stairs. She figured Bonnie had probably gone for one of her English neighbors—maybe Harold Reece who lived down the road.

The doorknob rattled; then everything got quiet. Esther leaned against the door. She hoped whoever was out there hadn't given up, because she didn't think she could stand being trapped in here with that bat much longer.

Esther heard some banging, which gave her a ray of hope. Suddenly the door came off, and she fell into a pair of strong arms. As a beam of light hit the man's face, Esther looked up. "Samuel?"

CHAPTER 34

S amuel, I—I didn't know that was you." Esther stammered. "Danki for getting me out of that attic."

He gave a nod, thinking how cute she looked as her cheeks turned a pinkish hue. Then he berated himself for having such a thought. Thankfully, she didn't know what he'd been thinking. "Bonnie came over to get me. She stayed at the house with my kinner so I could come over here."

"Th–there's a bat in the attic," Esther rasped. Her covering was askew, and she quickly pushed it back in place.

"A baseball bat?"

She shook her head "No, a bat that flies—and swoops—and. . ."

Seeing how shaken Esther was, Samuel suggested she go downstairs while he tried to capture the bat.

She looked up at him, eyes wide and wrinkles in her forehead. "Are—are you sure?"

"Jah. Go on down."

She hesitated but finally nodded. "Be careful, Samuel. Capturing a bat isn't the same as catching a fly."

"I'll be fine," he assured her.

As Esther started carefully down the stairs, Samuel stepped into the attic and hit the light switch, relieved when it came on. It would be much harder to try and capture the bat with only the light from his flashlight.

Whoosh! The bat flew right over his head.

Samuel ducked. Gathering his wits, he grabbed an

old sweater he spotted draped across a wooden trunk, and then he began a merry chase after the bat. After several foiled attempts, he finally captured the creature inside the sweater and hurried down the stairs.

"Got it trapped in this sweater!" he said to Esther, who stood shivering in the living room near the fireplace.

"Wh–what are you going to do with it?" she asked in a shaky voice.

"I'll take the critter outside and let it go." Samuel stepped onto the porch, opened the sweater, and gave it a shake.

When he returned to the living room, Esther pointed to the sweater and squealed. "It–it's still there!"

Samuel looked down. Sure enough, the bat was clinging upside-down to the sweater. He'd thought the bat had let go, but with it being so dark outside, he must not have seen it.

He rushed back outside and gave it another good shake. This time he saw the bat flap its wings and fly off into the night.

"Good riddance," Samuel mumbled as he headed back to the house. "You've caused enough trouble for one night."

———————

Just as Samuel stepped into the B&B, the telephone rang. Esther hurried into the kitchen to answer it. "Bonnie's Bed-and-Breakfast," she said when she picked up the receiver.

"Is this Bonnie Taylor?" a woman's voice asked on the other end of the line.

"No, this is Esther Beiler. I work for Bonnie, but she's not here right now. May I take a message?"

"I'm a nurse at a hospital in Portland, Oregon. I need to speak to Bonnie because her father's been admitted here after being involved in a car accident."

Esther's eyebrows squeezed together. "I'm sorry to hear that. Is he seriously hurt?"

"I can only discuss that with Bonnie. Can you please have her call me as soon as she returns home?"

Esther wrote down the number the nurse gave her and promised to give Bonnie the message. When she hung up, she returned to the living room and told Samuel about the phone call.

"That's too bad. I'd better get back to the house right away and let Bonnie know." Samuel said a hurried good-bye and rushed out the door.

———✺———

When Samuel entered his house with a worried expression, Bonnie felt immediate concern. "Were you able to get Esther out of the attic? Is she okay?"

He gave a nod. "She's fine, but while I was there, Esther got a phone call from a hospital in Oregon. It seems your dad's been in a car accident."

Bonnie gasped. "How bad is it?"

"I don't know. The nurse wouldn't give Esther any details. Just said you should call as soon as you got home."

Bonnie grabbed her purse and flashlight and then hurried out to her car.

When she arrived at the B&B a short time later, Esther gave her the phone message, and Bonnie called the hospital. When she hung up the phone, she turned to Esther and said, "My dad's injuries aren't life-threatening, but he broke several bones. I need to go to Oregon right away."

Esther nodded. "Of course."

Bonnie clasped Esther's arm. "Would you be willing to run the B&B while I'm gone?"

Esther's eyes widened. "Can't you close it until you get back?"

Bonnie shook her head. "Several people are scheduled to arrive in the next couple of weeks, and I wouldn't feel right about cancelling their reservations."

"I'd be happy to do it," Esther said, "but it might be

difficult since I'm supposed to go to Samuel's every day to watch his children."

"Maybe Samuel can bring the kids to the B&B in the mornings before he leaves for work, and you can watch them here. Since it's summer now and the weather's so nice, the kids would probably be happy to play outside most of the day."

Esther nodded. "If Samuel's agreeable to the arrangement, then I'm willing to do it."

Bonnie gave Esther a hug. "I appreciate it so much. Now I need to get a plane ticket and find someone to drive me to the airport in Nashville."

CHAPTER 35

Portland, Oregon

As Bonnie parked her rental car in the hospital parking lot, her heart started to pound. What if Dad didn't want to see her? When she'd returned to Oregon after Grandma's funeral and told him she'd decided to quit her job and move to Kentucky in order to open a bed-and-breakfast, he'd said that if she was going to do something that foolish, she may as well not bother to ever come home again.

Did he mean it? she wondered. *Will he ask me to leave?*

Things had been strained between her and Dad since Mom had died, and she'd probably made them worse by moving to Kentucky. But she liked it there and appreciated Esther, Samuel, and Allen, who'd become her friends.

She was pleased that Esther had been willing to handle things at the B&B while she was gone. Allen had taken her to the airport in Nashville, and Samuel had even agreed to come over every day and feed her chickens when he dropped the kids off for Esther to watch. That was surely proof of their friendship.

Bonnie turned off the car's engine and whispered a prayer. "Lord, give me the strength to face my dad, and help him to be receptive to my visit."

When Bonnie entered the hospital and spoke to the nurse in charge on her dad's floor, she was again told that the accident had left him with a broken leg, a broken arm, several broken ribs, and lots of nasty bruises.

"In order for him to be released, he'll need to have some help," the nurse told Bonnie. "His arm and leg will both be in a cast for at least six weeks."

Bonnie drew in a deep breath as she leaned against the nurse's station. She could take Dad back to Kentucky, but in his condition, she knew he wouldn't be up for that. Besides, as much as he hated it there, she was sure he'd never agree to go.

The nurse stepped out from behind her desk. "Would you like me to show you to his room now?"

"Yes, please."

Bonnie followed the nurse down the hall, and when she entered her father's room, she found him asleep.

"I'll just sit beside his bed until he wakes up," she whispered.

The nurse nodded and slipped quietly from the room.

Bonnie took a seat in the chair and winced when she saw the purple bruises on her father's swollen face. There was a cast on his left arm, and on his right leg, too. If not for the pain medicine the nurse said they'd been giving him, he'd no doubt be in a whole lot of pain.

Sometime later, Dad opened his eyes. He looked over at Bonnie and blinked a couple of times. "Wh–what are you doing here?"

"I came as soon as I heard you'd been in an accident."

"What for? You don't care about me," he said, looking straight at her.

She placed her hand on his shoulder. "That's not true, Dad. I love you very much."

"Humph! If you loved me, you wouldn't have run off to Kentucky."

"I went there for Grandma's funeral." *And you should have gone, too,* she silently added.

He turned his head toward the opposite wall. "You didn't have to stay."

"I like it there, Dad. Turning Grandma and Grandpa's

215

house into a bed-and-breakfast has been a challenge, but it's also quite rewarding."

"Humph!"

"The nurse said you're going to need some help after you're released from the hospital."

"I can manage."

She shook her head. "You'll be wearing your casts for at least six weeks."

"Yeah, thanks to the stupid driver who broadsided my car! That guy clearly wasn't watching where he was going."

"Is there anyone you'd like to ask about coming to stay with you during your convalescence?"

"Nope, and I'm not goin' to no convalescent center either."

"Then I guess you're stuck with me, because I'm not going back to Kentucky until you're able to manage on your own. Are you okay with me staying?"

"I guess so. What other choice do I have?"

She bit back a smile. He wasn't as tough as he liked her to believe. Now she just needed to give Esther a call to see how things were going and ask if Esther thought she could handle running the B&B for the next six weeks. She'd do that as soon as she visited with Dad awhile.

—m—

Pembroke, Kentucky

Esther had just finished polishing the hardwood floor in the downstairs hallway of the B&B when Marla, who was outside playing, hollered something. Esther whirled around, slipped on the floor, and dropped to her knees, bending her toe back. Today had not started out on a good note. First she'd cut her finger on a sharp edge while dusting the china hutch, then she'd gotten a splinter in her hand from the broom when she'd been trying to get some cobwebs off the outside of the house. Now she had a sore knee and a sore toe and needed to go outside and see what Marla was hollering about. This whole arrangement of watching Samuel's kids at the B&B and trying to handle reservations as well as guest accommodations was a bit more than she could handle. But she had promised Bonnie she would do it, so she'd manage somehow until Bonnie returned, which she hoped wouldn't be too long from now.

Esther started for the back door, but the telephone rang, so she dashed into the kitchen to answer it.

"Bonnie's Bed-and-Breakfast."

"Hi, Esther. It's me, Bonnie. How are things going there?"

Esther glanced at the kitchen door, where Leon now stood, holding a chicken. "Everything's fine. How's your dad?"

"He's pretty banged up and will need some help until his arm and leg have healed—probably six weeks."

"That's too bad. Does he have someone there to take care of him?"

"No, not really." There was a pause. "I said I'd stay to help out. Do you think you could manage that long without me?"

Esther glanced at Leon again, who had taken a seat in a chair at the kitchen table and held the chicken in his lap. "Umm. . . Yes, I'm sure I can manage. Feel free to stay as long as you need to."

"Oh, thank you, Esther. I really appreciate your willingness to take over for me, and I'll pay you extra for doing this."

"Helping others is what friends are supposed to do." Esther snapped her fingers to get Leon's attention, and then motioned for him to take the chicken outside. Leon frowned but did what she asked.

Esther had no more than hung up the phone, when Marla dashed into the kitchen. "Penny's up a tree, and she can't get down! I yelled before and tried to tell you she was goin' up, but you never came outside when I called."

"Why is Penny up a tree?" Esther questioned.

"She wanted to get Bonnie's fluffy gray cat down."

Esther moaned. *What more can go wrong?*

CHAPTER 36

"Stay in here and keep an eye on Jared," Esther instructed Marla. "He's in the living room playing with the blocks I got for him awhile back."

Marla hurried off to the living room, and Esther rushed out the back door. As much as she feared high places, she couldn't leave Penny stuck in the tree. She thought about sending Marla or Leon up after their sister but didn't think either of them was strong enough to help Penny down. Besides, they might lose their balance and fall. The last thing she needed was for another one of Samuel's children to get hurt.

Of course, I might get hurt, too, she reasoned. *And then what would I do?*

Esther tipped her head back and looked up at Penny, crouched on a branch high in the tree, with the gray cat perched on the branch next to her. "I'm going to get a ladder to get you down. Sit very still, okay?"

Penny gave a nod. "Hurry. I'm *vergelschdert.*"

"Try not to be frightened." Esther said in what she hoped was a voice of reassurance. Truth was she was probably as scared as Penny right now.

She headed to the barn and spotted Leon prancing around the yard with the chicken he'd brought into the house. "Please put that *hinkel* away and come steady the ladder for me," she said to the boy.

Leon hurried off toward the chicken coop while Esther went to the barn. Once she had the ladder in place and was sure Leon had a grip on the legs, she ascended it slowly. *First a bat in the attic that about scared me to death, and now this. How many other fears must I deal with? Help me, Lord,* she prayed. *Still my racing heart and help me not to be afraid.*

By the time Esther reached the branch where Penny sat, the fluffy gray cat had leaped to the ground.

"Slip your arms around my neck and wrap your legs around my waist," Esther told Penny.

The frightened girl's chin trembled. "I–I'm vergelschdert."

"I know, dear one. I'm scared, too," Esther admitted, "but we can do this. God will help us. You'll see." *Please, Lord, please help us.*

She thought about Philippians 4:13: *"I can do all things through Christ which strengtheneth me,"* and it bolstered her faith.

Penny did as Esther had instructed, and once Esther was sure the child had a good grip on her, she slowly and carefully descended the ladder. When she reached the bottom, she set Penny on the ground. "Please don't ever do anything like that again."

"Are. . .are you gonna punish me?"

"No. I think you've learned a lesson today." Esther gave Penny a hug, which helped her as well, because her arms and legs were shaking.

Tears dribbling down her cheeks, Penny nodded. "Jah, and I—I won't ever do that again." She pointed at the cat scampering through the grass. "He wouldn't come down when I called, and then when I went up the tree, he jumped down."

"You're a dummkopp, Penny," Leon said, stepping away from the ladder. "I told ya not to go up in that tree."

"I'm not a dummkopp. You're the dummkopp," Penny said tearfully.

Leon wrinkled his nose. "Am not!"

"Are so!"

Penny shook her finger at him. "Am not!"

Esther held up her hand. "That's enough. Neither one of you is stupid."

She motioned to the ladder. "While I put this away, I want the two of you to go into the house. When I come inside, we'll have something cold to drink."

The children scampered off while Esther picked up the ladder and headed for the barn. She longed to be a wife and mother, but after a day like today, she wasn't sure she was cut out for it. At least she didn't have any B&B guests checking in today.

Inside the barn, Esther was greeted by Bonnie's yappy little dog as it wagged its tail and bumped her leg with its cold, wet nose. "Not now, Cody," she said, pushing the dog away with her hand. "I don't have time to play."

Woof! Woof! Cody wiggled and continued to wag his tail.

"I said, not now." Esther pushed past the dog, put the ladder away, and hurried into the house. When she stepped into the kitchen, she halted. Marla sat at the table, reading Esther's journal! Esther had been writing it in earlier and had foolishly left it on the counter, never thinking anyone might read it.

Esther scooped up the journal and slipped it into a drawer. She hoped Marla hadn't read anything she'd written about Samuel. "It's not polite to read someone's private thoughts," she told Marla. "You should have asked me first."

The girl's face reddened. "S—sorry. I didn't know it was yours till I started reading."

Esther placed her hand on Marla's shoulder. "Next time you see something you're curious about, please ask before you touch it."

"I will."

"Where's Jared?" Esther asked.

"Sleepin' on the living room floor."

Esther was tempted to move him to the sofa or

Bonnie's downstairs bedroom but figured he might wake up if she did. Besides, the floor was carpeted, and he was probably comfortable or he wouldn't have fallen asleep there.

"Have Penny and Leon come inside yet?" she asked Marla.

Marla shook her head. "Did you get Penny out of the tree?"

"I did, and the cat came down on its own. I told Penny and Leon to come inside so we could all have a snack, but I guess if they're not in the house, then they didn't listen too well."

"A snack sounds good 'cause I'm hungerich," Marla said. Apparently she didn't care whether her brother and sister had come into the house or not.

"I'll fix some cheese, crackers, and lemonade as soon as your brother and sister come in. Why don't you go outside and see what's taking them so long?"

"Okay." Marla left her seat and hurried out the door.

Esther stepped into the living room to check on Jared. He was fast asleep on the floor, sucking his thumb and holding in his other hand one of the blocks Esther had found at the yard sale.

She smiled as she gazed at the child. What a precious little boy. How sad that he would grow up never knowing his mother. She wondered if Samuel would ever remarry, and if he did, would the children accept his wife as their new mother? Would they accept her if she was the woman Samuel chose to marry?

Esther shook her head. *I shouldn't allow myself to even think such thoughts. Especially when Samuel has given no indication that he has any interest in me. I'm still worried that he might be interested in Bonnie, but I don't have the nerve to ask.*

She moved back to the kitchen and had just taken a brick of cheese from the refrigerator when the back door swung open and Marla stepped into the room, followed by Leon and Penny.

"I found these two in the chicken coop," Marla announced. "They were lookin' for eggs."

"Did you find any?" Esther asked, directing her question to Leon.

Leon shook his head. "Nope, and I was hopin' there'd be some green ones today."

"Maybe tomorrow." Esther motioned to the bathroom down the hall. "If you three will go wash your hands, I'll get our snack ready to eat."

The children didn't have to be asked twice. They rushed out of the kitchen, tickling each other and giggling all the way.

By the time they returned, Esther had a plate of crackers and cheese on the table and was pouring the lemonade she'd made earlier.

"Can we go outside on the porch to eat our snack?" Leon asked. "That way we can watch for Daadi."

"I suppose that will be all right," Esther said. "I'll leave the door open so I can hear if Jared wakes up."

Esther handed the crackers to Marla and the plate full of cheese to Leon and told them to go outside and wait for her on the porch.

The children filed out of the house, and Esther came behind them with a tray that held the pitcher of lemonade and glasses. They'd just seated themselves around the table on the porch, when Samuel's horse and buggy pulled into the yard.

"Daadi's here!" Leon leaped off the porch and raced across the lawn. Penny and Marla followed. It did Esther's heart good to see the children so excited about seeing their father.

She watched as Samuel tied his horse to the hitching rail and headed to the house with the children. He walked with an easy gait and seemed to be more relaxed than usual. It was good to see him pick Penny up and laugh as he swung her onto his shoulders. When he'd first come to Kentucky, he hardly looked at the kids. Now it seemed he couldn't get enough of them. *Maybe the pain of losing his wife is lessening,* Esther thought. *Maybe Samuel's heart is finally healing.*

When Samuel and the children stepped onto the porch, Marla pointed to the table. "Esther fixed us a snack, Daadi. Will you sit with us and eat some, too?"

Samuel looked at Esther, as though seeking her approval.

She smiled and said, "There's plenty, and you're more than welcome to join us."

Samuel put Penny in a chair and took the seat beside Esther. "How'd things go here today?" he asked.

"Esther rescued me from a tree," Penny said before Esther could respond.

Samuel squinted at Penny. "What were you doing in a tree?"

"She went up after a dumb old *katz,*" Leon spoke up. "I told her not to, but she wouldn't listen."

Marla looked at Esther and smiled. "Even though Esther's afraid of high places, she was brave and climbed the ladder to get Penny down."

Esther's face heated. Marla must have read the part in her journal where she'd mentioned being afraid of heights. If she'd read that, what else might the girl have read?

Making no comment on Esther's fear of heights, Samuel looked at Penny and frowned. "You ought to know better than to climb into a tree. If you'd fallen, you could have been hurt." He looked over at Esther. "I appreciate you going up after her, and I'm sorry for the trouble she caused."

"It was no trouble," Esther said. "I'm just glad she wasn't hurt."

"The katz's okay, too, Daadi." Penny grinned widely. "He leaped outa that old tree and landed right on his feet."

"Just like I told ya he'd do," Leon said with a smirk. "You shoulda listened to me."

Fearful that the children might start an argument,

Esther quickly handed each of them a glass of lemonade, along with some crackers and cheese. Then she passed the plate to Samuel and gave him some lemonade, too.

He took a drink and smacked his lips. "Umm. . . This sure hits the spot on a warm day such as this. Danki, Esther."

"You're welcome."

"Esther's a real good cook," Marla said. She reached for a cracker and put a piece of cheese on top. "Tell Daadi about the raisin bread you made this mornin', Esther. He likes raisin bread a lot."

"There's still some left, if you'd like a piece," Esther offered.

Samuel shook his head. "I appreciate the offer, but cheese and crackers is plenty for me right now."

"I can send some home with you," Esther said. "Maybe you'd like it for breakfast tomorrow morning."

"That'd be nice." Samuel took another drink of lemonade. "Have you heard anything from Bonnie today?"

"Jah." Esther repeated all that Bonnie had told her when she'd called and ended it by saying, "So she'll be gone at least six weeks, and I'll be in charge of things here until she returns."

Samuel's eyebrows furrowed. "That will mean a lot of extra work for you. Maybe I should try to find someone else to watch the kinner till Bonnie gets back. That way you won't have so much to do."

"I'm sure I can manage." No way was Esther going to tell Samuel about the terrible day she'd had. If he thought she couldn't manage everything she was responsible for right now, he might look for someone to replace her. Esther loved being with Samuel's kids and didn't want to give that up, no matter how tired she was or how badly things might go on some days.

Marla placed both hands on her father's cheeks. "Please don't get no one else to watch us, Daadi. We don't want anyone but Esther."

Penny and Leon nodded in agreement.

"All right," Samuel said, looking at Esther. "But you must let me know if things get to be too much for you."

He turned back to look at the kids. "You must behave yourselves and help Esther whenever you can. And no more climbing trees, is that understood?"

All heads bobbed in agreement.

Esther smiled. *If I can prove to Samuel how capable I am, maybe he'll take an interest in me. Maybe someday he'll smile at me the way he does Bonnie.*

CHAPTER 37

For the next two weeks Esther kept busy watching Samuel's children and running the B&B. As she developed a routine, things seemed to get easier. The best part was that Samuel had agreed to go on a picnic supper with her and the children this evening. Esther really looked forward to that. She glanced at the clock on the kitchen wall. He should be here soon.

The back door flew open, and Leon rushed into the room, carrying a wicker basket. "Look what I found," he announced. "There was six eggs, and every one of 'em is green!"

Esther smiled at his exuberance. "Let's get them washed, and then we'll put them in the refrigerator."

"Can we boil some eggs and take 'em to eat with the other things you're fixin' for our picnic supper?" he asked.

She nodded. "Would you like plain boiled eggs, or should I make deviled eggs?"

Leon's blue eyes squinted as he looked up at Esther with a quizzical expression. "Don't want no eggs made by the devil."

Esther bit back a chuckle. "Deviled eggs aren't made by the devil, Leon."

"Then how come they're called 'deviled eggs'?"

"The fact that the eggs are seasoned with spice is what gives them the name 'deviled' eggs," Esther said as she took some eggs from the refrigerator that had already been boiled.

Leon just shrugged and placed the basket of eggs he'd gathered on the table.

Esther figured he hadn't really understood her explanation.

Just then Marla bounded into the room. "There's a car in the driveway, and some English folks are walkin' up to the house."

Esther glanced at the calendar and groaned. In her excitement over the picnic supper, she'd forgotten about the guests who were supposed to arrive this afternoon. Well, at least she didn't have to feed them anything until morning. She'd get them checked in, show them to their room, and then return to the kitchen to finish putting things together for their picnic.

"Could you go check on Penny and Jared while I tend to the guests?" Esther asked Marla.

"Jah, sure." Marla dashed out of the room, and Esther went to the door. When she opened it, a strong wind hit her full in the face, and then she noticed it had begun to rain. She hoped it wouldn't last, or they might have to cancel their picnic supper.

By the time Esther had the guests settled into their room and had returned to the kitchen, the rain was coming down harder.

"How we gonna go on a picnic when it's rainin' like this?" Leon frowned. "We'll get soakin' wet."

"We can eat in the house," Marla said when she entered the room with Jared and Penny. She looked at Esther. "Isn't that right?"

Esther nodded. "I don't see why not. We can have an indoor picnic right here in the kitchen."

Leon wrinkled his nose. "It won't be as much fun if we hafta eat in here. Me and Daadi was gonna do some fishin' if we went to the pond."

"We can go there some other time," Esther said. "That is, if your daed's willing to go," she quickly added.

"I'm sure he will be," Marla said. "Daadi likes to fish."

"He likes it when someone else does the cookin', too," Penny added.

Esther smiled. If she couldn't get through to Samuel any other way, maybe her cooking skills would reach him.

———w———

Samuel grimaced as he guided his horse and buggy down the road toward the bed-and-breakfast. Shortly before he'd gotten off work today, he'd developed a headache. He could usually tell when he got one of these headaches that rain was on the way—his sinuses started to plug up on him, and the headache followed. He'd been right, because it was not only raining like crazy, but his head felt like someone had been smacking it with a hammer all day.

When Samuel had arrived home from work, he'd taken some aspirin before showering and changing his clothes, but the headache hadn't let up. Now, thanks to the rain beating down, he was having a hard time seeing out the front window of the buggy. He hoped the kids were ready to go when he got there, because he was anxious to get back home. Due to the nasty weather, he knew they wouldn't be having a picnic supper this evening and was sure the kids would be disappointed, same as him. He'd begun to realize why his kids liked Esther so much. She was sweet, even-tempered, and real smart, too. And she cared about them as if they were her own. He'd been fortunate to have found someone like her to oversee the children when he was at work.

Samuel's stomach rumbled noisily, and he pressed his hand against it. "Sure wish I didn't have to fix supper tonight," he mumbled, taking his thoughts in a different direction. It wasn't easy working all day and then going home and having to cook a meal—especially when he wasn't that great of a cook. *Maybe we'll just settle for sandwiches,* he decided.

When Samuel pulled into Bonnie's yard, he was greeted by her yappy little dog. "Don't you have the good sense to get in out of the rain?" Samuel muttered when Cody started running back and forth, barking at his horse and leaping into the air like he was half crazy. The mutt sure had a lot of energy, and he liked to bark at nearly everything he saw. Samuel was surprised Bonnie didn't get rid of the dog. For that matter, he wondered what had possessed her to even take the stray in. Well, he guessed it was none of his business. He had enough to deal with when it came to Lucky.

Samuel climbed out of his buggy and hollered at Cody to get in the barn. It took several more times of him ordering the dog to go, but when the critter finally did as he was told, Samuel secured his horse to the hitching rail and hurried across the yard.

"Daadi, guess what?" Marla said excitedly when Samuel entered the house.

He bent down to give her a hug. "What?"

"Since it's raining, Esther said we could have our picnic supper in the kitchen."

"Is that a fact?"

She bobbed her head. "Please say we can stay, Daadi, 'cause she's fixed lots of good food, and I'm hungerich."

Samuel smiled despite his throbbing headache. "I guess we'd better stay then, 'cause I wouldn't want any of my kinner to starve to death, and I'm sure that whatever Esther's fixed for supper will be a whole lot better than the cold sandwiches I was going to make if we went home and ate."

"I get sick of sandwiches, so I'm glad we're not goin' home to eat." Marla tugged on Samuel's hand. "Esther's got everything ready now. Let's go in the kitchen so we can eat."

—◆—

Esther smiled when Samuel entered the room holding Marla's hand, and she was pleased to see that Marla was smiling, too. "Since it's raining, I thought we could have our picnic in here." She motioned to the table, which was fully set.

He gave a nod. "So I've been told."

Everyone took their seats, and after the silent prayer had been said, Esther passed the food around. There was chicken, fried golden brown; tangy potato salad; carrot and celery sticks; savory, maple-flavored baked beans; and spicy deviled eggs. She'd even thought to cover the table with a red-and-white-checkered tablecloth, so it seemed more like they were having a picnic. It did her heart good to see the children's smiling faces. This might not be the picnic they'd planned, but at least they were all together, and she was glad Samuel had agreed to stay. She hoped they'd have time after the meal to sit and visit while the children played.

Esther had just taken a bite of chicken when the telephone rang. She excused herself and took the portable phone that was usually in Bonnie's kitchen into the hall so she wouldn't disturb the conversation going on at the table. When she realized it was someone wanting to make a reservation at the B&B, she took a seat at the desk near the front door and wrote down the information in the reservation book.

Esther hung up the phone several minutes later and was about to return to the kitchen, when the phone rang again. "Bonnie's Bed-and-Breakfast."

"Esther, is that you?"

Esther recognized her mother's voice and she smiled. "Jah, Mom, it's me."

"How are you doing? Are you still running the bed-and-breakfast by yourself, or is Bonnie back from Oregon now?" Mom asked.

"I'm still on my own. Bonnie will probably be gone another four weeks," Esther replied.

"Are you managing okay by yourself? You're not tempted to watch TV, I hope."

"No TV, and I'm getting along fine and keeping busy."

Esther wasn't about to tell Mom all the trouble she'd had since Bonnie had left. Mom would be concerned, and she didn't need one more thing to worry about.

"How's Dan doing?" Esther asked.

"I'm sorry to say he's no better. He still tires easily, and he's using a wheelchair most of the time now."

"That's too bad. I'm sure he appreciates you and Dad being there."

"Jah. I know both Dan and Sarah are real glad we came to help out."

They talked a while longer; then remembering her guests in the kitchen, Esther explained that she needed to go. She'd no more than hung up the phone, when the middle-aged couple who'd checked into the B&B earlier came down the stairs asking for directions to one of the restaurants in Hopkinsville. By the time Esther finished talking to them and returned to the kitchen, Samuel and the kids were done eating.

"I'm sorry for taking so long," Esther apologized. "But I'm glad you went ahead and ate without me."

"It was very good." Samuel pushed back his chair. "I hate to eat and run, but I think we need to get home."

Marla's brows puckered. "Do we hafta go? We haven't had dessert yet, and I wanted to stay and visit with Esther awhile."

"Maybe some other time," Samuel said. "I've been fighting a sinus headache for the last several hours, and I need to go home and lie down."

"I'm sorry to hear you're not feeling well," Esther said. "Would you like some aspirin or willow bark capsules?"

He shook his head. "I took a couple of aspirin before coming here, but it hasn't helped. Think I just need to lie down awhile."

"Of course. I understand, and I'll just send the strawberry-rhubarb pie I made for dessert home with you." Esther was disappointed that she'd have to eat a cold supper by herself, but she felt bad about Samuel's headache. *So much for a fun evening with Samuel and the kids,* she thought with regret. The way things were going, it didn't look like she and Samuel would ever have a chance to really sit and visit.

Chapter 38

Wen Esther woke up the following morning, she felt disoriented. It had rained most of the night, and the constant Ping! Ping! Ping! against the window in the guest house bedroom had kept her awake for several hours. Some of the time it had rained so hard that she thought the roof might cave in.

She'd also been unable to sleep because she'd been thinking about Samuel and wondering how he was doing. When he and the children had left after supper, he'd looked exhausted. She knew that even though he had a headache, he'd have to do his evening chores and see that the children were put to bed. What Samuel needed was a wife who could help raise his children, but then Samuel might have other thoughts about that. Some widowed Amish men she knew had found another wife within the first six months, and they didn't even have any children. To be widowed and trying to raise four children by himself had to be very difficult for Samuel. Of course, he did have her and also Titus to help with the children, but if he had a wife. . .

Now don't let your thoughts take you where they shouldn't go, Esther told herself as she climbed out of bed. It was dark in the room, so she lit the gas lamp and then ambled over to the window and lifted the shade. The rain had stopped, and the sun shone brightly, spilling its warmth into the room. Since today was Saturday, and she wouldn't have Samuel's children to watch, maybe she could get some gardening done. Of course, the first thing on her agenda was to walk over to the B&B and fix breakfast for her guests, who would no doubt be up pretty soon.

Esther turned toward the dresser, picked up the hand mirror, and frowned. There were dark circles beneath her eyes—an indication that she looked as tired as she felt this morning. It hadn't been easy taking charge of things while Bonnie was gone. Esther knew Bonnie was where she needed to be right now, but she'd be glad when she came back and took over again.

What if she doesn't come back? Esther thought. *Maybe Bonnie will decide that her father needs her to stay there with him, and she'll sell the B&B. Then I'd have no place to stay, because it wouldn't be right to ask Samuel and the kinner to move out of Mom and Dad's house. If they moved back with Titus, it would cause problems between him and Suzanne again, and they might end up not getting married.* She splashed some cold water on her face from the basin she kept on the dresser, trying to clear her mind of the troubling thoughts. *It's best if I don't worry about this. I just need to trust that Bonnie will come back. I need to trust God to work everything out.*

—⁓—

Shortly after Esther cleaned up the kitchen, her two B&B guests, a middle-aged couple from Tennessee, headed out to do some shopping and sightseeing.

Esther stepped outside with a plastic container for the produce she planned to pick and was halfway to the garden when Allen's truck pulled in.

"I was in the neighborhood and decided to drop by and see how you're doing," he said when he got out of his vehicle and joined her on the grass.

"I'm doing okay." Esther pointed to the garden. "I was just getting ready to pick some green beans and tomatoes."

"Do you need some help with that?"

"Is your back healed well enough to be working in the garden?"

He gave a nod. "My mom went back home last week, and I'm good as new. She never would have left if I wasn't doing better."

"I'm glad to hear your back's not hurting anymore. Falling down the steps like that, your injuries could have been even worse." Esther thought of Samuel's wife, who had died because she'd broken her neck when she'd fallen down the steps in their home. Allen was fortunate that his back hadn't been injured seriously enough to leave him with any permanent disability.

"Since I have some free time this morning, I may as well help you," Allen said.

"I appreciate that." She handed him the plastic container. "You can use this and start on the beans if you like, while I go get another container for the tomatoes."

As Allen headed for the garden, Esther went to the house. When she returned a few minutes later, she found Allen kneeling beside a clump of beans.

"Have you heard anything more from Bonnie? Do you know when she'll be back?" he asked, looking up with a hopeful expression. Was Allen concerned about Bonnie or just making polite conversation?

"She called a few days ago." Esther moved toward a row of tomatoes. "Said her dad's getting along pretty well, but it'll be awhile before he's out of his casts."

"I imagine he'll need some physical therapy after the casts come off."

"I hadn't even thought about that." Esther picked a couple of ripe cherry tomatoes and placed them in her container. "I guess that means Bonnie might stay in Oregon longer than six weeks."

"That will probably depend on whether her dad can manage on his own when the casts come off." Allen wiped the perspiration from his forehead. "Whew! Sure is a hot, humid day. And look at the birds drinking from the birdbath over there." He pointed across the yard. "I'll bet they're feeling about as hot as I am right now."

"Are you thirsty? I could run back to the house and get you some water," Esther offered.

"Not right now. I haven't picked enough beans to earn a break yet."

She chuckled. "A quick drink of water wouldn't be much of a break."

"It would be if I drank it and then plopped down in that." He motioned to the hammock suspended between two maple trees in the front yard.

She smiled. "It does look inviting."

"It's been a long time since I kicked back and rested in a hammock."

"Do you have a hammock at your place?"

He shook his head. "But my folks had one when I was a boy."

"Well, feel free to take a nap in the hammock after you're done picking the beans."

He grinned. "I might just take you up on that."

For the next hour, they worked in silence, until each of them had their containers full. Then they carried them up to the house and Esther poured two glasses of lemonade and fixed a plate of cookies. "Should we take our snack outside?" she asked.

"Sounds good to me. My mother always says everything tastes better when it's eaten outside."

Esther smiled. "I think she might be right about that."

They sat in the chairs on the porch, and Allen took a drink from his glass. "This lemonade is sure good, Esther, and it does hit the spot."

"Yes, I agree." Esther handed him the plate of cookies. "Would you like to try one of these?"

"Thanks." He grabbed a cookie and took a bite. "Umm. . . This is really good. I've never tasted anything like it before. What kind of cookie is it?"

"They're called boyfriend cookies, and the ingredients include butter, whole wheat and soy flour, sugar, vanilla, and eggs. Oh, and there's also oatmeal, salted peanuts, and carob chips in the recipe."

He wiggled his eyebrows playfully. "Not only real tasty, but they're a healthy kind of cookie."

She gave a nod. "Boyfriend cookies are one of my all-time favorites."

"How come they're called boyfriend cookies?"

"I don't really know for sure. I guess maybe it's because they're good enough for a girl to serve her boyfriend when he comes to call."

"Speaking of boyfriends. . . Do you have a boyfriend, Esther?" he asked.

She shook her head. *No, but I wish I did.*

"That's odd. I would think a pretty girl like you, who's also a great cook with a pleasant personality, would have a string of suitors just waiting in line to court her."

Esther's face heated. She wasn't used to receiving such compliments—especially from an attractive English man like Allen.

"Sorry if I embarrassed you," Allen said. "I'm just surprised that you don't have a boyfriend, because you certainly have all the attributes most men would like if they're looking for a wife."

Esther stared out into the yard, thinking about Ethan Zook and knowing how he appreciated her cooking abilities and would no doubt start courting her tomorrow if she showed him the least bit of interest. But she wanted a man who would appreciate her for more than her cooking skills. She wanted someone who thought she was fun to be with and liked her personality. The man she wanted was Samuel, but he didn't seem to notice any of her attributes.

As Esther and Allen sat in pleasant camaraderie, they continued to visit. Allen told Esther about a new house he'd been contracted to build over in Trigg County. "It's going to be a big one," he said. "Over four thousand square feet."

"Will Samuel be doing the painting on that one?" she asked, curious to know if he'd be keeping busy, which would allow her to continue watching the children.

"I think he will." Allen set his empty glass on the table. "Samuel was a big help to me when I was recuperating. He worked extra hard and helped out wherever he could, and if he's willing to do the painting on the house, then as far as I'm concerned, he's got the job."

"Samuel seems to like keeping busy," Esther said. She remembered Bonnie saying she thought Allen was a work-aholic. Well, from what she'd observed, Samuel was one, too. But that was good in many ways. It allowed him to earn a living so he could support his children, and it meant Esther would continue to be employed by Samuel. At least she hoped she would. She'd be very disappointed if he ever found someone else to watch the kids.

"You're right about Samuel," Allen said. "With four kids to feed and clothe, he needs a good income." He set his empty glass on the table and stood. "Now that I've had a little snack, I think I'll take you up on that offer to relax in the hammock. . .unless you'd like to lay claim to it first."

"You go right ahead," Esther said. "I'm going inside to wash the produce we picked. Then I'll probably sit outside and listen to the birds awhile. When they sing, I like to think they're serenading me."

"All right then, if I fall asleep, wake me in an hour. I really should bid on a couple of jobs before this day is out."

Esther watched as Allen settled himself in the ham-mock. He looked so relaxed and at peace with the world. If Allen really was a workaholic, as Bonnie had said, then he probably didn't take much time for himself. She could relate to that, because here of late she hadn't been able to take much time for herself either, but she didn't really mind. She liked keeping busy.

—⁓—

Portland, Oregon

"Never thought I'd admit this, but it's been nice having you here." Bonnie's dad gave her a half-smile from across the breakfast table. "I appreciate you coming to take care of me. Sure couldn't have managed without you these weeks."

She reached over and placed her hand over his. "I love you, Dad, and I'm glad I could be here to help out."

He lowered his gaze to the table. "Don't know how you can love me. I haven't been the best dad." He pulled his fingers through the sides of his thinning brown hair. "It's hard for me to deal with the fact that you chose to move to Kentucky—especially when you knew how things were between me and my folks."

"Whatever the problem was between you and Grandpa and Grandma, you need to forgive them, Dad. Holding a grudge will only make you sick, and if you're not willing to forgive your parents, then God won't forgive you."

He blinked a couple of times. "Forgive me for what? I'm not the one who forced their only child to leave his friends in Oregon and move all the way to Kentucky, where he hated it."

"I can't understand why you'd hate Kentucky. I think it's beautiful there." Bonnie reached for her cup of coffee and took a drink. "Besides, from what you've told me before, you were only seventeen when your folks left Oregon. I'm sure you made other friends after you moved."

"I did make a few, but I was in my senior year of high school when we moved, and it was hard to start over again. It was even harder to leave my girlfriend, Trisha, because we planned to get married after we graduated from school and found a job." Deep wrinkles formed across Dad's forehead. "After I moved, she found another boyfriend and ended up marrying him instead of me."

Hearing the name Trisha caused Bonnie to remember the letter she'd found in Grandma's pie cupboard. She'd brought the letter along, planning to give it to Dad, but in all the busyness of caring for him, she'd forgotten about it until now.

"I'll be right back, Dad. I have something I think you need to see." Bonnie rose from her seat and went to get her purse in the other room. When she returned, she handed him the letter. "I found this in an old pie cupboard down in Grandma's basement. It was stuck in the middle of some newspapers."

Dad's brows furrowed as he stared at the envelope. "Was it open when you found it?"

She shook her head. "Since I wasn't sure what it was, I went ahead and opened it. Sorry. I didn't mean to be snoopy."

Dad pulled the letter from the envelope, and as he read Trisha's message, his eyes turned glassy. He sat silently for a while before he spoke, as though letting what he'd read sink in. "I—I had no idea Trisha was planning to break up with me even before I moved. If she'd only had the nerve to say so, I'd have probably been glad I was moving. All those years I spent mad at my folks were for nothing." He thumped the side of his head. "What a waste of time, and now it's too late. I can't bring Mom and Pop back, and I can't tell them how sorry I am for giving them such a hard time. I had a chip on my shoulder, and we argued about everything because I thought they were too strict. As soon as I graduated from high school, I joined the army. Then later, I came back here. By then, Trisha was already married of course, and soon after that, I met your mom."

"Did you love Mom?" Bonnie dared to ask. "Or did you marry her on the rebound?"

"Yes, I did love her, but I guess in my mind, she was second choice." He grimaced. "As you well know, your mom and I argued a lot. She never understood why I didn't want to visit my folks, and when she insisted on taking you there so you could get to know your grandparents, it caused even more friction between us."

"I'm sorry you disapproved, but I wouldn't have wanted to grow up never knowing your parents—especially since Mom's parents were no longer living by the time I was born. Grandma and Grandpa Taylor may have been a little strict and old-fashioned in some ways, but they were good people."

"Yeah, you're right. I guess your mom did a good thing by taking you to visit them in Kentucky, even sometimes when I refused to go along. I just wish you weren't living there now. I miss you, Bonnie."

"I miss you, too, and you're always welcome to visit me there. Of course, I'll come here for visits whenever I can, too."

He gave a nod. "I'll look forward to that."

"You know, Dad, since I've been living in Kentucky, I've gotten to know several Amish families there. They're family-oriented, and they've taught me a lot about putting God first and then the needs of family and friends."

"Guess that's something I've never really done," he said with a tone of regret. "I sure didn't put your needs first after your mother died, and when I forced you to give up your baby, I thought you might hate me for the rest of your life."

She shook her head as tears gathered in her eyes. "After I became a Christian, I forgave you for that. And looking back on it now, I'm sure that you did what you thought was right."

"Would you pray with me, Bonnie?" he asked as his own eyes filled with tears. "I need to ask God to forgive me for the ill feelings I harbored toward my folks, and I need His forgiveness for all the times I yelled at your mom." He took Bonnie's hand and gave her fingers a gentle squeeze. "I'm sorry for everything I've ever done to hurt you as well."

Bonnie swallowed around the lump in her throat. "I

forgive you, Dad. Now let's pray so you can seek God's forgiveness and find a peace in your heart that only He can give."

―∿―

Pembroke, Kentucky

Samuel had just dropped the kids off at the Zooks' home so they could play with Ethan Zook's younger siblings and was heading over to the B&B to pick up Marla's sneakers, which she'd left there last night. It seemed like his oldest daughter had become forgetful lately. This was the second time in less than a week that she'd left something at the B&B. He was beginning to wonder if she was doing it on purpose so he'd have to go after her forgotten items.

But why would she do that? he reasoned. *She sure can't enjoy watching me inconvenience myself.*

When Samuel pulled into Bonnie's yard sometime later, he was surprised to see Allen sleeping in the hammock. He was even more surprised to see Esther sitting on a blanket near the hammock, with a glass in her hand. They looked very cozy.

I wonder why Allen's here and why he's sleeping in the hammock. Could there be something going on between Esther and Allen? Samuel frowned. Come to think of it, while he and Allen had worked together a few times, Allen had mentioned that he thought Esther was very nice and would make a good wife for some lucky man. Could he have been talking about himself?

Samuel had never admitted it until now, but in the last few weeks, he'd begun to realize that his heart was beginning to heal. He still missed Elsie, of course, but the raw ache he'd felt for the first several months after her death had finally faded, and he felt like he might be ready to open his heart to love again. He'd even thought Esther might be the one. But if Esther was interested in Allen, then there was no hope for the two of them. Should he make his feelings known or keep quiet and see what happened between Esther and Allen? If Allen wanted Esther, then he'd most likely expect her to leave the Amish faith, because Samuel was sure Allen would never give up his modern way of life to become Amish. Or would he?

Chapter 39

The tail of Samuel's horse switched back and forth, letting Samuel know the impatient animal was tired of standing in the driveway.

"Okay. Okay." Samuel pulled up to the hitching rail, climbed out of his buggy, and secured his horse. "Be good now, Socks," he said, patting the horse's flanks. "I won't be gone long."

Samuel sprinted across the lawn and stopped in front of the blanket where Esther sat. "Sorry to disturb you," he said, "but I came to get Marla's sneakers. She told me this morning that she forgot to bring 'em home when I picked the kinner up last night."

Esther nodded. "They played in the sprinkler yesterday, and their shoes got wet, so we set them on the back porch to dry. I spotted the sneakers this morning and realized that Marla was the only one who didn't take hers home."

Samuel grunted. "That's because she's become so *vergesslich* lately."

"She's not the only one who's forgetful," Esther said. "I got so relaxed sitting here in the sun that I forgot about the rest of the produce I'd planned to pick in the garden today." She glanced over at Allen, who appeared to be asleep. "I think this warm weather made him drowsy, too."

Samuel was tempted to ask why Allen was in the hammock and not working today, but he figured it was none of his business—although he was quite curious.

Esther rose to her feet. "I'll get Marla's shoes now.

Would you like me to bring you a glass of lemonade or some iced tea?"

Samuel shook his head. "I appreciate the offer, but I should get back to the house. The kinner are over at the Zooks', playing with their youngest kinner, so I'm going to use this time by myself to get the laundry and a few other things done."

She nodded with a look of understanding. "I'll be right back."

When Esther went to the house, Samuel seated himself on the blanket where she'd been sitting. He'd only been there a few minutes when Allen's eyes snapped open. As he swung his legs over the hammock and sat up, he looked at Samuel and blinked. "Wh—where's Esther, and how long have you been here?"

"Esther's in the house, getting Marla's sneakers, and I got here a few minutes ago. I'm surprised you didn't hear my horse and buggy pull in," Samuel said. "For that matter, with Esther and me standing just a few feet from the hammock, I'm surprised you didn't wake up sooner."

Allen yawned and stretched his arms over his head. "Guess I was more tired than I thought, 'cause I never heard a thing."

"How's the pain in your back?" Samuel asked, instead of posing the question uppermost on his mind.

"Much better. In fact, I'm feeling so good that I picked some beans from Bonnie's garden. Esther's had a heavy load since Bonnie went to Oregon to take care of her dad, and I figured she could use a little extra help."

"Oh, I see." Samuel leaned back on his elbows and studied Allen. He was a successful businessman, nice looking, and seemed to be real smart about a lot of things. He was sure Allen could have any woman he wanted. The question was—did he want Esther?

"How come you're looking at me so strangely?" Allen asked. "Have I got dirt on my face or something?"

Samuel's face heated. "There's no dirt on your face, but

I do have a question I'd like to ask."

"What's that?"

"Are you interested in Esther?"

Allen tipped his head. "Interested in what way?"

Samuel scrubbed his hand down the side of his face. "Are you planning to court her?"

Allen's jaw dropped, and he nearly jumped out of the hammock. "Now what made you ask something like that?"

"Well, you're always saying what a good cook she is, and you've mentioned a few times that she'd make a good wife. So I figured. . ."

Allen grinned and thumped Samuel's back. "A good wife for you, my friend, not for me. It doesn't take a genius to see that you care for her. Every time I've seen the two of you together, it's written all over your face."

Samuel sat, dumbfounded. He couldn't believe how wrong he'd been. But even if Allen was out of the picture, there was still Ethan Zook to be concerned about. Samuel had noticed Ethan hanging around Esther after their last church service, and he'd seen Ethan talking to Esther several other times, too. Samuel was afraid if he didn't move fast he might lose Esther. But if he moved too fast, he might scare her away. Besides, what would his family back home think about him choosing another wife so soon? It hadn't even been a year since Elsie died.

"So what do you have to say?" Allen thumped Samuel's back again. "Are you in love with Esther or not?"

"I—I do care for her," Samuel admitted, "but I'm afraid it might be too soon for me to make a commitment to another woman. Besides, I don't know if Esther has feelings for me."

"Well, if the look I've seen on her face whenever you're around is any indication, then I'd say she definitely has feelings for you."

"You really think so?"

"If I was a betting man, I'd place a large bet on it. And if I was you, I'd take action soon, because any woman as

247

sweet, pretty, and capable as Esther is bound to turn some fellow's head, and I think that fellow ought to be you."

Samuel pondered that a few seconds, then nodded. "I'll give it some serious thought."

Allen grinned. "Glad to hear it. Well, I have a couple of jobs I need to bid, so I'd better head out. Do think about what I said." He thumped Samuel's back one more time and headed for his truck.

As Allen's rig pulled out, Samuel glanced up at the house, wondering what was taking Esther so long. Just at that moment, she stepped out the door and headed his way, carrying Marla's shoes.

"I'm sorry for taking so long," Esther said, "but I got a phone call from someone wanting to make a reservation at the B&B, and it took awhile to discuss the details."

"No problem. I was visiting with Allen."

She glanced at the spot where Allen's truck had been parked. "I see that he's gone."

"Jah. Said he had some jobs to bid."

"That's right. He mentioned it earlier, before he took his nap." Esther handed Marla's shoes to Samuel. "Guess I'd better get back to work in the garden, or it'll never get done." She smiled. "I'll see you and the kinner at church tomorrow."

Feeling as if he had a wad of sticky chewing gum in his mouth, all Samuel could do was nod. He wanted to ask if Esther would join him and the kids for supper this evening, but the words seemed to be stuck in his mouth.

Esther started walking toward the garden, and he moved in the direction of his horse and buggy. Maybe some other time would be better to ask Esther out.

Samuel had just untied his horse from the hitching rail, when Bonnie's dog darted out of the barn, barking and nipping at the horse's heels. Socks whinnied and kicked up his back feet, just missing the terrier's head. Not to be dissuaded, Cody kept barking and nipping at Socks's tail. Samuel tried to calm the horse, but the more the dog carried on, the more agitated Socks became.

"Cody, come here!" Esther clapped her hands as she raced across the yard. She was almost to the buggy, when Samuel's horse whipped his head around and knocked her to the ground.

Samuel gasped and raced to Esther's side.

Chapter 40

I'm fine, Samuel," Esther said after Samuel had carried her into the house and placed her gently on the sofa.

"Are you sure?" The deep wrinkles in Samuel's forehead let Esther know he was truly concerned.

"Yes, I'm fine. Nothing's broken, and the only thing hurt was my pride when I ended up face-down in the dirt."

He knelt on the floor beside her, and as he pushed a wayward piece of her hair back under the black scarf she wore as a head covering, a pained expression crossed his face. "It scared me real bad when my horse knocked you down. You should have stayed back, Esther. With those crazy animals carrying on like that, you could have been seriously hurt."

Esther was surprised at Samuel's concern and tenderness toward her. Was she imagining it, or was it possible that he cared about her in the same way as she did him? Oh, how she wished it were true. She'd give anything if. . .

"Esther, I—" Samuel looked away, as though unable to make eye contact with her.

"What is it, Samuel? What were you going to say?"

He lifted his gaze and said in a near whisper, "I've been thinking that it might be time for me to start courting again."

"You—you have?" Esther's heart hammered in her chest, and her mouth went dry as she waited for his answer.

"Jah, and I. . .uh. . .am planning to take the kinner out to supper in Hopkinsville this evening, and. . .well, I was wondering if you'd like to go along."

Esther smiled. Even though having the children with them certainly wouldn't be considered a real date, Samuel had asked her to go with them, and she was grateful for that. *He must not have feelings for Bonnie, after all. It really was my silly imagination.*

"I'd be happy to go out to supper with you this evening," she murmured, fighting back tears of joy.

He grinned. "That's good. Jah, that's a very good thing. I think the kinner will be happy about this 'cause they really do like you, Esther."

"I like them, too." *And you as well,* Esther silently added. *In fact, I'm sure I'm in love with you.* Esther knew that Samuel probably wasn't ready to make such a confession yet, but maybe in time he would come to love her, too.

They sat for several seconds, looking at each other and smiling, until loud barking, followed by a shrill—*Yipe! Yipe!*—pulled their gazes apart.

Samuel leaped to his feet and raced out the door.

Esther clambered off the sofa and quickly followed him across the yard, where Cody lay on the ground near Socks, whining.

"Ach! Looks like the dog's been hurt!" Samuel knelt beside Cody and did a quick examination. "I'm almost sure the poor critter has a broken leg. I'm guessin' Socks must have kicked him pretty hard." He grimaced. "Guess I'd better forget about doing any laundry today and call for a driver, 'cause I think we'd better take this poor little dog to the vet's."

─⟋⟍─

Elkton, Kentucky

When Esther and Samuel entered the vet's office, she was surprised to see Suzanne sitting in the waiting room.

"What are you doing here?" she and Suzanne both asked at the same time.

"I brought Samson in to have him neutered yesterday, and I'm here to pick him up." Suzanne looked at Samuel, who was holding Cody. "Isn't that Bonnie's little terrier?"

He gave a nod. "He was nipping at my horse and ended up getting kicked. I'm pretty sure his leg is broken."

"Oh, that's a shame." Suzanne looked at Esther. "Does Bonnie know about this?"

Esther shook her head. "I'll call her once I know something definite."

Samuel walked up to the receptionist's desk, and after she told him to bring the dog back to the examining room, he turned to Esther and said, "Why don't you wait here and visit with Suzanne while I take Cody in?"

"Okay." Esther was thankful Samuel was willing to do that, because she didn't relish the idea of watching while the doctor examined Cody. It hurt her to see anyone in pain—even an animal.

Suzanne motioned to the chair beside her. "Why don't you take a seat?"

Once Esther was seated, she told Suzanne how she'd been knocked to the ground by Samuel's horse and how Samuel had carried her into the house. "He had such a look of concern on his face," she said. "He even invited me to join him and his kinner for supper in Hopkinsville this evening."

"I knew it!" Suzanne's face broke into a wide smile. "And I'll have to say this—it's about time."

"You knew Samuel was going to invite me to join them for supper?"

"No, but I knew he'd get around to inviting you somewhere soon."

"How'd you know that?"

"I've seen the way Samuel looks at you whenever he thinks you're not looking. He's come to care for you,

Esther. I'm sure of it." Suzanne squeezed Esther's hand. "I think the two of you are perfect for each other, and I believe Samuel realizes that, too."

"I hope you're right," Esther said, "but I guess I won't really know unless he asks me to go someplace with him again." It was strange, but she'd never seen Samuel look at her in a special way. Usually when he was around, he looked the other way. But he had invited her out and seemed real happy about it, so maybe he did have strong feelings for her.

"Why wait for Samuel to ask you to go someplace else? Why don't you invite Samuel and the kinner over to the B&B for supper sometime soon?"

"I had them over not long ago when it rained and we couldn't go on a picnic, but if I ask them again, Samuel might think I'm being pushy, and I sure don't want that."

"I doubt that he would think that. Besides, what man in his right mind would turn down one of your delicious meals?"

"So you think I should try to win Samuel's heart with my cooking?"

"I think you've already won his heart." Suzanne chuckled. "But a little taste of your cooking from time to time wouldn't hurt either."

"Do you think Samuel's really ready to start courting again?" Esther asked, needing some reassurance. "I mean, do you think his heart has healed enough after losing his wife that he might actually consider marriage again?"

"I believe it has, but from what I know of Samuel, I don't think he'll rush into anything."

"No, and I wouldn't want him to."

"I have some news of my own," Suzanne said. "Titus and I have decided on the second Thursday in October as the date we'll get married."

"That's *wunderbaar*. Do both of your families know?"

"Mine know, and Titus was supposed to call his folks and give them the news this morning." Suzanne touched

Esther's arm. "I'd like you to be one of my attendants at the wedding."

Esther smiled and nodded. "I'd be honored."

"Maybe by next fall it'll be you and Samuel getting married," Suzanne said, gently nudging Esther's arm.

Before Esther could reply, Samuel entered the waiting room, this time without Cody.

"What'd the doctor say?" Esther asked, rising from her seat.

"Said the dog's leg is definitely broken, and it's a bad break, so he'll have to do surgery on it." Samuel slowly shook his head. "Guess Cody will have to stay here at the vet's for a few days."

Esther frowned. "Oh dear. I sure dread telling Bonnie this news."

—◊◊◊—

Paradise, Pennsylvania

"How are things going with you and Hannah these days?" Fannie asked Timothy when he and Abraham took a break from the fields and came to the house for lunch.

"They're a little better." Timothy reached for another piece of bread and slathered it with peanut butter. "I've been trying to do more things to help Hannah at home, and I've taken her and Mindy on a couple of picnics so far this summer."

"Is she still going over to her mamm's every day?" Abraham questioned.

"Nope. She goes over about once a week, and I'm okay with that."

Fannie smiled. "I'm glad to hear it."

Timothy nodded. "I just hope it lasts."

"As long as you keep working on your marriage, I'm sure things will only get better," Fannie said. "Oh, and by the way, while you two were out working in the fields this morning, I checked our phone messages, and there was one from Titus."

"What's new with him?" Abraham asked as he reached for the platter full of lunchmeat and cheese.

"He and Suzanne have set a date for their wedding. It'll be on the second Thursday of October."

"Did you tell him we'd all be there to witness their marriage?" Timothy asked.

She nodded. "I can't wait to see Titus again as well as Samuel and his kinner."

"Same here," Timothy agreed. "It'll not only be good to see everyone, but I'm anxious to see what Kentucky's like."

Fannie frowned. "I didn't see anything special about it when we were there last year."

Abraham bumped her arm with his elbow. "But Titus and Samuel seem to like Kentucky, so maybe they see something that you might have missed."

"Jah, maybe so." With a shiver of apprehension, Fannie sent up a silent prayer: *I know Timothy said he'd never move because of Hannah, but please, Lord, don't let him change his mind and take his family from here.*

CHAPTER 41

Pembroke, Kentucky

Esther hummed as she cleaned up the kitchen. Things were going so well in her life these days, she felt like pinching herself. During the last few weeks, she'd gone out to supper with Samuel and his children in Hopkinsville, they'd all gone fishing together twice, and she'd shared another picnic supper with Samuel and the children—this time at the pond. Tonight, Samuel and the children would be coming to the B&B for supper again, and she could hardly wait. While Samuel hadn't actually said he loved her, or was thinking of getting married again, the time they'd spent together so far had been quite pleasant, and he'd been very attentive to her needs. The children, of course, seemed to enjoy having Esther around, so she was fairly certain they would accept the idea of her marrying their father, should Samuel ever propose.

I shouldn't get my hopes up, Esther thought as she grabbed a sponge and began wiping the table. *As much as I desire to become Samuel's wife and the mother of his children, it might never happen. And if that's how it goes, then as much as it will hurt, I'll need to accept it as God's will.*

As she rinsed the sponge, Esther turned her thoughts to other things. Bonnie had called last night, saying her father was much better and that she'd be returning to Kentucky. In fact, her plane would arrive in Nashville late this afternoon, and she'd contacted Allen about picking her up.

If they get here in time for supper, we'd All ____ ould

lik ____ nce

the ____ en-

tio ____ so

she ____ by

aga

her ____ see

Eth

____ are

ratt ____ it's

gon

dow ____ ol ____ nd

stick

____ as

he s ____ by

is. . . ____ Walmart store in Hopkinsville

this afternoon and wondered if you'd like to go along."
He shuffled his feet a few more times. "Thought maybe after we're done shoppin' we could eat supper at whichever restaurant you choose."

"I appreciate your asking," Esther said, "but I have other plans for this evening."

Ethan dropped his gaze to the porch. "Sorry to hear that. I was hopin' you'd be free to go with me."

"Maybe some other time," Esther said, although she didn't know why. She had no interest in going anywhere with Ethan, and since it appeared that she and Samuel were courting, she probably should have told Ethan that she'd been seeing Samuel instead of letting him believe she might be available to go out with him some other time. But if she'd told him that, he may have repeated it to someone else, and if Samuel heard it and didn't really have courting on his mind, it could be quite embarrassing—for both her and Samuel.

Esther was about to tell Ethan good-bye, when he

leaned close to the door and sniffed deeply. "Have ya done any baking lately? I sure enjoyed that banana bread you gave my mamm awhile back." He smacked his lips noisily. "That was real tasty and moist."

Esther forced a smile. "I'm glad you liked it, but I haven't made any more banana bread since I gave the loaf to your mamm. The only baking I've done is just basic bread and some cinnamon rolls for the guests who've stayed here at the bed-and-breakfast."

Ethan's rather plain, hazel-colored eyes brightened, and he patted his portly stomach. "You wouldn't happen to have any cinnamon rolls now, would ya? I'm kinda partial to those, too."

She shook her head, trying her best not to let her annoyance show. She just wished Ethan would go. "The last of the cinnamon rolls were eaten by the B&B guests who were here earlier in the week. If you're really hungry for cinnamon rolls, I'm sure they probably have some at the bakeshop in our area."

"I might stop by there on my way home." For several seconds, Ethan stared intently at Esther, which made her squirm. Then he finally said, "Guess I'd better let you get back to whatever it was you were doin'."

She smiled. "I do have several chores I need to get done yet this morning. Bonnie will be back later today, and I want to have everything in good shape before she arrives."

"Jah, okay then." He turned and started down the stairs. When he reached the bottom step, he turned and said, "The next time I go to Hopkinsville, I'll let ya know."

Esther gave a forced smile and quickly stepped into the house. She had a hunch that Ethan's interest in her had more to do with her cooking skills than him enjoying her company. If there was one thing everyone in their community knew, it was that Ethan Zook liked to eat.

—⁓—

Nashville, Tennessee

"How was your flight?" Allen asked as he put Bonnie's luggage in the back of his truck.

"It went well. We didn't have much turbulence, and all my connections were on time." She smiled at him. "I really appreciate your coming to get me. I could have driven my own car here when I flew out to Portland, but not knowing how long I'd be gone, I didn't want to pay a huge parking fee if I ended up staying very long, which is exactly what happened."

"Picking you up was no problem at all. In fact, I was glad to do it," he said as she stepped into the passenger's side of his truck.

"So how's your dad doing?" he asked as he slid in behind the steering wheel.

"Much better. He's able to manage on his own now and will soon be back at work, I expect."

"I'm not sure if you ever said what he does for a living."

"He's the manager of a bank in Portland."

"Ah, I see. A big-shot, huh?"

She shook her head. "He's a pretty common guy. He's always had a good business head though. Kind of like you."

"What makes you think I've got a head for business?"

"I doubt you'd be a successful general contractor if you didn't."

Allen smiled and turned on the ignition. "Well, I do my best."

When they headed down the road a few minutes later, Allen looked over at Bonnie and smiled. "It's sure good to have you back. We've all missed you."

"I missed everyone, too." Bonnie fiddled with the handles on her purse, feeling suddenly uncomfortable. The tender expression she saw on Allen's face made her wonder if he might have missed her more than she knew. Had he come to care for her in a special way? A part of her wanted him to care, but there was the cautious part that said she must remember to keep her feelings to herself and put a safe distance between her and Allen so she wouldn't become emotionally attached to him. She'd allowed herself to fall in love once and had paid a huge price for it. Since then, she'd consoled herself with the fact that marriage wasn't what it was cracked up to be anyhow. Most married couples she knew argued all the time, the way her parents had done. Bonnie's friend Shirley, with whom she'd gone to high school, had recently been through a nasty divorce after a stormy marriage with a man who had promised to love and cherish her all the days of his life. So much for happily ever after!

When Bonnie lived in Portland, she'd focused on her job. Now she had the bed-and-breakfast to keep her occupied, so she hoped Allen didn't have any ideas of taking their friendship to the next level. She'd have to keep a handle on things—that was for sure.

CHAPTER 42

Pembroke, Kentucky

I t's nice to have you back," Esther said to Bonnie as they sat at the supper table with Allen, Samuel, and the children.

"It's sure good to be home." Bonnie smiled. "And I really do think of this as my home now."

"It must have been hard for you to leave your dad," Samuel said.

"Yes, it was, but he understands now that I'd rather live here, and he's promised to come visit me sometime—maybe this Christmas."

"I'm happy to hear that," Esther said. "I've been praying your dad would change his mind about coming to visit you."

"Dad and I talked about a lot of things while I was there, and I think everything will be better between us from now on."

"That's good to hear." Esther was anxious to hear more about Bonnie's visit with her dad but figured now wasn't the time to discuss it—not with Allen, Samuel, and his children sitting here.

"This fried chicken is sure good," Samuel said as he took another drumstick.

Esther smiled. "Danki, Samuel."

"This ain't one of them green-egg layin' chickens is it?" Leon asked with a wide-eyed expression.

Esther shook her head. "There's no need to worry. The

chicken I fixed is a fresh fryer I bought from one of our neighbors."

Leon's face relaxed. "That's good to know. Wouldn't feel right 'bout eatin' one of your hens."

"The chickens out there in the coop aren't mine," Esther said. "They belong to Bonnie."

"I knew that. Just seems like they're yours since you've been takin' care of Bonnie's place all these weeks."

Samuel tapped Leon's arm. "Why don't you eat now and quit talking so much?"

"Okay." Leon spooned some potato salad onto his plate and took a big bite. "Umm... This is sure tasty, Esther. You're a real good cook."

She smiled. "Danki, Leon. I'm glad you're enjoying the meal."

"I think we're all enjoying it," Allen said, wiping his mouth with a napkin. "Eating a home-cooked meal like this makes a man wish he had a wife." He glanced over at Bonnie, but she seemed intent on eating the biscuit she'd just picked up, and Esther couldn't help but notice that Bonnie's cheeks had turned a bright pink color.

"How's Cody doin'?" Marla asked, looking at Esther.

"He's getting along pretty well with his cast," Esther replied. She looked at Bonnie. "I'm glad you took it so well when I told you about his broken leg."

Bonnie shrugged. "I knew it was an accident, and it wouldn't have happened if the little troublemaker hadn't been bothering Samuel's horse. Hopefully, Cody learned a good lesson and won't chase after anyone's horse again."

"Some horses spook easier than others, especially when they're around dogs," Samuel said. "I'm afraid Socks is one of those horses that don't care much for dogs. He gets spooky around Lucky, too. Has ever since the dog was a pup and started barkin' at him."

"You're not gonna get rid of Lucky, are ya, Daadi?" Penny spoke up.

"'Course not," Samuel said. "Like it or not, the mutt's

part of our family, so he's here to stay."

The children looked relieved and went back to eating without another word.

"Did you hear that my brother's getting married in October?" Samuel asked Allen.

"Yes, Titus told me the other day when I stopped by the woodshop to see if they could make the cabinets and doors for a new house I'll be starting to work on soon."

"Will you attend Titus and Suzanne's wedding?" Esther asked.

Allen nodded eagerly. "It'll be my first Amish wedding, and I wouldn't miss it for the world." He looked at Bonnie and smiled. "I'll make sure you get an invitation, too, because I'm sure you'd enjoy seeing what an Amish wedding is like as much as I would."

"That would be interesting, all right," Bonnie said. "I hear it's a lot different from our English weddings."

"An Amish wedding is similar to the regular church services we hold every other week," Esther said. "Of course, in our wedding services, the bride and groom say their vows in front of the bishop, and the message that's preached is about marriage."

"How long does the service usually last?" Bonnie questioned.

"About three hours," Esther replied.

Allen's eyes widened as he released a shrill whistle. "Wow, that's a really long service. Most English weddings and church services don't last much more than an hour, and even then, some people complain about having to sit that long."

"You're right about that," Bonnie agreed. "It seems that some folks only want to give one hour of their time every week."

Esther thought about that for a while. She couldn't imagine anyone complaining about how long they had to be in church. She saw going to church as a privilege, and it was a Christian's duty. She'd never minded their three-hour services one bit.

They continued to visit about other things until the meal was over, and then the children scampered from the room and rushed outside to play.

"Why don't you and Esther go out and sit on the porch?" Allen said to Samuel. "Think I'll stay in here and help Bonnie with the dishes."

"Oh no, I should help her do the dishes," Esther was quick to say. "Allen, why don't you and Samuel go outside and visit?"

"No, Esther, I insist that you go outside," Bonnie said. "After all, you cooked this wonderful meal for us."

"But you just got home from a long flight," Esther argued.

"Well, I don't care who goes outside." Allen's chair scraped the floor as he pushed it away from the table and stood. "I'm going to be the one to help with the dishes." He grabbed his plate and silverware and quickly put them in the sink.

Samuel looked at Esther and said, "It's probably much cooler outside. Should we go sit on the porch swing?"

The thought of sitting on the swing beside Samuel was inviting, so Esther smiled and said, "That'd be real nice." After she'd cleared her own dishes, she followed Samuel out the door.

—⁓—

"Did Esther tell you that she and Samuel have started courting?" Allen asked Bonnie as he filled the sink with warm water.

Bonnie's mouth opened in surprise. "She never said a word; although I haven't been home long enough for her to say a whole lot to me yet. When did they start courting?"

"A few weeks ago. Samuel took Esther out for supper with him and the kids one evening, and I understand they all went fishing and also on a picnic together."

Bonnie handed Allen several dirty plates. "I'd hardly

call them going somewhere with Samuel's kids courting."

"Well, it's a start." Allen set the plates in the sink and snapped his fingers. "Say, I've got an idea!"

"What's that?"

"Why don't the two of us go on a double date with Samuel and Esther?"

Bonnie's hands became sweaty, and she quickly set the two glasses she'd picked up off the table onto the counter, fearful they might slip from her hands. "Wh–what kind of a double date?"

"How about if we four go to the Jefferson Davis Monument this Saturday? You haven't seen it yet, have you?"

Bonnie shook her head. "No, but. . ."

"Maybe Suzanne or even her mother would watch Samuel's kids for a few hours while we're on our double date."

Bonnie shifted uneasily. "Oh, I don't know. . ."

"Come on, Bonnie, please say you'll go. I'm sure Samuel wouldn't think to take Esther there by himself, and it'll be a lot of fun for all of us."

Bonnie was tempted to use the B&B as an excuse not to go, but she didn't have any guests scheduled to come in until the middle of next week. And since this was a double date and she wouldn't be alone with Allen, she guessed it would be okay.

"Oh, all right," she finally agreed. Secretly, she wished more than anything that she could allow herself to have some fun and not feel like she had to protect herself from more hurt. After all, it was just one date, and she was only going for Esther's sake.

CHAPTER 43

Fairview, Kentucky

Wow, would you look at that!" Samuel said in amazement as Allen pulled his truck into the parking lot at the Jefferson Davis Monument. "It looks even bigger up close than it does from a distance."

Allen grinned. "Wait until you go up inside and see the view from there. It's just amazing."

Esther's heart started to pound. She remembered how she'd come here with Titus shortly after he'd moved to Kentucky and had refused to go up in the monument with him because of her fear of heights. Titus had been nice about it, but she'd seen the look of disappointment on his face, and it had made her feel guilty.

What had she been thinking, agreeing to come here today? Surely Samuel, and probably the others, would expect her to go up in the monument, too.

I climbed up the ladder to rescue Penny when she was stuck in that tree awhile back, she reminded herself. *At least this time I'll be inside the safety of a building. Maybe if I don't look down I'll be okay.*

"What's wrong, Esther? You look upset," Bonnie said after they'd climbed out of the truck.

"I. . .uh. . . It's nothing. I'm fine," Esther said with a shake of her head, not wanting to reveal how bad her phobia was.

"Are you sure you want to do this?" Allen asked. "I remember the last time we came here you stayed below."

"I know I did, but I—I think I can do it this time." Esther really wasn't sure she could do it, but she had to try.

"Let's get our tickets bought and go up inside right away." Allen pointed to the visitor's center, which was where they'd need to go for tickets. "I can't wait to show everyone the great view from up there."

"This is going to be fun," Samuel said as he walked beside Esther. "Don't think I've ever been in a building that tall."

Esther shivered. Was it too late to say no? Would Samuel be terribly disappointed if she waited on a bench below while he and the others went up? She didn't want to do anything that might ruin her chances with Samuel, so she wouldn't let on how fearful she felt and was determined this time to go up in that building.

"How high did you say this building is?" Samuel asked their guide as they entered the elevator that would take them to the viewing area.

"The structure is 351 feet tall, and it was made from solid Kentucky limestone," the young man said.

"It was built in 1917. Isn't that right?" Allen asked.

"That's when it was started—built in honor of Jefferson Davis, the famous Kentuckian born June 3, 1808, right here on this site," the guide said with a nod. "But it wasn't completed right away. You see, steam was the principle source of power back then, and so the workers used steam engines to power their equipment, including steam-powered drills. A quarry was dug on the south end of the park site, and the stone was crushed in mixing cement. By the fall of 1918, the monument had reached a height of 175 feet. But then construction had to be stopped, due to rationing of building materials during World War I. Work on the monument resumed in January 1922, and it was completed in 1924. Of course, the monument has undergone major renovations since then," the guide added.

Samuel felt like his head was swimming with all that historical information. It was interesting to hear how the monument came about though.

When they stepped off the elevator and moved toward the viewing windows, Samuel noticed that Esther held back.

"Come on," he coaxed. "Shall we take a look?"

When she didn't budge, he took her hand. "Don't you want to see the view below?"

"Umm. . .sure. I guess so."

Looking none too thrilled about the idea, Esther let Samuel lead her to one of the viewing windows, where Allen and Bonnie already stood with their guide.

"The view from up here is breathtaking," Bonnie said. "I've been in plenty of tall buildings in downtown Portland, but to me, none of them had a view as nice as this. Just look at all those pretty trees!"

Esther clung so tightly to Samuel's hand that her fingernails dug into his skin. She was clearly not comfortable being up here.

"Are you okay?" he asked, leaning close to her ear.

"I—I'm fine. Just a little dizzy is all." She edged away from the window and leaned tightly against the back wall.

"I think we ought to go down now," Samuel said to their guide. "Esther's not feeling well."

The guide looked at Allen and Bonnie. "If you two aren't done looking yet, you can ride down in the elevator with us, and then I'll bring you back up. It's against the rules for me to leave you up here alone."

"No, that's okay. I've seen enough." Allen looked at Bonnie. "How about you?"

"I don't need to come back either," she said, as though sensing Esther's anxiety.

When they stepped into the elevator and started their descent, Samuel couldn't help but notice the look of relief on Esther's pale-looking face.

the HEALING

"Are you okay?" he asked when they stepped off the elevator.

She gave a quick nod. "I'm fine now. Just needed some fresh air."

"It was kind of stuffy up there," Bonnie said. "Of course, we're having another hot, humid day."

"Should we go to the gift shop and get an ice-cream bar?" Allen suggested. "Maybe something cold and sweet would perk us all up."

"That sounds nice," Esther said. She'd let go of Samuel's hand and was walking with a relaxed stride toward the gift shop.

Samuel smiled to himself. He enjoyed being with Esther and hoped they could do something fun like this again soon.

CHAPTER 44

Pembroke, Kentucky

As Esther sat on a blanket near the pond, holding Jared in her lap, a feeling of contentment came over her, like a warm, cozy quilt. She glanced at Suzanne, who sat beside her, and smiled. "It's a beautiful day, isn't it? Not so hot for a change."

Suzanne smiled. "Jah. It's a reminder that fall's not far off. You can really feel and see the beauty of God's creation on a day like this." She motioned to Samuel and Titus, sitting on the ground not far away with their fishing lines cast into the pond. "It's good that they both have this Saturday off and can spend some time together doing something they both like."

"You're right about them both liking to fish," Esther agreed. "From the eager expression I saw on Leon's face when his daed baited his hook, I'd say he likes to fish equally well."

"Everyone seems quite happy today." Suzanne motioned to Marla and Penny, who were giggling and taking turns throwing a stick for Lucky to fetch.

Esther leaned back on her elbows and sighed. "I can't believe Samuel and I are actually courting."

"Speaking of courting, how was your visit to the Jefferson Davis Monument a couple of weeks ago?"

"It was okay. I forced myself to go up inside, but I got dizzy and was glad that we didn't stay there long."

"Does Samuel know about your fear of heights?" Suzanne questioned.

"I think he does because Marla mentioned it to him that day when I rescued Penny from the tree. I made myself go up in the monument because I didn't want Samuel to think I'm afraid of every little thing, or he might stop courting me the way Titus did."

Suzanne's brows puckered. "I thought when you and Titus stopped courting it was a mutual agreement. You said you weren't seriously interested in him."

Feeling the need to reassure her friend, Esther shook her head and said, "I knew after we'd gone a few places together that we weren't meant for each other, but I think Titus knew it the day I wouldn't go up into the monument with him."

"Well, if Samuel really cares for you, I don't think he'll stop courting you because you're afraid of heights."

Esther shrugged. "Maybe not, but I didn't want to disappoint him by waiting below on a bench."

Suzanne squeezed Esther's arm. "I think it was good for you to meet your fear head-on. Maybe each time you force yourself to go somewhere that's up high, your fear will lessen."

"Maybe so, but I hope I'm not faced with challenges like the monument too often." Esther placed Jared on the blanket. The little guy had fallen asleep and was getting heavy in her lap. "Are you excited about your wedding?" she asked Suzanne.

Suzanne bobbed her head. "I can't believe it's only two months away. Summer has gone by so quickly, and there's so much to do yet before the wedding."

"You've finished sewing your dress though, haven't you?"

"Jah, but lots of other things need to be done—especially during the weeks right before the wedding."

"I'll be happy to help with anything you need," Esther offered.

"That's nice of you, but between watching Samuel's kinner and helping Bonnie at the B&B, you've got your hands full."

"I don't work at the B&B when we don't have guests, and most Saturdays, Samuel doesn't work, so that gives me some time to do other things."

"But don't you want to keep your Saturdays free for times like this, when you can be with Samuel doing something fun?"

"I do enjoy being with him, but we're not together every Saturday, and since you're my good friend and I'm going to be one of your attendants, I want to help with the wedding preparations."

The sunlight glistened in Suzanne's auburn hair as she smiled and said, "I appreciate that, and when it's time to start cleaning before our guests arrive, your help will be needed and appreciated."

"Do you know how many of Titus's family members will be coming?"

"I'm not sure, but I know his folks and his twin brother will be coming, because Titus talked to them both earlier this week. While Titus wants all his brothers and sisters and their families to come, he's a little worried about where they'll stay, because his place only has three bedrooms."

"Some of them will no doubt stay with Samuel. My folks' house is big enough to put up several people."

"Even so, if everyone who receives an invitation comes, we'll need to look for more places for them to stay."

"What about the B&B? I'm sure Bonnie would give them a discount on any of her rooms. Would you like me to speak to her about it?"

"That's a good idea. Let us know what she says, and then Titus can talk to his folks about it so they can spread the word." Suzanne nudged Esther and motioned toward the pond. "Looks like Samuel's heading this way. Maybe he's caught his limit of fish for the day."

—◆◆◆—

"Think I've done enough fishing for today," Samuel said, kneeling on the grass in front of Esther. "How would you like to go for a walk in the woods with me? If we're lucky, we might see some interesting wildlife along the way."

Esther motioned toward sleeping Jared. "If we all go for a walk, we'll have to disturb this little guy."

"I wasn't figuring on taking the kinner," Samuel said. "Thought it could be just you and me."

"Oh, I see." A blotch of red erupted on Esther's cheeks, but he was glad when she rose to her feet and didn't say no.

"Would you mind keeping an eye on the kinner for me?" he asked Suzanne. "I don't think we'll be gone too long."

"I don't mind one bit. After all, in just two more months, these sweet kinner will be my nieces and nephews." Suzanne smiled up at Samuel. "You and Esther enjoy your walk, and don't feel like you have to hurry back. Take your time, because we'll be fine here."

"I appreciate that. Oh, and make sure Lucky doesn't follow us. I don't want him scaring off any wildlife we might see." Samuel bent down and grabbed a bottle of water and a bag of pretzels from the box of snacks they'd brought along. "In case we get hungry or thirsty," he said, smiling at Esther.

She returned his smile and gave a little nod.

The birds chirped happily in the trees overhead as Samuel and Esther started walking along the trail near the water.

When they stepped into a clearing a short time later, Samuel pointed to a tall wooden structure that had been built for hunters to sit and watch for deer. "I'll bet if we climbed up there, we'd have a good vantage point and could keep an eye out for deer or any other critters, and they won't even know we're here."

Esther's eyes widened as she halted her steps. "You. . . you want me to climb up there?"

He gave a nod.

"How do you know that ladder's safe to climb? It looks pretty old."

"Esther, are you scared?"

"A little," she admitted.

"You climbed the ladder at the B&B to get Penny down from a tree."

"That was different. Penny's life was at stake, and the ladder I used was in good shape."

"I really don't think the tree stand's that old," Samuel said, "but I'll go up first and test the ladder. If I don't fall and break my neck, I'll come back and get you."

She swatted his arm playfully. "That's nothing to kid about, Samuel."

"Sorry." Samuel gave Esther's arm a reassuring squeeze and handed her the bag of pretzels and bottle of water. "I'll be fine. You'll see."

Slowly and carefully, Samuel ascended the ladder until he was standing inside the tree stand. He glanced down and saw Esther looking up at him. "The ladder's sturdy," he called, "and the view from here is really good. I'm coming back down to get you."

Samuel climbed down the ladder, took the water and pretzels from Esther, and tucked them both under one arm. "You go first, and I'll be right behind you," he said.

She hesitated but finally started up the ladder. Samuel followed, guiding her verbally with each step. When she reached the top, she drew in a sharp breath. "Ach, my! It's higher than I thought it would be."

"It's not that high," Samuel said, joining her on the wooden platform. "Compared to the Jefferson Davis Monument, this is nothing."

She inched away from the edge and closer to Samuel. "It is to me. I'm afraid of anyplace that's high up and have been since I was a kinner."

Samuel set the pretzels and water on the wooden floor and slipped his arms around Esther's waist. "You're safe with me, so don't be afraid," he murmured, leaning his head close to her ear. He felt her relax against him and was confident that her fear was abating.

They stood like that for several minutes, until Samuel spotted two doe nibbling on the leaves of some brush. "Look there," he whispered. "Do you see the deer?"

"Jah. They're beautiful, aren't they?"

"They sure are." *But not near as beautiful as you,* he thought.

Samuel kept his arms around Esther's waist as they continued to watch the deer. Then, when he was sure Esther was fully relaxed, he turned her to face him. "If you're afraid of heights, how come you went to the top of the monument with us that day?"

"I thought it would be good for me to face my fear, and I didn't want to disappoint you."

"It wouldn't have, Esther. I would have understood." He gave her a reassuring squeeze. "Are you afraid right now?"

"I was at first, but not anymore."

As Samuel enjoyed the quiet of the moment, he felt that with Esther by his side, he was right where he wanted to be. Giving in to his impulse to kiss her, he slowly lowered his head. Their lips were almost touching when— *Woof! Woof! Woof!*—Lucky bounded out of the woods and chased away the deer.

"Stupid *hund,*" Samuel muttered. "I shoulda left him at home. Guess I'd better go get him or he'll be running through the woods chasin' some poor animal for the rest of the day."

With a feeling of regret, Samuel climbed down the ladder, guiding Esther's footsteps as she followed. Maybe it was too soon for him to be kissing her anyway. He didn't want her to think he was too forward. If he could resist the temptation, he'd wait until they'd been courting longer to try and kiss her again. Until that day came, he thought it might be best if he made sure they were never alone.

CHAPTER 45

Paradise, Pennsylvania

You'd better hurry and start packing if we're gonna be ready to leave on time in the morning," Timothy said to Hannah after he'd put his own clothes into a suitcase. They'd hired four drivers with big, fifteen-passenger vans to transport the more than fifty relatives that would be going to Kentucky for Titus and Suzanne's wedding. Anxious to see Titus and Samuel, as well as the lay of the land in Kentucky, Timothy could hardly wait to get there.

"I've decided not to go," Hannah said, as she removed the pins from her hair and picked up the brush from her dresser.

Timothy whirled around to face her. "Just when did you decide that?"

"This morning when I found out that my mamm hurt her ankle."

"I'm sorry about that, but it's only a sprain, so I don't see why that should keep you from going to the wedding."

"My mamm's in a lot of pain, and she can barely put any weight on her leg, so she's going to need some help for the next several days."

Timothy ground his teeth together. Not this again. Was Hannah looking for an excuse not to go to the wedding, or had she once more latched on to her mother's apron strings?

"Look," Timothy said, trying to keep from raising his voice, "it's not like you're the only person who can help your mamm. She can call on one of her daughters-in-law if she really needs some help."

Hannah shook her long, silky brown tresses. "My brother's wives are all busy caring for their kinner. As you well know, Mahon and Betsy have five kinner, all under the age of ten, and my brother Paul and his wife, Sarah, have four kinner, two of them still in diapers. And of course my other brothers, Stephen and Clarence, live in New York, so their wives aren't available to help."

"Okay, so none of them are free to give your mamm a hand, but she has friends in our community. I'm sure she could ask one of them to help out."

Hannah shrugged. "Maybe they could, but Mom wants me. We do many things alike, so she'll know whatever I do for her is done right."

Timothy grunted. "If you want my opinion, your mamm's too picky about things, and she shouldn't expect you to stay home from my bruder's wedding to take care of her when she could ask one of her friends."

Hannah frowned as she set her brush down and turned to face him directly. "Are you forbidding me to stay here and help my mamm? Are you going to force me to go to the wedding with you, even though you know I won't have a good time because I'd be worried about Mom the whole time we're gone?"

Timothy shook his head. "I'm not saying that at all. I just think. . ." He lifted his hands in defeat. "All right then, you can stay home and take care of your mamm, and I'll take our *dochder* to Kentucky with me."

Hannah shook her head vigorously. "Mindy needs to be here with me."

"But you'll be busy helping your mamm, and Mindy will be underfoot."

"No she won't. I'll take plenty of things to keep her busy while I'm at Mom and Dad's house." Hannah's face softened as she placed her hand on Timothy's shoulder. "You know how frustrated you become whenever Mindy cries and you can't get her to settle down. I'm usually the only one who can make her stop crying and go to sleep."

"That's true." Timothy hated to give in, but Hannah was right—it would be hard for him to handle Mindy on his own. She'd probably wake up during the night, realize that her mother wasn't there, and start howling. Most likely, he'd be up all night trying to settle her down.

"Okay," he finally conceded. "You and Mindy can stay home, and I'll go to the wedding alone, but I really feel like you will be hurting Titus' and Suzanne's feelings by not showing up at their wedding."

"You won't be alone," Hannah said sweetly. "You'll have your mamm, your daed, and all the rest of your family there with you, and I doubt Suzanne and Titus will even miss me."

"I think they will, and it sure won't be the same for me without my fraa and dochder," he muttered as he closed the lid on his suitcase and placed it on the floor.

Hannah wrapped her arms around his waist and rested her head on his shoulder. "Mindy and I will miss you, too, but you'll only be gone a few days, and then we'll be together again."

That's right. We'll be together until your mamm needs you for something else, Timothy thought with regret. *And just when I began to believe things were going better between us.*

—⁂—

Pembroke, Kentucky

"I'm glad it's working out that some of Titus's family can stay here at the bed-and-breakfast," Esther said to Bonnie as they sat in the living room, enjoying warm apple cider before they went to bed.

Bonnie smiled. "Since I knew in plenty of time how many were coming and needed a place to stay, I was able to make sure I didn't schedule any other guests during the

the HEALING

time Titus's family will be here."

Esther finished her cider and set the cup on the coffee table in front of the sofa. "When I spoke to Suzanne the other day, she said Titus is really excited about seeing all his family again, and of course, Suzanne is, too. She met his parents when they came to Kentucky once, but the rest of his family she only met briefly when she went with Titus to attend the funeral for Samuel's wife. So hopefully, she'll get to know them all a little better while they're here."

"Allen told me about Samuel and Titus's brother Zach having been kidnapped when Samuel was a child," Bonnie said. "That was such an incredible story."

Esther nodded soberly. "Since Zach wasn't reunited with his family until he was twenty-one, they all suffered a good deal during those years he was missing."

Bonnie stared at the flickering flames in the fireplace across the room. Reflecting on Samuel's family being reunited with their long-lost son made her think of the baby girl she'd given birth to and never gotten to know. Where was her daughter now? Was she happy? Had she grown up in a good home? On more than one occasion, Bonnie had been tempted to search for the child, but she'd never followed through with the idea. She didn't want to come between the child and her adoptive parents, and she wasn't sure she could face her daughter and explain the circumstances of her conception or the reason she'd put the child up for adoption. No, she'd decided sometime ago to leave the matter alone. It was best for her and the child, who would now be a teenager.

Bonnie yawned and rose from her seat. "I don't know about you, but I'm tired and ready for bed."

"Guess I should head on out to the guest house." Esther stood, too. "It's been nice sitting here in the quiet, because in the next few days this old house will be filled with people who will probably be chattering away."

Bonnie patted Esther's arm. "I'm sure you're looking forward to meeting all of Samuel's family, because with the way things are going between you and Samuel, I'd say by this time next year, they may be your family, too."

Esther's eyes twinkled as she gave Bonnie a hopeful-looking smile. "I don't want to hope too hard for something that might never happen, but marrying Samuel would surely be an answer to my prayers."

CHAPTER 46

I t's so good to see you," Titus's mother said when she stepped out of the first van that had pulled in and hugged her son.

"It's good to see you, too, Mom." Titus hugged his father next and then went down the line, hugging his sister, Abby; her husband, Matthew; and their five children. Last, but not least, he grabbed his twin brother and gave him a big bear hug.

"Where's your family?" Titus asked Timothy. "Did Hannah and Mindy ride in one of the other vans?"

Timothy's eyes darkened as he shook his head. "Hannah's mamm sprained her ankle, so Hannah thought she had to stay behind and take care of her."

"Oh, that's too bad." Titus had a hunch Hannah's mother could have managed on her own, and from the look of irritation he saw on Timothy's face, he was pretty sure Hannah may have used her mother's sprained ankle as an excuse not to come. But why? What was so terrible about Kentucky that she didn't want to come here? Didn't Hannah want to get better acquainted with her new sister-in-law, or was she afraid that if she came to Kentucky, Timothy might decide he liked it here well enough to move? Poor Timothy must feel like a part of him was missing with his wife and daughter back in Pennsylvania rather than here with him, which is where they belonged.

The other three vans pulled in, so Titus pushed his thoughts aside and went to greet the rest of his family. All his brothers and sisters and their children had come for the wedding. If Hannah and Mindy had come, their whole family would be here, and it would be like a big family reunion.

"So now that we're all here, tell us where we're going to stay," Titus's mother said.

He motioned to his double-wide manufactured home. "Well, you and Dad are welcome to stay here with me, but I thought you might rather stay with Samuel, since I'm sure you're anxious to spend some time with your *kinskinner*."

"I would enjoy being close to the grandchildren," Mom said with a nod. "Maybe Mary Ann, Abner, and their four kinner can stay here with you. Then your daed, me, Naomi, Caleb, and their kinner can stay with Samuel."

"That's fine, and if Timothy doesn't mind sleeping on the sofa, I've got room for him to stay here, too," Titus said. "The house Samuel's renting is big, so I'm pretty sure he'll be able to put up several of our family members there. Some of the cousins can share a room with Samuel's girls and some with the boys."

"Where will the rest of us stay?" Titus's sister Nancy asked after she'd given Titus a hug.

"We're friends with a young woman who runs a bed-and-breakfast nearby, and she has six bedrooms, so some of you can stay there. Oh, and Suzanne's mamm wants some of you to stay with them because they have a few extra rooms as well."

"Sounds like you've got it all figured out," Dad said, clasping Titus's shoulder. "So why don't you ride in the van with us and show us the way to Samuel's place?"

"That's what I figured on doing." Titus smiled at Mary Ann. "If you and your family want to get settled in here, just go on in and look for the two bedrooms that have a pot of mums on the dresser. Suzanne's family grows 'em, and she gave me a couple of plants the other day."

Mary Ann smiled, and the depth of her love could be seen in her pretty brown eyes. "It's sure good to see you and finally know where you live, little brother."

"It's good to see you, too," Titus replied, giving his sister another hug.

—⁓—

"Mama Fannie. . .Dad. . .everyone. . . It's so great to see all of you." Samuel could hardly speak around the lump in his throat. He hadn't realized just how much he'd missed his family until seeing them right now.

Naomi gave him a hug. "You look good, Samuel. You've put on a few pounds, which you really needed, and I see a look of contentment and peace on your face."

He smiled. "Jah, I think moving here has been good for me. The kinner, too," he said, motioning to his four children, who were eagerly greeting their cousins.

She gave his arm a squeeze. "I'm so glad."

"Same goes for me," Naomi's husband, Caleb, put in. "We miss you and Titus, but we're glad you've begun new lives for yourselves and have found happiness here in Kentucky."

"I agree with that," Dad said, clasping Samuel's shoulder.

Samuel looked at Mama Fannie, hoping she would add her affirmations, but she merely smiled and said, "In the nine months you've been gone, the kinner have sure grown."

Samuel glanced across the yard to where his children and their cousins were playing with Lucky. "You're right about that. I can hardly keep 'em in shoes anymore 'cause their feet are growing so fast."

Titus motioned to the suitcases that had been unloaded from the van. "Why don't we take all the luggage inside, and then we can ride over to the B&B with those who'll be staying there? Mom and Dad are probably tired from the trip, so they can get settled in while we're gone, and all the kinner can stay here, too, if they like."

"I'd like to go along," Mama Fannie said. "Samuel's

told us so much about the B&B, and I'm anxious to see what it's like."

"Sure, that's a good idea," Samuel said. "It'll give me a chance to introduce you to both Bonnie and Esther."

———∿∿∿———

"I see a couple of vans pulling into the yard," Bonnie said, peering out her living room window. "I'll bet it's Samuel's family."

Esther's mouth went dry, and her palms grew sweaty. What if his family didn't like her? What if they disapproved of Samuel starting to court again?

"Come on, let's go outside and greet them." Bonnie hurried out the door, and although a bit hesitant, Esther followed.

Esther did a double-take when she saw two men who looked very much alike standing together on the lawn. It didn't take long for her to realize that one of them was Titus and the other was his twin brother, because the twin wore a beard, indicating that he was married.

"This is my brother Timothy," Titus said, motioning to the young man on his left.

Esther smiled. "It's nice to meet you, Timothy."

"Wow," Bonnie said, "you and Titus look so much alike. If Timothy wasn't wearing a beard, I probably couldn't tell you apart."

Titus chuckled and thumped his brother's back. "We've been hearin' that for most of our lives."

Timothy nodded with a grin. "We used to play tricks on our teacher when we were in school. Kept her guessin' many times as to who was who."

"That's not funny," said the older woman standing beside a tall man with gray hair and a matching beard. "I think you and Titus are the reason your daed and I have so many gray hairs today."

Samuel stepped forward and motioned to Bonnie. "Mama Fannie, Dad, this is Bonnie Taylor. She owns the bed-and-breakfast." He smiled at Bonnie. "These are my folks, Fannie and Abraham Fisher."

Bonnie extended her hand. "It's nice to meet you both."

Abraham smiled warmly, but Fannie barely gave Bonnie a nod.

If Samuel's stepmother is this unfriendly to Bonnie, Esther thought, *I wonder how she'll be with me.*

Samuel, red-faced and looking a bit uncomfortable, introduced Esther next.

Esther shook his parents' hands and was relieved when Fannie smiled and said, "It's nice meeting you, Esther."

After Samuel had introduced Esther and Bonnie to the rest of his family, everyone went inside.

"This house is so cozy," Samuel's sister Nancy said as Bonnie showed them around the B&B. "You've made it nice with so many special touches."

"Thanks, but Samuel gets the credit for a good deal of it," Bonnie said. "He worked really hard painting and fixing things that were broken, as well as remodeling most of the rooms before I was able to open for business."

"So we heard." Fannie's forehead wrinkled as she glanced at Samuel. Esther wondered what the woman's deep frown meant. Did Samuel's mother feel that Bonnie had worked Samuel too hard, or was she displeased because Samuel had moved his family to Kentucky? Esther had heard him mention a few times that his mother had tried to talk him out of moving, so maybe that was the reason for her apparent displeasure.

Samuel moved to stand beside Esther. "Uh—Mama Fannie, Dad, I've been wanting to tell you something."

"What's that?" Fannie asked.

"Not long ago, Esther and I began courting."

Esther held her breath and waited to hear their response. After several agonizing moments of silence, Fannie smiled and said, "I'm glad to hear that."

Abraham bobbed his head in agreement. "Jah, and I'd say that's a real good thing."

Esther released her breath in a sigh of relief. If Samuel should ever decide to marry her, maybe his folks would be pleased about that, too.

CHAPTER 47

"Well, this is the big day," Suzanne's mother said when Suzanne entered the kitchen. Mom poured a cup of coffee and handed it to her. "Are you naerfich?"

Suzanne nodded. "I am a bit nervous, but I'm sure I'll feel better once the wedding service starts." She glanced around. "I'm surprised none of Titus's family are out of bed yet."

"Oh, they're up," Mom said. "The men are outside helping Nelson and Chad with their chores, and the women and children went out to the barn to see the kittens that were born a week ago."

Suzanne smiled. "Kittens are always fun to watch—especially once they begin to move around and start wanting to cuddle." She moved toward the stove. "What do you need my help with this morning?"

Mom shook her head. "This is your special day, so I think you should just eat your breakfast and then go back to your room and get ready to become Titus's wife."

With a sigh, Suzanne dropped into a chair at the table. "Do you think I'm really ready for marriage, Mom?"

"Are you concerned about your cooking skills? Because if you are, I don't think you need to worry at all. Esther taught you well, and your new husband should have no complaints. Besides, as I understand it, Titus likes to cook, too."

"I wasn't thinking so much about my ability to cook. I'm more worried about how well Titus and I will get along once we're living in the same house."

Mom poured herself some coffee and took a seat beside Suzanne. "You get along well enough now, so I don't think it'll be any different after you're married."

"But I have my own opinion on things, and I know a wife is supposed to be submissive."

Mom gave a nod. "Being submissive doesn't mean you don't have a right to your opinion. When your daed was alive, we sometimes disagreed on how things should be done, but he always listened to my opinion. If we couldn't reach an agreement, then I respected his wishes and went along with whatever he decided." Mom patted Suzanne's arm. "Just remember what the Bible says in 1 Peter 3:1 about marriage: 'Likewise, ye wives, be in subjection to your own husbands.' I'm sure the ministers will be talking about that in the wedding service today."

"Danki for the advice." Suzanne smiled and clasped Mom's hand. "I hope that by next fall, Esther and Samuel will be the ones getting married."

Walking beside his father, Timothy headed to the Yoders' barn, where Titus and Suzanne's wedding service would be held, since the Yoders' house wasn't large enough to accommodate all the guests. He spotted the bride and groom waiting to be seated, and his thoughts went to Hannah. He could still remember how beautiful she'd looked on the day of their wedding, and how nervous and excited he'd felt sitting across from her, listening to their bishop's message on marriage and waiting to say their vows. He and Hannah had been so happy that day, and he'd been certain that was how it would always be.

But things were different now; it seemed like all they did anymore was argue. If only he could get Hannah away from her mother, he was sure things would be better between them. If Hannah had just agreed to come here for the wedding, maybe seeing the love Suzanne and Titus felt for each other would have caused her to remember that she'd promised to love and be faithful to her husband. Not that she'd been unfaithful, but Timothy was still convinced that his wife cared more about her mother's needs than his, and that had caused him to feel as if he didn't hold first place in Hannah's heart anymore. He felt cheated and hurt every time she wasn't at home when he needed or wanted her to be.

"Are you okay?" Dad whispered in Timothy's ear. "You look umgerrent."

Timothy shook his head. "I'm not upset. Just thinking about Hannah right now."

Dad gave him an understanding nod. "It's a shame she's not with you today."

Maybe things will be better when I go home, Timothy thought. *I've heard it said that absence makes the heart grow fonder. Since my birthday's next week, maybe Hannah will plan something special for me, but if not, it would just be enough knowing she truly missed me.*

———✦———

As Esther sat in a straight-backed, wooden chair next to Suzanne, tears pricked the back of her eyes. Her best friend would be standing in front of the bishop soon, saying her vows to her groom. She was happy that Suzanne was marrying the man she loved but wondered if things might change between her and Suzanne now that Suzanne was about to become a married woman. She'd be moving into Titus's house, and her responsibilities would increase. Once children came along, she'd be busier than ever. Would Suzanne continue working at the woodshop with Titus and Nelson, or would she give that up and become a full-time housewife?

I wish it was me getting married today, Esther thought as the bishop began to preach about the importance of communication in marriage. She glanced across the room and spotted Samuel, with Leon sitting on one side of him and Samuel's older brother Norman on the other side. Little Jared had fallen asleep and lay in a relaxed position across Samuel's lap. Esther noticed that Samuel's expression was nearly as sober as the groom's. It made her wonder what he was thinking right now. Her guess was he was probably remembering his own wedding day.

As the service continued, Esther's thoughts drifted back to the day she and Samuel had climbed up into the tree stand. She grinned, thinking to herself, *Did I actually climb that old thing?* But she knew at that point that no matter where their relationship was going, she would have climbed any height just to be with Samuel. Without any doubt—even high up in that tree stand—being next to Samuel was right where she'd wanted to be.

Whenever I'm with Samuel, I feel such joy and peace, Esther thought dreamily as she visualized Samuel lovingly stroking her face. *Does he feel it, too? Will he ever ask me to be his wife, or will today stir up memories of all that he had and lost?* She knew the next step would have to be up to him.

—————

Despite the chilly fall day, the Yoders' barn was hot and stuffy. It was probably from so many bodies being crammed together in one room, but Samuel figured it would have been worse if the wedding had been held in the house, because it wasn't nearly as big as the barn. Since Titus had such a large family, and most of them had come to see Titus and Suzanne get married, this was a bigger wedding than most that took place in this small Amish community.

Samuel glanced across the room at Esther, wearing a dark blue dress with a white cape and apron and looking as sweet and pretty as ever. He could no longer deny his feelings; he'd fallen in love with Esther and wanted to make her his wife. The question was, how long should he wait to propose marriage to her?

As Bishop King stood and called Suzanne and Titus to stand before him to say their vows, Jared stirred. Fearing the child might wake and start crying, Samuel began gently patting Jared's back. It seemed to help, for the boy relaxed and continued to sleep.

The bishop looked at Titus. "Can you confess, brother, that you accept this, our sister, as your wife, and that you will not leave her until death separates you? And do you believe that this is from the Lord, and that you have come thus far by your faith and prayers?"

"Jah," Titus answered with no hesitation.

The bishop turned to Suzanne then. "Can you confess, sister, that you accept this, our brother, as your husband, and that you will not leave him until death separates you? And do you believe that this is from the Lord and that you have come thus far by your faith and prayers?"

Suzanne answered affirmatively as well.

Bishop King looked at Titus again. "Because you have confessed that you want to take Suzanne for your wife, do you promise to be loyal to her and. . ."

The bishop's words faded as Samuel's mind took him back to the moment he and Elsie had become man and wife. He'd promised to be loyal to her—on the day of their wedding, and many other times when they'd been courting. He remembered one day in particular, when they'd gone for a ride in his open buggy. He'd pulled off to the side of the road to let several cars pass. Unable to resist the temptation, he'd leaned over and given Elsie a kiss. Following the kiss, he'd whispered, "I promise, I'll never love anyone but you." She'd smiled and said, "The same goes for me, Samuel."

"So go forth in the name of the Lord. You are now husband and wife."

Samuel's thoughts halted and he snapped his attention to the front of the room. Suzanne and Titus seemed to radiate a blissful glow as they returned to their seats.

Samuel looked at Esther and his heart sank all the way to his toes. Guilt invaded his thoughts, where moments earlier he'd felt free to hope. He couldn't break the promise he'd made to Elsie that day. He could not allow himself to love Esther. Their courting days must end. Maybe it would be best if he found someone else to watch the kids, because with Esther around so much it would be hard to keep his promise to Elsie.

CHAPTER 48

As Samuel took a seat at a table in preparation for the wedding meal, his gaze came to rest on Esther, sitting at the corner table with the bride and groom and their other attendants. She looked so happy today—almost bubbly, in fact. She was no doubt sharing in her best friend's joy over having just gotten married.

Esther's a wonderful woman, Samuel thought. *She deserves to be happy, and I hope she finds someone who will love her as much as I loved Elsie. She's good with children and will make a fine mother, so I hope she's blessed with lots of kinner someday.*

Samuel flinched, feeling as if his heart was being torn in two. His children loved Esther, and he was sure they'd be disappointed when they found out she would no longer be taking care of them. Of course, he had to find someone to replace her first. He sure couldn't go off to work every day and leave the two younger ones alone while Marla and Leon were in school.

Samuel felt a nudge on his arm. "Hey, aren't you gonna take this bowl of potato salad?" his older brother Jake asked.

"Oh, sorry. Didn't realize they were being passed yet." Samuel scooped some of the potato salad onto his plate and passed it along to his brother Matthew, who sat on the other side of him. Truth was, he didn't have much appetite. It was hard to think of eating when his stomach felt like it was tied up in knots.

I've got to stop thinking about Esther, he told himself. *I need to concentrate on something else.*

He glanced across the room to where his folks sat with his four children on either side of them. *Should I move back to Pennsylvania and let Mom take care of the kinner? That would make her happy, I'm sure. But if I moved, I'd miss Kentucky and the friends I've made here.*

He felt another jab on his arm and realized that Jake wanted to pass him something else. "This chicken looks pretty good, doesn't it?" Jake already had one piece on his plate, but he quickly forked another one before passing the platter to Samuel.

Samuel took the smallest piece he could find and then passed the plate on to Matthew.

"You're sure quiet today," Jake said. "Did it make you sad to see your little bruder get married?"

Samuel shook his head. "I'm happy for Titus and Suzanne."

"Jah. They make a nice couple. I'm sure they'll be very happy together." Jake passed a bowl of creamed celery to Samuel. "I've never cared much for this stuff, but you can have some if you like."

"Think I'll pass on it, too." Samuel handed the bowl to Matthew.

Matthew looked at Samuel's plate and squinted. "You're sure not eating much today."

"I'm just not that hungry, I guess."

Matthew spooned some creamed celery onto his plate. "With all this good-smelling food, I don't see how anyone could not be hungry."

"I think Samuel's saving up for the desserts," Jake said with a chuckle.

Samuel merely shrugged in reply. This wasn't the time or the place to tell his brothers that he was sick to his stomach because of the decision he'd felt forced to make. He'd have to tell everyone soon enough though. Sure couldn't let them think he and Esther might eventually get married.

—⁂—

"So what'd you think of the wedding?" Allen asked Bonnie as he passed her the platter of chicken.

"It was different. A lot different than any wedding I've ever attended."

He gave a nod. "That's for sure. Nothing at all like our traditional English weddings." He spooned some mashed potatoes onto his plate. "The thing I had the hardest time with was sitting on that backless wooden bench. Had to get up a couple of times and go outside so I could walk around and stretch my legs and back."

"I know what you mean." Bonnie lifted her water glass and took a drink. "Sitting there for three hours made me wonder how the Amish are able to continually do that during their weddings and biweekly church services."

"Guess they're used to it, since they've been doing it since they were kids."

She slowly shook her head. "I don't think I could ever get used to it. I think if I attended church with the Amish on a regular basis, I'd have to take a pillow to sit on, or maybe bring myself a comfortable chair."

"Yeah, me, too." Allen poured some gravy over his potatoes and took a bite. "Umm. . . The food they serve at their wedding meals is sure good."

"You're right, and can you imagine how many cooks and how much food it takes to serve so many people?"

"I couldn't even begin to guess."

They passed a few more dishes down the line, and then Allen concentrated on eating. He figured by the end of the day he'd have to loosen his belt a few notches.

"So what'd you think about the wedding service itself?" he asked, looking over at Bonnie.

"It was hard to understand, since almost all of it was in German."

"Yeah. Made me wish I'd taken German when I was in school instead of Spanish." Allen waited until the young Amish waiter pouring coffee handed him a cup, and then he turned to Bonnie again and said, "Did you notice there was no ring exchange or kiss between the bride and groom?"

"I did notice that," she said with a nod. "I also noticed that the father of the bride didn't walk his daughter down the aisle. Suzanne and Titus just walked to their seats with their attendants."

"Speaking of walking down the aisle, now that things are better between you and your dad, do you think he'd be willing to walk you down the aisle if you got married?" Allen asked.

"I suppose he would," Bonnie replied, "but that's not going to happen, since I have no plans to get married."

Allen wasn't sure how to respond. Did Bonnie feel that way because she hadn't had a proposal, or did she have something against marriage?

"You know, I've been thinking," he said.

"What's that?"

"I was wondering if you'd like to go out to dinner with me some evening next week. There's a new restaurant that just opened in Hopkinsville, and—"

"I appreciate the offer," Bonnie said, cutting him off, "but I'll be busy all of next week. The day after Samuel's family leaves, I have three couples checking into the B&B."

"How about the following week?"

She shook her head. "I'll be busy then, too."

"Oh, I see." Allen couldn't help but feel disappointed, and he wondered if Bonnie was giving him the brush-off. He'd thought the two of them were getting closer and that Bonnie might have come to care for him as much as he did her. Now he wondered if he'd been wrong about that. Maybe Bonnie only saw him as a friend and would never see him as anything more.

Allen thought about Connie, whom he'd gone out with a few times last year. The only similarity between her and Bonnie was their names, which rhymed. Connie was nothing like Bonnie, and he was glad he'd broken things off with her before either of them had gotten serious. Connie didn't want anything to do with religion and had made that quite clear whenever he'd brought the subject up. Allen knew what the Bible said in 2 Corinthians 6:14 about not being unequally yoked with an unbeliever. After he'd quit seeing Connie, he'd decided that if he ever found another woman he wanted to date, she would have to be a Christian. Bonnie was a Christian—he had no doubt of that—but she seemed to be holding him at a distance. For a while, he'd thought Samuel might be interested in Bonnie, but that idea vanished as soon as Samuel started courting Esther.

Allen glanced over at Samuel and noticed that he wasn't smiling. He looked like he might be upset about something. If he had a chance to talk with Samuel after the meal, he'd try to find out what it was.

———〰———

Feeling the need for a bit of fresh air as soon as the noon meal was over, Esther stepped outside. She spotted Bonnie sitting in one of the chairs under a maple tree in the Yoders' backyard.

"Looks like I'm not the only one out here on this chilly afternoon," Esther said, stepping up to Bonnie.

Bonnie looked up and smiled. "It was getting stuffy and warm in there, and after eating all that good food, I was afraid if I didn't get up and go outside I might fall asleep."

Esther laughed. "I know what you mean. I get drowsy after eating a big meal, too."

"It was a nice wedding," Bonnie said. "Quite a bit different than the weddings we Englishers are used to, but nice, nonetheless." Bonnie gave Esther's arm a little squeeze. "From the way things have been going between you and Samuel lately, I wouldn't be surprised if you two aren't the next Amish couple to get married."

Esther smiled but shook her head. "There are a few more Amish weddings in our community that will take place next month, but even if Samuel were to propose to me tomorrow, there wouldn't be enough time to plan a wedding for this year."

"Well, I'm sure you'll be a married woman by sometime next year," Bonnie said.

"I hope you're right about that."

Bonnie motioned to her left. "There's Samuel now, talking to Allen. Since you've had other obligations today, I don't imagine you've had much time to spend with Samuel."

"I haven't had any time at all," Esther said. "But since I'm not busy with anything right now, I think I'll walk over there and say hello. Would you like to come along?"

"No thanks. Think I'll sit here a few more minutes, and then I'll probably head for home."

"Okay. I'll see you back at the B&B later." Esther walked away, but before she got close enough to speak with Samuel, she was stopped by Ethan, who'd just stepped out of the barn.

"Wie geht's, Esther?" he asked.

She smiled. "I'm fine. And you?"

"Doin' pretty good." He gave her a wide grin. "Sure was a lot of good food served at the wedding meal, wasn't there?"

"There certainly was."

"That's why I came out here. . .to walk some of it off. I'll be back for the evening young people's supper, and I need to make sure I'm plenty hungry by then."

"I think everyone will be full by the end of the day," she said.

"Yep." Ethan gave Esther another big grin, and then he headed for a group of young Amish men who were gathered across the yard.

Esther started walking toward Samuel again, but by the time she got there, he and Allen had stepped around the corner of the buggy shed.

As she approached the shed, she heard Allen mention her name, so she stopped and listened. She knew it wasn't right to eavesdrop, but the men couldn't see her, and she was curious to know what was being said.

"How are things with you and Esther these days?" she heard Allen say.

"Umm... Well, okay, I guess."

"I had a lot of fun the day the four of us went to visit the monument," Allen said. "I was thinking if I can get Bonnie to un-busy herself soon, it would be fun for the four of us to go on another outing before the weather turns cold. Maybe we could go to the pond some Saturday afternoon and either do some fishing or just have a picnic lunch."

Esther heard Samuel's boots scrape across the gravel where he stood. "Well...uh...the thing is... I've decided not to see Esther socially anymore."

Esther pressed her weight against the side of the buggy shed, reeling with the shock of what she'd just heard. The sounds of activity, which moments ago were all around her, were drowned out by her own question. *How can this be?* Just a few days ago, Samuel had told his folks that he and Esther were courting, and now he didn't want to see her anymore? What could have happened between then and now to make him change his mind about her?

She no longer heard the children playing as they squealed with delight, chasing each other in a game of tag. She tried to focus on the women she'd seen earlier, relaxing under the shade trees and exchanging recipes, but their voices turned into murmurs and she no longer heard their words. She looked toward the buggies parked off to the side, with horses dozing as they stood waiting in the pasture. Even as tranquil as that scene was, it became a blur with tears she tried her best to hold in.

Esther covered her mouth with her hand in order to keep from sobbing out loud. Things had been going so well, and now, all of a sudden, they're not? She scolded herself for being so hopeful and believing in the happily-ever-after. She wasn't prepared to have her dreams evaporate right before her eyes. Fearing the truth, was there no chance of them ever getting married?

CHAPTER 49

When Esther woke up the following morning, she felt like she'd been kicked in the stomach by an unruly horse. Was it a bad dream, or had she really heard Samuel tell Allen that he'd decided not to court her anymore? No, it was true. She'd felt the pain of it all the way to her toes. She just didn't understand it at all. She'd been so sure Samuel had come to care for her.

Esther pushed the covers aside, climbed out of bed, and padded over to the window in her bare feet. Several of Samuel's relatives were in Bonnie's yard, loading their luggage into the van that was parked there. Those who had stayed at the B&B would be leaving today, and it was her understanding that a few, like Samuel's parents, would head back to Pennsylvania tomorrow. No doubt they wanted to spend a little more time with Samuel and Titus, as well as with Samuel's children.

Tears welled in Esther's eyes. From the short time she'd spent with Samuel's family, she'd concluded that they were a loving, caring group of people. It made her heart ache to think that if she and Samuel would no longer be courting, there was no chance of her ever being a part of his wonderful family.

Should I go to Samuel and talk to him? she wondered. *Should I tell him what I overheard him say to Allen yesterday?* Tears dripped onto her cheeks as she leaned against the window, *Guess I should wait until after Samuel's folks leave before I talk to him. When I go to watch the kinner the day after they leave, that's when I'll approach him about this.*

Esther wiped her eyes and turned away from the window, knowing she needed to get dressed and go up to the main house so she could help Bonnie with breakfast. But her heart just wasn't in it today. She wanted to crawl back in bed and shut out the world.

———

"Good morning, Mrs. Fisher," Titus said, standing beside Suzanne as she stood in front of the dresser, pinning up her hair.

She leaned into him, liking the sound of that. "Good morning, husband."

He nuzzled her neck with his nose. "Are you as tired as I am this morning?"

"Jah. Yesterday was a long day, and according to tradition, since we've spent our first night in my parents' home, we now have to help with the cleanup from the wedding, so we'll be even more tired by tonight, I expect." She set her head covering in place. "So I guess we ought to go downstairs and see if my mamm has breakfast started, and then we'll get busy cleaning the barn."

"We'll need to say good-bye to those in my family who'll be leaving today, too, and I think we ought to do that first," Titus said. "I know they want to get an early start."

She smiled. "It was nice having most of your family here for the wedding."

"It sure was, but I wish my twin brother's wife would have come with him." Titus's brows puckered. "I'm worried about Timothy. From some of the things he's told me, I think he's unhappy in his marriage."

"That's a shame. We'll have to remember to pray for Hannah and Timothy."

"You're right. Unless things change between them soon, they're going to need a lot of prayer."

—⁓—

"Now that you're here, I'll get breakfast started," Mama Fannie said when Samuel entered the kitchen after doing his chores.

"That's okay. I'm not hungry this morning."

"What happened? Did you eat too much at the wedding meal yesterday?" Dad asked as he shuffled into the room.

Samuel merely shrugged in reply.

"Is there something troubling you?" Mama Fannie questioned. "You've been acting kind of strange ever since we came home from the wedding last night."

"It's nothing," Samuel mumbled. He grabbed a mug from the cupboard, moved over to the stove, and poured himself a cup of coffee.

"I wish we didn't have to go home tomorrow," Mama Fannie said. "I'd like to spend more time with you and the kinner." She glanced over at Dad. "Couldn't we stay until next week? It would be nice if we could be here for Leon's birthday."

Dad shook his head. "We need to get back so Timothy and I can finish harvesting the fields. Besides, next week is also Timothy's birthday, and he'll want to be home with his wife and daughter."

"It's Titus's birthday, too, you know," she reminded.

"That's right, and I'm sure he'll be perfectly happy celebrating it with his new bride."

"Maybe we could stay here and celebrate Leon's birthday, and Timothy can go home without us."

"Nope," Dad said. "We need to get back for the harvest."

Deep wrinkles formed across Mama Fannie's forehead. "Sometimes I wish you'd give up farming. It ties you down too much."

"Farming is what I do." Dad took a seat at the table. "Wouldn't know what to do if I wasn't farming."

Mama Fannie sighed. "There are times when I wish you were still running the general store and I was managing the quilt shop. We saw more of each other then than we do now, that's for sure."

"Things change, Fannie," Dad said. "Naomi and Caleb are doing a fine job with the store, and Abby enjoys running the quilt shop."

Mama Fannie handed him a cup of coffee. "You're right, and I wouldn't take that away from them. I just wish—"

"Daadi, do something, quick! Lucky's chasin' Esther's katz!" Penny hollered as she raced into the room.

Samuel's heartbeat picked up speed. "Is Esther here?" Surely she wouldn't have come to watch the kids today. She knew Samuel's folks wouldn't be leaving until tomorrow.

Penny shook her head. "Esther's not here, Daadi. The katz I'm talkin' about is the one she gave us awhile back. Said it would help keep the mice down. Remember?"

"Oh, that's right," Samuel said with a nod. His brain felt so fuzzy this morning—probably because he hadn't slept well last night. He'd tossed and turned most of the night, his thoughts going from Elsie to Esther.

Penny stood on tiptoes and tugged on Samuel's shirtsleeve. "Are you gonna make Lucky stop chasin' the katz?"

He grunted. "There's no need for that. If the cat doesn't like being chased, he'll either climb the nearest tree or find a safe place to hide in the barn." Samuel pointed at Penny. "And if the cat does go up a tree, don't you get any ideas about trying to rescue him."

"I won't, Daadi. I know better than that now."

"Good."

Mama Fannie pulled Penny into her arms. "I'm going to miss you, sweet girl." She looked over at Dad. "Are you sure we can't stay a few days longer?"

Dad shook his head. "Nope. But we'll come back and visit again sometime next year."

Mama Fannie's shoulders slumped as she turned

toward the stove. Seeing how much she missed his children made Samuel wonder if he'd made a mistake moving away. Maybe it would be better if they moved back to Pennsylvania. At least then he wouldn't have to see Esther and be reminded of what he could never have. He'd have to think on that awhile; he didn't want to make another mistake. The kids had settled in here quite well, and they might not want to leave Kentucky. For that matter, he didn't want to leave either. He just wasn't sure how he could continue living here without seeing Esther all the time.

No matter what he decided about moving or staying, tomorrow when Esther came to watch the kids, he'd have to tell her that he wouldn't be courting her anymore and that he planned to look for someone else to take care of the kids. He just wished there was an easy way to say it. Better yet, he wished more than ever that he didn't have to say anything at all. Since his family had seemed so pleased about him courting Esther, he decided it would be best not to tell them about his decision until after they'd gone home. He didn't want to spoil the last of their visit with a bunch of questions, or worse yet, deal with Mama Fannie offering her opinion on things.

CHAPTER 50

Whe Esther arrived at Samuel's the following day to watch the children, she was surprised to see that his folks were still there. She'd figured they would have wanted to get an early start on their return trip to Pennsylvania and would have already left.

Do Titus's parents know he won't be courting me anymore? Esther halted her footsteps as a sickening thought popped into her head. *What if Samuel's parents are the reason he's decided to stop courting me? Maybe one or both of them told Samuel they didn't approve of him seeing me.*

She swallowed hard and drew in a deep breath, her feet feeling like lead with each step she took. *If I just knew why he'd made this decision, maybe I could do something about it.*

Esther stepped onto the porch and knocked on the door. It felt strange knocking on her own door, but with Samuel's folks still visiting, she didn't feel right about walking right in.

Marla opened the door and gave her a hug. "Sure am glad to see ya, Esther. Wish I didn't have to go to school today so we could do somethin' fun."

Esther gave the girl's head a pat. "We'll do something fun when you get home this afternoon."

When Esther stepped into the living room, she saw Fannie sitting on the sofa, holding Jared in her lap. Leon and Penny sat on either side of her.

"It's nice to see you again, Esther," Fannie said,

offering Esther a friendly smile. "The kinner and I were just talking about how much they like having you care for them."

Relief flooded Esther's soul. *If Fannie was being so friendly and had said such a nice thing, surely she couldn't have influenced Samuel to stop courting me. Maybe Fannie doesn't even know about the decision he's made.*

Esther smiled at Fannie and said, "I enjoy being with the children, too."

Fannie stroked the top of Jared's head and bent her head to kiss his pudgy cheek. "It's been nice being with them these past few days, but I wish we could stay longer. I really miss Samuel and the kinner."

Esther nodded with understanding. She missed her folks, too, but since Samuel and his children had come into her life, she'd been less lonely and had found a new purpose.

"I also wish we'd had more time to get to know you better," Fannie said. "Maybe when Samuel and the kinner come to Pennsylvania to visit us, you can join them."

Esther had to force a smile this time. If she and Samuel wouldn't be courting anymore, he sure wouldn't invite her to go with them to Pennsylvania.

"Abraham and I are very happy with Titus's choice for a wife," Fannie added.

"Jah. I think Suzanne and Titus will be very happy together." Esther removed her shawl and outer bonnet and hung them on a wall peg near the door. She was about to take a seat in the chair across from Fannie, when Samuel stepped into the room. He halted, and his face turned red when he looked at Esther.

"Oh, I. . .uh. . .didn't realize you were here," he said, dropping his gaze to the floor.

"I just came in a few minutes ago." It made Esther unhappy seeing his reaction, as if they'd just met.

He gave a nod and looked at his mother. "Dad and the others are bringing all the suitcases downstairs."

Fannie set Jared on the floor and stood. "As much as I hate to say it, I guess it's time for me to say good-bye."

—m—

When Bonnie stepped into the kitchen after feeding the chickens, she heard the phone ringing. She hurried across the room and picked up the receiver. "Bonnie's Bed-and-Breakfast."

"Hi, Bonnie. It's Allen. Thought I'd better check up on you this morning."

She shifted the phone to her other ear. "Why would you need to check up on me?"

"You looked awful tired when I saw you at the wedding, and after you said how busy you were, I wondered if there was anything I could do to help out."

"In what way?" she asked.

"I have a few hours free this afternoon, so I thought if you had some chores you needed to have done, I could swing over there right after lunch and do 'em for you." Before Bonnie could reply, he added, "On second thought, maybe I could pick up some deli sandwiches and we could eat lunch together before I do the chores."

Bonnie leaned against the kitchen counter and closed her eyes. As appealing as the thought of having lunch with Allen was, she wouldn't feel comfortable having him here today—especially when she'd decided not to spend any time with him alone.

"You still there, Bonnie?"

Her eyes snapped open. "Yes, I'm here. I...uh...appreciate your offer to bring lunch, but I really don't have time for that today."

"Oh, okay. How about if I just drop by later then and do whatever chores you need to have done?"

"That won't work either."

"Why not?"

"The types of chores I need to have done are things only I can do." Bonnie paused and waited for his response, and when he said nothing, she added, "I do appreciate your offer though."

"Sure. Any time you have something you need to have done, just let me know."

"Okay, thanks."

"Take care, Bonnie, and I hope you have a good day."

"You, too. Bye, Allen."

When Bonnie hung up the phone she went to the sink, turned on the cold water, and splashed some onto her face. She didn't know if she felt so hot and sweaty from her trek outside or from trying to get out of seeing Allen today. She'd allowed herself to care for him and knew the only remedy was to put a safe distance between them.

—∞—

Samuel stood on the porch with his children, watching as the vans transporting his family disappeared from sight. He and the kids had come outside to say their good-byes, leaving Esther in the basement to wash a load of clothes she'd volunteered to do. Now Samuel had to go back in the house and tell Esther what he'd decided about them. But he wouldn't do it until after Marla and Leon left for school. He didn't want them to hear what he had to say. The kids had come to care for Esther, and he knew they'd be disappointed to learn that she wouldn't be watching them while he was at work anymore. On second thought, maybe he'd wait to tell them until after he found a replacement for Esther. No point in upsetting them until he had to, at least.

"Well," Samuel said, squeezing Leon's shoulder, "you and your sister had better get your lunch pails and head for school. You don't want to be late."

"Are you gonna give us a ride today?" Marla asked.

Samuel shook his head. "It's a nice day with no rain in sight, and it'll do you both good to walk."

At first, Marla looked like she might argue the point,

but then she obediently went into the house.

A short time later, Marla and Leon headed down the road with their schoolbooks and lunch pails. Since Esther was still in the basement, Samuel gave Penny and Jared a couple of picture books to look at and instructed them to stay in the living room. Then, with a feeling of dread, he headed to the basement.

He found Esther bent over the washing machine, feeding one of his shirts into the wringer. Not wishing to startle her, he waited until the shirt had come through the other end and she'd placed it in the basin of cold water to rinse.

"Ah-hem." He cleared his throat.

She whirled around. "Ach, Samuel! I didn't hear you come down the stairs."

"Sorry. Didn't mean to frighten you."

She straightened and reached around to rub her lower back. "Did you need me to come upstairs and keep an eye on the little ones while you take Marla and Leon to school?"

"No. They're walking today, and Penny and Jared are in the living room, looking at some picture books my folks gave them."

"Oh, I see." Esther looked up at him and blinked a couple of times. "Samuel, I was wondering—"

"Esther, I need to speak with you about something," he said.

She gave a nod. "You go ahead with what you were going to say."

He cleared his throat again and popped the knuckles on his left hand. This was even more difficult that he'd thought it would be. "I've decided it's best if you and I don't see each other socially anymore."

"Why, Samuel? Have I done something wrong?"

Samuel winced. He could see the hurt on Esther's face, and it was almost his undoing.

"You haven't done anything wrong. I just think it's best

for me and the kinner if I don't get romantically involved with anyone." He shifted his weight and leaned against the wooden beam behind him, needing it for support. "You see, I'm still in love with my wife, and so—"

"I understand that there will always be a place in your heart for her, but I was hoping there might be a place in your heart for me, too."

There is, but I can't let it happen. I can't break the promise I made to Elsie.

"Samuel? Can we talk about this?"

He shook his head. "I've made my decision, and I think it's for the best."

Tears welled in Esther's eyes, and it was all Samuel could do to keep from pulling her into his arms. *How could I have been foolish enough to let myself fall in love with her?* he berated himself. *If I keep seeing Esther, I'll be breaking my promise to Elsie, and I can't live with that.*

"There's something else," Samuel said.

"What's that?" Esther's words came out in a whisper.

"I think it's best if I find someone else to watch the kinner."

Her eyes widened. "Why?"

"The more you're around them, the more attached they're becoming. Pretty soon, they'll start to think of you as their mamm."

"I'll make sure they don't," Esther was quick to say. "I'll make sure they never forget their mother."

"I've made my decision," Samuel said, drawing on all the strength he could muster. "You have plenty to do helping Bonnie at the B&B, so in the long run it'll be better if you don't have my kinner to watch."

"Oh, but Samuel, I—"

"I'll let you know as soon as I've found someone to take your place." Samuel turned and hurried up the stairs. If he stayed a minute longer, he might weaken and change his mind.

CHAPTER 51

Esther spent the next two days in a daze. It had been hard to go to Samuel's this week and watch the children, knowing it would all be over once Samuel found a replacement for her. What made it even worse was learning that next Saturday was Leon's birthday, and she was sure she wouldn't be included in the celebration.

"You look so tired this morning," Bonnie said, as she and Esther sat at the table in her kitchen for breakfast early Saturday morning.

"I am tired," Esther admitted. "I haven't been sleeping well lately."

"Since tomorrow will be an off-Sunday from your church, maybe you can sleep in."

"Maybe so." Esther was glad there would be no church tomorrow. She couldn't stand the thought of going to church and seeing Samuel sitting across the room with his boys beside him. It was bad enough to think about not watching the children anymore, but knowing Samuel didn't love her was breaking her heart.

"Esther, are you okay?" Bonnie touched Esther's shoulder.

Esther jerked her head. "I. . .uh. . . Actually, no. I'm not okay."

Bonnie's brows furrowed. "What's wrong?"

"I haven't said anything to you or even Suzanne because I've been too upset to talk about it, but Samuel and I won't be courting anymore."

"How come?"

"He still loves his wife, and apparently he doesn't love me." Esther gulped on the sob rising in her throat. "To make matters worse, he's looking for someone else to watch his children, so I'll soon be losing them as well."

"I'm so sorry, Esther, but maybe it's for the best."

Tears slipped from Esther's eyes and splashed onto the table. "H–how can it be for the best?"

"Think about it. If Samuel's still in love with his wife, then the memory of her would probably come between you. He might even compare everything you did to the way his late wife did things."

"I don't expect him to forget her. I just. . ." Esther's voice trailed off as she struggled not to break down.

Bonnie patted Esther's back. "I'm sorry Samuel led you on like he did. It wasn't right for him to start courting you and then drop you flat."

Esther looked at Bonnie's pinched expression, and for the first time since she'd met Bonnie, she saw a look of bitterness on her face. Could someone Bonnie once loved have hurt her real bad? Might she have suffered from a broken relationship that had left her with emotional scars? Esther was on the verge of asking when the telephone rang.

"I'd better get that." Bonnie stood and moved quickly across the room.

Esther pushed away from the table, too. It was time to get busy doing the dishes and quit feeling sorry for herself.

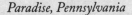

Paradise, Pennsylvania

"Suzanne and Titus said to tell you they were sorry you couldn't make it to their wedding," Timothy said as he and Hannah sat at the breakfast table, with Mindy in her high chair between them.

313

"Didn't you tell them my mamm had sprained her ankle?"

"Of course I did, but they still missed seeing you." Timothy reached across Mindy and touched Hannah's arm. "I missed you, too."

She smiled. "Well, you're home now, and just in time for your birthday next week."

"You mean you didn't forget?"

"Of course not. How could I forget my husband's birthday?"

He reached for a piece of toast and slathered it with strawberry jam. "You've been so busy helping your mamm, I wasn't sure you'd remember."

"Well, I did, and I'm planning to invite your folks and my folks over for supper that night."

"What about my brothers and sisters?"

Hannah frowned. "Our house isn't big enough for that many people. We'd have to go out to a restaurant for that."

He clapped his hands. "That's a good idea. Why don't we see if we can reserve a room at the Plain and Fancy Restaurant, and then everyone can be invited?"

Hannah handed Mindy a plastic cup filled with orange juice. "I don't think they have a room at any of the restaurants around here that would be big enough to accommodate all of your family."

"You may be right." Timothy took a bite of his scrambled egg and washed it down with a swallow of coffee. "I could clean out the barn and have my birthday supper in there."

Hannah shook her head. "That's too much work—not to mention that it would be a lot of trouble to haul all the food out there from the house. I think we should just stick with inviting your folks and mine and have a nice quiet supper here at the house."

"Okay, whatever." Timothy stared into his cup of coffee. Just like always, he was giving in to Hannah's wishes.

One of these days, he was going to have something go his way, and she'd just have to deal with it.

—⁓—

Hopkinsville, Kentucky

"Looks like you're making good progress on that house," Allen said when he showed up at the jobsite where Samuel had been working all morning.

Samuel gave a nod and kept on painting. "I'm hopin' to get done early today so I can have my driver drop me off at the Zooks' place on my way home."

"Are you talking about Ethan Zook?"

"Uh-huh. His younger brothers and sisters are friends with my kids, and I'm hoping that Ethan's mother might be willing to start watching my kids."

Allen tipped his head. "Why would you need Mrs. Zook to watch them when you have Esther? She's watching them today, right?"

"Nope. Since the woodshop's not open today, I left them with Suzanne." Samuel glanced at Allen then back at the house he was painting. "I need to find a replacement for Esther before next week if possible."

"How come?"

Samuel bent down and dipped his paintbrush into the bucket beside him. "Esther's got enough on her hands helping Bonnie at the B&B."

"They're only busy whenever Bonnie has guests, and with winter coming, things will probably slow down at the B&B."

Samuel shrugged and continued painting.

Allen moved closer to Samuel and looked him in the eye. "What's going on, Samuel? Is there a problem between you and Esther?"

"It's not a problem exactly," Samuel said. "We're just not going to be seeing each other anymore."

"Are you kidding me?"

Samuel shook his head and continued to paint. "I've decided it's the best thing to do."

"Best for who—you or Esther?"

"Both of us. Esther deserves someone who can love her with all their heart. I can't do that."

"Why not?"

Samuel stopped painting and turned to face Allen. "I made a promise to my wife, and I can't let myself forget what we had when she was alive."

Allen put his hand on Samuel's shoulder and gave it a gentle squeeze. "I think I understand a bit of what you're feeling. When I lived in Washington, I had a girlfriend whom I loved very much. In fact, I was hoping to marry her, but then she got hit by a car and died." Deep wrinkles formed across Allen's forehead. "A part of me died that day, too, and I was sure I would never fall in love again. But you know what, Samuel?"

"What?"

"I met Bonnie, and she's captured my heart." He frowned. "Now if I could only get her to see that."

"I'm happy for you, Allen, and I hope Bonnie loves you as much as you love her, but it's different for me."

"How so?"

"I promised Elsie that I'd never love anyone but her. I said that to her many times when we were courting and on our wedding day, too." Samuel drew in a deep breath and released it with a groan. "So I will not break my promise to Elsie."

CHAPTER 52

Pembroke, Kentucky

Daadi, why can't Esther come out to supper with us tomorrow tonight?" Leon asked on the morning before his birthday.

"Because tonight's just for our family," Samuel replied as they headed down the road toward the Zooks' house in his horse and buggy.

"But you said Aunt Suzanne and Uncle Titus are goin' with us," Marla put in.

"That's right. They're part of our family, and besides, this will be Uncle Titus's birthday celebration, too." Samuel glanced over his shoulder at Penny and Jared, sitting in the backseat, huddled together. It was a chilly fall morning, and he should have thought to bring a blanket along to keep the kids warm.

"I miss Esther," Marla said. "I wish she could be with us forever."

"Mama didn't stay with us forever," Leon said. "She ain't never comin' back neither."

Samuel winced. He didn't need that reminder this morning. Just when he'd begun to deal with Elsie's death and had been trying to move on with his life, all the old feelings had surfaced again. Now the kids were missing Esther, and so was he. If only he could let go of the promise he'd made to Elsie; but no, that wouldn't be right. Why had he even made such a promise, and why couldn't he let it go?

When they arrived at the Zooks' a short time later, Penny started crying, and Jared quickly followed suit. "I don't wanna stay here," Penny wailed. "I want Esther to take care of us like she did before."

Samuel picked Jared up and patted Penny's back, hoping to calm them down, but it was useless. They both continued to cry as he ushered them to the door.

"They'll be all right once you're gone," Mavis Zook said. "I'll find something fun for them to do."

Samuel gave a nod. "Marla and Leon will come here after school. I'll be back to pick the kinner up late this afternoon." He bent down and gave Jared and Penny a hug then hurried out the door before he felt any worse.

Samuel was almost to his horse and buggy when Ethan Zook stepped out of the barn. "I heard some hollering a few minutes ago. What was that all about?" he asked.

"My two youngest aren't happy with me right now."

"What's wrong? Did ya give them a bletsching?"

"No, I didn't give either of them a spanking," Samuel said with a shake of his head. "They're upset because Esther won't be taking care of them anymore."

"I wondered why you'd asked my mamm to watch 'em today." Ethan eyeballed Samuel with a curious expression. "I heard someone saying the other day that you won't be courtin' Esther anymore. Is it true?"

Samuel gave a nod. "You heard right."

"So then I don't suppose you'd have any objections if I courted her?"

Samuel hesitated but finally said, "You're free to do as you like."

A slow smile spread across Ethan's lips. "I hope ya know what you're doin'. Esther's a real fine cook, and she'd make a good fraa."

"I'm doing what I have to do," Samuel mumbled. Quickly, he untied his horse, stepped into the buggy, and directed Socks toward the schoolhouse.

He knew he had no claim on Esther, yet it irritated

him to think that Ethan was interested in Esther—especially since it was obviously for her cooking. Didn't the pudgy-looking fellow realize what a wonderful woman Esther was? She deserved better than Ethan, but it was her right to go out with him if she chose to. Maybe she'd even end up marrying the hungry fellow. Oh, but Samuel hoped not.

I just need to stay busy and keep my focus on other things, he told himself. *My business is staying true to Elsie and providing for my kids.* But could he do that if he remained in Kentucky? Could he deal with seeing Esther being courted by Ethan—or anyone else, for that matter?

When Samuel pulled the horse and buggy into the schoolyard, he turned to face Marla and Leon. "How would you two feel about moving back to Pennsylvania?"

"No way! I like it here," Leon said.

Marla bobbed her head in agreement. "Me, too."

"Why would ya wanna move, Daadi?" Leon questioned.

"I just think we might all be happier there, but I haven't made a decision yet, so we can talk about it more tonight." He motioned to the schoolhouse. "I think you may be late, so you'd better grab your schoolbooks and get inside."

The children did as they were told, and as they scampered across the grass to the schoolhouse, Samuel turned his horse and buggy around and headed for home. His driver would be there to take him to the jobsite soon, and he didn't want to be late.

———∿∿———

Esther had just taken a loaf of zucchini bread out of the oven when she heard the rumble of a vehicle coming into the yard. When she peeked out the kitchen window and saw Allen getting out of his truck, she set the bread on a cooling rack and went to answer the door.

"Hi, Esther, how are you?" Allen asked as he stepped onto the porch.

She gave a little shrug. "Okay, I guess."

"I heard about you and Samuel, and I'm real sorry things didn't work out."

"Me, too. Samuel's change of heart really knocked the wind out of me, but I guess it wasn't meant to be."

"Maybe Samuel will change his mind."

Esther sighed deeply. "I'd like to believe that, but he seemed pretty sure of his decision, and now he has someone else watching his children, too."

Allen's sympathetic look was almost Esther's undoing. "Is there something I can help you with?" she asked, needing to change the subject.

"I was hoping to talk to Bonnie. Is she here?"

"No, she went to Hopkinsville to run some errands."

"Oh, I see." Allen leaned against the porch railing and folded his arms. "Does Bonnie confide in you much?"

"What do you mean?"

"Does she share her innermost feelings with you?"

"Sometimes. She's told me some things about her childhood and how hard it was when she lost her mother."

"Does she ever talk about me?"

Esther wasn't sure what Allen was getting at, but she smiled and said, "She's mentioned you a few times."

"Do you think she cares for me?"

"Well. . .uh. . .I guess so. Why are you asking me this?"

"Because I care for her, and I thought we were getting close, but then all of a sudden she pulled away." He frowned. "I've asked her out several times, but she always says she's too busy. Makes me wonder if she's using it as an excuse."

"Bonnie does keep pretty busy here at the B&B. Seems like there's always something that needs to be done."

"I realize that, and I'm busy, too, but I'd make time for her if she'd let me."

Esther didn't know what to say, and she was relieved when the phone rang and she had to excuse herself to answer it.

"Okay, I'll let you go," Allen said. "When Bonnie gets

home tell her I stopped by, okay?"

Esther gave a nod and hurried away.

She'd no more than finished her phone call, when she heard a horse and buggy pull into the yard. Her heartbeat picked up speed. Could it be Samuel? Had he come to tell her that he'd changed his mind about courting her? She didn't want to be hopeful, but her heart betrayed her.

She hurried to the door, and when she stepped onto the porch, disappointment flooded her soul. It wasn't Samuel; it was Ethan Zook. She watched as he climbed out of his buggy and secured his horse, wondering why he'd be coming here.

"Wie geht's?" Ethan called as he strode across the yard toward the B&B.

"I'm okay. How are you?" Esther asked when he stepped onto the porch.

He grinned at her. "Doin' real good. I was on my way to the lumber mill to get some wood we need for our new greenhouse and thought I'd stop by here first and say hello."

She gave a brief smile.

Bonnie's cat scampered across the grass and rubbed against Ethan's leg. He bent down and rubbed the cat's head then turned his attention to Esther again. "I talked to Samuel Fisher awhile ago, and he said the two of you aren't courtin' anymore."

"That's true." Esther swallowed hard, barely able to get the words out.

"So since you won't be seein' Samuel anymore, I was wonderin' if you'd like to come over to our house for supper this Saturday night. My mamm's fixin' stromboli, and I know it's gonna be good."

Esther contemplated his offer a few seconds. While Ethan was a nice enough fellow, he really wasn't her type, so it wouldn't be right to lead him on. Still, going to supper at the Zooks' house might be better than sitting in the guest house feeling sorry for herself because she hadn't been invited to Leon's birthday supper. Yet if she agreed to go to the Zooks', Ethan might get the idea that she was interested in him and keep pursuing her.

"So what do you say?" he asked. "Would you be free to come over to our place for supper?"

Esther smiled and slowly shook her head. "I appreciate the invitation, but not this time, Ethan." Even though she knew she had no chance with Samuel, she wasn't ready to begin a relationship with anyone else right now—maybe never, truth be told.

"Would ya be willing to come some other time?" he asked with a hopeful expression.

She gave a quick nod and grabbed the broom that was propped in one corner of the porch, hoping to appear busy.

Ethan stood silently for a few seconds. Then he smiled and said, "See you at church on Sunday, Esther."

Esther returned to the house to finish her baking and clean all the downstairs rooms. By three thirty, Bonnie still wasn't home, so Esther peeled some potatoes and carrots to add to the pot roast she had simmering on the stove. She'd just put the last potato in when she heard a knock on the door.

This must be my day for visitors, she thought as she dried her hands on a towel. When she opened the back door she was surprised to see Marla and Leon on the porch, holding their backpacks and lunch pails.

"What are you two doing here?" she asked.

"Came to see you." Marla grabbed Esther's hand and gave it a squeeze. "We miss you, Esther."

"That's right," Leon said. "And we'll miss ya even more when we move back to Pennsylvania."

The shock of Leon's words made Esther feel lightheaded. She leaned against the doorway for support. Samuel must really want to get away from her if he was planning to move back to Pennsylvania. But why? What had she done to turn him away? "I—I had no idea you were moving back," she stammered. "When will you leave?"

Marla turned her hands palm up. "Don't know. Daadi

just told us this mornin' that he thought we oughta move back."

"We told him we don't want to go, but Daadi probably won't listen to us." Leon looked up at Esther with imploring eyes. "Can't ya talk to him, Esther? Can't ya do somethin' to get Daadi to change his mind?"

Esther knelt down and pulled both children into her arms. "I don't want you to move either. You've come to mean so much to me, but I don't think there's anything I can do to make your daed change his mind."

The children looked up at her with tears glistening in their eyes, which only made her feel worse. If Samuel moved back to Pennsylvania, there would be no chance of them ever getting back together.

CHAPTER 53

A re my kinner ready to go?" Samuel asked Mavis when he stopped by her house that afternoon to pick up his kids.

"Penny and Jared are," she said, "but Marla and Leon aren't here."

"What?" Samuel's spine stiffened. "Where are they?"

"When my Daniel and Eva got home from school, they said Marla and Leon had told them they were going over to Bonnie's Bed-and-Breakfast."

"What'd they go there for?"

Mavis shrugged. "You'll have to ask them, because since they never showed up here, I assume they're still there."

Samuel ground his teeth together. He did not need one more stop to make. After his driver had dropped him off at home, he'd hitched his horse to the buggy and come over here. He'd worked hard all day and was anxious to get back home and take a shower. Besides, if he went to the B&B, he was likely to see Esther, and he wasn't sure he could deal with that.

"Guess we'd better get going," Samuel said, knowing he had no other choice but to go get Marla and Leon. He motioned for Penny and Jared to follow him out the door.

After they were settled into his buggy and headed down the road, he glanced over his shoulder and said, "Did you two behave yourselves today?"

Penny nodded soberly. "Mavis said she'd give us a bletsching if we wasn't good."

Samuel grimaced. When he'd asked Mavis to watch the kids, he hadn't expected her to threaten his kids with a spanking. If they'd been bad, would she have made good on her threat? As far as he knew, Esther had never been harsh with the kids, and they'd never mentioned her threatening them with a spanking either.

Samuel shook the reins to get Socks moving faster. He'd be glad when this day was over.

When he pulled his horse and buggy onto the driveway of the B&B a short time later, he spotted Esther hanging clothes on the line. Marla and Leon were nearby, playing in a pile of leaves.

"I want you and Jared to stay in the buggy and wait for me," Samuel told Penny. "I'm going to get Marla and Leon, and it shouldn't take me long."

"Can't we get out?" Penny asked. "I wanna say hi to Esther."

Samuel shook his head. He knew if he let Penny and Jared out of the buggy he'd have a hard time getting them back in. They would either hang onto Esther, run around the yard, or play with Bonnie's cat or the dog.

Samuel turned to Penny and said, "Remember now, stay right here."

As he headed across the yard, dry leaves crunched beneath his feet. He was almost to the clothesline where Esther was hanging a lace tablecloth when she turned and looked at him.

"Samuel."

He swallowed hard. Why'd she have to be so beautiful and sweet? Why couldn't he stop thinking about her all the time? And there she went again, being so cute when her cheeks flushed that light shade of pink.

He pulled his gaze away from Esther and pointed at Marla. "What are you and your bruder doin' here? You know you were supposed to go to the Zooks' after school."

"We wanted to see Esther," Leon said before Marla could reply. "We miss her, Daadi."

I miss her, too. Samuel resisted the urge to say the words. Instead, he marched over to Leon and pulled him to his feet. "Let's go. It's getting late, and we need to get home now."

"I'm sorry if they bothered you," Samuel said, glancing at Esther and then looking quickly away. "It won't happen again."

"Oh, they were no bother," she was quick to answer. "I enjoyed spending a little time with them."

"Didn't they tell you they were supposed to be at the Zooks'?"

"Yes, and I was going to take them over there as soon as I finished hanging these things on the line."

"It's kind of late to be doin' laundry, isn't it?" Samuel didn't know why he was being so irritable, but he couldn't seem to help himself. Was it the fact that the kids had come over here when they should have gone to the Zooks', or was it because he'd been forced to see Esther?

"I was busy doing so many other things today," Esther said, "and since there's such a nice wind blowing this afternoon, I figured they'd be dry before it gets dark."

"Oh." Samuel jerked his attention back to the kids. "Say good-bye to Esther, and let's go."

Marla ran to Esther first and gave her a hug, and Leon did the same. Then they both turned and walked slowly to the buggy, heads down and shoulders slumped.

Samuel glanced at Esther once more and mumbled, "Have a good rest of the day."

"You too, Samuel." She smiled, but her expression appeared to be strained. Was she having as hard a time looking at him as he was at her?

Samuel whirled around, and as he sprinted to the buggy, he made a decision. He was glad his house in Pennsylvania still hadn't sold, because whether the kids were in agreement or not, he was moving back home.

CHAPTER 54

On Saturday morning when Samuel woke up, he lay in bed, unable to decide when he should tell the kids about his decision to move. He didn't want to spoil Leon and Titus's birthday supper this evening, so he'd wait until Sunday to give them the news. The kids wouldn't like it of course; they'd already made it clear that they didn't want to move. But once they got back to Pennsylvania, where they could enjoy both sets of grandparents and all their cousins, he was sure they'd be fine.

I wonder how Titus will feel about us moving, Samuel thought as he crawled out of bed and stepped into his trousers. *Will he try to convince me to stay, or will he be understanding and give me his best wishes? I'm sure he'd like to have some of his family around, but he's married now, and he and Suzanne will be starting a family of their own.*

Samuel ambled over to the window and stared into the yard, where Lucky ran back and forth through the scattered leaves, chasing a fluffy gray cat. *Once we move, Esther can have her house back, and she won't have to live in that little guest house at Bonnie's anymore.*

He moved away from the window and sank to the edge of the bed. Why couldn't life be simple? Why'd there have to be so many hurts and frustrations? If only Elsie hadn't died, they'd still be living in Pennsylvania, and he would never have met Esther.

Samuel's gaze came to rest on the cardboard box pushed against the wall on the other side of the room. It was the box full of Elsie's things that he still hadn't completely gone through. Samuel didn't know why, but he felt compelled to do that right now.

He rose from the bed and knelt in front of the box. When he opened it, the first thing he saw was one of Elsie's white head coverings. He'd give that to Marla when she was older. Next, he found some of Elsie's handkerchiefs. Maybe Penny would like those. Then he discovered the yellow blanket Elsie had bought for the baby they'd lost when she'd died. That would go to Jared.

Under the hankies was Elsie's Bible. Maybe he could give it to Leon. A lump rose in Samuel's throat as he lifted it out and opened the first page. Elsie's name had been written there, along with Samuel's name and their children's names. There was also a place to write in the date of Elsie's birth and her death. Elsie's birth date had been filled in, but her date of death was still blank.

Samuel picked up the Bible and carried it across the room to the dresser, where he kept a notebook and pen to keep track of his paint jobs. Tears blurred his vision as he wrote the date of Elsie's death. She'd died just a week before Thanksgiving. It was hard to believe it had been eleven months already.

Samuel stood staring at the Bible for several seconds; then he opened it to a page she'd marked with a yellow ribbon. He noticed that Psalm 147:3 had been underlined, and he read it out loud: " 'He healeth the broken in heart, and bindeth up their wounds.' "

Samuel had thought his heart was healing, but when he'd reminded himself of the promise he'd made to Elsie, the pain of her death had become real again, like a wound that never completely heals.

Oh Lord, he silently prayed. *Please give me a sense of peace. Help me to keep my focus on my kinner and not on Elsie or Esther. Elsie's gone, and she's never coming back. Esther's here but can never be a part of my life. I just want to be free of this pain.*

When Samuel's prayer ended, he made his way back to the box. He'd go through the rest of Elsie's things and be done with it, once and for all.

He pulled out a few more items—an apron, Elsie's reading glasses, and a poem Marla had written and given to Elsie on the last Mother's Day she'd still been alive.

The next thing he removed from the box was a leather journal. Inside, he saw that Elsie had posted entries about once or twice a month. Strange. He hadn't even realized she'd been keeping a journal.

He turned several pages, reading with interest as Elsie described some of the events that had happened that last month she'd been alive. When he heard the patter of feet coming down the stairs and realized the kids were up, he quickly turned to the last page Elsie had written, curious to know what her final entry said. The lump in his throat became thicker as he read her words silently.

> *I don't know the reason, but this pregnancy is different than my other four were. I feel so tired all the time and have been terribly sick to my stomach. Sometimes I feel dizzy, too, and I have a horrible feeling that something might be wrong with me or the boppli. Am I going to die? Or maybe the boppli will die or be born with some kind of birth defect. I need to speak to Samuel about this—need to tell him what's on my heart. Samuel has promised me many times that he'll never love anyone but me, but that's not fair to him. I need him to know that should I die before he does, he's free to love again. I want my beloved husband to find another wife—someone who will love him and our kinner as much as I do.*
>
> *I must close now, as Jared is awake from his nap and crying. I'll talk to Samuel about what I've written when he gets home from work tonight.*

The words on the page blurred as Samuel sat in stunned

silence. Elsie had sensed there was something wrong with her or the baby. Would one or both of them have died even if Elsie hadn't fallen down the stairs?

He drew in a shaky breath and swiped at the tears running down his cheeks. Elsie had released him from his promise. She'd actually wanted him to find someone else if she died.

Tap! Tap! Tap!

"Daadi, are you in there?" Leon called through Samuel's closed door.

"Jah." Samuel could barely get the word out, his throat felt so clogged with emotion.

"We're hungerich. Are you comin' out to fix us some breakfast?"

"I–I'll be right there." Samuel pulled a hanky from his pants' pocket and blew his nose. He knew he needed to fix the kids their breakfast first, but then he was going over to Bonnie's Bed-and-Breakfast to see Esther.

———※———

"I want you to get your teeth brushed, put on a jacket, and meet me outside," Samuel told his children after they'd finished eating breakfast.

"How come?" Marla asked.

"I'm going to see if Suzanne and Titus will keep you for a few hours, because I have an important errand to run." Samuel figured he could take the kids with him, but he wanted to be alone with Esther when he told her how he felt.

"Will ya be back in time for my birthday supper?" Leon questioned.

Samuel ruffled the boy's hair. "Don't you worry about that. I'll be back in plenty of time for us to go to supper."

"I'm glad to see you're smilin' today," Marla said. "You looked so sad yesterday."

"If things go well today, like I hope, I'll be doing a lot more smiling from now on." Samuel tweaked the end of her nose. "Now hurry and get ready to go."

The children scampered out of the kitchen, and Samuel put all the dirty dishes in the sink. He'd wash them later. Right now he had something more important to do.

—m—

Paradise, Pennsylvania

"There's something I need to talk to you about," Timothy said to Hannah after they'd finished eating their breakfast.

"What's that?" she asked as she turned the water on at the sink to do the dishes.

"I stopped by Naomi and Caleb's store yesterday afternoon, and Naomi was pretty upset."

"How come?"

"She said she'd heard about my birthday supper tonight and wondered why she and her family weren't invited."

Hannah turned to look at him. "Why are you bringing this up now?"

"Because when I got home yesterday, you were at your mamm's, and then Mindy was fussy all evening and you kept busy tending to her. By the time you came to bed, I was sleeping."

She shook her head. "I wasn't asking why you didn't tell me sooner. I wonder why are you bringing this up when it's already been decided. When we had this discussion a week ago, we agreed that only your folks and my folks would be invited here for supper tonight."

"We didn't actually agree on it." Timothy tapped his fingers on the table. "More to the point, you pretty much said how it was going to be, and I just went along with it so we wouldn't end up in another argument."

"Then why are you bringing it up now?" She turned back to the sink.

"Because Naomi was upset about not being included."

"If we had invited her family, we would have had to

include your other brothers and sisters and their families, and you know our place isn't big enough for that."

"We could have used the barn like I'd wanted to do."

Her head snapped around, and she glared at him, crossing her arms. "I told you before—that would be too much work."

He stiffened. "Anything that has to do with me is too much work, but if your mamm wants something, you don't seem to mind."

"You don't have to bring my mamm into this. She has nothing to do with it."

"Jah, she does, Hannah. You two thinking you have to be together all the time has been a source of trouble between you and me for a long time. I'm so tired of it!"

Hannah grabbed a towel, dried her hands, and hurried across the room. "Let's not argue," she said, placing her hands on his shoulders. "Mindy's in the living room playing, and I don't want her to hear us shouting at each other."

"I don't want that either."

Hannah stood silently and started rubbing his shoulders. Normally, it would have felt good, but right now, Timothy was too irritated to feel good about anything.

"We'll have a nice time tonight; you'll see."

"I'm glad you think so." He pushed away from the table and headed for the door.

"Where are you going?"

"Outside. I need some fresh air!" The door banged shut behind him.

CHAPTER 55

Pembroke, Kentucky

W hat would you like to do today?" Bonnie asked Esther after they'd cleaned up the kitchen. "I think we could both use a break from the usual cleaning we do on Saturdays."

"But if you have guests coming, we'll need to clean the rest of the house," Esther said.

Bonnie shook her head. "No guests scheduled until next Tuesday, so we'll have Monday to clean." She poured two cups of tea and handed one to Esther. "Should we take this into the living room or would you rather put a jacket on and sit outside on the porch?"

"Let's go outside," Esther said. "It's a bit chilly, but the sun's out. We may as well enjoy it now, because it won't be long before winter is here with its cold weather and probably some snow."

They slipped into their jackets, picked up their cups of tea, and went out to the porch.

"Let's sit over there so we can look out into the yard." Bonnie motioned to the wicker table and chairs on the far end of the porch.

After they were seated, Esther said, "I should have brought out some of that gingerbread I made last night. Do you want me to go get it?"

Bonnie shook her head. "I'm fine with just the tea, but if you want some, go ahead."

"Maybe later." Esther took a sip of tea and let it roll

around on her tongue before swallowing. "This is so good. Peppermint is my favorite kind of tea."

Bonnie took a drink, too. "It is quite flavorful."

They sat in companionable silence for a while; then Bonnie looked over at Esther, and with a most serious expression she said, "There's something weighing heavily on my mind, and I'd like to share it with you, but only if you promise not to repeat what I've said to anyone."

"I won't say anything."

Bonnie took another sip of tea and set her cup down. "I—I hardly know where to begin."

Esther waited, figuring Bonnie needed time to think about what she wanted to say.

"As you know, Allen's asked me out several times lately, and I've said no."

"Because you're not ready for a serious relationship, right?"

Bonnie nodded. "But I'd like you to know why." She paused and stared into the yard, watching the shadows appear as a cloud drifted over the sun. After several seconds, she looked back at Esther with furrowed brows. "When I was a teenager I did something I'll always regret."

"What was it?" Esther dared to ask.

"I had a boyfriend, Darin, who said he loved me and insisted that if I loved him too, I'd be willing to. . ." Bonnie stopped talking and drew in a sharp breath. "Before my mother died, she'd talked to me about keeping myself pure and waiting for marriage to be intimate with a man, but Darin kept insisting that if I loved him, I'd do what he asked."

Esther reached over and touched Bonnie's arm. She was almost sure what Bonnie was about to say and wanted to offer her some reassurance.

Tears welled in Bonnie's eyes. "I weakened, Esther. I gave in to my feelings, and several weeks later, when I realized I was pregnant, I told him about it."

"What'd he say?"

"He laughed and said it wasn't his problem—that I'd have to deal with it on my own because he was moving to a different state and didn't care if he ever saw me again." Bonnie reached into her pocket for a tissue and blew her nose.

"What did your dad say about your situation?" Esther asked.

Bonnie swiped at the tears running down her cheeks. "Dad blew like Mt. St. Helens and said in no uncertain terms that I'd have to give the baby up for adoption."

"Did you?"

Bonnie gave a slow nod. "I felt that I had no other choice. I was only sixteen, still living at home, and with no job or money of my own."

"Could you have come here to live with your grandparents?" Esther asked.

"I suppose, but since I was still underage, I'm sure Dad would have come and got me. Besides, I didn't want Grandma and Grandpa to be disappointed in me, so they never knew about the pregnancy." She gulped on a sob. "It was hard enough to live with myself."

"Was the baby a boy or a girl?" Esther dared to ask.

"A girl. I only got to see her for a little bit, and then they whisked her away."

"Do you know who adopted her or where she is today?"

Bonnie shook her head. "Dad made sure it was a closed adoption."

"I'm so sorry," Esther said. "I'm sure it must have been difficult for you to give up your baby."

"It was, and I grieved for my little girl, like I had when my mother died." Bonnie sniffed deeply. "I can't tell you how good it feels to be talking about this with you. I've kept my feelings bottled up all these years, and it's affected me in so many ways."

"When you returned from Oregon, you said things were better between you and your dad. Did he apologize for making you give up your baby?"

"Yes, and I think I do understand his reasons. Dad was still dealing with the grief of losing my mother, and between that and the stress of his job at the bank, there was no way he could help me take care of a baby." Bonnie reached for her cup and took a drink, although Esther was sure the tea had gotten cold.

"I'm a Christian now, and I know I should have forgiven myself, as God forgave me," Bonnie said, "but I still struggle with the guilt for having gotten pregnant, not to mention giving my own flesh-and-blood child away." She paused and drew in a quick breath. "I'll never let my emotions carry me away again, and I don't think I could ever trust another man not to hurt me the way Darin did."

"Is that why you haven't gotten serious about Allen?"

Bonnie gave a nod. "I don't think the scars from my past will ever heal."

A verse of scripture Esther had read a few days earlier crossed her mind. "Psalm 147:3 says, 'He healeth the broken in heart, and bindeth up their wounds.'" Esther placed her hand on Bonnie's arm and patted it gently. "God will heal your heart, if you let Him."

"I—I've tried."

"But you have to put your faith and trust in Him and become willing to forgive yourself for the things you've done in the past, just as He forgives us."

More tears sprang to Bonnie's eyes. "Funny, but that's pretty much what I told my dad when he opened up and told me how he felt about his parents. Isn't it amazing that we humans can dole out advice, but when it comes to ourselves, we need someone else to make us see the truth?" She squeezed Esther's hand. "Thank you for helping me see the light."

"It wasn't me who opened your eyes to the truth," Esther said. "It was God's Word. That's how He speaks to us."

"I know, but God often uses others to show the truth of His Word."

Their conversation was interrupted by a horse and buggy coming up the driveway.

"It's Ethan Zook," Bonnie said. "I wonder what he wants."

Esther grimaced. "He probably came to see me."

"What makes you so sure?"

"He asked me to have supper with him tonight, and I said no. He probably came by to ask me again." Esther rose from her seat. "Guess I'd better go out and talk to him."

She hurried across the yard and joined Ethan at the hitching rail, where he'd just tied his horse.

"It's good to see you, Esther," he said with a nod. "I came by to see if I could talk you into havin' supper at our place tonight."

Esther shook her head, trying not to let her irritation show. Didn't Ethan know when to take no for an answer? "I'm really busy, so if you'll excuse me. . ."

He motioned to the porch, where Bonnie still sat. "When I pulled in just now, I saw you sittin' up there with Bonnie. Didn't look like you were busy to me."

"We were taking a break," she explained.

Ethan leaned close to Esther—so close she could feel his warm breath against her face. "Isn't there any chance you might change your mind? I'd really like the opportunity to court you, Esther."

Esther didn't want to hurt Ethan's feelings, but she didn't want to be courted by him either. Without knowing it, he'd managed to irritate her more times than not, and she couldn't get close to someone like that. So she forced a smile and said, "I'm sorry, Ethan, but I don't think we're meant to be together."

When Samuel pulled his horse and buggy into Bonnie's yard, the first thing he saw was a horse and buggy parked in front of the hitching rail. As he drew closer, he spotted Ethan standing real close to Esther.

Oh no. Am I too late? he wondered. *Has Ethan already begun to court Esther?*

Samuel debated whether he should turn around and head out, but when he saw Ethan climb into his buggy and pull away from the rail, he changed his mind. He was here now, and he had to speak to Esther, even if she turned him down.

Samuel held his horse steady until Ethan had pulled out of the yard; then he eased his horse up to the hitching rail and climbed down from the buggy. When he approached Esther, she looked at him strangely.

"I'm surprised to see you here, Samuel. Where are the kinner?"

"I left them with Suzanne and Titus." He took a nervous step toward her. "I wanted to talk to you alone."

"What about?"

Samuel swallowed a couple of times. "I. . .uh. . .was wondering if we could start over."

Esther stared at him with a curious expression.

He took another step toward her. "I made a mistake saying I didn't want to court you anymore, and I almost made the mistake of moving back to Pennsylvania."

"The kinner mentioned that yesterday. I was afraid you might move and wished you wouldn't," she said in a voice barely above a whisper, never taking her eyes off his face. "What made you change your mind?"

"It was something I read in Elsie's journal this morning. She wrote that she wanted me to love you, Esther."

Esther's eyebrows lifted high. "But your wife didn't even know me."

"You're right, but she was afraid she was going to die, and she wrote in her journal that if she did, she wanted me to find someone to love again. She wanted me to find someone who would love me as much as she did and who'd love our kinner, too." He touched Esther's arm gently. "I think that woman is you. Fact is, I never thought I could fall in love again until I met you."

Tears sprang to Esther's eyes and dribbled onto her cheeks. "Oh Samuel, I love you, too—and your kinner as well."

Samuel glanced around, worried that someone might be watching them. When he was sure no one was, he took Esther's hand, and they stepped around the corner of the shed, where he pulled her into his arms and kissed her sweet lips. She fit perfectly into his embrace, and he knew at that moment he would never let her go. "I don't think we should rush into anything, but after a proper time of courting, do you think you might consider marrying me?" Samuel murmured against her ear. His heart pounded, awaiting her answer.

Esther nodded and rested her head against his chest. "I know that Elsie will always have a special place in your heart, and I'd never try to take her place, but I promise to love you and the kinner with my whole heart."

They stood that way for several minutes; then Samuel tipped her head up so he could look at her pretty face. "The kinner and I are going to supper tonight to celebrate Leon and Titus's birthday. It would make the evening more special if you could be there, too."

She smiled. "I'd be happy to join you."

Samuel closed his eyes and said a silent prayer. *Thank You, Lord, for helping my heart to heal and for giving me this special woman to love.*

Epilogue

One week later

There's something I want to share with you," Samuel said to Esther as they sat on his front porch one evening, visiting as they drank some coffee.

"What is it?" she asked.

"It's a letter I got from my brother Timothy today." Samuel pulled an envelope from his pocket and took out the letter. "Listen to what it says:

> *Dear Samuel:*
> *Things still aren't going well between me and Han-nah, and I've decided it's time for a change. I had a talk with Dad the other day and asked if he thought he could find someone else to help him farm his place. He was agreeable and has asked Norman's two boys, Harley and John, to take over for me, because I've decided to sell my place and move to Kentucky. I'll be in touch soon to discuss the details with you.*
>
> > *As ever,*
> > *Timothy*

Samuel looked over at Esther and squinted. "What do you think about that?"

She sat for several seconds, letting the words from Timothy's letter sink in. "This is a surprise. I had no idea Timothy was thinking of moving here."

"When he came for Titus and Suzanne's wedding, I

could tell that he liked it here, but I never expected he would move. With the way Hannah's tied to her mamm's apron strings, I'm surprised he talked her into it."

"Are you sure she's in agreement with this? Timothy didn't say so in his letter."

Samuel stroked his beard thoughtfully. "You're right about that, but I don't think he'd up and move unless she'd agreed. Timothy's always done pretty much whatever Hannah wanted."

Esther placed her hand on Samuel's arm. "I hope it works out for them as well as it has for you."

He nodded and clasped her hand. "I came here and found healing for my broken heart when I met you. I wonder what Timothy and Hannah will find."

Esther's Recipe for Boyfriend Cookies

Ingredients:
1 cup butter, softened
¾ cup granulated sugar
¾ cup brown sugar, packed
3 eggs
1 teaspoon vanilla
¼ cup whole wheat flour
¼ cup soy flour
3½ cups quick-cooking oatmeal
1½ cups salted peanuts, coarsely chopped
1 cup carob chips

Preheat oven to 350 degrees. Cream butter and sugars. Add eggs and vanilla, beating until fluffy. Sift flours and add to creamed mixture. Fold in oatmeal, peanuts, and carob chips. Drop by teaspoon 2 inches apart on greased baking sheet and bake 8 to 10 minutes. Yield: 7 to 8 dozen cookies.

DISCUSSION QUESTIONS

1. When Samuel Fisher's wife died, he was so deeply grieved, he could barely function. After a short time he made a hasty decision to move to Kentucky where his younger brother Titus lived, hoping to leave the past behind and heal his broken heart. How long do you think someone who has lost a loved one should wait to make a major decision such as moving to another location?

2. Besides getting a fresh start, another reason Titus encouraged Samuel to move to Kentucky was because there were fewer tourists in the area near Hopkinsville. How do you think the Amish who live in the larger tourist areas cope with the curious stares and questions from people wanting to know more about the Amish way of life? What are some ways tourists can learn about the Amish without infringing on their privacy?

3. When Esther Beiler's parents sold their store and moved to Pennsylvania, Esther made a decision to stay in Kentucky. Even though she had no other family living there, she didn't want to leave her friends or the area she had come to know as her home. How would you feel if you needed to move, and your only daughter chose to stay behind? Would you try to convince her to move with you, or allow her the freedom to live where she chose?

4. As soon as Esther met Samuel, she was attracted to him, but she kept her feelings to herself, knowing he was still grieving for his wife. She tried to help Samuel through his grief by caring for his children and being his friend, even when

Samuel didn't reciprocate. What are some ways we can help someone going through grief?

5. During Samuel's time of grieving, he often ignored his children and was sometimes short-tempered with them. How can a person who has lost a loved one cope without letting it affect their relationships with family or friends? How can we help the children of a grieving parent deal with their loss and not feel rejected by the remaining parent?

6. When Esther saw Samuel neglecting his children, she became concerned. Without being pushy, what are some ways we can help a grieving parent let their children know that they still love them?

7. When Samuel and his children first moved to Kentucky, they lived with his brother Titus. After a while, this caused a rift between Titus and his girlfriend, Suzanne, because Titus spent so much of his time with Samuel and ignored her. Suzanne was also concerned that when she and Titus got married they'd have to share their home with Samuel and his family and wouldn't have the privacy a newly married couple needed. Is it ever a good idea for more than one family to live in the same house for an extended period of time? If so, what are some ways they can learn to cope?

8. When Esther believed that Samuel was interested in Bonnie Taylor, the English woman who ran the bed-and-breakfast in the area, she became jealous. How can a person deal with jealousy and not let it affect their friendship?

9. Samuel's step-mother, Fannie, became concerned when she heard that Samuel had been spending a

lot of time with an English woman. She was afraid that if Samuel became romantically involved with Bonnie, he might leave the Amish faith. When a parent has concerns about one of their children's choice for a mate, what is the best way to deal with it?

10. How would it have affected Samuel's Amish family living in Pennsylvania if he had married an English woman and left the Amish faith? If Bonnie joined the Amish faith and gave up her modern way of life, what challenges might she face?

11. After reading *The Healing*, did you learn anything new about the Amish way of life? What differences did you notice between the Amish living in Christian County, Kentucky, and the Amish in Lancaster County, Pennsylvania?

12. Were there any spiritual applications from *The Healing* that helped you deal with a difficult situation? Which verses of scripture in the story spoke to your heart?

About the Author

Wanda E. Brunstetter is a *New York Times* bestselling author who enjoys writing Amish-themed as well as historical novels. Descended from Anabaptists herself, Wanda became deeply interested in the Plain People when she married her husband, Richard, who grew up in a Mennonite church in Pennsylvania. Wanda and her husband live in Washington State, but take every opportunity to visit their Amish friends in various communities across the country, gathering further information about the Amish way of life.

Wanda and her husband have two grown children, six grandchildren, and two great-grandchildren. In her spare time, Wanda enjoys photography, ventriloquism, gardening, reading, stamping, and having fun with her family.

In addition to her novels, Wanda has written several Amish cookbooks, two Amish devotionals, several Amish children's books, as well as numerous novellas, stories, articles, poems, and puppet scripts.

Visit Wanda's website at www.wandabrunstetter.com and feel free to email her at wanda@wandabrunstetter.com.

Collect the Trilogy!

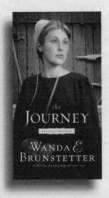

The Journey
by Wanda E. Brunstetter

Until Titus Fisher learned wood-working skills, he'd never been able to stick to a job. Now living in Kentucky, life has a whole new outlook, but can a heart once torn by love's rejection find new life and choose between two women who are as unique as night and day?

Paperback / 978-1-68322-365-8 / $6.99 / December 2017

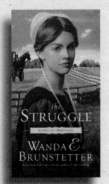

The Struggle
by Wanda E. Brunstetter

Lancaster County Amish man Timothy Fisher has moved his wife, Hannah, and daughter, Mindy, to Kentucky, the land of tomorrow. But when a tragic accident occurs, their marriage seems splintered beyond repair. What drastic measures will God take to salve their grief and heal their breach?

Paperback / 978-1-68322-368-9 / $6.99 / February 2018

Other Books by Wanda E. Brunstetter

Let's Keep In Touch!

Want to know what Wanda's up to and be the first to hear about new releases, specials, the latest news, and more? Like Wanda on Facebook!

Visit facebook.com/WandaBrunstetterFans